T0356443

BY PAISLEY HOPE

Holding the Reins
Training the Heart
Riding the High

Riding the High

Riding the High

A Silver Pines Novel

PAISLEY HOPE

DELL
NEW YORK

Dell
An imprint of Random House
A division of Penguin Random House LLC
1745 Broadway, New York, NY 10019
randomhousebooks.com
penguinrandomhouse.com

A Dell Trade Paperback Original

Copyright © 2025 by Paisley Hope

Penguin Random House values and supports copyright.
Copyright fuels creativity, encourages diverse voices,
promotes free speech, and creates a vibrant culture.
Thank you for buying an authorized edition of this
book and for complying with copyright laws by not
reproducing, scanning, or distributing any part of it
in any form without permission. You are supporting
writers and allowing Penguin Random House to
continue to publish books for every reader.
Please note that no part of this book may be used
or reproduced in any manner for the purpose of
training artificial intelligence technologies or systems.

DELL and the D colophon are registered trademarks
of Penguin Random House LLC.

ISBN 978-0-593-98245-7
Ebook ISBN 978-0-593-98246-4

Printed in the United States of America on acid-free paper

2 4 6 8 9 7 5 3 1

The authorized representative in the EU for product
safety and compliance is Penguin Random House Ireland,
Morrison Chambers, 32 Nassau Street, Dublin D02 YH68, Ireland,
https://eucontact.penguin.ie.

If the mood ever strikes to save a horse
and there are no cowboys in sight, don't worry, darling.
The always gorgeous, sometimes moody, sometimes sweet
town sheriff will do just fine. (And besides, cowboys
don't carry handcuffs.)

Warnings

Open door sexual content.
Light discussions of grief (nothing on page).
Dirty talk, mild degradation.
Handcuffing, anal play, cum play, hand necklaces.
Dealing with a flighty, pain-in-the-ass ex-wife on occasion.

Riding the High

PROLOGUE
Ginger

MAY, THREE YEARS AGO

"I think I want two pizzas. Extra pepperoni," the voice I know almost as well as my own sounds from behind me.

I roll my eyes, take a deep breath, and turn to face the other side of the bar. "Good—when *you* call to order it, you can let them know." I toss him a cutesy kind of grin.

"Just don't forget my bacon and pineapple when you order for me, Law Daddy."

Fucking Yankees fans, and in particular, the *most* annoying Yankees fan there is: Cole Ashby.

His wide eyes stay on mine as he sips his beer, their deep amber flecks pulling me in. He's the only Ashby with those eyes, and I don't know where they came from, but, damn, they anchor me every time their focus is on me. I watch him push the sleeves up on his flannel shirt with large, sculpted hands, showcasing a little more ink on his left arm than the last time I saw him.

He sets his beer down and leans over the bar, drumming his fingers against it, and gives me the same smirk he's been giving me for years, the one that makes my knees go a little weak. *Get your shit together, Danforth.*

I mentally berate myself for falling victim to his charm. Every single time.

"I think we both know I won't be the one ordering," he says, his deep baritone clear in the noisy bar.

I do my best to brush him off, but I am a woman, and there are times when that intense stare turns me into temporary mush. I've given up trying to figure out why.

"Let's just get through the first inning before you start shit talking." I turn to break his hold on me and help my next customer, wishing it was busier in the bar so I could avoid Cole altogether.

I hear Cole chuckle from behind me as if he knows my team will be fucked with the first pitch before he heads back over to the table he's been sitting at with a co-worker.

He's so damn cocky, so damn sure his Yanks have us beat, but I guess most of the time they do. I'm used to my team losing to the Yankees, because I am a tried-and-true Cincinnati Reds fan, though not really by choice. It was simply ingrained in me.

My first solid memory is eating nachos with my grandfather at a Reds game when I was six. My granddad is no longer earthside, but he was the best man I've ever known, and the only man who's never let me down. My mother never inherited his love for the game, so he passed his passion on to me. Sadly, these days the Reds don't play quite as well as they used to.

An hour later, the bar is bustling, and my Reds are losing by three runs. Not late enough in the game for Cole to gloat, but late enough that when he returns for another beer, I question why I put myself through this suffering for the sake of tradition. Cole and I have been doing this since my second year of college, when we ended up at the Horse and Barrel the weekend our teams played each other. I had to open my big mouth about a shitty play the Yankees made, saying we could beat them with our eyes closed. Cole had looked at me with that frustrating smirk, then said, "Wanna bet?"

That was four years ago, and every year I come back like a sucker believing my Reds will pull through. I've only won the honor of paid-for pizza once.

I look over at Emma, my co-worker, and gesture for her to serve Cole when he saunters back up. I'm not in the mood to listen to him yet. She grins and makes her way over to him at the other end of the bar, tossing her blond hair over her shoulder as she goes. Even from over here, I can feel his smug attitude.

"Avoid me all you want, Vixen. Won't change the outcome of the game," he calls out, loud enough to grate on my nerves.

"We'll see," I retort without looking up. I'm laser focused on cleaning the draft tap, but I can't help but try to put him in his place.

"And I know it's hard to believe, but it's not all about you, deputy. Truth is, I've simply dealt with enough children today. Had my fill, ya know?"

Cole raises his fresh beer and nods at me like he knows he's getting to me before leaning forward to talk to Emma with a grin. I roll my eyes in response.

I really *am* exhausted. Today was the last day of school, marking the end of my first year as a teacher at our local high school. I'd love to say I'm sad to see the school year end, but that would be a lie. I need this break. Shaping young minds all day, every day, maintaining a relatable vibe, *and* keeping teenagers actually engaged is damn hard work. But toss in the fact that you're expected to make them actually learn something? Nearly impossible.

This summer, I plan to sit by my parents' pool by day and make as much extra cash as I can at the "seedy bar" side job my dad lectures me about during the evenings. No matter how much he warns me about getting into trouble here, I'm not giving it up. Rocco Pressley is a great boss, and the tips are excellent.

Emma makes her way back over to me and grabs a clean glass for filling.

"He said—*and I quote*—he'll be back and don't feel bad, Ginger, it's not your fault you always pick the losing team."

I want to smack him. Emma senses my annoyance and starts to laugh.

"I don't know how you're friends with him," she notes.

"I know, he's damn frustrating," I retort.

"No," she continues, tossing a glance his way. "I mean, I'd be waiting exactly *zero* days before trying to jump that man's bones. Those arms, that grin, those dimples. Oh my."

"We're not friends. He's my best friend's brother," I correct her, and *I know he's hot, trust me.*

"You're just new to town, so all the men around here pique your interest. I'm desensitized."

"Either way, that man is pure fire," she says over her shoulder as she serves another customer.

I turn to face him and toss him a haughty look, praying my Reds can pull off a miracle just to shut him up, but by the end of the ninth, it seems no one has heard my prayers.

I glance over at him and can't help myself. When he raises his drink to me in a cheers, I smile back.

Guess I owe this fucker a pizza. *Again.* I watch him in my periphery and wonder if he even had the option to spend the night with his wife, or if he has completely given up in the marriage department. I can't say I really blame him, since Gemma seems like she isn't interested in making things work or focusing on her daughter at all these days. As I wipe down the bar, I remember the first night he texted me a few months ago, the night he knew he and Gemma probably weren't going to make it.

"She's in Lexington with friends, again," Cole says, his eyes focused on the little outside TV running sports highlights. "Thanks for coming. I need someone outside the situation to talk to, and my brother won't understand. He'll tell me to stay with her, to do the right thing, but I can't."

"What's going on?" I ask, sitting beside him in my sweats and oversize T-shirt. The sound of crickets fills the air as I slide my sandals off. This man. Wearing sweatpants and a T-shirt, feet bare, and holding a baby monitor in his lap with one hand, wondering what his wife is doing at one A.M. on a Thursday night. He's such a great dad, and he's always trying to give his daughter a family that just doesn't seem as though it's meant to be.

"Gemma was too young to become a mother. She's always struggled to put Mabel first, and it's only gotten worse as Mabes has become more independent. Gemma's started hanging around the wrong crowd, and she doesn't make an effort with either of us anymore."

I nod but don't say anything. Cole and I haven't really been close since he married Gemma, but of course I'll be here for him when he needs me. Laurel Creek is a small town, and I've heard that Mabel's care has fallen on Cole over the last year or so while Gemma finishes school, but I didn't realize she was leaving him at night too.

"Weekly nights out with the girls have become almost every night." He sighs. "She's drinking too much, and the rift between us has grown. There's no place for that with Mabel. I don't understand how her social life can be more important than her daughter. We fight about it constantly."

"What do you want, Cole? Have you tried talking to her? Laying out an ultimatum?" I ask.

"I want a wife I can trust. But let's face it, we didn't really know each other when she got pregnant. We gave it our best shot, but it's clear Mabel isn't her priority anymore. I'm not sure she ever was."

I pull the bottle of bourbon off the weathered side table and pour myself a little into the second glass Cole brought out with him. Mabel's swing set blows gently in the breeze in their tiny yard as he presses on. "I called her out before she left tonight. She actually said that she wasn't meant to be a mother." He scoffs in disbelief. "Said she wants to experience more before she settles down." His jaw tenses and he looks out to the yard. "I don't even know what that means."

He turns his amber eyes to meet mine, his brow furrowed, as he sips his whiskey.

"I don't trust her, but I'm going to give her one more chance when she comes home, whenever that is. But I refuse to give up Mabel."

I reach over and place my hand over his. The same live wire feeling I've always felt when I touch him zings up my arm.

"This isn't the fifties anymore, Cole. Just know if you want something different, you have options as Mabel's main caregiver."

He nods but says, "I'm not ready to go there yet. I have to have a little faith she'll come around."

"Even if it means you face a lifetime of unhappiness?" I ask, pulling my warm hand from his and taking a much-needed sip of my own bourbon before adding, "Do you love Gemma?"

"No. But Mabes is getting older quick. I'd live in an unhappy marriage until she's eighteen to keep her family together if Gemma can turn this around and we can quit arguing."

He blows out a deep breath, and my heart breaks for him as he sets his wide jaw and turns to face his yard, knocking back the rest of his shot.

"Got any popcorn?" I ask, changing the subject as a distraction, since I'm pretty sure that's what I've been brought here to do. "I started watching that show you told me about, Brooklyn Nine-Nine. I'm just starting season two if you want to watch with me?"

Cole turns to me with a grin that says he's grateful I'm here.

"I'll get a bag going. Oh, by the way, see your Reds take a dive tonight?" he asks as he gets up to make the popcorn, running a hand through his wavy, dark hair. I shoot him a dirty look and flip him the bird. When he turns his back and heads into the house, I smile to *myself. If giving him a mental break from this is all I can do, I'm going to do it right.*

I restock the beer in the cooler now, as the game officially ends. I know Cole will be coming to gloat without even looking up to confirm he's on his way. There's always been something about him that tells my body he's arrived before I see him. Of course I go the mature route and ignore him for as long as I can, serving as many people as possible, taking my sweet time as I chat to one of my regulars. I don't usually let him flirt, but tonight I do just to piss Cole off. At his end of the bar, Cole soon loses his patience and clears his throat. I finally turn to glare at him.

The worst thing about trying to be friends with Cole? He's gorgeous. He's an easy six foot three, big hands, broad shoulders and strong, muscular arms, an ass that only comes from playing sports all through high school and working on his family's ranch most of his life. His straight, Roman god–like features and dark, wavy brown hair are only enhanced by his big eyes, which are framed by thick lashes. Those eyes turn to whiskey fire when he is up to no good, and they've had my attention since I started hanging around his baby sister, CeCe, at school. Cole is older than us by three years, which meant I spent hours sitting in the stands watching him play hockey, baseball, or football every weekend with the Ashby clan. I was a lovesick teenager the moment I realized my first and true love, Zac Efron, had nothing on Cole Ashby.

Back then, I was constantly stumbling over my words and getting caught staring at him. A few torturous years passed like this, but then something changed. I grew up and into my God-given curves. After that, it felt as though Cole was staring back a lot more often.

Mr. World's Biggest Yankees fan pats his throat now, his beautiful face beaming with cocky victory.

"Thirsty . . . so thirsty," he mouths at me.

Cole spreads his hands out over the bar and leans in. His jaw is covered in a light scruff and his Yankees hat sits backward on his head, letting a few dark tendrils of his perfectly imperfect hair escape it.

"I'll take those pizzas piping hot, and make sure I get them before the end of the national anthem tomorrow night," he brags. The scent of Cole washes over me when I get close enough; weathered cedar and spice from his trademark cologne mixed with a hint of mint. He leans into me, his voice low. "I know I don't have to give you my address, Vixen."

I glare at him. "Perks of being your number one distraction," I offer sarcastically. He places a hand over his heart like I've shot him.

"How dare you? I pay you well with snacks and incredible company, Ginger."

"Debatable," I retort jokingly, sticking out my tongue before cracking and passing him his favorite—Kentucky Bourbon Barrel Ale—before he even asks for it. He pulls the bottle from me, and his fingers brush mine. There's no stopping the heat that spreads up my forearm with his touch.

"Extra mushrooms on that pizza, right?" I grin, knowing he hates mushrooms, and then turn back toward the back of the bar.

Cole chuckles behind me. "Don't even think about fucking around," he warns as I wave overhead and continue to the back for a break from both my job *and* his eyes.

The Friday night crowd is difficult to clear out tonight, but we manage. I stay with two other servers and our boss, Rocco, until every last peanut shell is off the floor, my Dolly Parton playlist getting us through. When it's finally time to lock up, I feel my phone buzz in my pocket.

LAW DADDY

Favor? Brooklyn 99? 🤠🍺

I stare at the message Cole left when the bar closed, and I know Mabel is staying at the ranch. Gemma must not have come home again, and Cole's gotta be at his wits' end after dealing with this for so long.

I'm so tired, but I instantly make up my mind. I can always sleep in tomorrow.

I make my way to the kitchen where our line cook is finishing her sanitization of the space. When she sees my face, she gives an all-knowing smile.

"Honey garlic or barbecue?" She grins as she pulls open the massive refrigerator door. She always keeps a stash of leftovers in there for the staff to munch on.

"Barbecue, and any chance you have some wedges too?" I ask, slinging my purse over my shoulder.

"Sure thing, honey." She pops a hefty Cole-sized meal into a to-go box and passes it over to me with a smile.

"I'll say it again. I hope he appreciates you," she adds as I turn to leave.

"I'll say it again." I grin as I turn to go. "He's just a friend."

I sigh as I breeze through the door into the warm late-night spring air, pulling out my phone.

ME

On my way.

CHAPTER ONE
Cole

NOW

"Do you want to get some food or something . . . ?" the blonde in my bed at the Vienna Hotel in Lexington calls to me as I head to the bathroom. I try to remember her first name with certainty. I toss the condom in the bathroom trash, swinging the door closed to take a leak while she continues talking in the next room. I only half hear her. In my mind she's already gone, and I'm already showered and ordering room service. Running a hand through my sweaty hair, I blow out a breath, then head back into the room.

She's got the wrong idea, alright, curled up in the center of my bed in her underwear.

"I, uh, have to be up early in the morning to head home remember? So I think I'm just going to get some sleep," I remind her, picking up her slinky black dress and passing it to her.

I never understand why women say they're only looking for some fun, but then the moment I pull my cock out of them, all of a sudden their expectations change.

"So you really meant just . . . *actual* fun." She looks up at me with puppy dog eyes as if that will make me reconsider. She is pretty, and the sex was alright, but any sense of "us" always ends when the sex does.

"Look . . ." *What the hell is her name? Stacey?* "I had fun, but we only met two hours ago, and we live on opposite sides of the country. I really do have an early morning tomorrow."

Lacey?

"Tracey is the name you're looking for," she deadpans. *Shit.*

"Of course, Tracey," I say. In my defense, it was loud in the bar.

I pass her shoes to her and glance at the clock. My phone call is coming in five.

I don't even have to get her an Uber because Tracey has a room here, six floors down. Reaching out, I take her hand.

"I meant what I said in the bar. It's not personal, and you seem great. I'm just not looking for anything right now," I tell her as sincerely as I can.

"Well, you have my number, so if you ever do find yourself in Colorado, don't be a stranger," she says as she opens the door to my suite. I'm only here because my whole family came today to watch my brother Wade's horse compete in her first prep race ahead of next year's Kentucky Derby. We all opted to stay the night except for Wade. His girlfriend, Ivy, is six months pregnant. I never thought Wade would find someone who would put up with his grumpy ass, never mind *want* to put up with it. Ivy wanted to stay in her own bed after the race. and what Ivy wants in Wade's world, Ivy gets. They left right after the race to head back to our hometown, Laurel Creek, about an hour away. The rest of us, including my sister, CeCe, and my best friend/soon-to-be brother-in-law, Nash, had dinner together before CeCe and her friends started their typical drink-more-and-dance-more routine. That's when I decided to find some fun of my own. Hanging around to watch Ginger

Danforth shake her perfect ass while every man in the bar watches her is a bad idea when I've had a bourbon or two. So, like I always do, I searched for a distraction—and found Tracey.

"Thanks for a great time," I say to her in my most sincere tone, patting her awkwardly on the shoulder. She smiles and nods, heading out the door and down the long hall to the elevators, allowing me to finally breathe out a sigh of relief. I fucking hate the awkward goodbye.

As she steps into the elevator, Ginger breezes out. She looks at Stacey, *fuck*. Tracey raises an eyebrow, then turns back to me.

"Still incognito? Giving these women your middle name, *Weston?*" she asks quietly, hiking a thumb over her shoulder as she passes by. A smile plays on her full, rosy lips, and her chocolate eyes dance as she gets closer.

"No idea what you're talking about," I scoff. I haven't done that in at least a year. Never should've told Ginger I used to give women my middle name after Gemma and I split up to make sure my business stayed my business.

She sashays right by my room to her own, and like a helpless fool, I watch her go because no one walks like Ginger. Her whole body moves in sync as if she was born on a goddamn runway. I don't know if it's a confidence thing or her body just gets the message from her brain that she's sexy as hell. Either way, it's goddamn mesmerizing.

"Don't even think about looking at my ass, fuckboy," she calls behind her without turning back to see if she's right.

She is.

"Flattering yourself as always." I avert my eyes and head back into my room to the sound of both our doors closing at the same time. Until right now, I had no idea she was staying next door to me tonight. Our rooms are fucking adjoining. Good thing she was out for the last hour.

The moment I close my door, my phone starts to buzz. Nine o'clock on the dot. I toss a T-shirt on and pick up my cell, answering the FaceTime call from the only full-time girl in my life.

"Half pint," I greet as my daughter Mabel's perfect little face comes into view. She's like a happy cherub with long, dark hair and my eyes. I miss her, and it's only been five hours since I saw her last. There wasn't a chance she wasn't going home from the race with my mother, her nana Jo. The two of them are the very best of friends, and Mama promised Mabel all the junk food and movies. She beams at me now through the screen.

"Hi, Daddy. Can I have M&Ms in my popcorn?"

I lean on my side on the bed and make a face.

"Who on earth thinks you should do that?"

"Auntie Ivy." Mabel smiles the toothy eight-year-old grin that makes my heart squeeze, the one where her big girl teeth are still sparse and there is another wiggly baby tooth what seems like almost every day.

She pans the phone to Ivy, whose feet are on the coffee table at the big house at Silver Pines, our family ranch. I can't help but chuckle. She looks exhausted, and she's getting a more pronounced baby bump by the day. My brother comes into view as he cops a squat beside Ivy and passes Mabel a bowl of popcorn.

Wade shrugs at me. "Don't knock it till you try it."

"I make Wade try all my cravings." Ivy giggles as she shoves some popcorn and M&Ms into her mouth. I still can't comprehend how happy Wade looks these days. Still grumpy as fuck with us most of the time, but with Ivy, there isn't a moment that goes by when he isn't making googly eyes at her.

"It's yummy!" Mabel says happily. I chuckle back, slightly cringing that she's eating chocolate at night, but she's happy and I'd do anything for that smile. "When you come home tomorrow, can we go get my new fishing pole for the cabin?" Mabel asks, switching gears the way kids do. She's excited for our annual trip to Lake Charles.

"Sure can, and some new lures that are easy to put on and off so you don't prick your fingers."

Wade snickers. "When you were eight, you were at the river in your bare feet hooking worms by yourself. Relax, chopper dad."

I grin at him through the camera of my phone.

"I can't wait until you get here," I say smugly. He has no idea what it's like to have your heart walk around outside your body every damn day.

"We're going to watch the movie now, Daddy!"

"Okay, buddy," I tell her. "I love you, Mabey Baby."

"I love you, Sir Peanut Butter Cups," Mabel replies in her best monster voice. She loves calling me by the nickname I earned after I held two peanut butter cups up to my eyes to make her laugh when she stubbed her little toe in the kitchen last winter.

We say good night and more *I love you*s so that when I hang up, the silence is deafening. I clean up the room and draw my bed back. I make a point to never fuck a stranger between clean sheets.

I get in the shower, and a million thoughts run through my mind as the hot water soaks my skin.

I'm officially the sheriff of Laurel Creek as of next Monday, although my swearing-in ceremony isn't until mid-June. Which means my shenanigans with different women need to stop. Our county is old-school. Real old school, and even though I've been elected, all the public needs to oust me within the first ninety days is one small scandal. After the way my predecessor was recently pushed out when he got caught stealing money, the older sticklers in town will be watching me like a hawk.

Not to mention that my deputy sheriff, Brent Wilson, is Gemma's on-again, off-again boyfriend and would happily throw me under the bus if he thought he had a chance at my job. When I'm through with my shower and back in the main room, I hear Ginger's TV through the wall.

I grin as I decide I want to ruffle her feathers. Knowing she has a love/hate relationship with scary movies, I search up cheesy ghost sounds on YouTube and crank my phone's volume up to full blast, pressing it to the hollow door between our spaces. I wait. The sound must be getting through to her; these walls are paper-thin. Sure enough, my phone buzzes in my hand seconds later.

> **VIXEN**
> You have my attention, Michael Myers. I'm currently hiding in the closet waiting for my demise.

I can just hear the sassy tone she'd use.

> **ME**
> You watch your TV at a ridiculous volume level.

> **VIXEN**
> Well, I had to be on the safe side. Didn't know if you'd be hauling in the next conquest.

> **ME**
> I'm on a break, what are you doing, smartass?

> **VIXEN**
> Eating Skittles and thinking about room service.

> **ME**
> They got 99? Wanna come over?

VIXEN

Ew no. Not stepping one foot in that pussy-scented love den.

I blow out a breath. Fuck, why can't I ever just keep it in my pants?

VIXEN

Come here. Hose yourself down and bring your wallet. You can buy me a late night snack. These Skittles aren't cutting it.

I toss on a hoodie. She doesn't have to ask me twice.

ME

Deal.

VIXEN

Try to make it without picking some poor unsuspecting girl up on the way.

ME

Well, if I'm late you know why.

VIXEN

I don't wait. The offer expires in 3, 2 . . .

I unlock my adjoining door and knock at hers between our rooms just as the last text comes through, and she swings it open with an eyebrow raise and a sexy smirk.

"Such a good boy. Hope you brought that wallet." She smiles, reaching up to pat me on the head as if I'm five. Her tone is full of her trademark sass but zero judgment, and just walking in here feels like entering a safe space. Her club attire is long gone, and she stands in the middle of her tidy room, hair piled high on her head, fresh-faced, wearing sleep shorts and a tank.

"You would've let me in anyway and you know it." I pinch her shirt playfully on the way in and let out a breath I didn't know I was holding until the moment I saw her pretty face.

CHAPTER TWO
Ginger

Of course he was pushing some woman to the elevator when I got off. Typical Cole *Weston* Ashby. To say he's never been a real one-woman man since his disaster of a marriage would be an understatement. I'm not sure if he'll ever settle down again and I'd be okay if he didn't at least for a little while. I like what we have. Over the last couple years we've become friends, sort of. I mean, he's definitely the one who pushes all my buttons, but he's also the first person I'd call to bail me out of jail.

Our friendship is unique and it's enough. After all, sometimes I get lonely too. Hookups are easy, but finding someone you don't hate watching TV with? Someone who actually puts the *comfortable* in comfortable silence? Not so much.

"I ordered room service. Pizza and nachos. Figured you'd need to replenish your carbs after your 'workout,'" I tell him as he breezes through the door. His sweatshirt sleeves are pushed up to his elbows, his arm bearing Mabel's name in ink. He's wearing gray Nike sweatpants that fit him just right, his wet hair from the shower touches his forehead, and he smells so damn good. Too good.

If he wasn't Cole . . . I would be having totally different thoughts about how this night should go.

"You tracking my every move?" he jokes. "What are the odds you walk off the elevator the second she leaves?"

I laugh and tighten my messy bun.

"It's programmed into my psyche to not be around when you're in the middle of . . . that." I wrinkle my nose. "I'm not sure my body would recover if I had to listen to you and your lady friends." I hold my hands to my heart.

"Oh, *Weston*," I fake-moan in my highest-pitched voice. "I *never* do this. Tell me again how you don't either," I mock. "That's it, right there . . ." I fall back on the couch in a fit of giggles. Cole grimaces in response.

"Alright, that's enough," Cole says, a tinge of annoyance in his voice. "Just put the show on, woman."

Cole makes his way to my minibar and grabs himself a Coke, then settles on the sofa beside me.

"Seriously, though, she re-up your cup?" I ask him.

He gives me a way-too-serious look.

"It's hurtful that you think so little of me. How do you know I don't have feelings for Stacey? An instant connection neither of us could fight?" he asks.

I laugh in spite of myself, then pat him on the head. "Well, for one, because I met her at the race, and her name is *Tracey*."

Cole chuckles in defeat.

"And two, because *she's* not here. Instead, you're spending your Saturday night watching Andy Samberg." I toss a Skittle at him. "With me."

He picks it off his sweater and pops it in his mouth. "She was alright."

"What's her story?"

"Kept telling me to call her Miss Riverbend County." Cole

snickers as he cracks his soda. I let the ridiculousness of that scenario play out in my mind.

Cole lets his head fall back on the back of the sofa and groans.

"Fuck, I have to get my shit together. I'm the sheriff now. Nights like these need to stop." He's muttering to himself like he does sometimes when we're together.

I pull my legs up to my chest. I'm used to him talking like this. I try to be the only person who doesn't judge him. He is who he is, and when the hell else is he supposed to get laid with a daughter to care for 24/7?

"You have a lot on your shoulders. Tomorrow is a new day." I smile at him as the knock at the door tells us our pizza is here.

"That's what you say every time." He smirks and gets up to grab our food.

We watch our favorite reruns of *Brooklyn Nine-Nine* for the next hour while chatting about everything and anything: my summer, Nash and CeCe's wedding, our friend group's trip to Vegas next weekend. Conversation flows easily, but, then again, it always does.

"Truth or dare?" I ask him as we watch an episode we've seen at least five times before.

"Truth?" he mutters as he leans back on the sofa. "I'm too tired for a dare."

"You never choose dare." I toss a pillow at him. "Real talk, do you ever give any of these women a fighting chance? You never know, one of these days any given Tracey could be the one," I say, genuinely curious to hear his answer. "But you'd have to actually try."

Cole shrugs his broad shoulders and extends his hands behind his head.

"I enjoy women. I make sure they enjoy me. That's where it ends."

"TMI . . ." I retort, although there's really nothing that is too much for me when it comes to Cole. "But glad to know you're just cocky enough to consider yourself advanced in the women's enjoyment department."

He gives a half grin but doesn't say anything.

"Maybe you're choosing too many amateurs," I push on. "You should start screening them first to make sure they're on your level so they don't bore you. You could have a sign-up sheet, or hold auditions."

Cole's grin grows wider, but he keeps his eyes on the TV.

"I could wear a T-shirt when I go out that says 'Not for beginners'?" he counters.

"Title of your sex tape?" I retort, referencing *Brooklyn Nine-Nine* one-liners.

He looks over and leans in, a wide smile on his lips.

"Or 'Advanced Users Only'?"

"Fuck," I say, although it comes out a little breathless. "Please stop."

There's a beat before we both laugh, and I toss another Skittle at him.

He scrubs his freshly shaved jaw with the back of his knuckles.

"I'm used to women telling me to do anything *but* stop, Vixen," he says in a low voice and pinches my calf. It's meant to be playful, but his tone is too low for my lady bits to handle.

"Gross," I say, averting my eyes from his.

"Look, the truth is, everyone needs their thing, and the women I meet, they're my only vice. Though sometimes I wish I'd chosen better the first time around. But the moment that thought goes through my head I feel like shit. Because Mabes wouldn't be who she is if she had a different mom."

I nod. I want children, but I can't imagine the weight of a human being's life on your back. Cole turns his whiskey eyes on mine. There's a glint in them that tells me the serious talk is over, and he's about to say something mischievous.

"Your turn. Truth or dare?"

"Dare. Always," I answer confidently as I take a sip of my water, readying myself for whatever Cole tells me to do.

"You sound so sure of yourself." He tilts forward, his elbows resting on his muscular legs as he thinks.

"You're tired after all that advanced sex, remember? Probably can't come up with much at this hour. I'd say a dare is a safe bet."

The glint in his eye comes back as he picks up the remote to the TV.

He opens YouTube and searches "Macarena dance" before handing me back the remote. It's the song I performed junior year with CeCe and Liv as part of our talent show routine, and he knows it as it starts to play. He also knows I hate it.

"Grr." I grunt at him but stand anyway.

"Backing down already?"

I narrow my eyes at him.

"A dare is a dare, so . . . start dancing," he commands like a drill sergeant. "And I'll be judging your technique."

Cole leans back and folds his thick arms behind his head, relaxed and ready to watch me thoroughly embarrass myself. But he should never underestimate my willingness to beat him at his own game. I smooth my tank and take my place in the middle of the room.

"Atta girl." He grins.

The beat kicks in, and I throw him a small smile.

This is about to become the sexiest macarena dance he's ever seen, all in a plot to make him uncomfortable as hell and call it off.

I slink closer to stand right in front of Cole's legs. I cock a hip and pull my hair out of its bun, it tumbles down around my shoulders. Then I blow a real slow kiss at him.

"The fuck are you doing?" he asks, recoiling, shock lining his face. *Excellent.*

"What you asked, darlin'," I say sweetly. "Just playing out my dare."

Cole's throat bobs as he swallows hard, but he doesn't take his eyes off me.

I begin to roll my hips smoothly as the beat continues. The dance doesn't call for a sexy hip roll, but I do it anyway. Like I said, he asked for it.

I extend my arms, palms down, palms up, palms to my shoulders, the back of my head, giving him the sexiest gaze I can. I'm staring into this man's goddamn soul. I look right at him and move as seductively as possible, crossing one arm to my left hip then the other to my right. His hazy gaze takes hold of me for a split second, and for a moment, it feels as though he's reeling me in as much as I am him.

I force myself to look away, tossing my hair around like I'm dancing for grocery money. I swear I hear Cole gulp, and I smile internally. *Gotcha.*

I watch my own movements carefully then look up to meet his gaze.

One hand to my left ass cheek, one to my right with a loud snap. I roll my hips slowly and part my lips. I wait for him to call it, but my plan is backfiring, because Cole doesn't tell me to stop.

Instead, his eyes are dark, stormy, and raking over me with a vengeance. I've never seen him look at *me* like this before. The dance that was meant to be a joke continues because I'm more stubborn than he is, though this is quickly becoming the riskiest game of chicken I've ever played.

Just as the singer croons the chorus line, I complete a jump to swivel my ass right in front of where Cole sits. He clears his throat and stands, giving in before I do.

"Alright, fuck, *enough*," he growls.

I stop dutifully and start laughing, knowing I pushed the weirdness level too far but not giving a shit. He deserved it.

"Always gotta win, don't you?" he says defeatedly.

I point the remote, nixing the hideous song, and put our favorite show back on.

Ginger 1. Cole 0.

"Always, Law Daddy," I answer, pretending the way he just looked at me didn't settle right into my memory for all eternity. *"Always."*

CHAPTER THREE
Ginger

"Favor?" I ask in a squeaky voice. Considering it's the middle of the night, I'm sure he already knows what that favor is.

I hear the sound of his latest fling ask who it is. Shit.

I continue giving him a plethora of excuses.

"He's wasted, and I didn't, I mean, I am not calling my dad. I'd rather hitchhike." I pull my phone away from my ear and check the battery: 12 percent.

Please say yes . . .

"How many times have I told you not to rely on him? You know he's gonna get shitfaced and either leave you hanging or pass out."

I should've known I couldn't call Cole Ashby for a ride without a lecture. As if I need it. I know my boyfriend, Silas, is a dick, especially when he drinks. I blame his chiseled abs. All he has to do is flash them, and I lose all train of thought. Plus, being the girlfriend of the upcoming University of Kentucky football star has its perks, namely the envy of every mean girl at school who's ever called me fat or made fun of my hair, my braces, or my height.

"I don't need a lecture right now, Cole. I need a ride. Can you come, or do I have to hitchhike?"

"I'll be there in ten," he huffs out before I hear the phone click. He's pissed. He just started dating Lindsay Billings, who probably won't like that he's leaving to pick up his little sister's friend at two A.M., but I don't have anyone else to call. CeCe is God knows where. She and Olivia left with two football players an hour ago when I told them I was staying with Silas, and I would've walked the three miles home before calling my dad.

I don't go back in to tell Silas I'm leaving. He took some kind of psychedelic with two of his football buddies an hour ago. They're on their offseason now and taking full advantage.

I'm practicing how I'm going to end things with Silas tomorrow when the headlights of Cole's pickup truck round the corner of Second and Williams Street.

I wave a hand so he sees me.

"I am starting a job at Jennings Décor tomorrow for the summer," I say as I get in and grab my seatbelt. "I told him I didn't want to stay late, but he never listens."

Cole looks at me with a stern face, which I hate. He's only three years older than me but he thinks he's so much more mature. He's just got his own cabin at his family's ranch too, which doesn't help. He really has his life together. We weren't surprised when he chose something other than ranching as a career. CeCe said he never really liked ranching much, and that he wanted to make a difference in the community instead. He's attending the Police Foundation's program at our local technical college, which he's almost finished. As if he needed a boost in the hotness meter, becoming a cop definitely does it for me. Something about a uniform and him ready to serve and protect makes him even sexier than before.

I sigh and look out the window. I'm used to being attracted to Cole; I just don't usually let the thoughts roll through my mind, but what can I say. Four vodka coolers later and here we are.

"You can't be surprised he didn't listen to you. In case you haven't noticed, guy's a dick." Cole grunts.

"Thanks, Captain Obvious."

"Look, I'm leaving for Grosvenor in a couple of days to work for the summer, and CeCe is going to Seattle soon. You won't be able to call me for a ride. And besides, it's going to get weird if I'm leaving to pick you up like this when my sister doesn't even live here anymore. Lindsay was pissed tonight." He mentions his current fling.

"Can't you just tell her I'm like your sister? It is very brotherly of you to come get me." I grin at him, but he doesn't return my smile.

"I don't think she would buy that. This is the second time since I started dating her that you've called me after midnight. Last time she accused me of screwing you on the side."

I make a weird scoffing noise. Lindsay is jealous? Of me? She looks like a Victoria's Secret model. Long legs, thin, silky straight hair. I am the polar opposite of that. Short, curvy, and my hair is wild and out-of-control curly. Unless he was looking for how far he could stray outside his type . . .

"Well, obviously that's not happening. As if you'd ever try to hook up with me. She's drop-dead gorgeous." I laugh at how ridiculous it sounds. Cole's jaw sets and he wears that annoyed look again.

"And you know, you don't have to answer when I call," I continue because it's true, he doesn't. But he always does. "One day you'll be asking me for help."

He laughs in disbelief.

"I'll believe it when I see it, but I'm not going to have you walk home. What kind of almost cop would I be?" His annoyance melts into a soft grin, and my heart flutters in my chest.

God, he's gorgeous. He was always solid playing sports and working with Wade in the barns, but since he started training to be a cop, he's filled out even more. CeCe says he works out like two hours a day. I sigh.

"Well, thank you, Cole."

"Y'owe me. What's that now? Eight? Ten favors?" He playfully pushes at my shoulder.

He turns onto my street, Royal Oak Drive, the large spread of *traditional Cape Cods and colonials on perfectly manicured, tree-lined streets. We live in the part of town that is dubbed Pill Hill, because most of the people who live here are doctors, shrinks, or lawyers. You'd think I would love it, but the truth is I can't wait to have my own place. Something small, off the beaten path, maybe boho chic, messy, and a little chaotic.*

"Eleven actually," I tell him, keeping my gaze out the window.

"When it's my turn to cash in, I'm gonna collect big time," Cole says as he pulls up to my house. It might be the only one on the street that still has its front lights on. My dad is up, and probably waiting to berate me for my life choices, tell me how everything I do affects him and our family. Same old, same old.

I grimace as I look up at our six-bedroom colonial, one of the biggest on the street. My dad is a wealthy man. He was a successful lawyer before becoming local alderman last spring. Now he has congressional aspirations. He's running for the third district. Small business affairs and he also owns commercial properties in downtown Laurel Creek. He didn't become this successful by missing details. Edward Danforth never misses anything that could affect his reputation, especially not the fact that his only daughter is two hours past her curfew. But my feelings, or what's going on in my life? If it doesn't fit well into his plan for me, he doesn't mind missing that.

"Well, looks like this night's just about to get even better," I say sarcastically.

"He still on you about college?" Cole asks, putting the truck in park. The muscles in his forearms ripple as he does so, and I do my best not to stare.

I fail as always.

"Yeah, he says horticulture isn't a career." I've always wanted to be a florist, maybe own my own shop someday. "Wants me to do something noble and serving. Like teaching or law. Funny thing is, I would never want to be a lawyer."

"Would you want to teach?"

I shrug. "I don't know. I love kids, I've had some good teachers. I have the grades to do it. But sometimes I feel like no matter what I do, it will disappoint him just a little."

"There is nothing about you that should disappoint him," Cole says sincerely.

He wets his lips, and I wonder what it would be like to be Lindsay, to have that beautiful, warm body press up against me, plant kisses down my neck, murmur sweet things to me—

"Ginger?" Cole snaps me out of my daydream. Am I panting?! *Shit. Cole and alcohol are a bad mix.*

"Uh—thanks again, for picking me up. Sorry to interrupt whatever you were doing with Paris Hilton," I say, fiddling with my purse strap.

Cole looks over at me.

"Meh, no biggie. I'm not really feeling it anyway. She gets kind of needy to be honest. You did me *a favor if you want the truth." He chuckles.* Typical Cole. Never stays with one girl for too long.

I check my invisible watch. "Well, I mean it's been what? Three whole weeks? You're way past due."

"Fuck off," he scoffs. I smile and make to get out of the truck.

"Hey, Vixen?" Cole's hand darts out to stop me. He's been calling me that more often this year, mostly whenever he's bailing me out of one harebrained situation or another, like this one. He doesn't have a nickname for any of CeCe's other friends, so I take it as a win. I turn to face him.

"Hmmm?"

"Don't let that fucking Silas prick treat you like that." He slides his large hand downward, placing it on my knee. I try to ignore the way his touch sends heat to every cell in my body, how it feels too close, even through my jeans. I look at his hand then back up to his eyes. His normally amber hue is molten. He's so close I can feel the heat from his skin, smell his minty breath, and my insides turn liquid.

"I mean it. You deserve better than that bullshit," he mutters, flexing his grip lightly on my thigh.

"Why, thank you for the advice, officer," I say dutifully, mocking him, trying to sound a lot cooler than I feel.

"I'm calling in my first favor," he blurts.

I gulp and raise an eyebrow. "Oh?"

"Yeah, oh," he says. "Just, fuck. You don't . . . see yourself the way other people do."

I laugh nervously and look out the front window.

"Are you complimenting me, Cole Ashby?"

He shakes his head. "I mean it, Ginger. I'm telling you this so that, even though I give you a hard time, you know your worth. And I'll always come when you call, okay? Just . . . find someone better."

I don't know if it's his hand still on my thigh, the intense way he's looking at me, or the vodka. Maybe a combination of all three? But something inside me breaks. I very slowly and intently inch my body closer across the bench seat, notching myself against him, alcohol-induced confidence taking over. I reach my hand to the side of his face and look deep into his eyes, like I'm asking permission. He doesn't move. He doesn't speak, so I tilt my head, slide my hand around his chiseled waist, and pull him close, capturing his lips with mine.

The moment we connect, static lines every part of me. I'm no longer liquid, I'm pure fire, every inch of me burning for him. I moan as Cole's hands circle my waist, and I press my body closer against his. For one second, everything feels so right, perfect even. For one second.

Until those hands push me away.

The buzzing sound continues like a leaky faucet, interrupting my dream of one of the most embarrassing nights of my life. I open one eye and see my phone five feet away on the coffee table.

The room is bright. Almost midday bright. I stretch my

legs out on the couch and feel the warmth of Cole's arm under my toes. We fell asleep again. I give him a nudge as I pick up my phone and flip it over. I groan.

"Father."

"Darling," he replies curtly, all business.

"It's almost noon. Are you just waking up?" he asks. I can hear the displeasure in his voice. "You weren't out doing anything you shouldn't be, were you? You know the primaries are coming up."

Yes, Father, I do. One wet T-shirt contest for charity in college, and I'm ruined for life, it seems.

"No, I've been up for hours," I lie.

Cole yawns like a yeti at the other end of the couch, not realizing I'm on the phone. I kick him. His eyes flit open, and my core twinges. I try very hard not to fall asleep with Cole because the way he looks in the morning, hair ruffled, warm and toasty against my body is just—

"You sound like you're half asleep. Are you still coming for dinner tomorrow night? Your mother is trying to figure out how many places to set."

As if I have a choice.

"Yes, of course I'll be there."

"Are you bringing anyone?" he asks hopefully.

"Wasn't planning on it," I say dryly, rolling my eyes.

"Hmm, I see. See you at seven sharp. Be punctual."

"Yes sir," I mock before hanging up. I flop back on the couch and groan.

"Don't you have your own room?" I ask Cole as he stretches.

"I tried to leave, but you were sleep talking." He grins. "Begged me to stay."

I kick him harder and put my hand to my ear.

"What's that now? You have to go? Such a shame," I say, standing and grabbing my toiletries. Cole chuckles and sits up, working the knots out of his neck from the uncomfortable couch.

"That's it, use me and kick me to the curb before I've even had a morning coffee." Cole goes to adjust himself and, even though I try not to look, it's hard not to.

"You know, I think that's what *she* said." I wink, ignoring the way morning Cole seems to get to me every damn time.

Cole laughs in spite of himself.

"Fuck, *she* is staying here. I can't even go downstairs for breakfast. I was supposed to leave early this morning."

"Not a chance I'm feeling sorry for you and your first-world fuckboy problems." I roll my eyes. "And you're going to have to find someone else to share a couch with when we're in Vegas next weekend. The family might think it's weird if you sneak out of mine and Olivia's room in the morning. And I'm also not about to explain your need to hang out with me all the time to CeCe right now when she's a bit of a bridezilla," I say without looking at him as I rummage through my overnight bag for my yoga pants.

Cole laughs from behind me.

"Guess I'll just have to find some other grumpy, non–morning person to hang out with while we're there."

"Good, then your knees can dig into someone else's back all night."

I gather all my items into a pile in my arms, balancing my clean socks between my chin and my toiletries because I'm a one-trip bitch.

"Don't worry about CeCe. She's too involved in her own life to notice anything we do." He points at me. "And don't act like you don't enjoy my company."

He stands and tosses his hoodie back on over his T-shirt. When his head pops through, he's wearing a big, dimpled smile.

"I feel the way you snuggle your feet into my side when you're falling asleep and snoring like a little freight train."

I narrow my eyes at him and decide to give up my stack of perfectly gathered items in exchange for tossing my socks at him. They hit him square in the face. *So worth it.*

"I cannot be held accountable for any snuggling I do when I'm unconscious. And I do *not* snore," I say heatedly. "Now I need a shower and a coffee. Time to go pursue your next victim. Toodles, Law Daddy."

I gather my items again and head to get ready without so much as a glance back.

"You definitely snore!" I hear him retort as I shut the bathroom door behind me. I take my time in the shower, mulling over the impending dinner with my parents, particularly my father. He hasn't invited me because he wants to spend time together. He wants to go over his primary schedule and anything he might "need" from me.

I know my father was hoping I would bring David Black with me. He's the son of a colleague, a lawyer just like him, and for some reason when he introduced him to me last month, he thought we were a match made in heaven. David was nice enough, tall, dark, and handsome, but also a little arrogant and self-absorbed. The entire dinner my parents awkwardly arranged was spent listening to him tell me how many cases he's won and how he's going to make partner soon. Not my type, but it's becoming increasingly clear that my parents think he is the kind to "settle down" with. The last guy they loved like that was the son of my dad's newly appointed political advisor. Brock. The good guy. The guy who seemed as though he'd do anything for me. My parents adored him, and I even kind of fell for him, thought he may have been the one, until he broke my heart. I found him in the shower of my dorm with a girl from down the hall. It had been going on for weeks while I busted my ass at my placement study. Ever since then, I've only casually dated now and then. I don't really see the point of anything more until Mr. Sweep Me Off My Feet comes around. Aside from the obvious, and I have enough vibrators for that.

When I finish in the shower, Cole is gone, probably already checked out to get back to Mabel.

I'm just packing everything into my suitcase when there is a knock at my door as my phone buzzes on the bedside table simultaneously.

I go for the door first.

"Good afternoon." A concierge flashes me a smile as I swing open the door.

"Oh, I didn't order anything—"

"This is from Mr. Ashby," he cuts in, pushing the cart into my room.

He hands me the slip of paper, and I read the breakfast menu: coffee, Greek yogurt with berries, and granola.

I pull a five out of my purse and thank him as I close the door. Making my way over to my phone, I see texts from Cole and Liv, my and CeCe's other best friend.

LAW DADDY

Don't drive on an empty stomach. Also probiotics and berries will help with that really miserable mood you were in when I left.

ME

Your fault for trying to talk before coffee. Did you get out of here without being spotted?

LAW DADDY

Barely. Till next time, Grandpa.

ME

Grandpa?

LAW DADDY

Shit, sorry, all that snoring, got you confused with my pop.

ME

In that case till next time, Professor Fitts.

A few seconds go by.

LAW DADDY

Did you just name the Laurel Creek High biology teacher? I'm not going to ask.

ME

Oh sorry, I was just remembering the last man that made me fall asleep from just talking, like you did last night.

LAW DADDY

Terrible attempt at a joke. Enjoy your breakfast, asshole.

Yes sir. I grin and start happily munching on my strawberries, opening Liv's messages as I do.

LIV

Look what I scored.

I open the image. It's a photo of two silky sashes that read "The bride's bitches." I smile. This weekend will be one for the ages. Nash has chartered us a private flight to Vegas, and we're all heading down for his and CeCe's "together" bachelor and bachelorette party. "Together" because they are disgustingly obsessed with each other and can't bear to spend one night apart.

ME

Perfect.

LIV

I thought so.

LIV

What are you doing? Lunch? Sage N Salt?

I look at the time. Twelve-thirty.

ME

I am just leaving Lexington now, so about an hour?

LIV

You're just leaving now?

I sip my coffee.

ME

I slept in.

LIV

It happened again didn't it.

Liv is the only person in the world who knows about my and Cole's rather unique friendship.

ME

See you in an hour.

LIV

You know you're like a girlfriend without the

perks. In porn they call that a fluffer. Just saying.

I roll my eyes and do my best to end this conversation.

ME

See you soon, porn expert.

Precisely an hour later, I'm seated at the outdoor patio in the sun at the Sage N Salt, the hot lunch spot in our quaint little town of Laurel Creek with Olivia giving me a stare that says, "The jig is up."

"*What?*" I ask defensively as I sip my iced tea.

"Look, I got it when his marriage was falling apart and he needed a friend. I got it when they split, even, and he didn't want to be alone."

I push my sunglasses farther up my nose.

"But what is the reason you guys still do this *now*? He's been separated from Gemma for over two years. How do you always end up back together but never *together*?"

She eats a forkful of her pasta as I push my quinoa and chicken around on my plate.

"He's like a stray dog." I grin.

"Uh-huh." Liv smiles back. "And it has nothing to do with the fact that you've always been semi-infatuated with him, and whenever he calls, you come running?"

I think back to all the times I've been there for Cole when he's needed me over the years.

"He was in the room next to mine. We watched some TV. We're friends," I say simply. "And he was always there for me too." I hold a finger up. "Before you ask, I don't know why."

"I do." She smiles, tightening her ponytail high on her head. "You're the only woman in this town he hasn't stuck his dick in."

"He worked through this town years ago. We're *just* friends," I reiterate for the hundredth time.

"Whatever gets you through the day." She winks.

"But just so we're clear, you have no thoughts whatsoever about him hovering his strong body over the top of you? And I won't find you two together in the morning this weekend in Vegas?"

I scoff as the picture she paints washes over me. I think of the way he looked this morning. His brow knotted in sleep, his full lips slightly parted. I clear my throat as my heart rate starts to accelerate.

"Not a chance," I lie.

CHAPTER FOUR
Ginger

I enter my parents' front hallway the next night and take a deep breath. Nothing here is ever out of place. The flowers that adorn the table in the center of the large space are replaced weekly, the circular staircase is polished to perfection, and the marble floors glimmer as if they've been shined by hand. I'm instantly greeted by the smell of my mother's famous coated chicken marsala—the recipe she still hasn't officially given me. I only know it by watching her sift spices into the bag before she tosses in the chicken. She says she'll leave it to me when she dies, and I tell her by then I'll be too old to cook it.

"Bella," she greets when I enter the vast all-white kitchen. Her long, dark hair, not unlike mine, is loose, her smile is bright and youthful, and she's wearing a tight floral top and leather-looking pants. The sound of Kenny Chesney, always Kenny Chesney, croons to me as she walks around the island to pull me into a warm hug. My mother is the free spirit in this house, always flitting about, trying some new hobby she's excited to share with me. I never understood how she and my father ended up together, a thought reiterated now as he waltzes into the kitchen in a shirt, tie, and dress shoes. A uniform in his own house. He's the epitome of old money and my mother's polar opposite. His father owned the pulp and paper mill outside of town, and when he died, my father sold it off to the highest bidder. He never had any use for it, going into law. Now, readying to enter his second term as a congressman, he never stops working and is the most organized, critical man I know. Just being in the same room as him makes me stand up straighter.

"Good evening, darling," he says as he kisses me on the top of my head. "I'm still disappointed you didn't call David back. He was quite interested in you when you met."

Nice to see you too. I'm well, thank you for asking.

"I will never do well with being set up on a surprise blind date."

"It wasn't like that." My mother eyes me with disapproval. "We just want you to find your person sooner rather than later so I won't be an old biddy of a nonna."

"That won't happen." I roll my eyes. "You'll outlive us all."

I walk around the island and pour some of my mother's homemade wine into a bowl-shaped glass. If there's one thing this woman can do, it's create the most delicious concoctions. Italian roots for the win. I take a sip and survey our home, modern but decorated with my mother's heritage in every room. In the kitchen it's the backsplash, a bold navy and white fleuret design to the ceiling, adorned by maple wood beams. Well, that, and the line of spices over the stove, dried orange and lemon zest, bay leaves, oregano, garlic, capers—the flavors of my childhood.

"*Mia cara,*" my nonna says as she enters the kitchen. The hug she gives me is soft and full of love. She came to America with her parents from Sicily when she was twelve, and they worked together at Scoops, our local ice cream shop, until the summer before her senior year, when she met my granddad. She tells us it was love at first sight, and they married, and she had my mother before her nineteenth birthday. I'm blessed beyond measure to have her still so youthful in her late sixties. Her stature is small like mine, and she has short, naturally dark hair even at her age. She wears glasses and has a twinkle in her eye that never dims. My granddad simply died too young, and I always hope there may be someone for her yet. CeCe and I often joke about matching her up with Papa Dean Ashby. Until we remember Papa Dean wouldn't know what to do with someone as spicy as her.

"Are they giving you *tutta la merda*—all the shit—before the dinner salad has even been served?"

"Of course." I grin at the fact she still says *shit*, and every other curse word, in Italian, regardless of the fact that she's lived here for fifty-seven years. She grips both sides of my face.

"You're lovely just the way you are. Don't let them rush you. When you find the right one, you'll know." She pats the side of my face and raises her voice so my mother can hear.

"Your mother should've had more children. Instead, she pins all her hopes on you to give her grandbabies."

"Is that such a terrible thing?" my mother calls back while tossing a green salad. "I just want my baby to be happy and give me babies to love in return. There could be worse things."

"Preferably she will find a man who has some business experience and a good strong work ethic. Like that David," my dad says in a curt tone, wagging a finger as he sips his wine. I take a giant gulp of mine.

"Both of you, please," I mumble.

As if living alone with an excellent teaching career at twenty-six makes me a spinster.

"Pay them no attention, honey," my nonna says as she pats

my hand and takes a seat at the island. "Tell me all about what you'll do this summer."

I prop my face onto my palm and think for a moment.

"I'm going to help CeCe with the wedding, tan, maybe do some cleaning and redecorating, or take up a part-time job to help bridge the gap from my pay dock."

I only get partial pay during the summer months, which is why I normally take on extra classes, but I need a break from teaching this year.

"I've been thinking about maybe helping Liv out at her boutique. But I'm *not* going to look for a husband," I say, glancing at my father. He eyes me over his glass.

"These things have to come naturally," I say, getting up to refill my glass and kiss him on the head.

"Ginger, please, it's never too early to start looking. You must think of the future." And *some man to help bolster your political career.* "There's a young man out of Tennessee. I met him at a dinner a few weeks ago, an alderman. If you come to the fundraiser this weekend in Lexington, he'll be—"

"I'm going to Las Vegas this weekend with Nash and CeCe," I cut him off.

"Hmphh," he grumbles. "City of sin and overindulgence. Remember trouble can follow you no matter where you go. There is always a video waiting to be posted somewhere."

"I will try very hard not to get knocked up, knocked out, or strip in the middle of the strip," I say with a grin as I pop an olive and a piece of cheese into my mouth from a platter on the island.

"Ginger Lily! We're just looking out for you," he says, his brow furrowed.

"And criticizing me," I fire back.

"We just don't want you to end up an old woman all alone," my mother says dramatically.

"Like me." My nonna grins. We lock eyes, she waggles her eyebrows, and we giggle conspiratorially.

My mother ignores our laughs and wags her salad tongs at my father. "Oh! Didn't you say Emilio Cruz's son is recently divorced?" She turns her bright brown eyes to me. "He's got two kids already. You could be a stepmama!"

I look at my nonna and roll my eyes. This is exactly the reason I don't come home for dinner very often.

CHAPTER FIVE
Cole

"**P**lay nice, kid," my office administrator, Bev, warns as I enter the reception area on my way to my next meeting.

I've known Bev since I was a rookie. She's in her late fifties and keeps everything in this building in order, including me. She's the only one I trust enough to vent to about Brent, who she thinks is "like a little weasel with an agenda." A weasel that always needs some busywork.

"Always." I grin as I hand her a freshly brewed coffee from our mediocre machine.

She accepts it eagerly.

"Have you eaten today?" she asks. Some men have a work wife, I have a work mother.

"Not yet. I'll grab something quick after this meeting," I say, glancing at my phone for the time. How is it after one already?

"How's it going this morning, deputy?" I ask, playing nice, when I enter Brent's office a few minutes later. He's been asking for this meeting since last week. He's a fairly big guy and looks like your typical Kentucky farm boy. I've known him for years and, while he used to be strong and fit, judging by his beer gut now, I'm guessing he sucks back a few too many after work.

He sits up in his chair when he sees me, puffing up his chest as he pulls documents out of his drawer.

"I wanted to talk to you about the policy I think needs changing," he says, attempting an authoritative voice.

Here we go . . .

I grit my molars.

"Which policy?"

"Your spending policy." *Sounds about right.*

"Well, that will be easy. Seeing as this is my third day, I haven't spent anything."

I scrub my jaw.

"Oh, wait, grabbed Bev some label tape yesterday when I left the courthouse." I grin.

"I mean for the future." He sneers. He hates that I'm his boss. "After what happened with Sheriff Sims, I think we need to open everything up. Currently we only report the general account online. That is because any money he was using to pad his own pockets came from the facilities fund. He was allotting a huge budget for food for inmates and then buying the bare minimum. Instead, he'd purchase gift cards at the local grocery store to gamble online."

I nod. I know all this already, of course.

I lean back in my chair across from him. Fuck it, I have nothing to hide.

"Great idea," I say, nodding. His tensed jaw falls slack with my agreement. "Why don't you head a financial responsibility committee?"

If I don't pick my battles, it's going to be a long-ass four years.

"Okay. I can ask Tucker, Bates, and . . . Fuller to help."

I nod. "Sure. And you'll keep monthly spending reports of every cent you spend too. Everyone will. Let's show this town we've got nothing to hide. Oh, and you can start by getting me a detailed report of every place we can save. Let's do what's best for the county." I stand and get ready to head out to the planning meeting I have next for some new training programs I'm thinking of running for the deputies. "Oh, and Brent. I'll expect those reports with weekly logs of your time Mondays by nine A.M."

"That seems like a waste of your time to read through all that," he says. Brent hates paperwork, never getting to his statements and reports when they need to be on time. "I can just handle this for you."

Yeah, or do his best to twist what's going on here and make it look like I'm doing something I'm not. I don't trust this guy as far as I can throw him, and I know firsthand from loyal constituents he was spreading rumors about me after Sims was fired, hoping to take the top spot over me.

"I'm sure you can handle it." I put my hat on. "But what kind of sheriff would I be if I didn't have a hand in everything my staff was doing?"

He doesn't answer before I breeze back by Bev on the way to the boardroom.

"That should keep him busy and out of your hair for a few days," I tell her with a grin.

"Your facilitator for the safe work environment class is already in your office. There's sandwiches there if you're hungry," she calls out as I head down the hall.

"You're the best, Bev!"

This sheriff gig is going to take a lot out of me, but as long as I leave this place better than I found it, I'll be satisfied. Even if that means I have to make nice with Brent.

The rest of my week flows effortlessly with Brent knee-deep in last year's expenses, and by mid-afternoon on Friday, as I'm driving to pick up Mabes from the ranch, I find myself actually looking forward to our Vegas weekend. I haven't been away in . . . forever. The last time was a few years ago when Wade and I went to watch Nash play in game five of the playoffs for the Stanley Cup in Dallas.

I pull up to the house and see my girl on the porch munching on a huge ice cream cone next to Harley, our family dog. My mama's Johnny and June plays through a Bluetooth speaker softly as she rocks and reads on the double porch swing, the trees sway in the fields beyond the house, making for a picture-perfect backdrop. I suppose I should be appreciating how settling it is, but the only thing I'm thinking is, *There goes Mabel's lunch.* My mother raises her hands when she sees me as if to say she's not guilty for giving my eight-year-old an ice cream the size of her head.

"We've talked about this," I say as I shut my truck door.

"It wasn't me. Pop made it for her," Mama replies, standing to give me a squeeze.

"She helped me weed the whole back garden," Pop says, coming through the door with an ice cream of his own, somehow even bigger than Mabel's. "Don't be such a hard ass. A little ice cream won't kill her."

"That's another dollar in my swear boot, Great Pop." Mabel reminds him he owes her a dollar every time he swears. We all do.

"I put ten in your boot when you got here. I'm all paid up." He winks.

"You guys really don't get the idea of the swear boot, do

you?" I ask my grandfather as I shake my head, leaning against the old wooden porch rail. "And, Mama, please try to keep the sugar to a minimum when I'm gone this weekend."

"What do I always say?" she asks, folding her arms over her chest and reclaiming her seat beside Mabel. "When she's here, she's my girl. Not yours." She grins at Mabel, and I remind myself to be grateful I have my family so close and willing to help. I watch my daughter wink back at my mother. I laugh and lean forward to ruffle her hair. When the hell did she get so grown up? A pang of guilt hits my chest for leaving her this weekend. I don't like being away from her, even if I know she's going to have the best time with her nana.

"You're going, Cole," my mama says sternly, reading my mind.

"We're going shopping for my dress," Mabel says as she finishes her ice cream and begins crunching down on the cone.

"Are you now?" I ask.

"Yeah, her mama called, said she has to work and probably wouldn't have time to take her before your swearing-in." Mama eyes me carefully, signaling this means Gemma is missing her weekly visit again. She's been talking about taking Mabel shopping in Lexington for two weeks. I eye Mabel, who doesn't seem to care that my mama will be the one taking her. I tell myself that with all the people around her who love her and *are* there for her, maybe she won't notice if one isn't.

I gather Mabel's backpack and load it into the truck.

"We'll be back in two hours," I call, backing out of the driveway. I'm fucking exhausted. The idea of forgoing this whole trip, getting a good long run in, then sitting my ass on my couch with a pizza and some TV flashes through my mind before I give my head a shake. Fuck, what am I? Forty-nine instead of twenty-nine? Maybe I need this weekend after all.

We get home in just under ten minutes. Our house is on the other side of town, near Cave Run Lake, and the place I feel the most comfortable. It's not a huge property but sits on the curve of a tree-lined court with a big pie-shaped lot. Sycamores and catalpa trees frame the yard and create a sense of privacy for our in-ground pool during the summer. It's the perfect place to raise Mabel. She can ride her bike, chalk in our long concrete driveway, and even venture into the court without worrying about any traffic. Most of my neighbors are retired and treat her like the little princess of the street. Our house is a smallish red ranch-style brick home with a big front picture window, three bedrooms, and a double car garage. The best part is that it's all mine. Paid for from years of saving and the allotment my dad left each of us kids when he died. He wanted us to spend it while we were young, and I couldn't think of anything better to invest in than a stable home for Mabes.

Mabel drops her backpack on the bench in our entryway the moment we get in the door.

"Wash up," I tell her as I toe my boots off before heading into the kitchen to start on a late lunch.

I hear the familiar buzz of my phone on the kitchen counter as I enter and start pulling out some meats, cheeses, and fruits from the fridge. When in doubt, a little smorgasbord will do the trick.

There are multiple messages from pretty much everyone I know, including Ginger.

VIXEN

Is this what I can expect from the good sheriff this weekend?

She's attached a video of some kind of Vegas male stripper show. A row of about ten "cops" dance a choreographed routine before ripping their fake uniform shirts from their bodies. I laugh. Christ, this woman never ceases to surprise me.

> **ME**
>
> I don't want to know what you searched to get this. But to answer your question, this is exactly what you can expect. Though I'm a better dancer.

> **VIXEN**
>
> Don't forget to pack those handcuffs and your dancing shoes then, twinkle toes.

> **ME**
>
> Do you know me? I've been packed for two days.

> **VIXEN**
>
> Yeah, I should probably start packing.

> **ME**
>
> I would say that I'm shocked you're not packed, but I'm not. You'll probably start ten minutes before we have to leave and then make me go buy you toothpaste or something when you forget it.

> **VIXEN**
>
> I am not a child, Cole Ashby. But thank you for the toothpaste reminder. 😉

> **ME**
>
> A toothbrush is always good too.

VIXEN

Just worry about yourself and don't forget that sequined Speedo, sheriff.

I scroll through the rest of my messages as I slice up a watermelon and place the food on a platter. I am not the world's greatest chef, but I can pull off an easy lunch on the fly.

SARGE

Is there a luggage limit on this plane? I'm pretty sure Ivy is packing her weight in M&Ms.

NASH

Anyone else excited to see this baby come out candy coated and scowling?

SARGE

Still be better looking than you.

NASH

If he looks like Ivy.

QUEEN JO

Be good kids this weekend. Break hearts, not the law.

I fire back some messages while finishing off Mabel's lunch, also thinking of everything Mabel will need for the weekend. I glance at the clock: ten minutes to clean if I want to have time to pack her stuff and get out of here on time.

"Half pint, lunch's ready!" I call down the hall.

"Coming," Mabel singsongs as she skips into the kitchen.

"I helped," she says with the world's most adorable smile, holding a grocery bag in her tiny hands.

"What did you do, buddy?" I grin, genuinely curious.

"I packed." She holds up her bag. "Two pairs of pajamas, clothes for tomorrow, my toothbrush, Cowey, and socks and underwear. I'm all ready. Oh, and Nana said to bring my slippers." She holds up her stuffed cow, aka Cowey, who goes everywhere with her.

I smile as I pick her up and squeeze her tight.

"You're my favorite girl."

Mabel leans back and holds her hand up for a high five. I give her one.

"We're a team, right, Daddy?" she asks, always knowing my answer.

"You know it, buddy, the best team," I say, kissing her squishy cheek before I set her down at the old weathered kitchen table.

Carrying everything on my shoulders might be overwhelming, but, fuck, I wouldn't change this life for anything. Every time I look at my daughter's face, I know I'm one hundred percent the luckiest man in the world. Mabel eats while I clean and we talk about her weekend. I make sure we both have everything ready to go and check the clock.

It's sin city time.

CHAPTER SIX
Cole

N ash doesn't flash his money around, ever. Dude wears fucking Levi's jeans every damn day. If you didn't know he was an NHL player for nine years, you'd never know he was a multimillionaire.

Walking out to the runway ready to board the private Gulfstream G450 he chartered for our four-hour flight to Vegas, it feels like we're all multimillionaires.

"This how the other half lives, brother?" I ask him and CeCe as they stand in front of the plane's stairs.

"Something like that," Nash replies as we do the brotherly clasp of hands mixed with a half hug. "Only for one weekend," he adds. I can tell he's feeling sheepish about openly spending this much money.

Inside, the plane is luxury wood and ivory leather. It fits fourteen even though only ten of us are flying tonight. Already seated are Wade and Ivy, my sister's other best friend, Olivia Sutton, and Nash's two hockey buddies. Newly retired Stars center Cory Kane and his wife, Anna, talk with another former teammate of Nash's, Chris Bell, who now plays for the New

York Rangers. I've met them both a few times, so I shake their hands easily when I get to an empty seat beside them and drop my bag.

"Banner year so far for you," I say to Chris as I sit. He scored fifty-eight goals in the regular season. He's a grizzly fucker, always fighting dirty. The fans love him.

"Thanks, man. Unfortunately, it wasn't enough to get us past the first round, though." Suddenly, Chris's jaw falls slack, and I lose his eye contact.

"Holy hell, no ring. Dibs," he says, looking over my shoulder. I start to turn to take in the view, but I already know who he's looking at before I see her. Because I hear her, and I *smell* her. Ginger always smells like she has just walked in from the ocean on a Caribbean island. Some mix of coconut, vanilla, and citrus.

"Damn." She pats Nash on the shoulder. "Letting us live in style this weekend, Nashby?"

"God, I'm going to regret this," Nash says, scrubbing his face and eyeing CeCe, who ignores him and makes her way to Ginger for a hug. Ginger releases CeCe and looks back to the rest of the plane. I watch her through Chris's eyes, and her beauty crashes right over me like a fucking tsunami wave. Her normally curly hair is styled in long, layered waves that make her look . . . almost freshly fucked. With those almond-shaped, light brown eyes against her dewy tanned skin, she just looks unreal. I turn away, stopping myself from staring. I won't fall back into that old pattern, not when I've spent years keeping myself in check.

"Well? Who's ready to tear this town up?" she calls out, causing the girls to hoot and holler.

She struts over to the minibar and bends down to grab a bottle of open champagne. Fuck me. She's wearing royal-blue yoga leggings, Nikes, and a white tank top. It's a simple outfit, but she looks downright stunning. Those leggings would take any man out at the knees. They hug every single curve her body offers, and put her heart-shaped ass on display. Ginger is hard not to stare at on a regular day but in *those* leggings. Goddamn. I swallow and turn my eyes back to Chris. He's fucking eating her up.

"I can't believe we haven't met yet. I'm Chris Bell, Nash's friend." Chris addresses Ginger, extending a hand to her for shaking. She turns mid sip to look up at him with her chocolate eyes and a dazzling crimson-painted smile. He's instantly a goner. Yeah, that's gonna stop. I don't like Chris Bell looking at her like that.

"Ginger," she says, shaking his hand back. He smiles wide. *Uh-uh. Nope. No way.*

"When you're settled, come take a seat so we can get acquainted." He says it like he's sure she's all his.

I stand and move into Ginger's sight line, pulling her eyes from Chris to me.

"She won't sit this entire flight," I assume, breaking their back-and-forth. "She'll be treating this jet like a disco the whole way to Vegas, won't you, Vixen?"

I'm not normally one to stop her from hooking up with anyone, but she has been on the plane five minutes. *Dibs?* Who the fuck says that about a woman?

Ginger winks. "Why would I sit, Cole? If this plane is destined to go down, I'm going down dancing, not sitting like a square firmly buckled into my seat."

I look into her eyes. *That's right.* I know she'll be dancing, or at the very least fidgeting the whole way to Vegas. Ginger hates heights after a bad experience coming home from spring break one year in college. Her plane had some really rough turbulence, and she vowed in the moment never to fly again. It took her a couple years, but she eventually got back on a plane.

You'd never know she's nervous because she does sit as we

take off and is the picture of cool as she talks to Chris. I flex my fists involuntarily as I watch them.

"Well, if you're up for a road trip, next time we play Nashville I can get you tickets," he says to her.

Just say no.

"Maybe! Thanks for the offer. I'm going to catch up with my friends now, though." She nods as the unbuckle your seatbelt sign flashes, and she heads toward Liv and CeCe in the next row.

"Don't stay away too long," he calls after her with a cocky grin I hate.

Ginger just smiles at him as she breezes by, patting me on the shoulder on her way past.

"Remember those handcuffs, Law Daddy?" she asks, with a sultry voice that for some reason goes straight to my cock. I give my head a shake and make my way to the minibar in search of a fucking drink. A double.

Almost four hours into the flight and Chris is still trying to make eyes at Ginger from the other side of the plane. Someone turned on the Shania Twain and the girls are all dancing in the small cabin. As Chris watches her, he looks ready to make a meal out of her.

I get up to pour myself another drink and pass by Ginger, CeCe, and Liv. The way she moves tells me she might be getting a little tipsy, and tipsy Ginger might just go along with whatever this Chris guy is searching for.

"Hey. Uh . . ." I say, awkwardly interrupting the girls. Ginger turns to face me, her flushed cheeks and thrumming pulse making me stare a little longer than I should.

Focus, Cole.

"Remember last Sangria Sunday when you asked me to never let you drink like that again?" She looks at me like I'm crazy. You'd think I'd give up and walk away, but apparently I've lost my goddamn mind.

"How many of those fruity numbers have you had?" I push on. "'Cause being in the air, it can make you intoxicated faster. Just so you know."

Her mouth falls open, and she glances from CeCe and Liv back to me with a *what the fuck are you doing* face because I'm pretty sure my sister doesn't know I drove Ginger home last Sangria Sunday.

Awkward.

"Uh . . . you're not *my* brother, remember?" she says, laughing, even though her eyes are begging me to shut up.

"Just saying, save some for Vegas maybe . . ." I mutter.

Fuck. *Even more awkward.*

I give up and take my drink back to my seat as Ginger continues to dance. Chris is still watching her, practically licking his lips. When the captain tells everyone to take their seats for the descent, I breathe out a sigh of relief. Longest four fucking hours of my life.

The lights of Vegas are a neon-colored bright spot in the middle of a black abyss as we head for Harry Reid International Airport. It's the strangest thing to pop a full-fledged city in the middle of the desert, but a thrill runs through me whenever I see it. Because here, anything goes.

"What a fucking crew. Best behavior, hooligans," Nash says as we travel through the gate, wagging his finger. His smile is wide as we pass some airport slot machines.

We have a plan to check in at the Paris Hotel before heading down for dinner, after which we'll separate from the girls for the night.

The rooms Nash and CeCe have booked us are all stunning, each one newly renovated and a Versailles executive suite. I enter mine and close the door.

The view is incredible. From my window I look out onto the Sphere and the High Roller.

I take a few minutes to unpack and call my mother. She tells me Mabes had the best night watching *Trolls* in the backyard on the old projector beside the campfire. I thank her again for watching my girl, say good night, and hop in the shower.

When I'm done in the bathroom fit for a king, I pull on a pair of navy chinos and a crisp white button-down that makes me look a lot more tanned than I should for May, but weekends in the yard and helping on the ranch tend to do that. I pair the outfit with a brown leather belt and matching shoes before giving myself a final glance in the mirror. We're going uptown high rent for this dinner, and when I get down to the common area between Paris and Horseshoe, my eyes immediately flit to Ginger. She's standing in the open bar drinking a martini. A chocolate martini, I'm betting.

Her hair is doing that wavy thing it was doing earlier, but now it's half up, and little pieces frame her pretty face. She's wearing a black, strapless dress that looks classic, like something out of the sixties, with a red belt around her small waist. She's finished the look with gold stilettos. She looks like a pinup model. I grit my teeth as she chats easily with Chris.

"Have some hair trouble? That why you're late?" Wade smirks as I approach the group, the last to arrive.

"I had to check on my daughter, fucker." I clap him on the shoulder.

"Maybe a little of that and fucking with your hair. You can admit it, we won't judge."

"This is all natural, bud, no fucking with required. Don't be jealous 'cause you're rocking your dad hair era."

I hear Ginger laugh. She's got a weekend-in-Vegas glow to her and seems more comfortable around Chris than on the plane.

I clear my throat loudly enough to make my presence known.

"Thank *God* the supermodel has arrived. I'm starving." Ginger grins when she sees me and, as we start to walk, she falls in step beside me. We're heading across to Brasserie B. Nash used his celebrity to get us a private area, and Wade is frothing at the mouth to eat at world-famous chef Bobby Flay's restaurant. He thinks he's a Bobby in training.

"You clean up pretty nice, Law Daddy, even though it took forever," Ginger says to me, a playful smile on her lips. "Ready to prowl for unsuspecting tourists?"

I lean down to respond so only she can hear.

"Nah, I had to practice my dance for the all-cop revue." I waggle my brows at her, and she laughs in response.

"Makes sense. Wasn't sure if you fell asleep up there."

"Not gonna lie, I thought about it."

"Game face, buddy. It's all for them." She squeezes my upper arm, and a feeling I've had under control for years fires through my body. I look over at the Bellagio fountains as we walk, trying to get my head around my thoughts. Maybe it's just the stress of knowing I need to clean up my act. No more one-night stands—or at least not as many. Maybe that's what's making me look at Ginger differently? Because she's safe? I decide that must be it as I eye up Nash and CeCe, whispering in each other's ears as they walk. I make a gagging sound. "They're way too fucking happy," I mutter.

"Sickening, isn't it?" Ginger grins back up at me.

"Horrifying," I retort. "Reminds me what a fucking train wreck my own love life is."

"Fucking same. You know what? I say we have fun this weekend. Let loose. Partners in crime?" She offers, "Or as you cop types call it, PICs?"

"I'll be your PIC, but you can't dip out on me last minute." I nod to Chris. "Because it seems like you have someone else willing to take my position."

"He's alright." She wags a ruby-red nail in the air. "But he's no PIC. He actually told me his shoe size three times. Who just fits that into conversation?"

"Pricks trying to get laid," I scoff without thinking. "And if he's bragging about it, there's no way it's as big as he's implying."

"Exactly!" she exclaims as we cross Las Vegas Boulevard. "And gotta stay true to my own rules. I don't get down with fuckboys."

I nod, but those words sober me right up. Because she's talking about guys like me.

CHAPTER SEVEN
Ginger

My feet are killing me. We've danced and dragged our asses all over this strip tonight, going from one club to the next. Well, all of us girls except Ivy, who went with the boys because Wade wasn't about to leave his pregnant almost-wife on the streets of Vegas. It's just before one A.M. Vegas time and I'll admit I'm tipsy, and thoroughly jet-lagged, as we leave the Cosmopolitan.

When we meet back up with the boys in front of Caesars, everyone is chatting away, but it all fades into background noise when I lay my eyes on Mr. Cole Weston Ashby approaching me. He's gorgeous; his wavy hair still perfectly imperfect in the Vegas heat, and his freshly shaved jaw is looking like the ideal place for me to plant my lips. I can usually block out his hotness and remind myself of who he is, but the way he's looking like the ultimate tall, dark, and handsome snack in that fitted white button-down, his sleeves rolled up to his forearms revealing his inked left arm that ripples with vein and muscle, is . . . shit, it's a lot.

I continue to watch Cole until my thoughts are interrupted by Chris Bell.

He's full of *I might let you fuck me* charm. Don't get me wrong, he's nice enough, and I can tell why he fits in with Nash's old hockey crew, but it's clear he couldn't care less about anything I say, not really.

As we all cruise the strip, Chris keeps in step with me, asking all about the clubs we went to, telling me about a night he had when he played here in the winter, and some trouble they got into at Vdara. He's also telling me how beautiful I look, "Much more beautiful than any woman I've seen tonight in Las Vegas," as his hand migrates down toward my lower back.

"Thanks," I say nonchalantly, scooting away from under his hand.

He seems a little more loose than the other guys, and I'm guessing he's had more to drink.

"You know what they say about Vegas?" he coos in my ear.

"They say a lot of things, Chris," I retort flatly.

He laughs off my lack of interest. "What happens here stays here. Let's be something that happens here, baby." He makes an effort of wrapping his long arm around my waist this time and pulling me close. I remove his hand and shoot him a warning look that tells him not to grab me like that again.

"So, this is our stop, yeah?" Cole posts up unexpectedly beside me, grasping my elbow and nodding to the Flamingo Hotel and Casino beside us. "You wanted to do some gambling tonight. Remember?"

He's trying to get Chris to let up, and if I didn't know better, it almost seems like he doesn't like him hitting on me.

"You need me to teach you how to use the slot machines, Cole?" I ask, one eyebrow raised questioningly.

"I think judging by the way your words are starting to blend, I'll be showing *you*."

I weigh up my options. Nash and CeCe will definitely be stalking off somewhere soon, so it's either spend the rest of the night warding Chris off from touching me, give up on the night completely, or hang out with Cole.

It's an easy choice, but I don't want Cole to know how easy.

"I don't know, Law Daddy. You're rather stiff and boring tonight. You'll need to convince me a little harder."

He rolls his eyes but ignores my teasing before calling to the group, speaking for me. "Okay, we're gonna do some gambling, we'll see ya'll later."

I try to protest but end up stifling a giggle as I look back at Chris's grimace. CeCe turns around with Cole's words and launches her drunken self into my arms.

"My *bestest* maid of honor ever. I love you," she says, slurring her speech.

"Jesus, let's go get you to bed, firefly." Nash grabs her around the waist and pulls her out of my arms, chuckling at her behavior.

I can't help smiling at the happy couple as I turn to hug Liv good night.

"You two going to be okay together?" she whispers in my ear.

"Yes, *Mom*," I say, letting her go. She looks at me with the glint in her eye that tells me she may not quite believe me.

I stick my tongue out at her just as Chris makes his way over to me, leans in, and gives me a too friendly hug.

"Sleep well, beautiful. I'll see you tomorrow," he says in my ear, lingering longer than warranted.

I hear Cole clear his throat behind me as he tugs me away by my elbow and pats Chris on the shoulder a little harder than warranted. Chris doesn't notice. He backs up to blow me a cheesy kiss before heading off with the others. Yep, he's definitely had a few too many.

"How many favors is that now, Vixen?" Cole says in a low voice as we make our way onto the Flamingo casino floor.

Wait.

"How did you know I didn't want him?"

Cole starts to laugh. "It was obvious."

"How so?" I ask, stopping dead in my tracks, genuinely curious.

Cole turns to face me, curving a finger under my chin. He lifts it to assess me. The feel of his warm skin against mine strikes me differently when we're alone and I've had a couple of drinks. Warning bells start ringing in my head.

Dangerous. Off-limits. Do not look into those eyes.

Too late.

Cole's amber pools bore into mine, and it feels like forever before he speaks. When he does, his voice is deep and full of gravel.

"I know when you're comfortable around someone, Ginger, and that look you were wearing when he put his arm around you told me everything."

I swallow. He leans down to hover his lips near my ear.

"You were practically begging me," he says in a low voice.

Goose bumps break out over my flesh, but alcohol gives me courage.

"For what?" I challenge, turning my face up.

He pulls back and smirks. I hate how stunning he is. "To give you just what you need."

I narrow my eyes, and he drops his finger from my chin.

"And just what is it that I need, sheriff?" I ask, folding my arms over my chest.

Cole scrubs his jaw while he thinks. "A burger and fries, wait, nope—" He nods surely as he starts to walk. He looks back at me over his shoulder. "Nachos and . . . somewhere that has some country music."

"Goddammit," I mutter, taking off to keep up with his long, lean legs.

"Don't pretend I'm not right." He says it as sure as the sun rises.

I roll my eyes. Apparently, Cole Ashby does in fact know just what I need.

CHAPTER EIGHT
Cole

O ne hour, an extra chocolate martini, and a tray of nachos later, Ginger is up line dancing at Gilley's Saloon in Treasure Island, and she's a fucking sight as the house band fires up "Boot Scootin' Boogie" by Brooks & Dunn.

I sip my bourbon at the side of the dance floor because not only has she befriended a rogue bachelorette party, but it is genuinely as if every fucking guy in here can't stop staring at her. I can't just leave her to the wolves in a strange and wild city. Who fucking knows where these assholes have been. So I keep watch. It's mesmerizing the way her smile lights up her whole goddamn face while her full, pert ass moves under the structure of her dress. I swallow the rest of my bourbon and take a minute to run a hand through my hair and compose myself.

I have no clue what's gotten into me tonight. Ginger looks back at me over her shoulder with a little smirk, lifting her hair off her sweat-slicked back before returning her gaze to the packed dance floor in front of her. I picture myself making her even sweatier, and then I picture myself licking her clean, and my mouth turns to sand.

It's at this very moment that I tell myself it's probably time to stop drinking and get to the clarity of my own room. Stat.

I walk onto the dance floor to collect her and, because I just can't help myself, take a moment to watch the way her hips roll as she moves. She turns to face me, and I hear her breath hitch. That sound is enough to send all the blood in my body to my cock.

"Ready? You must be wrecked," I say, averting my eyes from those perfect tits.

"Booo. Can't I finish the song, *Daddy*?" she pleads in a teasing tone, tweaking my chin as she continues the sexiest fucking dance I've ever seen to country music. She wraps her arms up around my neck.

"Dance with me," she whispers. She's had too much to drink. She flutters her lashes as she looks up at me in a pout, taking her juicy bottom lip between her teeth. "Pleeease?"

Fucking hell. Those lips.

No . . . I berate myself to get my shit together.

She's your sister's best friend.

Hell, she's your friend.

I don't listen to my inner voice and, instead, put my hands around her waist, loop my fingers under the belt in her dress, and pull her gently to me for the rest of the song.

She must be able to tell by the end of it that I'm looking at her like I don't understand why my cock is thickening by the second because she tilts her head to the side and backs up a little in confusion.

"What's wrong?" she asks, her words blending together slightly.

"Nothing," I reply, trying to sound cool but failing miserably. She backs up a little and the distance she's created sobers me slightly. Ginger and I may not always see eye to eye, but over the last couple years we've built a connection I care about. I can't ruin it now, no matter how much her body looks like magic moving this way in front of me, or how her pretty brown eyes watch me curiously. It can't happen. End of story.

"Hey! We thought you guys were gambling?" I hear from my left. Turning, I watch as Chris Bell, now draped with a random blonde in all black leather, and Cory Kane and his wife, Anna, approach. All of them are well past drunk. A smile plays on my lips. Chris is showing Ginger his true colors. Not like she didn't already know, but this moment makes me happy nonetheless.

I grip Ginger tight at her waist. "We just stopped in for some nachos. We were heading out. Busy day tomorrow." Looking down at Ginger, I ask, "Ready, Vixen?"

She nods and laughs. "Ready, Dad."

The way we moved together is still front and center in my mind as we say our good-nights and begin walking the short ten minutes back to Paris, taking in the sights and sounds as we go.

When we reach the lobby, I press the button for the elevator. The door opens and a leggy redhead steps out, looks me over, and smiles. I give her a friendly, uninterested nod as we step inside.

"I'm sorry saving me from Chris has really cut into your ability to find a Vegas one-night stand." Ginger giggles.

Ouch.

"You know," I say, "I'm not a total manwhore. I don't really want to be the one-night-stand type anymore. It just seems difficult to stop."

We light up floors twenty and twenty-five, then begin to rise.

"You mean you just keep falling into their pussies? It's hard not to, I suppose—"

"Look, it's simple." I turn to face her, *little brat.* "Mabel is my priority. I don't ever see myself putting anyone in front of her, but I like human connection, and I like . . . sex." I shrug, not embarrassed to admit it, at least not to her. "It's the only time I can just be me. Free. Hence, double life."

She nods like the shit I'm spewing actually makes sense.

"My life with Mabes is my life, and the life I live on the side is a form of release. Not real. I never lie to women about my intentions. I tell them exactly what I'm looking for. But the problem is, most of them only seem to want the same thing until the act is over."

Ginger nods, thinking.

"I just hope one day you find both, Cole. Someone you can be with who fits into your life. Your *real* life."

I shrug. "Who has time for the love story? I spend my days battling my ex and her dick of a boyfriend who I'm pretty sure is hot to take my job the second he can."

Ginger readies to get off as the elevator dings. I motion for her to go first and begin to follow.

"This isn't your floor," she says.

"No, but you aren't walking to your room alone."

"I'll be fine, Cole. It's right there." She points to the end of the hall. "You're giving me tenth grade flashbacks," she adds, and I instantly know what she means. "CeCe and I weren't even allowed to walk into the mall without you following us to make sure we were safe."

"Then you'll know there's no point in arguing. You're like a people magnet. Horny drunk men specifically. Not a chance I'm leaving you alone."

"Suit yourself," she muses as we walk. It only takes a minute to get to her door.

She turns and looks up at me one last time and I'm thankful that soon she'll be out of my view. How the fuck does someone drink and dance all night and *still* look like this? All I can think about is getting away from her so my hard-on that's been making an appearance every time she touches me for the last two hours will go away.

Ginger turns and places her hand on my forearm. Her skin is warm and soft as fuck. The smell of her overwhelms me, that sweet coconut and the sun. All I want to do right now is bring her to my mouth and—

"Don't worry about Brent. You've got this sheriff thing, Cole. You know that, right? Fuck the town. We're lucky to have you."

Her pink tongue darts out as she smiles up at me and wets her juicy bottom lip. She's so fucking close and she's always on my side. Maybe for just one night, away from reality, I could afford to see if she tastes as good as she smells—

"I thought I heard voices! God, I didn't expect you to stay out so late. You haven't answered my texts," Olivia says as she opens the door to their room. Ginger drops her hand from my arm and backs up.

"My phone died."

I look at Olivia, who has her arms crossed over her chest. Ginger reaches up to give me a hug. Her perky tits press into my chest, and I angle myself so she doesn't feel . . . anything she shouldn't.

"Nighty night, Law Daddy." She winks happily, her voice like pure smoke as she turns and heads into her room.

My eyes drift to her hips before she disappears behind the door. Olivia clears her throat and my eyes snap up to meet hers. *Busted.* She gives me the two-finger point from her eyes to mine.

"I'm watching you, Ashby," she says, and before I can answer, she's closed the door.

CHAPTER NINE
Ginger

"You two are playing with fire. And if I'm being honest I don't like keeping this little friendship a dirty secret," Liv says from behind me the next morning.

"It's not a dirty secret," I say as I spread lip gloss on my bottom lip with my ring finger. "It just doesn't come up in conversation, and I think CeCe would be . . . weird about it. She overanalyzes everything and would never stop asking questions. Questions I don't have answers to."

"Can you blame her? It's her brother, and, as much as you joke around with her about wanting him, I don't think she actually believes you do." Liv stares at me with a mom face.

"I *don't*, I didn't . . . I mean . . . shit."

"Please, on some level you always have, but after the 'dreaded kiss' you can't admit it to yourself." She grins.

"Because it was the most embarrassing moment of my life! He *rejected* me. Pushed me away mid-kiss. Told me it wasn't a good idea, remember? It sent the message loud and clear. Cole Ashby doesn't think of me that way. It took me over a month and a boyfriend in tow before I could even show my face at the ranch after that." I put my head in my hands with the humiliating memory.

Liv snickers and fiddles with the bow of her paper bag shorts. "He was dating someone then, and that was eight years ago. Hell, you two were barely legal. Do you not understand the way he looks at you *now*? Or how he does anything he can to get under your skin? Do you think he does that because he *isn't* attracted to you?"

I shrug and toss my lip gloss in my clutch. "I never thought of it. It's *Cole*. He looks at me half the time like I annoy the shit out of him and the other half like I'm a loose cannon."

"Maybe so, but there's a part you're forgetting, the part that never takes his eyes off you. Especially when you aren't looking."

"That's a bit dramatic." I look up at her and blow out a raspberry. But Olivia's not entirely wrong. Cole looked at me like that last night, and just the thought of his eyes on me sends heat through my core.

My thoughts are interrupted by a little knock that could only be CeCe's.

"We'll talk about it later, but be careful. I warned him and I'll warn you. I don't want to see you or CeCe get hurt. This is *her* wedding summer, remember," she scolds playfully and makes her way to the door.

"Are you guys ready? God, I feel like shit. Never let me drink again," CeCe moans, looking perfectly put together in the cutest little yellow romper. Her long blond hair is pulled up onto her head in a bun. It's going to be a hot one today. I look at my outfit one last time.

"This okay?" I ask her of my blue linen sundress with spaghetti straps.

"You look like a hot tourist. I'd do you." CeCe grins. "What happened with Chris last night? You weren't feeling it?"

I avoid Olivia's gaze.

"I saw him at Gilley's Saloon with some random blonde," I blurt out. "He's exactly who I thought he was."

"What time did you and Cole get home?" CeCe changes the direction of the conversation.

"Around two," Olivia cuts in, hiking a thumb at me. "Apparently this one needed nachos."

"I made Nash take me for middle-of-the-night pancakes . . ." She starts into a story about the pancake house at three A.M., clearly thinking nothing of Cole and me hanging out. I avoid Liv's eyes as I take a deep breath and look away. Liv may be on to me, but of course CeCe isn't. Why should she be? After all, I've been hiding the way I look at Cole for years.

"Alright, let's get this show on the road," Nash calls out. "We have a little surprise for you all!" He's wearing a huge grin and raises his voice so we can all hear. "Chartered two copters so we aren't crammed together and can all get a good view. We'll split up when we get there."

Excited chatter ensues as I start to panic. I don't like planes on the best of days, but a helicopter? And nothing separating me from the rocky depths of the Grand Canyon but a little tin box? *No thank you.*

The moment we arrive at the small private airport, and I see the copter on the pad, my breathing accelerates, and I start to feel lightheaded.

No one notices because they're all so excited to get in this box of terror and plummet to their imminent demise. I'm about to pass out or run, or run until I pass out, when I feel a large hand settle on my lower back.

"You're safe," Cole says into my ear. I shake my head.

"This is too much."

Cole grins at me reassuringly. "Remember last summer when Mabel asked you, CeCe, and Liv to go on the Ferris wheel with us at the county fair? You held your breath the entire time. I think you actually turned blue." He chuckles like it's funny. "But you made it through."

"That was different. Mabel was there, and I didn't want to scare her. And in a Ferris wheel I have a fighting chance at least. I could grip something on my way down."

He gives my waist a squeeze.

"You are safer on this helicopter than on the Ferris wheel, trust me."

"How so?" I ask.

"Well, for starters, the pilot isn't a carny, so there's that."

"I'm serious," I plead.

"Listen, you have to think about it logically. They probably do ten of these a day. Just this copter. Think of all the other companies that do it too. Have you ever heard of one going down?"

I scoff, a sort of hysteria lining the sound.

"Have you asked all the people who have crashed in a helicopter? Tragedies happen every day, Cole."

"Maybe so." He says surely, "But you can do this. I've got you. If you fall, I fall and you can land on me. I'll starfish right out."

"Oh, yeah?" I laugh. "You'll give me a nice soft landing a billion feet down? How sweet of you."

I swat at his shoulder, but he grabs my wrist and pulls me to him.

"There's nothing soft about me, baby," he says in his best fake sexy voice as he flexes an arm.

His cocky playboy words do their job, and I laugh even harder.

"Well, a whole lot of good that hard body will do when you're a *pancake*," I say nervously, looking out at the two death carriages in front of me. I bite my lip watching all my friends make their way to their respective copters, weighing my options.

Cole dips his head down so he can speak low. His joking tone is gone, and his voice is encouraging.

"Come with me, Ginger. Trust me, you don't want to miss out on the view. And if you somehow manage to survive"—his smirk is back—"you'll be so proud of yourself." He slides his hand down my arm to my hand, and an involuntary shiver runs through me.

"You've got this," Cole challenges over his shoulder, starting to walk.

Fuck it. Here goes nothing.

CHAPTER TEN
Cole

By the time we get through a helicopter tour where Ginger death-gripped my thigh for most of it and a late afternoon lunch in Caesars Palace, I've had a few shots with the boys to try to loosen up and forget how much I liked the feel of Ginger's nails biting into my skin. Which basically means I'm doing my best to stay sober at four in the afternoon.

I head to the bathroom before we seat ourselves for our after-dinner showing of *Indecency*, the newest show Caesars offers, to splash some cold water on my face. All day I've tried to focus on another woman. *Any* other woman, but none of them are fucking doing it for me. The only thing I can manage to pay attention to is how close Chris Bell sits to Ginger, how she smiles politely at him as they talk, how he bought her a drink (okay, he bought all the girls drinks), and how she laughed at something he said.

I look at the man in the mirror. He looks calm and collected.

"Get your shit together, Ashby. Anything with her would complicate years of keeping things platonic, and you care about her in ways that have nothing to do with sex." I give myself a pep talk.

"You talking to yourself?" Wade breezes into the bath-room.

I flinch. "No."

"Sure sounded like it." He chuckles, heading to the urinal. We're the only two people here. "Your fist is a sure bet, you don't have to sweet talk it, you know. Gotta say I can't believe we're in Vegas and I haven't seen you with some unsuspecting tourist yet, feeding her some bullshit story."

I wash my hands as he joins me at the sink and does the same.

I shrug. "Just not feeling it, I guess."

"Uh huh." Wade grins but keeps his eyes on his hands. "Doesn't have anything to do with the way Chris is doing his best to charm Ginger?"

He reaches for a paper towel, drying his hands while he speaks. "Your gaze's been burning a hole right through her all weekend."

"Ginger is free to flirt with whoever she wants. Even if the shithead has a different woman on his social media practically every day. That's her choice."

"Right," Wade says. He pats me on the back. "And you just called a guy you barely know a shithead, so . . . Whatever gets you through the day, bud."

"Fuck you."

"Might be a good idea to stay back a few minutes, tug one out in here. I just gave the woman you couldn't care less about her ticket to the show. You're sitting right beside her."

"So?" I retort. Wade's pissing me off, as if I'm some sort of lovesick teenager who can't sit next to someone I've spent countless nights with.

"So . . . do you know what this show is about?"

I raise my eyebrows. "Uh . . . indecent people?"

Wade snorts.

"Let's just say if you aren't turned on before the performance, you probably will be by the end of it. But, you know, it's only Ginger. You'll be just fine sitting beside her."

I give a low laugh and follow behind him.

"I will be just *fine*."

Well, fuck, I wish I'd taken Wade's advice. The show is sexy as hell, just as he'd said. But that's not what has had me bricked up beside Ginger for the last forty minutes. It may be the hottest burlesque show in Vegas; and I'll be honest, it's pretty fucking impressive. But it's not the show that has my attention, it's Ginger, practically *panting* beside me.

I lean down to whisper in her ear. "Need some ice? I have extra in my drink."

She closes her mouth and nudges me with her elbow but doesn't turn to face me. She lays her palms out on her thighs and I wonder how warm and wet she is where they meet—

"A literal play-by-play of you and Miss Riverbend County last weekend at that whiskey bar?" She interrupts my thoughts with a little smirk.

I laugh a little too loudly. Wade smacks the back of my head.

I try to make it through the rest of the show without watching Ginger, but I can't. She's mesmerizing, the way her chest rises and falls with shallow breath, how her pulse hammers away in her throat, the feel of her leg against mine as she shifts in her seat. I should be watching the stage, but this view? The one where I get to watch Ginger's every expression, every reaction, is downright fucking captivating. For no reason I can understand, I'm finding it hard to ignore the feelings I haven't let myself feel in a long damn time. Suddenly, it's Ginger I don't want to miss one second of.

Fucking Christ, Cole.

I need to get my head straight. Actually, I need a workout. And my fist, since no woman in this town, other than the one I shouldn't want, seems to be doing it for me right now.

The group is ready to party by the time we're done. The atmosphere is charged, and Chris brings all the girls, except Ivy, another drink from the bar. I clench my fists involuntarily when Ginger happily accepts hers.

Does it make me see red when Chris leans down to whisper something to Ginger I can't hear? Fucking right it does. And that is exactly why, after cruising the strip and having to watch Ginger command every red-blooded male's attention, I decide to bow out early and head to the gym instead.

"Getting old, Cole? Can't hack it with us youngens?" Ginger challenges. Normally I would give her some witty retort, but the truth is it's *her* I can't hack it with. Not tonight. Last night I didn't trust Chris around her, but tonight I don't trust *myself. And* I like her too much to change anything between us.

"Must be it," I reply with a rueful smile.

After saying my goodbyes and heading back to my room to get changed, I'm in the hotel gym. The facility is state of the art and has everything I need to push Ginger and her perfect curves from my mind. By the time I've sat in the steam room, then moved to a cold shower, I feel better. Refreshed. Thinking clearly. Thinking like myself.

This is *Ginger.*

We can barely go a day without rattling each other. Not to mention, we're totally different. I need order and stability. I do the same things every day. I have a calendar on my fridge that maps out laundry days and bath nights. But Ginger, Christ, she's the opposite of routine. She is unpredictable. She's sarcastic and feisty, and she drives me fucking crazy.

But as I'm making my way back through the lobby and I see her sitting at the bar with a sort of sad look on her face and deep into what I'd bet my left kidney is a chocolate martini, not *one*, not even a *glimmer* of one of those fucking reasons stops me from making my way right over to her and dropping onto the stool beside her.

CHAPTER ELEVEN
Ginger

WARDEN

I trust you're making smart choices?

ME

I've only been arrested once; I'll do my best to cover my face when the news team following me catches up.

WARDEN

I don't find this kind of humor suiting, Ginger.

ME

Who says I'm kidding?

WARDEN

Good night. Remember the family.

*H*ow could I forget?

I set my phone down and eye the old world European allure of the Café Americano bar.

Should I mess with my father? Probably not; he'll only have a million questions later. Should I have another martini? Again, probably not, but I don't hesitate when the bartender asks.

Instead, I nod a firm yes. I've definitely had too much to drink because I've started to feel sorry for myself. Nash and CeCe made their escape before CeCe drank too much, and because they couldn't keep their hands off of each other. Wade and Ivy left after the show, tired and ready for ice cream. Liv has gone with Cory and Anna to the Venetian. I could have joined them, but I wasn't feeling it, telling them all I had enough for the night.

I just can't get Cole out of my mind. Everywhere I look, people are finding their someone, but not this girl. *This girl* eats cereal for dinner in her underwear and is trying to figure out how to attract a man who might actually want to spend more than one night with her.

I take another big gulp of my martini and rest my heels on the weathered rung of the wooden stool beneath me.

I'm being honest, I haven't been looking hard enough for my someone. Because if I find a man who wants more from me, that means I have to give up whatever it is that Cole and I have been doing, this odd friendship that's grown deeper over the last two years when I was the only one he felt he could turn to about the divorce. No judgment. And I'm not ready to throw that away.

By the time I've drained my glass, I can feel it—the tears that creep in sometimes when I think I'll end up alone forever in my tiny apartment, long after Cole has found his soulmate.

I recall my mother's words from the other night when she asked if I was still spending time with Cole Ashby. She always liked Cole, but after realizing nothing would ever happen with him, she's encouraged me to put distance between us.

"The right one will come. Stop giving your best years to the play-boy 'friend' that doesn't ever want to settle down."

After spending the weekend around Cole like this, without the distraction of TV or Mabel, I know she's right. I have been pining for him for years, and it's self-sabotage at its finest. How many other opportunities am I ignoring on the off chance Cole texts me and asks me to come over?

It has to stop. Right here, right now. I pull the paper menu off the bar beside me and flip it over, then snatch a pen from my purse.

> I, Ginger Lily Danforth, hereby commit to stop thinking about Cole Weston Ashby. ~~I will stop coming when he calls.~~
>
> I will only come when he calls if it's important. I will stop wanting him. I will ignore the way he brushes his hair off his forehead, and how his incredible eyes sometimes turn me into a melty puddle of scientific matter.
>
> Read this every day so you don't end up alone for the rest of eternity.
>
> PS No matter how old you get, your ass still looks hot.
>
> Ginger

"Writing your memoirs?" I jump when I hear Cole's voice and instantly smack a hand onto the paper, spinning around on my stool.

Well, fuck, he looks devastatingly gorgeous. He's wearing a pair of gray sweats, a black Nike workout T-shirt, and his Yankees hat. And I've just vowed to stay away from him.

"The life and times of Ginger Danforth, challenging fools and taunting strangers by way of a blue sundress." Cole says it like it's up on the silver screen, framing his words with his hands.

He drops his workout bag with a thud to the floor and sits down on the stool beside me, folding his arms across his chest and stretching out his long legs. They're almost touching mine.

"Am I anywhere close?"

"Hardly." I sniff.

He closes the short distance between us and swipes away the rogue tear that's escaped onto my cheek. I close my eyes when the calloused pad of his thumb caresses my skin. Cole looks worryingly at me, then spins around to get the bartender's attention. As he glances away, I shove my written pact into my purse.

He turns back with a questioning stare.

I sigh. "I'm just contemplating how everyone I know is happy and in love, and I still live in a studio apartment with absolutely zero prospects in sight."

"Knock it off," Cole says, his jaw tense. "If *you're* feeling like this, how should I feel?"

"Cole, you've got a beautiful daughter," I say in an almost whisper, my words beginning to blend together. He smiles, and the warm buzz of the martinis makes it look that much sweeter.

"You're definitely right there. But, as you so eloquently put it every chance you get, I also can't seem to stop sleeping around."

I pat him on the shoulder. "I have hope for you yet, Law Daddy."

"At least you're smiling now. Can't have you crying . . . over?" He tilts his head in question.

"Oh, just having a self-reflection moment. Thinking about the pressure my parents put on me."

"Still trying to control your every move?" he asks.

"That and telling me I should be trying to meet a nice man this summer since it will be the first one I haven't worked at the bar and I have the whole thing free. '*Your mother and I aren't getting any younger, you know,*'" I say in an impersonation of my dad.

"Your parents should be proud of what you've already accomplished. Which is a lot. What you do is important. I see kids in their teens every day. A good teacher guiding them through those years makes all the difference. Plus, you're for sure the hot teacher, and every kid needs one. Shapes their formative years."

He smirks.

"You always know just what to say," I fire back sarcastically. "Here lies Ginger Danforth. Cereal connoisseur and hot teacher." I look up at him, hating the way I wish that he would touch me.

Fuck it. I accept the thought the moment it enters my head. One more night of Cole before I give up on him cold turkey.

"What?" he asks, eyeing me suspiciously,

"I didn't say anything."

He points a finger at me, then turns his hat backward. "You got that vixen look on your face. Like you're going to ask me to do something I'll regret."

I stick my tongue out.

"Favor," I say, propping my elbow up on the bar and resting my chin on it.

Cole looks at me. "Knew it." The bartender approaches, and Cole flicks his eyes to him. "Water, please."

"Nope," I say, "two chocolate martinis."

The bartender looks between us, unsure of who to listen to.

"Favor," I reiterate firmly, keeping my gaze on Cole. He sighs.

"Two chocolate martinis," Cole confirms without taking his eyes off mine.

"Your favor is that I drink a god-awful chocolate martini with you? Pfft. Pretty dull, but okay."

"Nope," I say again, suddenly feeling like precisely what my misery needs is some company. "You, Cole Ashby, are going to get roaring drunk with me, and we're going to dance the entire night away at every bar on the strip, a farewell to my youth before I make it my mission to go home and find myself someone who looks at me the way Jake looks at Amy."

"Bringing *Brooklyn Nine-Nine* into this? Really? Look, it's been a long time since I got 'roaring drunk.'" Cole adds air quotes around my words. "Since before Mabes at least."

"Get your ass upstairs right now then, change into something that showcases those hard-earned muscles, and I'll order us an extra."

"Fuck sake, Ginger. This seems like nothing good can come from it." Cole takes his hat off and rubs his forehead.

"I think that's precisely why we should do it." I look up into his eyes, sobering up for a second. "I need this, Cole. For one night. Let's just . . . have fun. Plus you can't say no. A favor is a favor and we're PICs."

Cole looks at me, then to the bar, then back to me.

"Fine," he says.

"Fine?" I reply. "That's it? God, you're easy."

Cole leans in closer, spreading his hands onto his thick thighs, fingers wide.

"When was the last time I said no to you, Ginger?"

"I—" My mouth falls open slightly.

The reality that I can't remember a time when Cole said no to me hits me square in the chest. Going against my pact with myself, I launch myself into his hard warm body and sling my arms around his neck. I grip him tightly in appreciation and whisper, "Thank you, Cole."

What I'm not expecting is his response. Cole circles his strong arms around my waist and pulls me closer between his legs. Every crevice of my body melts with his. I sigh and breathe in the spicy clean scent of his chest. If I didn't know any better, I'd almost think he needed that hug too.

Before he releases me, he leans in to my ear and whispers in a low, deep voice, "Don't make me lose control tonight, Ginger. Promise me."

A shiver runs down my spine, and I lean back to look up into his amber eyes. "I promise. It's us, Cole, what could go wrong?"

CHAPTER TWELVE
Ginger

Pain.

The kind of pain that you're subconsciously aware of before you even open your eyes. It's everywhere. My feet, my head, my thighs, my . . . pussy?

My actions from last night snap into place in my groggy mind.

The smell of commercial detergent and last night's perfume fills my senses. I crack one eye. Afternoon sunlight blinds me. Nope. Not a chance in hell that is happening.

I groan. I'm sure I must be dying.

The clearing of a man's throat causes me to shoot up in bed immediately. I grasp for the sheets to cover myself, realizing right away that Cole is perched at the end of it.

Oh, shit, I'm still naked?

I cover my bare breasts and bravely open both eyes. Bad idea. My head feels like it weighs a thousand pounds.

Cole sits across from me, dressed in his gray sweats and a white T-shirt. His chiseled arms are on full display as he flexes then releases his large, folded-together hands. His hair is mussed and morning perfect. Something stirs deep inside of me, and my pussy aches at the sight.

More details come flooding back to me. Us. I definitely was drunk but not any more than he was. Pictures pass through my mind in flashes; his hands on my face, the look in his eyes. His words. Oh, *God.* I blink to bring me back to the present. Even that hurts.

His elbows are propped on either knee, and the look he's wearing as he stares out the window is somewhere between anger and confusion. I realize briefly I'm not in my room, I'm in his. I glance at the clock. One P.M.

Cole leans back in the chair, relaxing his legs and scrubbing his face with his hand as I panic. This is it. Too much alcohol and we let it happen. The one thing I always said I wouldn't. The worst thing we could do. The thing I knew would ruin our friendship. There's no going back now, we've gone and done it—

"Good afternoon, *Mrs. Ashby.*" Cole's eyes lock onto mine and hold them. "In case you don't remember, we have a big fucking problem."

CHAPTER THIRTEEN
Ginger

What. The. Fuck?

Cole's voice is low and deep and his words echo in my ears. *Mrs. Ashby.*

Everything comes crashing down around me as memories from last night continue to play in my head like a foggy reel.

The dance floor, his mouth on mine. How I told him I wouldn't be his one-night stand. His hands, my hands . . . everywhere. Him . . . everywhere . . . us.

"How adventurous are you feeling tonight?" he asks, a drunken smirk on his face.

"Always adventurous," I answer almost instantly. Cole brings his lips down to hover over mine. The incredible scent of him this close washes into me.

"Prove it," he taunts. *"Truth or dare?"*

A challenge.

"Always a dare, Cole," I whisper.

Challenge accepted.

I look down at my ring finger. The simple white gold band feels cool and foreign against my skin. I glance to his and see the thicker, more rugged version of my own. The way my body goes completely weak when I see that might live in my mind rent-free for a hell of a long time.

A ring that represents *me*? On Cole's hand? Holy hell. Even now, in my near-death state, seeing that ring breathes life into me.

"Gatorade and Tylenol beside you," Cole says, interrupting my hazy recollections. I see us making it into the licensing bureau just before they closed, holding it together so we wouldn't appear as drunk as we were. The chapel. What happened afterward when we got back to his room. More than once. All of it hits me with the weight of the world crashing down around me.

"If you don't want to be my one-night stand, then it's a good thing we're in Vegas. I dare you to marry me, Ginger, so I can properly fucking worship you."

"Everything coming back to you?" he asks.

He looks stone-cold sober. How long has he been awake?

Cole stands and looks down at me with his hands on his hips. Scary dad mode. Why is this doing it for me? Oh, God, *I slept with Cole.* And while I don't remember everything, the one thing I do recall is that it was . . . so fucking good.

I shake my head, and nausea washes over me.

"Oh my God, Cole. What are we going to do? Can we just go down and ask them to reverse it, fuck, annul it? Fuck . . . fuck . . . fuck."

"We only have two hours before we have to fly back," he states in a monotone. Why is he calm? He's way too calm. "You better wake up, have a shower. We need to figure this out."

I nod, then swallow down a Tylenol, closing my eyes and silently begging for relief. I blow out a breath before inhaling another. Repeat. *That's it. Breathe, Ginger.*

"This is a solvable problem. It might be one of the craziest mistakes I've made. Alright, it takes the fucking cake, but there's an easy solution. People do this all the time. It's Vegas. We'll just . . . yes . . . that's what we'll do, we'll get an annulment," I say, rubbing my temples.

Cole starts to laugh, then turns to stare out the window. He suddenly doesn't seem as calm as he did two minutes ago.

"I'm a cop, Ginger, remember? Pretty sure you have to not have sex, prove fraud or lack of consent to get the marriage annulled. We *definitely* had sex, and we definitely both consented."

"Tell me something I don't know," I mutter, still rubbing my aching head, squeezing my thighs together to stop the ache between my legs with the memory of him between them.

Images of his rough hands all over my body take over. The way he touched me like he simply couldn't get enough. How his lips never stopped searching my skin, his mouth on mine, worshipping me, just like he said he would. The things he said as he pressed me up against the hotel door the moment we shut it and he dropped to his knees, burying his face under my dress, tearing my panties aside.

"They can't see you out there, Vixen, but they can hear you. Let them hear how much you like my tongue buried in your sweet cunt. Scream my name. Let this whole fucking city know whose wife you are."

I clear my throat, wishing the one and only night I got to be with Cole I wasn't drunk, wishing I could remember it more clearly for future self-care reference. I blow out a breath, pushing what we did from my mind.

"Yeah, uh . . . definitely had sex," I say, looking away, feeling the blush of my cheeks. "Don't really remember it, though," I lie, finding it easier to pretend I don't know what he felt like than admit it.

Wait—

"But we were so drunk, which has to count for something?"

"Fucking Christ," Cole bites out as he rubs his temples. "I

know enough to know we can't apply here. We have to do it where we live. Right next door to where I work." He shakes his head. He's definitely angry, but he doesn't seem angry at me. He seems angry at himself.

"I haven't even been sworn in yet. One week on the job and the single dad sheriff goes to Vegas, gets drunk, and gets married to the incumbent congressman's daughter? If that doesn't scream small-town scandal, I don't know what does."

Oh, God, my dad.

"Fuck," I say, picturing my father's face when this hits the local news.

I can't take this in right now. I move quickly to swallow the rest of my Gatorade and stand, wrapping the sheet around me. Cole grins.

"This is not funny," I say, struggling to conceal my body.

"It's a little funny that *now* you're shy? After . . ." He looks away from me before he finishes his sentence. "The things we did."

Yep, definitely going to throw up. My head buzzes as I make my way away from the bed. *Where the fuck is my dress?*

"I'm allowed to be shy when I don't remember anything from last night," I say, peddling my lie again.

Every part of me remembers him buried inside me. That part I'll never forget.

Fuck, I'm so proud of you, Ginger, so determined to take all of me. And you're going to, Vixen. Every last fucking inch.

The memory of the dirtiest words any man has ever spoken to me mixed with Cole, *my* Cole? Something about that affects me in a way I can't put into words. I look up to his deep amber eyes. He's still waiting expectantly, taking in every stretch of my sheet-clad body.

"Look, Cole, I just need my head to stop pounding, and then we'll figure this out. Okay? No one ever needs to know." I make a beeline for the bathroom, ready to pass out or be sick.

I hear him mutter something, but it fades as I shut the bathroom door behind me and drop to the floor, a million thoughts running through my mind. Holy shit, did we just ruin everything? And worse yet, why does this ring on my finger not scare me as much as it should?

Twenty minutes later, I feel semi-human and slightly calmer, ring buried in my purse. My shower provided me with the thought process I need to solve this. I'm going with my earlier play: denial for the win. I can simply pretend I don't remember how it felt to have Cole's body hovering over mine. Nothing will change. We can deal with this quietly, my father never has to know, the town never has to know. We can handle this. *We can handle this.*

I make my way back into the room, wrapped tightly in a towel, searching for something to put on other than my wrinkled blue dress.

"We'll go for the annulment. There has to be a clause for intoxication. I can't even believe they let us get married in that state."

"I left you a pair of my sweats and a T-shirt." Cole points to the chair. "And it's Vegas. Drunken weddings are their bread and butter."

"Thank you." I gratefully grab the clothes and disappear behind the bathroom door to put them on.

When I get back out to the main room, a knock at the door makes my eyes flit to his. I expect to see them worried too, but instead they're traveling slowly over my curves in his sweats.

"Thank you for the clothes," I say, folding my hands in front of me at the same time he says, "It's room service." *Oh, God, this is going to be awkward.*

He pulls his eyes away and lets the server in.

I pace the room and wait as Cole tips her. When the door is closed again, I make my way to the table and slump down across from him.

"I'm sorry," I say. "I promised we wouldn't lose control, and we—"

"It's not your fault, Ginger. I chose to drink that much. I chose to come up with the bright idea of getting married. Clearly I wanted you last night. This is my fault. It was a drunken moment of weakness, and I should have known better."

"This doesn't have to change anything . . ." I mutter, desperately wishing I could rewind time.

He sighs and reaches across the table to grab my forearm. He pulls it to him, sliding his hand down over mine and stroking my ring finger. He looks down at it, then back up at me.

"My receipt says I got the gold package. There will be photos to prove it, so I'd say everything has changed." His eyes grow serious. "But, Ginger, me and you, we're in this together. And *us*? There's not a shot in hell one reckless night could ever ruin that."

I breathe out a sigh of relief.

"I'll handle it all," he continues, my hand still in his. "I'll find out everything I can tomorrow. I'm going to text Bev in the morning, have her pull all our options together. I can't have any scandal right now. It's for the best that we keep this to ourselves. *Everything* that happened last night. We can't tell a soul."

I nod, grateful for him in this moment. The last thing I need is for news of this to get out and provide my father with the primary disruption he is so desperately trying to avoid. He'd never let me live it down and would give me a lifetime of lectures I don't need. I'm twenty-seven years old and sometimes I still feel like I'm a kid when it comes to him.

I look around the room, taking the space in for the first time. It looks like a tornado has torn through.

It was us. We were the tornado.

My phone starts to ring, Olivia's ringtone. Looks like I'm about to get a lecture anyway.

When I return to our room, it takes me a half hour of lying to Olivia to calm her down.

"So you two got drunk, slept together in his bed, and want me to believe *nothing happened?*"

"Cole and I have fallen asleep together before," I say so I don't have to lie to her.

I don't like keeping this from Liv, but I can't risk CeCe finding out about last night, at least not right now. I won't cloud her wedding summer with my stupid life choices. Besides, there's no point. It will all be a distant memory before we know it.

As we make our way to the plane, the heaviness of the weekend hits me.

I left Laurel Creek ready to blow off some steam with my girls and I'm coming home Cole Ashby's wife.

CHAPTER FOURTEEN
Cole

The drive home from the airport in Lexington is too quiet. My mind is racing and won't fucking settle. How could I let this happen? I have a daughter to raise, a new position I just started. The uptight old biddies in this town will have my nuts in a vise for this faster than I can blink, as will my deputy chief if he ever finds out.

But even though I know it was wrong, last night plays on repeat in my mind. I thought of nothing else during the silent plane ride home with Ginger beside me. For four fucking hours, I laid my head back in my seat with my eyes closed, pretending to be asleep with my headphones on. Pretending the feel of her so close to me was doing nothing to me. Pretending that burying myself deep inside her didn't feel like finding the holy fucking grail.

As I turn in to Silver Pines now to pick up Mabel, the gravel drive spits the occasional rock from my tires as I take in the evening sun. There are horses loose in the paddock, and one of the maintenance crew is cutting the lawn on a riding mower. I breathe deep as the smell of freshly cut grass fills my senses. No matter what is happening in my life, no matter what challenges I face, the rolling hills of Silver Pines and Sugarland Mountain bring me a settled kind of peace. One I'll never find anywhere else on earth.

"Sir Peanut Butter Cups!" Mabel calls when I come through the big house door. I smile and put on my best brave face.

"How was your weekend, half pint?" I ask as I squeeze her tight, kissing her squishy little cheek in a million places as she giggles. The smells of the old wood cabin walls and my mother's meatloaf fill the air. Breathing it in and holding Mabel instantly centers me.

She puts her chubby hands on both sides of my face. "Me and Nana watched movies and fed the horses and Harley ran away after a bunny, I ate four chocolate chip cookies—" She continues her stories as I gather all her things and thank my mama for looking after her with a hug. I'm about to head out the door when Nash and CeCe come through it, rambling something about a list of photographers my mama's compiled for them.

"Auntie, come and see the princess dresses Nana saved for me on her computer!" Mabel tells CeCe. My sister envelops her in a little side hug.

"You're going to be the cutest flower girl ever," she says, ruffling Mabel's hair and following her to the den.

Nash smiles after them. "You look wrecked, bud," he says, rolling his sleeve up and heading for the bar. "What a fucking weekend. And now it's only five weeks until the big day. I can't believe it."

I nod. "You can say that again."

He motions to pour me a bourbon. I shake my head, the thought of drinking any more alcohol turning my stomach. I just want to get home, relax, and sleep for twelve straight hours.

"Have a little too much last night?" he queries, taking a sip of his own.

I fiddle with my hat and then turn it backward while I finish packing Mabel's crayons into a container.

"Yep," I answer.

"Heard Ginger did too. CeCe said she drank all night and danced at Chandelier. Funny thing is I can't see her going there alone, so someone must have been with her." He rubs his jaw as though he's a goddamn detective. "Can't imagine it was Chris since she shot him down, and Cory said Liv was with them all night—"

"What do you want from me?" I look over at him. He's leaning back in his chair like the cocky all-knowing prick he can be.

He leans forward. "Look, I get it. There's something between you two. If you think I don't know you've been fighting this for years—" I scoff, interrupting him. He pauses before continuing. "But just know what you're getting yourself into. If I was a betting man, I'd say something happened this weekend."

"And why would you say that?"

"Because I missed your usual fucked-up foreplay banter all the way home. It was awfully quiet up there in seats 4A and B. The kind of quiet that follows a night of unplanned sex."

"Don't you have a wedding to plan?" I ask tersely.

"Yeah, I do, one where I want to keep the bride happy and focused. *Not* in the middle of some drama between her best friend and her brother. Capeesh?"

I sit down across from him. Fucking guy knows me too well. I take my hat off and rest it on my knee.

"I've got everything under control," I say. Nash narrows his eyes at me as CeCe comes back into the room.

Grateful for the distraction, I stand and let Mabel say her goodbyes. I say my quick goodbyes too. I need to get the fuck away from my family. I need some space to sort this shit out.

I grab Mabel's hand. "Let's go have some dinner, my little best friend."

She smiles up at me. "Okay, Daddy. Pizza?"

"Sure, buddy, anything you want."

I smile down at her, hoping I can get my shit together and be a good example for her. 'Cause, fuck, right now I don't feel like one. You know, considering she has a new stepmom she doesn't know about. A new stepmom I'm having a real hard time getting out of my head.

Once we're home, I unpack Mabel's weekend bag, prepare her dinner, throw a load of laundry in the wash, and pack her a new bag, ready for the ranch tomorrow. It's where she'll be while I work. I make a note to do a search for summer camps or play groups between sorting the annulment to keep Mabel entertained.

My job is so much more demanding now as sheriff. Between managing the deputies and my new town obligations, I'm feeling stretched to the max. I should be working with the community and spending time listening to the public about their concerns. But instead, all my energy is going into keeping the local office and my deputies running. I could work twelve hours a day and still never have all my tasks complete. Now that school is out, keeping Mabel entertained on the ranch all day won't be easy, nor is it fair to have my almost sixty-year-old mother have to spend all day every day doing so.

VIXEN

> So are you contemplating your life with me tonight, sheriff?

I see her name and message light up the screen. I lean forward on the sofa and pick up my phone. If I'm trying to forget what her tight little body feels like pressed up against mine, I should probably avoid talking to her, but it's Ginger, so it's hard to do that.

> VIXEN
>
> Too soon?

ME

This isn't funny, Ginger.

> VIXEN
>
> I assume you didn't tell my new stepdaughter about me?

When I don't reply after a minute, another text comes through.

> VIXEN
>
> Listen, if I don't laugh, I'll think about all the ways my father is going to murder me if he finds out and how the town will come after you with shovels and pitchforks.

> VIXEN
>
> Do you think Brent will be leading the pack, with Gemma screaming "off with his head"?

I smirk. Somehow even this doesn't seem so bad when Ginger is in it with me. So I decide to give in and play along, guessing it's better than stressing myself out all fucking night.

> ME
>
> Yep. Told Mabel I found her a new mommy who loves housework and wants to come over and do all this goddamn laundry after a weekend away for me.

I huff out a breath. Never thought I'd use *Ginger* and *mommy* in the same sentence in relation to Mabel. I pick a fluffy white beach towel out of the overflowing basket and start folding, snapping a photo to send to her in the process.

VIXEN

That's a lot of towels.

VIXEN

Is it weird that seeing you do domestic things like laundry is doing it for me?

Just the thought of doing it for her makes my cock wake up.

ME

Enough to want to come help fold?

I breathe out a sigh of relief as we fall back into our usual back-and-forth.

VIXEN

That depends.

ME

On what?

VIXEN

The way you fold your towels.

VIXEN

Quarters or thirds?

VIXEN

Careful, if you get it wrong, I will be forced to divorce you.

I chuckle and scrub my face. The insanity of this situation momentarily consumes me, and I start to laugh.

ME

Quarters. And if I got it wrong, we had a good run.

VIXEN

True. Because we're done. It has to be thirds, and it serves me right for getting married before I've ever even had a real date.

ME

You've never had a date?

VIXEN

Nope, picked some real winners, didn't I? It's okay though, they always said it wouldn't last. 🙈

I watch as text bubbles pop up, then disappear, then pop up again.

VIXEN

But seriously, thank you, Cole.

ME

For what?

VIXEN

Sorting all this out. If I had to accidentally marry anyone, I'm glad it was you. PICs still?

ME

Always, Vixen.

I finish folding my laundry and set my phone down, breathing out a sigh. I lean back into my sofa and close my eyes. Exhausted after the last two days doesn't even cover how I feel right now.

Tomorrow I'll get the process started. Tomorrow everything will go back to normal. Tomorrow I can stop thinking about the way her silky skin felt under my hands.

But tonight? I just want to remember.

CHAPTER FIFTEEN
Cole

"What do you mean, don't get it annulled?" I ask, completely baffled as to why Bev would suggest I stay married.

"Because I don't actually think you can annul it, at least not as easily as you think."

She waits for me to speak up. I don't. Instead, I take my hat off and place it on my knee.

She leans forward, pressing on. "Because you would be lying, kid. There's no way you got that drunk, got married, and kept it in your pants. Sorry." Bev says all this in a whisper even though her office door is shut. She leans back in her chair and folds her arms over her chest, her short white hair shining under the fluorescent lights.

"Fuck sakes," I say, taking a sip of my water.

"I haven't always been old, okay? The town is small and nobody ever stops talking. I hear things too," she says, looking coy. I pick up my buzzing phone. It's Brent, so I silence it. He'll just call me back in an hour anyway. I'm lucky if a day goes by where he doesn't call me ten times. I look back at Bev.

"You didn't deny it. So the way I see it, you've got three options to get you through the next few months. I've done all the research you asked for this morning, so here goes. And listen up, I don't repeat myself."

I nod. Noted.

"One. You can get an exemption due to intoxication, but you have to prove you were drunk. It's a lengthy process that isn't done quietly." She looks at me sternly. "Two. You can just flat-out lie and say you didn't consummate the marriage. Which is fine, but that sorta goes against everything you stand for, you know? The law? There's also always the chance your new wife gets angry because you want an annulment, or she has feelings for you so she tells someone who tells someone, et cetera—"

"Ginger doesn't feel like that." I cut her off.

She looks at me like my mother would in this instance, like she knows a fuck ton more than I do.

"Honey, you never know how a woman really feels. It's a possibility, trust me."

I turn my head to the side and roll my eyes at her assessment, but images of us on the dance floor, against the shower wall of the bathroom in Vegas, Ginger on her knees in front of me all roll through my mind.

Okay, maybe she felt *something*.

"Or there's option three," she says, cutting through my pornographic thoughts.

My eyes snap back to hers.

She grins. "You get creative."

"What the fuck does that mean?"

"It means you have exactly eighty-three days left in this probationary period. So, I say, the easiest thing to do is just stay married, quietly." She taps the end of her pen on the desk in thought. "But you might want to come up with a way to do that gracefully, on the off chance Deputy Digs-a-lot happens to find out."

I look up at the ceiling, wondering how the fuck I let any of this happen.

"You know he's just waiting to find anything to gossip about to the public that proves you're irresponsible."

She's right. Brent would jizz in his too-tight pants to get the word out about me getting drunk and marrying Congressman Danforth's daughter. Irresponsible? Check.

"How the hell can I do that? I have a daughter, Bev. I will not fake anything where Mabel is concerned. That's a hard fucking no."

Bev leans forward and wags a finger at me.

"That's up to you. Like I said, get creative. But if you and your new bride can get through the three months, then quietly divorce sometime after your probation and her father's election are up, you're covered either way."

"How so?"

"Either no one even finds out, best-case scenario, though they probably will because you're the sheriff and her dad's a congressman. The good news is that by then it's believable for you to say you fell in love, and maybe you wanted your privacy. Is Ginger shy?"

I start to laugh. "Not a chance."

"Okay, so maybe you just didn't want to share the news with anyone. But after a few months you realized you couldn't make it work. Say you're too different."

I shrug. "That would make sense."

"Right, then no one is the wiser, and no one can accuse you of being flaky or irresponsible. Besides, if anyone finds out after the probationary period, it will be way trickier for them to come at you with something personal."

My phone dings on her desk, and I glance at it. It's an email letting me know the summer camp I wanted to get Mabel into is a bust.

"Three months," I repeat, the wheels in my head turning. "Late August."

Bev nods.

"When school starts up again." I drum my fingers along the arms of my chair. "And after Edward's primary election."

I think back to the conversations I've had with Ginger over the last few weeks.

Her first summer with no classes. Wanting to earn some extra money. Not wanting to disappoint her father, not wanting anything to change between us.

I pick up my phone, telling myself not to overthink this.

ME

I need you to come over tonight.

VIXEN

You know vows don't actually say obey anymore, right?

ME

Could you please come over tonight? I have an idea I want to run by you.

VIXEN

Last time you had an idea I ended up married.

ME

True, but you said yes so what's that say about you?

ME

Six o'clock don't be late.

VIXEN

You better be feeding me.

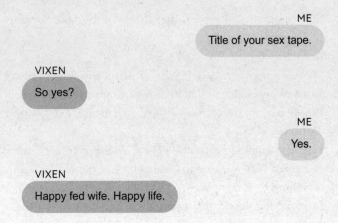

ME

Title of your sex tape.

VIXEN

So yes?

ME

Yes.

VIXEN

Happy fed wife. Happy life.

I smirk and put my phone in my pocket. I look up to find Bev eyeing me carefully from the other side of the desk.

"You have an awful gooey look on your face," she notes, closing her notebook and placing her pen on top, "which I'm hoping means you're going to take my advice. I like you, Cole, and I don't want that jackass for a boss." She nods her head to the left where Brent's corner office sits three doors down.

I stand, put my hat back on, and grin at her.

"Time will tell, and thanks, Bev. You're an angel," I add before heading out the door. My plan circulates and grows as I go back to my own office. Because suddenly, I feel creative as fuck.

CHAPTER SIXTEEN
Ginger

I don't even get the chance to knock on Cole's glass front door before Mabel is pulling it open at 6:05, squealing my name and attaching herself to my leg immediately.

"Did you bring me another piece for my garden kit?" she asks, her eyes that match her dad's glimmering with excitement.

"Mabes, don't ask someone if they bought you a gift," Cole calls from the kitchen. His space is open, aside from a half wall, so I can see him puttering around, popping dinner ingredients on platters. The house is always cozy and tidy but could use a bit of help in the décor department. A few generic scenic prints hang on the walls, and there is a large art sculpture over the living room sofa, which Cole made in his senior year of high school. The floors are rustic barnwood, and fishing and sports magazines line the wrought iron coffee table in front of the overstuffed sofa. Through the back window, maple trees frame the yard and, beyond that, Sugarland Mountain creates a breathtaking backdrop.

"Of course I did," I say, winking at her, and pulling the newest addition to her kit out of my bag.

"This one is a flower press," I tell her. "We'll have to do it together, but any flowers you see that you want to preserve from the garden can go in here. Once we press them, you can keep them forever."

This kid is always outside and has been collecting rocks, bugs as pets, sticks, greenery, and flowers for the last year. She's a child after my own heart. I was the same when I was young.

"I want to plant some flowers. Daddy doesn't know how to grow things."

"Hey, that's not fair, I didn't kill the succulent Nana gave you," Cole says as he rounds the corner from the kitchen.

"That's 'cause you don't ever have to water it!" Mabel retorts. He shrugs, and I smile at their adorable dynamic.

Maybe it's the new husband factor, or the dad factor, or some combination of both, but tonight, Cole looks *way* too good. He's tanned, clean-shaven, and the color of his blue T-shirt against his amber eyes makes him look just about perfect. But the best part of Cole's getup? The grilling apron he's wearing that says *Grillmaster's Motto: It's not burnt, it's flavor.*

I run my hand down Mabel's hair.

"Go easy on him, he's a busy guy, your dad," I say. "Besides, it's not his fault he's terrible at taking care of plants." She laughs as I tweak her chin, and Cole grunts at my insult. "Why don't you show me where you want to grow flowers?"

Her eyes light up, and she takes my hand, leading me toward the yard.

"Nana said maybe she can help me. Sometimes her back bugs her, though," Mabel rambles as we head through the back door. Cole follows.

"Been meaning to get on that garden. We'll do it this summer, okay, Mabes?" Cole says, keeping pace behind us.

"Daddy tried to grow tomatoes before, but it's just full of weeds now." Mabel presses on.

Insects buzz, and the water in Cole's pool shimmers as we walk by. It's like a little backyard oasis here, intimate and private, with a huge concrete patio that runs the length of the house covered by a wooden pergola. The entire perimeter of the yard is surrounded by trees, but the pool is wide open to all-day sun. I can see why Cole chose this house for him and Mabel. It has the same quiet, peaceful feel of the ranch where he grew up and faces the same direction for that view of Sugarland in the distance.

We make our way to the "garden" at the back of the yard and take in the sad state of affairs. It's a bordered plot about eight feet by ten feet, and sits beside a potting shed. The beginnings of a garden remain, but Mabel is right, it's mostly weeds now.

"Could I press that flower?" Mabel asks, pointing to one lone little blue violet poking up amid the mess. I smile when I see it; a beautiful bloom among the weeds always reminds me of nature's persistence.

"There's hope for you yet, garden," I say, before plucking the lively flower from the earth and handing it to Mabes.

"We'll press it after dinner, okay?"

She grins up at me in response. "Okay."

We kneel down together to sort through what is already here: some volunteer potato stalks, carrots and rhubarb, a lot of overgrown clover and thistles.

"This could make a great little garden, you know," I tell her, sifting my fingers through the soil as an earthworm disappears below. "It has good soil."

"Will you help?" Mabel asks, smushing dirt between her chubby fingers.

"Sure, I will. If it's okay with Daddy," I reply as Cole yells over that the burgers are ready.

We sit outside under the wooden pergola, enjoying the evening sun. It's the beginning of a beautiful night and, as we dig
into Cole's barbecue, I watch as a hummingbird hops around
on the feeder by their back door.

"This might be the first time you've ever made me dinner,
Cole Ashby." I sigh contentedly, listening to a neighbor cut
their grass a few houses down.

"And?" he asks, one eyebrow raised from his end of the
table.

"It's quite impressive. Not burnt at all." I smile and take
another bite of my burger.

Even with the unspoken secret between Cole and me, the
air tonight is comfortable. Just as it always is. Which gives me
hope that all is not lost the moment we sign on the dotted line
and dissolve this marriage. Through the rest of dinner, we
have easy chatter back and forth. Mabel tells me what she's
doing this week—going to the zoo in the next county with Jo,
a playdate with her friend—and, when dinner is done, Cole
heads back inside to do some chores while Mabel and I set up
to press her violet. By the time we're done, Cole is all cleaned
up from dinner, and Mabel wastes no time in looking for more
flowers (or anything else that will work) to press. It's a typical
night in the Ashby house. And all the while I'm wondering
what the hell I'm doing here.

"She's asleep," Cole says as he comes out from the back of the
house at nine o'clock with a basket of laundry. I glance up at
him, taking a break from watching the lightning bugs dance as

the sun finally sets, sending an orange glow through the cedars and holly bushes. He drops the laundry on the floor and heads for the kitchen to grab us each a drink.

"What's this?" I ask, taking the amber liquid from him and sipping it.

"Pa's bourbon. I'm trying to loosen you up before I cash in on a favor."

My stomach drops.

"I gotta say, all this buildup makes me think I might not want to know what you're going to ask," I note, moving to help him fold the laundry.

"Probably not, but I'm hoping you'll remember all the nights I picked you up when you were in trouble. Plus all the stops for food on drunken Saturday nights. Every last favor, Vixen. Remember them all."

"Jesus, Cole. Just ask already. It can't be worse than convincing me to marry you." I laugh, setting down the fourth towel I've folded to his two.

"Well, I found out some answers today . . ."

He starts to fill me in on everything he found out from Bev—about proving intoxication or lying—and I let the news sink in.

"So, we'd have to get a divorce?" I ask. "In which case, I'm taking half."

I laugh; he does not.

"I'm being serious, Ginger. Divorce is public knowledge. And when you're in my position . . ."

My chest tightens. If I didn't know any better, I'd say Cole almost looks nervous. Cole never looks nervous, which makes me . . . well, very nervous.

He starts pacing the length of his six-panel front window that's almost floor to ceiling.

"I do have an idea that I think will help us both," he starts.

I lean back against the couch but say nothing. Cole takes

that as his invitation to keep talking. "What if we stayed married?"

My mouth falls open and, for at least ten seconds, that's how I stay until I realize I should say something, anything, but it's impossible to form any words, because *the fuck?*

"I . . . For . . . ever?" I ask, gulping.

"No, not forever." Cole chuckles before making his way over to sit down across from me on the ottoman.

"You don't want this to affect your father, and I don't want to give Brent one reason to pick away at my position *or* for the public to find out." He takes a breath before continuing on. "I remember you saying you may be a little short of money this summer, and I am struggling to keep Mabel busy. What if I can offer something that suits us all? Mabel included. That's why I wanted you to come over early this evening. So you could . . . so I could see how you fit."

Everything adds up as I realize *why* I'm here tonight. Anger rushes through me.

"This was a nanny interview?!" I ask incredulously. "That's fucked up, even for you."

"No, not an interview!" He reaches out and grabs my arm before I can stand. "Christ, Ginger, I know you are more than capable. I just . . . *fuck*."

I pull my arm back and raise my eyebrows expectantly.

"Start talking, Ashby."

Cole rises, takes a sip of his drink, and continues walking the length of the room, bourbon in hand. He pauses in front of the window, staring blankly into the distance, before turning back to face me.

"Ginger, you're great with Mabel. Amazing, actually."

"That's a good start." I wait for him to continue.

"I just, I'm trying to figure out if this could be an option. This isn't easy for me. I don't . . . let people into our world.

Ever." He comes to sit back down across from me. He looks me in the eye, drains his glass, and continues.

"Hear me out. You move in here for the summer, so you can help me take care of Mabel. I'll pay you the going rate, whatever that is, plus ten percent. It will only be part-time, but I'll pay you for full-time. My mom likes to help when she can, and Mabel will be gone for over a week to Gemma's parents' cottage too. Mabel will have an explanation for why you're here without her needing to know what's really going on. And it covers our tracks in case anyone, mainly Brent, ever finds out. We can divorce quietly later, perhaps sometime in the fall. This way, it will be a lot easier to make the town believe we meant to get married but chose to keep it private."

I don't answer him immediately, so Cole starts rambling about my accommodations.

"The in-law suite would be yours, so you'll basically have your own wing. I redid it a few years ago, and it's never even been used. You can spend the summer swimming and relaxing at the house . . ."

Cole trails off and walks over to me, sinking to his knees and placing both his hands on my thighs. I tense. I'm not used to this Cole, the one who isn't afraid to touch me. For years, ever since the night we kissed, it's been like both of us were on a mission to show each other who wanted who less. But this Cole? The one that makes me dinner, touches me freely, and looks at me like I'm his only hope . . . I'm not really sure what to do with *him*.

"If word gets out, we'll tell them all we thought it could work, but we realized we were too different." He smirks, like that much is obvious.

"That's believable," I say with a shrug.

"I thought so." He removes his hands and sighs. "Look, I know in terms of favors this one is big—"

"Huge," I say, putting my head in my hands. "The hugest."

"The hugest," he repeats, swiping my hands away and using his finger to tilt my chin up, "but, Ginger, I need this. Sometimes, fuck, I feel like I'm holding everything in my life together by a single thread . . . that someone just coated in gasoline and set on fire," he deadpans.

"You're doing a great job, Cole."

"It might seem that way. But I barely have time to cut my own lawn. There's so much mess to clean up from what the last sheriff left behind at work. *And*, on top of that, I'm trying so fucking hard to be a good example for my daughter. This job I have is her future. I need to be good at it."

I eye him for a beat.

"You better get me another drink and some sort of notepad, 'cause I'm gonna have some ground rules."

The smile Cole gives me in response takes up his whole face. His full lips curve up over his straight white teeth, and his dimples settle in his wide jaw. He stands.

"Yes, okay . . . whatever you want." He grins then kisses my cheek. "And . . . you're the best PIC ever."

"Settle down with the flattery, Ashby. I already agreed." I swat at him as he starts into the kitchen.

I chew my bottom lip as a rush of excitement flows through me. I'm going to stay Cole Ashby's wife, even if it's just for a little longer.

I remember the written pact sitting somewhere in my purse that says I will no longer come when he calls. Should I be surprised I haven't followed my own rules? Probably not. When it comes to Cole Ashby, I'm starting to wonder if there's anything I *wouldn't* do.

CHAPTER SEVENTEEN
Cole

H oly fuck, I can't believe she's in.

I pour her another drink and head back toward the living room, shaking out the energy I have coursing through me. As I re-enter, Ginger crosses one curvy tanned leg over the other.

I try not to remember what it felt like to slide my tongue along it, but I fail. Every single time I close my eyes, I see every part of her.

"Alright, ground rule number one," Ginger says. "No funny business while I'm here, which means, and I know this is going to be tricky for you, Sir Weston, no Lexington and no other women."

Fucking easy.

I place the glass of bourbon in her hand. My fingers brush hers as I do, and I raise my eyes to meet her gaze. "I wouldn't do that while you're here, Ginger. I'm not . . . a total fucking animal."

"That remains to be seen. But I just want to make it known,

fake wife or not, I will not be cheated on," she scolds, wagging one perfectly manicured finger at me.

"Of course." I nod. Fuck, what does this woman think of me?

"Two: No funny business here either." She waves her first two fingers over her form. "The other night's drunken encounter aside, I am off-limits."

I raise my eyebrows, swallow, then nod. That one might be a bit harder.

"If we want to come out the other side of this in some sort of normal capacity, we have to go in like it's a business arrangement."

"A business arrangement." I repeat her words, drilling them into my thick skull as deeply as they'll go.

"I take care of Mabel when you need me to, which means CeCe or your mama won't need to have her when you work the afternoon shift. And yes, I'll take over your in-law suite."

I nod. "I can play by the rules. It should be easy for both of us. What happened in Vegas was a result of alcohol and bad decisions. We've been platonic for years. We're both adults, now is no different," I lie.

"Agreed. My ring is zipped tight in the secret pocket of my purse, along with the memories of that night. We're friends," she says quickly, and I can't quite decide whether her denial of what happened between us makes me annoyed or just makes me want her more.

"I won't tell my parents anything different from what we're telling Mabel. But we'll need to work out what we're telling your family."

I sigh. Yes, we will. They're the nosiest fuckers in this town.

"We'll tell everyone the same thing. You're moving in to help with Mabes. They know these new policies I'm drafting, plus the mentoring program I'm launching for new deputies, leave me burning the candle at both ends."

"It's believable for Liv too, she knows we . . . spend time together sometimes." She shrugs, avoiding eye contact.

I can't help myself. Smirking, I lean back to eye her up.

"You talk to Liv about me?"

Definitely don't hate that.

"Wipe that smug look off your face, Law Daddy, we're friends and I've mentioned it to her once or twice."

She's playing dumb, but I'm not having it.

"I'm about to cut the shit, Ginger. Judging by what happened in Vegas, I'd say we like each other a little more than we let on."

Ginger's cheeks start to turn a shade of the lightest pink under her golden skin. She's flustered, and I like that it's me making her that way.

"Don't go puffing your chest, loverboy. You can be friends with someone and find them . . . attractive. I don't *gush* about you to her. I tell her where I am when I come over. You know, in case anything ever happens. Like you snap and turn me into a lamp shade."

This fucking woman.

"Mmmhmm. Makes total sense."

I don't buy one ounce of the bullshit she's peddling, and the way she's looking at me tells me she's just as confused as I am about the way we are with each other. The way we've always been.

"We are the wild cards out of all of them. If nothing else, they probably wouldn't be surprised if they did find out what we did," she says, abruptly changing the subject.

I let her off the hook, for now.

"For once I wish I wasn't the impulsive one who slept around, or the one who already failed at one shotgun marriage. For once, it would be nice not to be the rogue Ashby sibling." I sigh as Ginger swallows the last of her bourbon.

"Hell, I hear that. At least we can be wild cards and PICs

together." She grins and stands to go. "Okay, sheriff, we'll call a dinner this weekend to tell your family the plan for this summer. I've done my obligatory once-a-month dinner with my mom and dad already, so my relay to my family is a text."

"I'll tell Mabel in the morning. She should be the first to know."

"Oh, and I have one more rule . . ." Ginger looks at me, placing a hand on her hip.

"That is?" I ask.

"I know we haven't always seen eye to eye . . ." she starts.

I chuckle and rub my jaw. *Understatement of the year.*

"But when it comes to Mabel, don't pick at everything I do, and don't undermine me. If you have a problem with how I care for her, talk to me in private. And for the love of GOD, Cole, let us have fun. I take care of kids for a living, I did my placements in elementary schools, so I sorta have some expertise in this department."

I sigh. "I promise I will do my best."

Ginger nods. "Oooh, I've got it. You can have a safe word. A veto if you really don't like what I'm doing."

The thoughts that run through my mind imagining another scenario where we would have a safe word are as vivid as the image of my cock sliding into her tight pussy. I let out a low laugh.

"What?" she queries.

I don't say anything, and instead, just shake my head.

"Get your head out of the gutter, roomie. I'll expect your safe word by tomorrow."

She winks at me before sauntering toward the front door. I don't take my eyes off her as she goes, even as she bends over to place her purse into the back seat of her white VW bug.

Eighty-three days with no sex. Holed up in my house with *that* ass?

I run a hand through my hair and take a breath. Something tells me I'm going to need to brace myself to live with the sexual storm that is Ginger Lily Danforth Ashby.

My wife.

CHAPTER EIGHTEEN
Cole

EIGHTY-ONE DAYS TO GO

"You two are shacking up together? But you're not knocking boots?" Papa Dean asks two days later. He's talking in a low tone so Mabel won't catch the conversation as we sit in the backyard of the big house. "And we're supposed to believe that?"

His bushy white eyebrows rise to signal that, no matter what I say, he's going to think I'm full of shit.

"Jesus, Pop," I choke out, scrubbing my face, "can't there be a time in this family where we don't say exactly what we're thinking? And no, we're not. Purely platonic."

The rest of my family waits for someone else to speak while Pop's stare cuts through me. I turn away from him and look out to the massive red barn in the distance decorated with our ranch logo. It's where we store a lot of equipment. Two ranch hands are hosing out a tractor's wheels. I'm not interested in what they're doing, but I'm set on watching them to avoid Pop's gaze. Ginger looks at me and shrugs. I notice the lilac bush behind her. It's a stunning backdrop for her deep brown curls.

Fucking hell, am I turning into Nash?

"I need some extra cash this summer, and Cole needs help," she says, breaking my stare and grinning mischievously. "I'm his last resort. Turns out he's got a little too much history with every other woman in town."

She just can't help herself.

"That tracks," Nash says with a chuckle.

"Laugh it up, fuckers," I tell them all, watching Mabel play with the dog. "It's a win-win situation. It doesn't always have to be drama."

"I for one think it's a great idea," my mama cuts in, winking at Ginger as she pours her sweet tea from a glass pitcher. "Gives me lots of time to sort some bits around here. I've just introduced Glenda to a few new weekly clubs, and now I'll be able to go with her, ease her into town life."

Glenda is Ivy's mother, who moved to the ranch a couple of months ago. She's recovering from alcoholism and is thriving here at Silver Pines. She visits the horses daily, walks the trails around the property, and spends a lot of time sitting on her front porch watching the ranch hands go about their daily chores while she crochets. She's even started a little business selling hats and blankets.

"It's very sweet of you to take this on, Ginger," Mama carries on. "I was worried about how I was going to balance looking after Mabel with taking care of the books. Especially with Wade and Ivy so focused on making sure Angel's Wings is ready for her derby run. But I still want my Mabel and Nana day once or twice a week."

"Of course," I say, nodding.

I'm so lucky to have a mother who wants to spend so much time with her grandchild. In fact, over the last few years, she's almost been like a second mother to Mabel. Especially when Gemma bails on her weekly visits.

"Well, Mabel must be thrilled," CeCe chimes in from across

the table. "About time you realized how good Ginger is with her. You're lucky to have her all summer."

My sister grins at Ginger, but I can see the guilt in Ginger's eyes for lying to her best friend.

"Mabel is thrilled," I say.

At least that much is true. She literally squealed when I told her yesterday morning that Ginger would be with her for most of the summer.

"You're gonna live with Cole, though? Good luck," Nash scoffs. "You two usually don't get along for more than twenty minutes."

"We've been working on that lately, actually, and I'll have my own quarters at the house. I can stay far away from him and, besides, we have strict rules."

"Sounds like a great plan for a few months. A real win for everyone," Liv says with her chin resting on her palm. She's looking at Ginger like she sees right through her as she tosses her copper hair over her shoulder.

"It will be," Ginger fires back, a little too sharply, and I get the feeling she's trying to convince herself.

"Good girl for making rules," Ivy says, giving Ginger a high five from across the old barnwood table. "I hope it includes your coffee made every morning."

"Settle down, over there," I reply, watching as Wade stops spicing our steaks and walks over to Ivy to lazily slide his hand over her growing belly. It's like he can't not touch her. He takes a drink of his bourbon then bends down to kiss her.

"How's that steak coming along?" Ivy asks as he lingers with her long enough to torture us all.

"Mama wants to eat?" he says.

Fucking hell.

"Get a room, for shit sakes," I say louder than I should, tossing a napkin at them.

"Dollar, Dad!" Mabel yells from the yard. She's sitting in

the thick green grass with Harley and her coloring, but she looks about done with that now. "Auntie, come play ring toss with me!" she calls to CeCe.

"Call her in to clean her room, she doesn't hear me. Say *shit* above whisper level and she does?" I say quietly.

My mother giggles in response. "She's a businesswoman. Takes after her nana."

"I'm coming, baby," CeCe singsongs, before kissing Nash and turning to Ginger and Liv. "Come with me, you two."

Both women dutifully stand, and they all walk over to where Mabel is waiting. I watch as they retreat into the middle of our massive yard; the natural fescue grasses swaying in the breeze beyond serve as the precursor to the pond my dad installed at the edge of the space. This was my dad's favorite place to sit. He loved cooking out like this in the summer. He'd take charge of the big outdoor kitchen covered with a pergola under the Edison lights, or have all of us sit around the large stone firepit, drinking bourbon and making s'mores. I know he would love to be here with me and watch Mabel play.

The familiar pang of grief tightens in my chest as I remember the last time we were together out here. It was the fall before he died, and we were watching Mabel chalk on the patio. All the leaves had turned, and the lawn was littered with them. He was struggling to rake them, and we had to call in some ranch hands to help. We sat and watched them while he gave me advice. I was pissed that Gemma had missed Mabel's school play. He told me not to sweat the small stuff, to stop chasing perfection for Mabel, and just live in the moment. He urged me to let my daughter put down her own roots. Her childhood didn't need to look like mine to be memorable or special, it just had to be hers.

"Looking mighty forlorn over there, bud. Sad you don't have a woman of your own to kiss?" Nash says, turning his Stars hat backward and grinning at me.

"Christ almighty. Just trying not to be sick. Whipped is what you are, the both of you!" I point between Wade and Nash. They laugh, signaling they couldn't give a fuck that they are. For one tiny second, I feel a touch of jealousy at how settled and content my brother and best friend are.

"Hey, don't hate the players just 'cause you ain't joining the game," Pop says, putting his glasses on, folding his hands behind his head, and leaning back in his wooden chair.

"Take it easy, old fella." I chuckle. "I've been there, done that. Clearly wasn't for me."

"So did I. But it wasn't like this because I wasn't with the right person," Wade says, angling his almost empty glass of bourbon at me and turning to the grill with our steaks. "Yours could be right around the corner. You never know."

"Or in your own backyard," Pop adds with a smug grin.

"Christ," I whisper, looking back over at Mabel to make sure she didn't hear me. "What a bunch of shit disturbers."

I stand and walk from the big house patio that runs into the wide, flat yard to watch the girls play. It's an open space with a view of all the barns to the left, and the highway in the distance through a big field of crabapple trees to the right. I take a deep breath once I join them. Yep, this view is much better.

The smell of grilled steak fills the air, and I can't help but laugh as the girls compete like their ring toss game is an Olympic sport. I watch as Ginger lands her third ring on the spike, before turning to give Mabel a high five. Mabel is smiling from ear to ear, and I can tell she's so fucking happy to be surrounded by so many people who love her. People I want to keep in her life. The only job I have for the next couple months is remembering this is a business arrangement; I cannot get used to having Ginger around.

CHAPTER NINETEEN
Ginger

EIGHTY DAYS TO GO

"That's the last of it," I say happily as Cole grimaces. He's carrying in my last tote of clothing as I carry in my "tool box," a secret home for my spicy novels and vibrator collection.

"Christ, woman, how many outfits do you need?" Cole grunts out, dropping my clothes onto the bed.

"My apartment is on the other side of town. I don't want to go back and forth more than I have to. Plus I want to dedicate all my time to Mabel."

"Bullshit. It's because you're an over-packer and are afraid you might need that one pair of socks you didn't bring."

I bite my bottom lip and consider any socks I've forgotten, like the over-packer I actually am. He shapes the brim of his Yankees hat, and his upper arms flex as he does so. I eye the ink dancing down his left arm. It's a full sleeve decorated with vines, Mabel's name, his father's birth and death dates, and various pictures and phrases.

It briefly occurs to me that I haven't seen Cole shirtless in years and find myself wondering what lies under those clothes.

It was so dark when we were together in Vegas, I didn't get the chance to sneak a good look.

I'm still mid ogling Cole when Mabel bounds into the room and passes him her American Girl doll, dressed in a floral romper that matches her own.

"Can we start the garden tomorrow?" she asks me with the world's most excited look on her face. I can't help but smile at her enthusiasm.

"Absolutely!" I say, tucking a piece of her hair behind her ear. The more she grows, the more she looks like Cole. CeCe, really, but with dark hair.

"And you're really going to have breakfast here with me every morning?" she asks, switching direction.

"That's the plan. We're going to have lots of fun this summer, my Mabes."

I look more closely at her and realize she's covered in some form of dirt and sticky matter from what I assume is the backyard, judging by her muddy bare feet. Cole must be thinking the same thing.

"God, you need a bath, half pint. You've been making mud pies again?"

She nods with a smile and holds up her dirty little hands.

"Yes, but I don't want a bath. I want to play with Ginger." She adds a little pout into the mix, the one *she knows* makes Cole turn to mush every damn time.

I laugh. "Maybe we can do two things at once. You know, when I was little, and I didn't want a bath, sometimes my mom and dad let me have a pool bath. Maybe Daddy will let us do that."

"What's a pool bath?" Mabel's eyes light up as if I just told her I was taking her to Disneyland.

"Well, you put your bathing suit on and scrub your hair really, really well but with no soap and no shampoo. Almost like a pretend wash."

I wink at her, and Cole shoots me a disapproving look.

"I'm getting my bathing suit!" she says, running from the room before her dad can protest.

"It's Thursday. Which means it's hair wash night." Cole says this with such a serious look on his face I can't help but laugh.

"Oh, no, what *will* we do?" I reply, feigning shock. "I know . . . wash it tomorrow? And, excuse me, but you have *hair wash* nights? What kind of prison are you running here, sheriff?"

"The predictable kind. Sundays, Tuesdays, and Thursdays are hair wash nights. Don't fuck with the system, Vixen."

I eye him, registering that he's being serious. I swallow down my laughter.

"Fuck," he says. "My safe word. I'm choosing it. It's *authority*. If I say it, you immediately wait to talk to me first."

"*Authority?* Over a hair wash?"

I can't help it. It's one of those moments where you know you shouldn't laugh so it makes you want to laugh even more. The stern look Cole is wearing, his hands on his hips, an American Girl doll slung under his arm. It's too much.

I flop down on my new bed, throwing my head back and letting the laughter take over. When I open my eyes, they're damp, and Cole looks just as pissed as before, a real contrast to the happy doll he's holding.

"Cole, please put down . . . put down the doll if you're going to look that annoyed."

"Ginger, you can't just change everything we do . . . This was a bad—" He opens his mouth to say more, but he stops dead in his tracks because Mabel is back in the room, already in her suit and holding her life vest. I stand up, trying to remember what bathing suits I brought.

"Why aren't you ready?" she asks, looking between me and

Cole before turning and running toward the back door, her little feet thwapping against the hardwood floor as she goes.

"I have no control in my life, apart from between these four walls," Cole says to me in a hushed tone.

"Let us have a little fun this summer, Cole," I challenge. "It's good for her."

He grimaces.

"Fine," he grunts in response. "We'll delay hair wash night, and since this was your idea, suit up."

He turns to leave before stopping himself.

"Ten-four, sheriff," I giggle.

He tosses me a devastating Cole smirk as he drops Mabel's doll on my bed, and I stand, backing up toward the wall as he approaches. He looks like he may yell . . . or kiss me . . . or both?

When he's only a few centimeters from me, he looks down from his imposing full height and places his hands on my shoulders. I gulp, and just when I'm prepared to ask what he's doing, he brings his face down to hover his lips over my ear. He's so close I can smell his skin and minty breath.

"You good and warmed up, Vixen?"

I look up at him. *Hell, I am now.*

"F-for what?" I stutter, which makes him grin.

"For me to beat what I assume will be some sort of a bikini bottom right off that sassy little ass at pool volleyball." His hands drop from my shoulders, and he backs away. I let out the breath I was holding.

"You're burning daylight, woman," I hear him call down the hallway as I stand there stunned.

This man just comes near me and I buckle. How in the hell am I making it through this summer?

CHAPTER TWENTY
Cole

Something I never thought about when I asked Ginger to swim with us? Bathing suits. Ginger's curves usually do things to me no other woman's does. But it was a lot easier to withstand when I didn't know what she felt like wrapped around my cock. Thing is, she's not even wearing anything skimpy like I assumed she might. It's as though she's wearing the most modest bathing suit she owns because she's in the pool with Mabel. But despite its coverage, the hot pink one-piece with a halter-style neck and an open back is still hot as fuck. As the last point of pool volleyball is scored, Mabel cheers. "We beat Daddy!" she says as the two of them high five. But it doesn't end there. I'm dumbfounded as they high five with the other hand too, then clap their own hands together, turn sideways, and bump elbows before landing a high ten in perfect sync.

They have a handshake?! When the fuck did that happen?

I laugh, incredulous.

"Alright, Mabes. Time to get ready for bed," I tell her as I climb out of the pool and grab a towel from the pile I placed on the outdoor table earlier. Miraculously, she doesn't argue, which tells me we wore her out, and she might actually be ready for bed on time. Maybe pool baths aren't so bad after all? I'd never admit it, but it isn't so bad to step outside my comfort zone once in a while.

Ginger gets out behind me, and I feel like I'm watching her in my periphery in slow motion. The way the water trickles down her skin is almost like it doesn't want to let go of her any more than I would if I had her in my grasp. I hand her a fluffy white towel and follow her gaze that rakes over the raised G in cursive nestled under my rib cage.

When she's this close to me, there's no way she doesn't see it, and I can see the question in her eyes when they meet mine. I was already in the water with Mabes when she came out, so it wouldn't have been visible earlier, but I'm not hiding it now. It's been there since the summer she kissed me. Since the summer she flipped my world upside down and turned into the only woman I've never been able to stop from invading my head, a reminder of the summer I thought about her every goddamn night at Grosvenor. How I never said no to her, how I always compared other girls I knew to her. How she was the light in any room she entered. Those ten seconds she kissed me fucked me right up and showed me why I could never let myself *really* ever fall for her. I knew in those ten seconds if I did, I'd never get back up.

CHAPTER TWENTY-ONE
Cole

SEVENTY-NINE DAYS TO GO

I string my umpteenth calf of the day by his hind legs with a quick loop and pull him into the branding area. I'm used to the smell now. In fact, I don't think I even have a sense of smell anymore. I'm six weeks into this job at Grosvenor Cattle Ranch, the one my dad had Wade and me take on this summer because the Grosvenors were struggling to keep up and "we're all part of this community together." We've done a round of branding already, and we're on to our second. There are thirty of us moving about, working methodically, not speaking. I wait for Carson, my workmate, to pull his calf in and spot the long metal rod leaning into the hot embers; the fancy-looking G I've become accustomed to all summer. The end is slightly red and smoking hot.

That fucking G has been staring me straight in the face day in, day out, on every notepad and invoice, over every barn door, on the side of every truck, and at the end of the iron.

Each time I see it, I think of her.

I left to come here for the summer two days after Ginger shocked the shit out of me and kissed me when I drove her home. I haven't fucking been right since.

At first, I blamed being away from home, worrying about my placement and my last year of school, not having any semblance of a girlfriend for the first time in, well, ever, after I ended things with Lindsay.

But now, I know. I'm hung up on Ginger Danforth, my little sister's best friend.

I spent the first two weeks being angry at her. She had to fucking do it. She had to kiss me, and it had to feel like that. Like nothing I've ever felt before. But she's CeCe Rae's friend, and she just turned eighteen. Not to mention her dad scares the shit out of me. I've only met him three times, and every single one of those times he's looked at me like he thought I was lunch meat when his daughter deserved wagyu.

And she does. She deserves everything.

"Two more coming in now." Carson nods to me and, as if on cue, two calves are pulled in. I lift the hot metal out of the resting area, check the end, and singe the G that looks too pretty to be a brand into one of their legs. The sickening scent of burning fur and flesh fills the air in a small plume of smoke, and I wonder if the way Ginger's lips felt on mine will be branded into my mind the same way that G now lives in this cow's hide.

Something tells me the answer might be yes.

Intense heat against my rib cage wakes me, and the feeling disappears just as quickly as it came when I sit up and grip my side, expecting warmth, but the raised flesh under my fingers is cool. My room is dark, and I hear birds already chirping outside my open window. I check the time, 4:45 A.M. I turn and sit up on the edge of the bed, I have an early day today, so I may as well get up and get going. The floorboards creak under my bare feet as I pull on only a pair of sweats and head down the hall to my kitchen, rubbing my eyes as I walk. I expect to be alone, but when I reach the living room, I realize I'm not.

"Oh, sorry, did I wake you?" Ginger asks, sitting up straighter as her eyes slowly blaze a trail from the deflating morning bulge in my sweats to my face. Suddenly I'm feeling very exposed, but I don't mind her gaze, I welcome it. Something about it feels charged with electricity.

She's sitting on my sofa in a matching silk pajama set, little shorts and a crop top that reveals the tiniest sliver of skin at her navel. Her hair is piled high on her head, and her feet are nestled in a pair of fuzzy gray slippers. She is sipping a coffee and watching TV in the dark.

"No, the birds woke me. I didn't expect you to be awake."

"I couldn't sleep either. I've never wished I had a stun gun more than when those sparrows started chirping at four o'clock," she says.

I chuckle as I move closer to her, imagining her taking aim out her window.

"Refill?" I ask, outstretching my hand. She smiles up at me, looking so soft and so beautiful before taking her last sip from her mug. She must do it too fast, because a tiny bit of coffee escapes her lips and she darts her tongue out to catch it.

"Oops," she says, as I take her mug from her. My cock must like the way her tongue meets her lips, because he wakes back up and I question my sanity as I head to the kitchen to pour us both a fresh mug.

Turned on by coffee? That's a first.

I make her coffee the way she likes it and then fill my own cup.

The sky is just starting to lighten as I reenter the living room. Ginger's knees are pulled up to her chest as she giggles over something someone just said on *Brooklyn Nine-Nine*. I look at the TV.

"Is this a Halloween Heist episode?" I ask, handing her the steaming mug.

"Yep, the one where Holt's husband joins in," she answers as I take my seat beside her. We sit just like this for the next half hour, sipping our coffees next to each other as the sun comes up. I sneak glances at her as she laughs at the parts of the episode we both know so well. I can't help think about how much I like the way Ginger looks in skimpy pajamas on my sofa in the wee hours of the morning and how nothing about it feels strange or unfamiliar. In fact, the only word that comes to mind is *comfortable*. Being with Ginger is oddly comfortable. It hits me that I think I've always been more comfortable with Ginger than most other people, even when she gets under my skin. It also hits me that sitting in the early light with her, drinking our morning coffee together, might just be my favorite way to wake up.

CHAPTER TWENTY-TWO
Ginger

SEVENTY-SIX DAYS TO GO

The whole house smells like sugar and vanilla. I pull the last batch of cupcakes out of the oven and place them on a cooling rack while Mabel mixes icing on the other side of the kitchen peninsula. It's hot today but not sticky, and there's a beautiful breeze coming through the open window facing the backyard. Five days in, and I'm starting to learn where everything is in Cole's very orderly house. For a single man he keeps everything extremely neat, and Mabel seems to know where everything goes as we wash dishes.

We've spent the better part of the afternoon decorating the living room, baking cupcakes, setting up snacks, and readying the house to resemble Cole's worst nightmare: his house, covered in Cincinnati Reds décor. A fuck ton of it. Tonight the Yankees play my beloved Reds, and what kind of a stepmom would I be if I didn't share my love of the game with Mabel? I secretly can't believe she agreed so easily to wear the T-shirt I bought her with one of my favorite players, Jonathan India's, name and number, 6, on the back. It might earn me a divorce before I've even made it through my first week, but I can't wait to see the look on my husband's face.

We are just getting the pizzas in the oven when we hear Cole walk through the door. Mabel and I look at each other and wait.

"*Vixen! Authority!*" Cole's voice booms. He must be taking in the Reds banners, red balloons, and giant 6 balloon, which Mabel and I spent the morning picking out. We break into a fit of giggles and, when he comes into the kitchen, I hold the plate of cupcakes up, trying to ignore how goddamn good he looks in his sheriff's uniform. The dark brown T-shirt-style button-down clings to his strong upper arms and is tucked into tan, fitted uniform pants. The way everything molds snugly to his body has my heart rate increasing just looking at him. Add in the badge on his chest, and the holster against his narrow hip, and I'm practically panting. Damn it, this night was supposed to be about torturing *him*.

"We made you some cupcakes," I say sweetly, though a little breathlessly.

Cole's jaw sets. "You corrupted my house? My *daughter*?" he snarls.

Mabel laughs. "I like Ginger's team. The shirt is a prettier color than my Yankees one. But look, Daddy, Ginger put my scrunchie in," she says, turning her head so he can see the Yankees scrunchie Mabel tells me he bought her for Christmas in her hair. He brings his gaze back to me.

"I'd never corrupt her, Cole. I can't help it if she knows greatness when she sees it." He grunts in response, but I push on. "Red really is a pretty color."

He looks down at the jersey I'm wearing. It was my grand-dad's custom Barry Larkin jersey. This afternoon I've paired it with my denim cutoffs. I turn to show him the back, signed by Larkin.

"Where'd you get that?" he asks, his tone curious.

"My granddad," I reply softly.

"Ginger's granddad used to take her to all the games," Mabel says. "They ate lots of nachos, and he taught her how to play baseball. Just like how you taught me!"

His face instantly softens.

"Cute. But this is still unacceptable," Cole says, pointing around at the décor. He looks down at the plate in my hand and hesitates, as though he's trying to decide if the cupcakes might poison him.

"But these do smell really good."

He picks up a cupcake, pulls the pick out, and tosses it behind him dramatically.

"Daddy!" Mabel laughs as he stuffs the little cake into his mouth.

I smile smugly.

"Still unacceptable," he says as he chews. "It may take some time, but I'll be plotting my revenge."

He points back and forth between Mabel and me with a mock-serious look on his face before heading for the shower, but I don't miss the look he gives me from behind her back.

"Fucking. Done. For," he mouths slowly, and the dark look in his eyes brings my core to life.

I turn to Mabel the moment he's out of sight, and we both break out into uncontrollable fits of laughter.

"I can hear you two!" he calls from down the hall, which makes us laugh even harder. Torturing Cole is way more fun with a little teammate.

Cole returns ready for the game thirty minutes later in his Yankees jersey. He sits on the opposite side of the couch from us, announcing it's the home team's side and muttering something about us being traitors.

By the time we've reached the end of the sixth inning, dinner is long done; it's pushing eight-thirty and Mabel is getting tired as she settles into the massive pillow fort she and I created earlier. Cole follows Mabel into the fort to cuddle with her. He's been surprisingly quiet since his Yankees started losing by two runs.

"Come inside, Ginger?" Mabel asks with a yawn. She's against one side of the fort and Cole is in the middle, which means the only place I can lie down is beside him.

Cole watches me with a face I can't place. Though he seems just as unsure as I am about us being in such close proximity, I give my head an internal shake and tell myself not to think twice about it before making my way in.

Mabel and I really did a number on the fort; it's covered in twinkle lights, and the opening is the perfect size to allow us to see Cole's entire TV.

"You've jinxed my Yanks," Cole whispers to me as we all settle in.

I tip my face up to look at him. "I think it's time you admit the Reds are better this year."

He pinches my shoulder.

"It's okay, really, we won't judge you for switching teams," I continue playfully. "We welcome everyone, even Yanks fans."

"Over my dead body," Cole scoffs as he strokes Mabel's hair.

There's something so nurturing about the tiny movement, and clearly Mabel thinks so too as she cuddles under his strong arm and closes her eyes. A tightening I've never felt takes over my chest, then moves through my entire being as I watch him with her. So strong. So loving. I gaze at them, letting myself soak in their love for a beat.

The seventh inning starts, and the atmosphere in the pillow fort is almost magical as we watch. An early summer breeze blows, and the sounds of the crickets outside echo through the open windows. The glow of the TV, mixed with the spicy clean scent of Cole, fills my senses. Mabel's out cold, and I'm having a hard time concentrating on the game because, somewhere during the last inning, Cole shifted his arm behind me and started using his free hand to trace my shoulder lazily. The pads of his calloused fingers slide down my skin and I shudder. There's nothing sexual about what he's doing, but my body reacts regardless, and I lose my train of thought as his fingers move up from my skin and through my hair.

He's talking about the Yankees' season and why, even if the Reds win tonight, they don't stand a chance at taking the weekend. I tilt my head up to him, ready to argue with him. But, this time, his head is positioned much closer to mine. His eyes bore into mine. I gather the will to keep my thoughts straight.

"You can't mean that. They're at home and Greene is at his best," I say, reminding him what a good year our pitcher has had.

"Ginger." He growls like it's a warning, his lips hovering dangerously close to mine.

I try to remember how to swallow. "Yes, Cole?"

"Thank you for making today very fun for Mabel, but if you ever, *ever* vandalize my house with Reds shit again, I'm going to do fucking ungodly things to you."

I smirk and look back at the TV, feeling safe and brave because Mabel is on his other side. "Don't make promises you can't keep, Cole."

He pulls my hair in response. It's meant to be playful, but all I can think is, *Please pull harder.*

"You won't always have Mabes to protect you," he adds.

I force myself to focus and tell myself not to read too much into his touch. I know enough from watching him with Mabel that Cole's just affectionate, and this doesn't mean anything.

We stay in the fort for the rest of the game as the Reds continue to beat the Yankees by three runs. But I don't see the end, because I fall asleep, curled into Cole like it just might be where I belong.

CHAPTER TWENTY-THREE
Ginger

SIXTY-SIX DAYS TO GO

LAW DADDY

Bring warm sweatshirts. It gets cold up there.

ME

I've been packing for myself for like fifteen years at least. I also checked the weather and have packed extra socks, my pillow,

ME

and a partridge in a pear tree.

LAW DADDY

Always gotta be a smartass. All this from the woman who doesn't even wear a coat in the winter.

ME

It was one time. I also helped Mabes pack. So she's good to go. All you have to do is worry about yourself.

I watch the three little dots pop up, then disappear, then pop up again, but still, nothing. I stare at my phone. It's been fourteen days since I moved in, and Cole has been leading two new courses in citizen interaction techniques and report writing. On top of this, he's also been covering for two deputies who are on vacation. We spent the other night on the front porch drinking a bottle of my nonna's homemade wine while he went over Mabel's summer schedule and told me where he'd need me to fill in as he takes on this extra load. He needs this Lake Charles holiday to reset and recharge before another busy few weeks.

As Cole has been working all hours, Mabes and I have fallen into a great routine. We both get up early, and I make her breakfast. Some days Cole wakes early and has coffee with me, some days he gets up when I'm already making Mabel's waffles or muffins, which she tells me are far better than her dad's boring cereal. Once everything is ready, we sit outside in the sun and count the painted lady and viceroy butterflies vying for the milkweed bush in the corner of the yard while we eat.

Our garden project is in full swing now too. Over the last week, we've managed to dig out the entire back garden and refill it with fresh topsoil. Mabel is a very go-with-the-flow kind of kid but, at the same time, a little workhorse when she wants something. She spent three days straight with me outside, filling one side of the plot with starter plants: new tomatoes, some peppers, intermittent flowers, spinach, and lettuce. It's all in the beginning stages, but to see Mabel's face light up every time a new sprout appears has been magical. She's drawn a picture of the garden in her notebook, and every time something new pops up, she adds it to the sketch.

Most nights over the last two weeks, Mabel has already had dinner by the time Cole gets home. We talk while he eats, then we play board games or swim until Mabel is ready for bed. By the time his routine with her is done and he's showered, it's late. Which means, aside from a couple nights we watched TV together, and the evening we spent on the front porch, I've mostly been hiding in my room with my romance novels and one of my "tools." Normally I have more self-control, but seeing Cole come through the door every day in that damn uniform, and hugging his daughter like the perfect family man he is, I'm really being pushed to the limit.

Now, as I'm zipping up my suitcase, I glance down at my phone. Still no answer from Cole. We're heading to the lake cabin he rents every year an hour outside of Lexington as soon as he gets home and showered. Cole says staying at the cabin is like being the only people on earth. We'll be gone for four days over the weekend, and I'm just hoping for a comfortable bed and a good place to read my book.

My phone buzzes as I pick it up.

> **LAW DADDY**
> Thank you for helping her pack.

> **ME**
> It took you that long to say thank you?
> Awkward.

> **LAW DADDY**
> You're awkward.

> **ME**
> Real mature.

> **ME**
> You'll be happy to know I'm almost packed and I have sweatshirts.

LAW DADDY

I was packed two days ago.

ME

We can't all be Captain Organized.

LAW DADDY

You could be somewhat organized though . . .
Second Lieutenant Organized maybe?

ME

I live my life one day at a time, Ashby. I don't
worry about organization or rules.

LAW DADDY

Exactly what you want to hear from the woman
in charge of caring for your child.

Whatever. I scoff and put my phone in my pocket just as I feel it buzz again. I can't help myself and pull it back out with a smirk.

LAW DADDY

Are you doing some sort of wifely thing and
ignoring me?

ME

Sure am.

LAW DADDY

Atta girl. Shows that maturity you made me
realize I'm lacking.

LAW DADDY

Now get that ass packing. I'll be home soon.

I shake my head and, this time, firmly place my phone in my shorts pocket. Oh, I'll get packing alright.

I peek into the living room and spy Mabel sitting at the coffee table doing a sticker book and watching the movie I could probably speak from memory after the last two weeks, *Annie*. The newest one with Jamie Foxx. She's obsessed.

I decide I'm safe for mischief, so I head into Cole's room. His walls are cream and empty, and his bed is covered in an army-green duvet and ivory throw blanket at the bottom. The wood tones of his headboard match his dresser, and the items that sit on top are sparse; some wooden boxes, cologne, a watch box housing way too many watches for one person, a glasses case, and a framed photo of him and Mabes the day she was born. I smile at the picture and sigh like a cartoon character with hearts for eyes because the image of him holding the tiniest little bundle in his arms, and the look of love he's giving her, is bewitching.

Focus, Ginger.

I spy his suitcase easily in the corner and hoist it up onto the bed. When I unzip it, I stand in shock. This suitcase looks like something I'd pin on Pinterest.

Every single thing has its place. His socks are folded perfectly in one section, boxers in another. The entire suitcase is a sort of masterpiece as it opens further, and I discover shorts, sweats, and jeans in an underside compartment. I think of how I tossed a few bathing suits, some shorts and tanks, alongside my toiletries and books, into my own case. No rhyme, no reason. It's official, Cole and I are polar opposites in every way.

I get to work unraveling each pair of socks and do my best to mix them up. They're all crisp and white but have different colored Nike swooshes on them. I put navy with gray, black with red, and so on. I unfold his boxers and flip them inside out, before placing everything back exactly where I found it, so he won't notice until he unpacks. I stand back and smile, then remember the joke Reds boxers I gave him one Christmas. I wonder if he still has them. I make my way to what I assume is his boxer drawer.

I pick right. Top drawer: at least twenty-five pairs of perfectly folded boxers, mostly black. I shuffle around for a few moments before I find the Reds pair. I quickly pull them out and replace them with one of the pairs he'd packed. I smile as I consider the fact he'll have to wear them one of the days we're away.

I go to close the drawer, but my sweater catches in the handle, and I knock a small wooden box off his dresser in the process. It spills to the ground with a clanging sound. I freeze, waiting to hear if Mabel is coming.

What am I doing in Cole's underwear drawer?

I move to pick up the items that have fallen out of the box and realize they're handcuffs. Four or five different pairs. I pull two out for inspection just as Mabel comes bounding into the room. I quickly stuff them into the pockets of my loose gym shorts and pull my oversize tank down to cover them.

"What fell?" she asks. "What are you doing?"

I smile. "Just making sure Daddy has everything he needs."

"Can I help?"

"Of course," I answer. "Do you want to help me zip up the suitcase?"

She nods, and we push down on the case to close it. When we're finished, I hear the oven timer sound and realize our early dinner is ready. I move to the kitchen in my bare feet and pop on Cole's fluffy oven mitts to pull out the lasagna that we assembled this afternoon. It's perfectly bubbly, just the way my mother and Nonna make it.

I'm just getting the table ready as Cole comes through the front door an hour early from work. Only, unlike most days, he isn't empty-handed. Instead, he's carrying two of the biggest bouquets I've ever seen: dahlias, roses, lilies, carnations, a real stunning mix of blooms. Mabel runs over to him as he places both bouquets in one hand to pull his sheriff's hat off and hang it on the hook at the front door.

"You got flowers for Ginger too?!" she exclaims as he bends down to kiss her cheek and hand her her bundle of flowers.

Cole's rugged masculine beauty stuns me. The slow, steady grace with which he toes his large boots off, the slight scruff along his wide jaw, his ass in those tan uniform pants. I'm a sucker for it all.

His eyes flit to mine across the room, and I almost drop the freshly baked lasagna as the corners of his perfect lips turn up into a grin.

"Of course, I couldn't let her room be lonely while we're gone any more than yours," he says as he approaches me.

Am I still holding the lasagna?

I blink and set it down on the warming board on the stove. When I turn around, Cole is right there.

"I wasn't sure exactly what kind of flowers you liked, so I just got one of everything Cindy had," he says, mentioning the owner of the flower shop in town.

"I . . ." I manage to croak out, fumbling like an idiot. Cole chuckles, pulling the oven mitts from my hands and placing my bouquet in my arms as Mabel comes into the kitchen with hers.

"I picked my spot!" she says, and I struggle to keep up with this little unspoken piece of their life.

I watch as Cole pulls out two vases from a kitchen cupboard, unwraps her flowers, and fills one vase with water.

"There's one for you there . . ." He gestures to the pretty crystal vase left on the counter as he heads off with Mabel to her room. He's back inside of a minute and finds me in the same spot, staring down at my flowers as I take in their heavenly scent. He laughs lightly.

"Somewhere along the line of Gemma and me splitting up, Mabel developed a kind of anxiety around leaving home for any length of time. Sometimes it's only when she leaves, but other times it's when we both do . . ." he explains as he takes my flowers from me.

"That's understandable," I say softly as he pulls the wrapping from them and arranges the stalks carefully in the vase before filling it with water.

"She even has a bit of an attachment to our house itself. Our holistic doctor called her an empath, which basically means she feels everything. She worries the house will be lonely when we're gone, so we put flowers in her room to keep it company. They usually go in the window in the sun. I don't know why, but it makes her feel better about leaving. Doc says it's a phase and that it will pass."

My heart swells at the effort this man makes to keep his daughter settled.

"Thank you, Cole, they're so pretty," I manage.

"Go pick your spot in your room while I serve up this delicious dinner," he says, rubbing my shoulder.

I look down at the blooms then back up at him as Mabel bounds into the room.

"You guys made this?" Cole says to her.

"Yes! Ginger taught me her nonna's recipe."

"Looks so good," I hear him say as I head to my room in search of the perfect place for my flowers. I place them on my end table and stand back to admire them. Cole could never know that this is the first time any man has brought me flowers. It's a simple gesture that shouldn't affect me as much as it does. I push down my heart in my throat as I make my way back to Mabel and Cole. I head to the counter and serve myself a slice of lasagna.

"I already got you one, and some salad," Cole says, pointing to the table, where a plate of food waits. He leans back in his chair and makes all sorts of exaggerated, grunty noises over the dinner we made. For some reason, they lead my brain to all the wrong places.

"Mabel did the hard work. That perfect layering is all her."
I smile as I take a bite.

"Ginger made the sauce. We crushed up tomatoes," Mabel
tells her dad proudly, "and I squished them with my hands."

"Hope it wasn't after you made mud pies in the yard." Cole
grins at her.

"I did wash my hands, Daddy!"

He turns to me. "You made the sauce from scratch?"

I nod. "My nonna would disown me if I used jarred pasta
sauce, Cole. And, trust me, she'd find out somehow."

I can't bring myself to look at him. The picture of Cole
seated at the table in the late afternoon sun is giving me all
sorts of feelings I'm not prepared for.

Once we're finished eating, we move to clean up as Mabel
disappears to watch the end of *Annie*.

"Be careful, sheriff. Keep being so nice and I'll expect flowers every time I have to leave," I blurt as we put the last clean
dishes away.

Cole looks at me with a face I don't quite understand. He
leans down to kiss me on the cheek, taking his time before
pulling away.

"Keep making lasagna like that, and I won't let you leave,"
he says into my ear, sending goose bumps down my spine before backing away and heading off to the shower.

"Out the door in thirty, ladies!" he calls out over his shoulder, oblivious to the way his words have just rendered me
speechless.

As the door to his room shuts, I remind myself this is a business arrangement, then I realize his handcuffs are still in my
pocket. *Not very businesslike, Ginger.*

The drive to Lake Charles passes quickly and, in just over an hour, the blue expanse of the lake comes into view in the distance.

"I don't know how I've never been here before, it's so close to home," I say, looking out the window.

"It's a hidden gem," Cole says. "Dad brought us fishing here every summer from the time I was thirteen until I finished college. We'd stay for a week, usually in this cabin we're heading to, and always planned to come back after I became an officer. We never did. So, the summer he got sick I organized a weekend trip for the three of us. Mabes was only four when she came here for the first time. Gemma was . . . away," he says cautiously, which tells me she was MIA. If I remember correctly, that was the summer before they split up.

"Papa is here," Mabes says in a matter-of-fact tone. So surely, in fact, I almost believe her.

"Mabes thinks he's a butterfly," Cole explains. "We always see the monarchs flying around the same bush in the yard. They never used to be there, but now they fly around right in front of where my dad sat every morning. He loved it here. Said he would get his own cabin here when he retired."

A look settles across Cole's face. It's something between fondness and grief.

"We'll see him. He always comes," Mabel states.

I look back at her and smile. Sometimes I wonder if she's really a grown woman living in a little girl's body. I am sure we could leave her on her own for the day and come back to the house clean and dinner ready. A real-life Matilda.

"Well, I, for one, am excited to see this magical place!" I say, propping my feet up on the dash as I watch the town roll by. My jean short cutoffs are sticking to the leather seat of Cole's truck as we drive with the windows open. I throw a silent prayer up to the universe. *Please let there be air-conditioning.*

We weave our way through the windy streets of Lake Charles. It's a beautiful harbor town with a marina that runs alongside the main road and goes for a few miles. The whole strip is lined with boats of all shapes and sizes, and boaters who have taken up a sort of residence at their slip. There are gazebos and sun shelters everywhere, housing people cooking out and sitting on patio furniture. It's a small town, with one grocery store facing the harbor, quaint shops, and an old-fashioned drawbridge for boats to escape into the lake. The moment we pull through town I take a deep breath. Cole's right; it's relaxing and feels almost coastal even though we're in midland Kentucky. The only thing that reminds me we're still here are the rolling green hills in the distance.

"I love it already," I tell them.

The three of us are chatting away as we round a hill and start up to the top. After a few minutes more of driving, we pull up a long, hidden driveway.

"Home sweet home," Cole says as the house comes into view. When it does, I gasp. It's not overly big but is a good-size log cabin ranch. The property is framed with trees and pristine landscaping around the front porch, but it's the view behind it that takes my breath away: the lake itself, glittering in the midevening sun as far as the eye can see, sailboats bobbing on the still water. I'm speechless as we pull up to the garage, which is attached to a basketball hoop and bucket with balls ready to play. I can see Cole grinning at my reaction in my periphery.

"It's . . . beautiful," I whisper.

"Wait until you see the back," he quips.

As we get out of the car and walk up the cobblestone walkway to the front door, Mabel stops behind me.

"Hi, Papa," she says like he's sitting right there, and sure as shit, right there in the bush at the side of the porch is the prettiest monarch, settled and calm, its wings barely moving as it perches right beside us. Just as my skin breaks out in goose bumps Cole leans down and whispers in my ear. "Told you, Vixen. Magic."

The overwhelming sense of calm continues as we move through the house. It's a center hall plan with two bedrooms on one side of the house and two on the other. All are equally as big as one another and have full bathrooms between them. The whole place is made of wood, not unlike the cabins at Silver Pines, only much less rustic and more modern. The kitchen has clearly been renovated and boasts a huge center island with stone counters and stainless-steel appliances. The main living area is open plan, and features floor-to-ceiling tinted windows to showcase the hot tub that sits on the back patio, and the lake behind. When my tour of the interior is complete, Cole and Mabel lead me to the back of the house, beyond which is a large, flat yard with the greenest grass I've ever seen. Stone inlay leads through the center to a set of stairs that drop down fifty feet, providing access to a private beach with little wisps of crabgrass shooting up through the sand, and a weathered red dock complete with a little silver skiff. The water is clear and shallow to the end of the platform, and the sand is lined with beach glass and shells.

"Can we boat, Dad?" Mabel asks.

"After we unpack," Cole replies, ruffling her hair. "We can't do everything at once."

I feel my phone buzz in my pocket as he shows me around the rest of the yard, but I decide to ignore it until I'm back in the privacy of my room.

LIV

How's the love den?

ME

If you mean the cabin with Mabel, it's beautiful.

LIV

And you're there why? Because Cole needed a nanny on a trip he takes every year?

ME

Because Mabel asked me in front of Cole to come and he agreed. And why would I turn down a free vacation?

LIV

Uh huh.

ME

Nothing is going on.

LIV

I'm on to you, Danforth.

LIV

Just . . . be careful. Okay?

LIV

This is Cole. Don't forget.

ME

How could I? It's all I think about. Trust me.

LIV

Did you at least equip yourself for a weekend with a hot, probably shirtless, outdoorsy dad?

I pull out my spicy why choose novel I'm partway through and Mr. Always Ready, my favorite purple silicone wand that hits all the right spots. I snap a photo.

ME

Armed and ready.

LIV

You dirty little slut.

ME

A girl's gotta do what a girl's gotta do.

LIV

Unless she gets some help from a willing hot sheriff.

ME

FRIENDS

LIV

Whatever gets you through the day. 👍

A sharp knock at the door momentarily scares the shit out of me. I shove Mr. Always Ready behind the pillow and spin around, tossing my phone onto the bed just as the door opens.

Cole walks in. "You unpacked? We're going to take a boat ride. Make sure you bring a sweater. It gets chilly out there just before the sun sets."

He eyes the cover of my book on the bed.

"Uh huh," I say, gulping down my anxiety.

"You okay?" Cole's eyebrows rise. His navy sleeveless Nike workout shirt shows his muscular upper arms and hangs low enough under them that I can almost see the outline of his abs and the curious branded G under his ribs. It's hard to spot, encompassed by so much ink, but it looks like the Grosvenor logo from a ranch two counties over where he worked one summer when we were kids. I wonder what sort of crazy shit he got up to there.

I force my eyes to his face. His hat sits backward on his head, and he has a dishtowel slung over his shoulder, which somehow makes him look even hotter.

"Yep," I croak out.

"Maybe you're quiet because you snuck into my suitcase and fucked with all my shit"—he moves a little closer—"and you're feeling guilty?"

I laugh and breathe out in a huff. "No idea what you mean."

"Uh-huh . . ." Cole's eyes rake over me suspiciously. "I'm tossing those Reds boxers into the campfire, by the way. I'll go fucking commando before I wear them."

I don't laugh, and Cole looks at me expectantly. I'm pretty sure he can see me sweating from ten feet away at the idea of him and no boxers.

"Not even a grin, Vixen?" he asks. Yep, he's on to me. "Why are you being so weird?"

"What's that G on your side?" I ask in an attempt to distract him, but also because I'm curious.

"Nah, that's not going to work," he says playfully, moving toward me to analyze me better, and tugs one of my curls gently.

"You're not changing the subject; why are you acting like you got caught with your hand in the cookie jar?"

I sigh and throw my hands in the air, deciding he needs a dose of reality.

"You know, Cole, when a woman is acting strange, it usually means she's trying to hide something."

I reach behind the pillow and pull Mr. Always Ready out, holding it in my hand so he can get the full view. He looks from it to my book, which I'm sure he can guess is smutty from the woman chained to a bed on the cover, aptly titled *Sinner's Paradise*. His jaw falls open. Any embarrassment I may feel is suddenly totally worth it.

His mouth snaps up and he gulps. "In *my* cabin?"

"Technically not your cabin," I say as I drag my case out from under my bed. "I didn't see the 'no vibrators' sign on the door. And please, you're the furthest thing from a prude."

Cole folds his arms over his chest. "Here's an idea . . . maybe *not* get yourself off for one weekend?"

I tip my head to the side. "Aww, baby, where's the fun in that?" I say, stuffing the vibrator into my bag and putting it under the bed. "Close your mouth, Cole." I smile sweetly, patting him on the chest as I walk by him.

"Shouldn't have to put a sign on the door, Vixen," he says, as if my behavior is shocking, but I didn't miss the way his throat bobbed or the way he eyed Mr. Always Ready up.

Men. Show them a vibrator, and they lose all train of thought.

After dinner, Cole boats the three of us around the inner lake. The homes that back onto it are just as beautiful as the cabin we're staying in. Most of them are floor-to-ceiling glass, and the last of the day's light reflects off their windows. Green and rocky bluffs jut out into the water on either side, and the lake has turned into a deep mercury pool as the orange sun sinks below the horizon. I breathe in the fresh lake air and watch as seagulls roam overhead to land on the beach beyond, still busy with visitors enjoying the sunset. But though the landscape is stunning, I can't take my eyes off Cole as we cruise along the water. He's in command, operating the motor and steering the boat in his backward hat and sunglasses. He looks gorgeous, and I'm finding it hard to watch anything but him.

By the time we get back to the house, it's dark, and Mabel is already dozing. Cole carries her up the steps, and she snuggles in against him, her dark hair hanging down over his strong arm. It's obvious she knows she's in the safest spot on earth, and I wonder if it's possible to crush on this man any more; my baby-making equipment feels like it might burst at this sight alone. *Plus*, he doesn't even break a sweat on the fifty-foot climb to the top.

He turns back to me before he enters the house to tuck her into bed.

"Hot tub and a drink?" he asks.

I glance over to the tub on the deck. Just behind it is a bar area, with built-in solar lighting, that sits against a wooden privacy fence.

Getting inside the tub might be the worst idea ever when I'm trying not to jump this man's bones.

I should retire to my room and work at getting myself off to push through this weekend. I should say no, but instead I say, "I'll get changed."

CHAPTER TWENTY-FOUR
Cole

Well, fuck me.

This bathing suit is not like the one she wore in my pool. *This* bathing suit threatens to ruin me when Ginger emerges in what may as well not even be a cover-up because I can see right through it, revealing the outline of the skimpiest yellow bikini ever.

I sink further into the water as she approaches, and the sun says its final farewell to the day. Ginger shrugs off her cover-up and tosses it onto a waiting lounge chair. I swallow hard. Her full breasts are barely covered. The thin spaghetti strings are doing the Lord's work holding them up, and the sides of the bottoms match the top. One thin strap runs over each of her flawless hips, leaving the tiniest scrap of fabric to cover the place I instantly wish my face could make a home in. My cock throbs against my swim shorts with the thought, aching to be freed. I've never felt more like staking a claim to someone in my life as I do in this very moment.

Bad idea. This was a bad idea. I avert my eyes to a safer view, the bar area beside me, as I think of the way horseshit sits on my boots in the barn, or how the cell block floors look after a night of a bunch of drunkards in the tank. Anything to bring my inflated cock back down to earth.

I clear my throat.

"Drink?" I ask.

"Is the sky blue?" She doesn't miss a beat.

I chuckle and pour her a glass that equals mine from the tub-side bar stocked with plastic whiskey glasses and the bourbon I brought. This place truly has everything for the perfect stay. There's even a container of little paper umbrellas for cocktails on the bar, which runs a whole side of the sunk-in hot tub. Above it sits a black metal cursive sign that says *"It's five o'clock somewhere."*

I pass her the drink as she steps her pretty red toes over the side. Even her feet are fucking spectacular. I would settle to fuck *them* right about now.

The stress I've been feeling, both at having Ginger live under my roof, constantly wandering around in her jean shorts and bare feet, *and* dealing with my new position as sheriff, trying to keep the townspeople happy and run the office properly, has me sucking back this bourbon and pouring myself another as quickly as possible.

My swearing-in is on Tuesday night, along with three new deputies we've recently hired, and then it will be official: I'll be Laurel Creek's sheriff and will have sixty-one days before life goes back to normal.

"Oh my God, that's nice," Ginger half moans as she takes a seat.

The curse of her tits floating up to the perfect level so I can see her pearled nipples through her suit, coupled with the noise she just made, have me feeling like a crazed man. I stiffen and look out to the dark, murky lake.

"Chasing after her all day makes you crave this type of relaxation," she continues as her head tips back. She holds her dark mass of curls above her head and lets them drop over the edge behind her onto the deck. Hot water laps against my body as she settles herself in the water beside me. It's a six-person tub, but we're less than a few feet apart.

"Try chasing her for eight years." I let out a low laugh and run a hand through my damp hair. I sneak a glance at her as I shift to pour myself more bourbon. Her arms are spread wide, and she glances up to take in the view of the stars.

"You're right, it really does feel like you're the only people on earth out here," she says, as I take in the sight of the moonlight grazing the column of her throat. She's so exposed like this. So open. So free.

"I like being out on the water. It reminds me of my childhood." She hums as she shifts, her toes brushing my calf. She doesn't look at me when it happens, but the simple action sends a jolt of heat right up my leg to my still inflated cock.

"I can't picture the great Edward Danforth out on the water in a little skiff," I say, keeping my tone light. The whole town knows him. He's robotic to the core. Ginger was always a lot more like her mother and grandmother than she was her father.

She laughs.

"Definitely not. My dad sailed and tried to teach me the best he could. My granddad taught me how to boat. We fished a lot in Cave Run when I was young too, and he showed me how to hook a worm when I was Mabel's age." She smiles at the memory. "I really miss him."

She whispers her last words and I feel them.

I nod, aware of her love for her granddad and how rare that tiny admission was. She doesn't talk about him much and I, more than anyone, know why. There isn't a day that goes by that I don't think about my dad. But sometimes it's easier to keep that grief inside, rather than talk about him.

"My dad used to take us to Cave Run all the time too. I wonder if we were ever there together," I say casually.

"Probably. I would've been the only girl in bare muddy feet and a baseball hat. I never saw girls out there fishing much." I smile when I think of her like that, a flash of a daughter of her own one day runs through my mind.

"Didn't you have any girl friends?" I ask, genuinely curious.

"Not really. Not until CeCe and Liv sat next to me in homeroom. They're the only girls I've ever been friends with that didn't hurt me, or make fun of me, or backstab me in some way." She has a faraway look in her eye. "But they're my everything now. The only reason I'm keeping this marriage from them is because CeCe has enough to concentrate on with her wedding and the festival. I don't want to disrupt that with our recklessness. But I'm going to have to tell her or Liv at some point."

The slow swallow of her throat pulls me into a hazy trance, and I feel my mouth water.

"You're allowed to keep things private if you choose to. I know you all have girl code, but CeCe kept things to herself when she was sneaking around with Nash last summer."

I'm trying to distract myself from my thoughts of tearing that scrap of a bathing suit off her. But all hope is lost because as she talks, she unties the neck and re-ties it a little tighter, pulling her tits up above the water. I flex my fists in an attempt to keep myself on this side of the tub.

"That was different," she says, picking up her glass from the deck. "She and Nash were in a relationship. We're not. And Liv and I had it figured pretty quickly. CeCe can't hide emotions. I know her and Liv better than anyone else." Her eyes meet mine. "Except maybe you."

She grins, turning her eyes to mine and bringing my gaze back from roaming her body.

"I'm not that easy to read," I retort, making a weird laughing noise. *Smooth, Cole.*

"Yes you are." She bites her plush bottom lip and assesses me for a few seconds. "Like right now, you're worried that I'm not going to last, that I'm going to spill the tea, and this marriage scam will fall down around your feet."

Damn. She's not wrong.

"But I'm not bailing." Her eyes move back out to the water. "I told you I'm in, which means I'm in a hundred percent. I just hope CeCe understands why I didn't tell her."

She turns to me like she's reading the rest of my thoughts.

"You're also a little extra tense these days with work and wondering if we can make it through the rest of the summer together. Mabel gets dirty every day now, she has scrapes, but"—she holds one finger in the air—"she can bike without her training wheels now. The world is a scary place."

"Something like that," I reply to her sarcasm. My lips curl into a small smile, and I swallow the last of my bourbon.

Ginger holds my gaze for a beat before saying, "I think I'll teach Mabes how to drive the boat this weekend."

I recoil. "Like hell you will. She's too young."

She waves a graceful hand. "It's fine. Breaking the law for a simple learning experience won't hurt her. It's high time Mabel knows when it's safe to get away with things or not."

I grimace at her.

"Authority," I say, which makes her laugh.

"Come on, what's wrong with a little rule breaking? She's the sheriff's kid, isn't she *supposed* to break the rules?"

The glint in her eye tells me she's kidding, but still . . .

"Every time you say something like that, you make me regret this arrangement a little more," I tell her.

A grin spreads across her face.

"Take it easy, Sheriff by the Book."

She pushes herself off the tub and swims closer. I slide slightly to let her in as she reaches over to the bar and pours herself another bourbon.

"I was only joking anyway," she says with a smirk.

The need I feel to put her in line consumes me as the small of her back rises out of the water. I let my eyes ravage her while she isn't looking, taking in the curves of her arms to her upper back, the line of her spine, every single vertebrae, to the little dimples just above her bikini bottoms. The perfect place for me to anchor my thumbs while I spread her wide and fuck into that tight little pussy I can't forget.

Ginger pours the bourbon as her tits rest against the ledge of the tub. It almost fucking breaks me, but she places the cork back in the bottle and is back to her spot a few feet away before I completely lose control.

Once she's settled, she spends the next half hour telling me all about her granddad and their fishing superstitions, how he taught her to drive the boat and to read the weather patterns. He even showed her how to clean the fish when they caught them. I sit and listen intently because even hearing about old fishing stories from Ginger is captivating. She has a way of painting a picture when she talks that I haven't experienced with any other person before.

When we've had enough of the heat and my hard-on has subsided enough for me to make an honorable escape, I help her step out and do my best not to let the slippery feel of her skin brick me right back up.

I hand her a towel to cover up, mainly for selfish reasons. I don't know how much longer I can remain this kind of gentleman with her.

She wraps it around herself, but the moment it's secure, she uses one finger to reach out and skim down my ribs, running it over the raised letter at my side. Her eyes move over me, blazing a trail as they go. After what feels like eternity, she steps into me, and when her eyes finally meet mine, her lips are parted, her cheeks flushed from the heat and bourbon. Her hair rests against her wet skin, making the ends stick to it. *Fuck*, I reach up and tuck a lock of it behind her ear. I've never seen anything more beautiful in my life.

She opens her mouth to speak—

"Daddy?" a small voice says from the patio door, causing us both to flinch and step out of each other's space.

I look at my daughter, who is rubbing her eyes with the heels of her palms. I expected her to wake up at some point but not before midnight. It's only eleven.

"Will you lie with me until I fall back asleep?" she asks.

"I'm coming, buddy. Go back to bed, I'll be there in a second," I say to her.

I look back at Ginger, suspended between two worlds: my wants and needs as a man and my duty as a father. I don't even say good night before leaving Ginger on the patio and heading inside.

Forty-five minutes later and Mabel is fast asleep again, which allows me to silently sneak out of her room. She must be exhausted. The fresh air always does her in.

I make my way to the other side of the house. I need to apologize to Ginger for not saying good night. It's not her fault she's so fucking enticing, and I have no self-control. It's almost midnight now, so I don't expect her to be up. But as I walk toward her room, I see the light from under her door. I'm just preparing to knock when I hear it, the shuffle of her bed and the slight hum of—*No fucking way*. I lean in to listen a little closer, my ear almost to the door.

She moans, a soft, breathy sound that brings me right back

to *that* night. I'd know it anywhere. I hear it once more as the hum continues. She's definitely getting herself off with the vibrator she brought to my cabin.

Holy fuck.

My cock instantly grows almost painfully hard as I hear her heavy breathing increase along with the quiet hum of her vibrator. I instinctively adjust myself as a tiny moan escapes her. I flex my fist once, then twice before forcing myself to the safety of my own shower. It's either that or take care of myself right in the fucking hallway.

I let the hot water wash over me, hoping the space will wash some sense into me.

But it doesn't.

The idea of her making herself come under my roof is all-consuming. Is she still in her wet bathing suit? Is she fresh from the shower? Is she stark fucking naked on the bed? My mind is a clusterfuck of images, mainly imaginary ones and pictures from the night we spent together as I run my hand over my cock. I slap a hand to the shower wall and give in. Just this once.

Closing my eyes, I let the night in Vegas flood my mind for the thousandth time. I remember how those moans sounded below me, a longer and more drawn-out version of what I just heard in the hall. I continue to stroke my cock. Ginger is all I see: the way her shorts sit just above that little curve where her ass meets her thigh, how her eyes grow wide with shock when I say something that surprises her, the face she makes when she eats something delicious. How she looked on that dance floor in Vegas; the smooth roll of her hips, her hands moving that little black dress up just enough to hint at the apex of her thighs.

I bite my bottom lip to contain a groan as I imagine the way she looked on all fours while I drove into her again and again. The sound of the toy she was just coating in her arousal spurs me on. I could hear her getting close, just as close as I am now. In my mind, I'm back in our hotel room. I tip her head back with both my hands and smear her crimson lipstick across her cheek before holding her mouth open. Her tongue darts out to wet her lips, so ready and willing to accept me. I slide into her, my fingers tangling through her thick, wavy hair. It's so fucking soft. Her mouth is warm and, as she looks up at me, her cheeks hollow out before she gags and sputters around my cock. She works herself up and down my shaft, and I grip her head tight, giving her something to choke on every time I hit the back of her throat. The memory is so visceral, and I'm pretty sure my bottom lip is ready to bleed as I hold in the deep sounds begging to escape my chest. I press my free palm even harder against the shower wall, imagining my name on her lips as she comes in a breathy moan.

"*Cole . . .*"

"Fucking Vixen," I breathe out in a heady sigh as I spill into the shower basin. I take a second to re-center, pushing my wet hair from my forehead. As my cum disappears down the drain, I wonder how the fuck Ginger Danforth has managed to throw my years of practiced self-control out the window, reeling me in while I'm totally helpless to stop it.

CHAPTER TWENTY-FIVE
Ginger

SIXTY-TWO DAYS TO GO

The next three days are a blur of sun, sand, fishing, barbe-cuing, cornhole barefoot in the thick green grass, pro-vided by the rental, and catching all sorts of insects on the cabin property with Mabel. Vacation Cole is irresistible, and I've given up trying to tell myself otherwise. He's totally relaxed and wanders around shirtless with Mabel like he lives on the lake.

It's late Monday morning, our last day, and I'm perched in a lounge chair on the dock watching Mabel and Cole fish off it, using my sunglasses to hide the fact I can't stop staring at Cole.

I'm stretched out in my black one-piece bathing suit, which almost exactly matches Mabel's. It wasn't planned, but she was thrilled when we came out of our sides of the cabin and into the living room, wearing nearly the same thing. Right down to the single braid in each of our hair. Even Cole couldn't help but laugh.

We've had a blissful three days at the lake and, to be honest, the last thing I want to do is head back to town later. But it's inevitable. Cole has a big day tomorrow, and I've already readied Mabel's dress to go watch her dad get sworn in with the entire family.

"That's it, buddy. Give him some line," Cole says as Mabel starts to reel in a catch.

She squeals in delight as the little rock bass flops up onto the deck. Cole's jaw is set as he works to help Mabel unhook the fish, his strong legs supporting him as he crouches down beside her. I can't get the vision of his naked torso out of my mind from our late-night hot tub meetups.

Cole works to help Mabel unhook the flapping fish and, for the millionth time, I take in how gorgeous he is. I rake my eyes over the wisps of dark, sweaty hair that poke out from under his hat and stick to the nape of his neck, and the furrow in his brow as he removes the hook from their catch with steady patience. He's even better looking than normal after three days in the sun, and the landscape of his muscled chest has turned a golden brown. But it's the dip in his lower back, the two dimples just above the band of his bathing suit shorts, and that perfect ass as he squats down on the dock, that have me breathing faster.

It's a wonder Mr. Always Ready hasn't died this weekend from overuse.

I'm pulled out of my trance as Cole pats Mabel on the back.

"That's it, now we'll let the fish go," he tells her.

"Can we go on the boat now?" Mabel asks.

"A little later. I've got to run to town to refill one of the propane tanks for the cabin owner. You can come with me."

"Can I stay with Ginger instead?" she asks.

"Ginger looks pretty comfortable where she is, Mabes. Let's leave her be."

I prop myself up on my elbows. "It's fine, she can stay with me. We can keep catching fish, can't we, Mabes?"

Mabel's eyes light up before she turns to face Cole.

"Okay, I'll be back in less than an hour," he replies, kissing Mabel on the head and turning so our eyes meet. I feel the pull to him like he's got his hooks in *me*.

"See you, sheriff." I wink at him.

"Be good, girls," he says as he starts to walk up the stairs. Something about the way he calls me his girl charges my heart rate as I watch him go.

"Can you stop staring at my dad now and help me cast?" Mabel asks, loud enough for Cole to hear. He looks back over his shoulder to flash his signature cocky Cole grin.

My face heats, and I wish I could sink between the deck boards on the dock.

"I—yes." I rise to help her, while knowing I'm totally busted. I'll never hear the end of that one.

We cast out a few more after I hear Cole's truck leave the driveway but don't catch anything else.

"Can we go in the boat now?" Mabel asks. "I've been waiting all day."

"I think we should wait for your dad to get back, honey," I tell her.

"Why? You know how to drive the boat, right?" she responds.

"Yes, I suppose so."

"I'm bored of the dock," she says, fiddling with her fishing pole.

I think for a moment. I can drive the boat. Especially as the bay is as calm as glass.

"Let me call your dad," I say to Mabel, pulling my phone out of my pocket.

Mabel waits expectantly as it rings, but it goes to voicemail.

She looks up at me with pleading eyes, and I feel grateful that, after the last two weeks spent together, she still likes me.

I smile at her. "Okay, but only if he texts back to say it's fine."

"Yay!" Mabel jumps up and down and launches herself into my leg. "I know he'll say yes to you!"

I give her a little squeeze as she continues, "I like having you for my dad's friend."

I get us both ready to go, and pack a bag with water, snacks, and life vests. Just as I'm about to try Cole again, he texts back.

LAW DADDY

This goes against everything I'd normally allow.

ME

That's why you should do it. Step outside your comfort zone. I've managed bigger boats than this. We'll be fine.

A few seconds pass as I watch the little dots pop up.

"Can we go now?" Mabel asks, as she stands on the dock in her life vest.

LAW DADDY

I'm putting a huge level of trust in you to take my daughter on the water. Make sure her life vest is secure and stay in the bay. There's a bit of a wait here to fuel up, I might be a bit still.

ME

We'll be back before you are. I'm just taking her down the harbor and we'll stop in the reeds so she can cast a few.

LAW DADDY

Don't make me regret this, Ginger. Please stick to the plan.

I like his message, roll my eyes, and shove my phone in my pocket.

"Let's go!" I tell a happy Mabel as we climb in and take off into the crystal-clear bay.

I check the time on my phone and am surprised to see we've already been on the lake for an hour. Mabel and I have been having so much fun. We're a little farther out than I expected we'd go. We spent a lot of time looking at all the homes that line the shore and seeing Mabel smile makes me feel . . . happy too. We've been drifting in the reeds on the other side of the harbor for ten minutes or so, but I'm not liking how the sky looks in the distance. The entire bay seems to be coated in a greenish haze as a bank of gray clouds roll in, as if they're about to unleash a rainy fury upon us. I try to text Cole to tell him we're heading home, but it bounces back. No service.

"Come on, Mabes, pull that line in. We should get going."

Mabel does as I say, and we pack up all the fishing stuff. Within just a few minutes, I notice how much closer the clouds are. Note to self: Next time, leave as soon as you see them. I've been out on the water when a storm has started before. Granted, never this quickly, and I was always with my dad or my granddad, both boating experts.

I start the motor, and we begin our journey homeward. The wind has picked up slightly, and the water is definitely a little rougher than when we left. A small ripple of fear trickles up my spine when I hear a boom of thunder in the distance. Mabel looks at me and I at her.

"Is it going to rain?" she asks.

"No, I think we'll be back before it does, babe."

We ride along with ease even though the water is choppy, staying as close to the shore as possible without ruining the prop. It's still too far away to reach by swimming, but at least we can see it. I try to take solace in the fact that we're not out in the middle of barren water.

"I don't like thunderstorms," Mabel tells me.

I'm silent for a moment. I don't usually mind them. From the safety of my covered balcony, I sometimes even enjoy them. But not when I'm out on a lake with a child, a child whose father will kill me for being even half an hour late.

I glance down at my phone in my lap as I steer. Still no service.

More thunder sounds, and lightning and wind follow a few seconds later. Both Mabel and I jump at the deep, rumbling sound. I reach my hand over to cover hers.

"It's okay, we're already halfway back," I tell her as we pass the midway point I marked on our way out. I know we still have several minutes left going at the speed we are. But by the time we make it to the first row of cabins I recognize, it starts to rain. The water is getting really rough now, and all I want to do is get back to the house so Mabel isn't scared.

"Almost there, babe. Don't worry," I try to reassure her as the wind howls even harder. We finally round the corner for our shoreline, but we're both soaked and I'm holding Mabel in my lap to make sure she's as sheltered as possible. I keep the boat moving at a slower, steady speed to navigate the choppy water. I talk to Mabel the whole time, telling her about my granddad and the things we did together when I was young.

Another deep crash of thunder sounds, and Mabel jumps.

"I'm scared," she says as I hold her close.

I look into her eyes.

"I will keep you safe. I promise. Okay, brave girl? Five more minutes and we'll be home," I tell her, praying I'm right, "and when we're back, we'll dry off, because right now we look like a pair of wet puppies. Then we'll have something to eat, and Daddy will probably make that face at me, you know, his angry one, because we got caught in the rain."

"That's the one my nana calls his cranky pants face," she says as she cuddles into me to stay dry.

"And then tonight we'll go home and, if you aren't too tired, we'll get all cozy and watch *Annie*. Okay?"

"Will you watch with me?" she asks.

"Of course I will," I promise. "I'll even make us popcorn."

I push her to keep talking as the rain pelts against my skin. I ask her to tell me all the things she wants to do when she goes with her grammie Trudy to the cottage, and what she thinks we should make her dad tomorrow for his special day breakfast. Anything to keep her calm and keep myself from crying.

My heart sits firmly in my throat as the wind increases, and I fight with all my strength against it to keep the boat moving straight and heading toward the row of cabins, one of which is ours. The beach is empty as we cruise by, and the waves close to the shore are intense. How did I get myself into this situation? Oh, I know, because I *never* ever follow the rules. I always have to push it, and now I've broken Cole's trust. I should've gone back when I said I would. I should've stayed closer to the house.

The water hitting the boat is so loud that I almost cry with relief as I finally see our cabin come into view in the distance. I will myself to stay steady and calm.

As we get closer to the house, I spot Cole pacing under the gazebo on the dock, cellphone in hand. The sheer look of panic he's wearing that turns to utter disbelief when he sees us tears at my heart. No matter what he says to me when I get off this boat, he'll never make me feel worse than I do right now.

I brace myself. The look on his face is one of both intense relief and one that says he's about to murder me.

CHAPTER TWENTY-SIX
Cole

I don't like the look of the sky as I exit the store after getting the tanks filled. In the time I was in there, a bank of clouds started to roll in, and fast. I hop into my truck just as I hear the first sound of thunder. I try to call Ginger. Straight to voicemail. I check my service. Full bars. I send her a quick message before I fire up my truck.

ME

Hopefully you're back. Pack up and head inside straight away. The storms here have been known to get rough quickly.

I start the drive back to the house, looking up at the sky whenever I can. It's almost black now, and rain has started to pelt against the windshield. I keep myself calm by telling myself Ginger and Mabel are at home, that they're huddled inside together, and I don't need to be worried about anything.

I curse myself as I drive with the wipers at full speed. I should've told Ginger about the chance of this happening. I should've made her wait to take the boat out until I got home. This bay is notorious for sudden storms. *Fuck.*

I pull down the drive to the cabin as the rain and wind whip against the truck. I don't even think about getting the tanks out. I just toss the truck in park and make a beeline into the storm, burning through the front door as soon as possible.

"Mabes? Ginger?" I call out, but it's too quiet. It's clear they're not here.

I tear through the house and out the back door, but when I get to the stairs, all the blood drains from my body. There's no boat at the dock. The level of panic that rolls through at the thought of Mabes in danger is a form of adrenaline I've never felt in my life. Right now, I would nuke the entire fucking earth and leave it to char and ashes if it meant bringing her back to safety.

I run so fast down the stairs my feet are a blur. I pull my phone to call Ginger again, but it goes straight to voicemail, and I see now that my earlier message didn't go through.

"Fuck!" I call out, frantically pacing. She must have gotten caught off guard. *If anything happens to either of them . . .*

Just as I'm ready to dial the number for the Coast Guard, my fingers shaking, I see them. My legs give way, and I drop to my knees on the dock as relief washes over me.

As they get closer, I can see Ginger holding her T-shirt over Mabel to try to shield her from the rain. She's left in only her bathing suit and must be freezing as the wind and heavy water droplets pummel her skin. Mabel is huddled into Ginger, but when she looks up to find me, she's not crying like I thought she'd be. She seems okay. Fine, even. Slow and steady, I watch as Ginger brings them in. I jump into the water as they get close to the dock and pull the whole fucking boat the rest of the way.

The rain is already subsiding when I nestle the boat up beside the dock. These storms are usually fast and turbulent. Ginger looks at me but says nothing as I hoist Mabel onto the platform and move onto it to help her up. Mabel has no idea of the danger she was just in. I bring her to me, burying my face in her hair, on the verge of tears as the adrenaline starts to wear off.

"Ginger drove us through a roller coaster!" Mabel exclaims. "We pretended we were at Disneyland." She smiles and wrinkles her nose, reaching up to my cheek. "You're all wet, Daddy."

"So I am," I say, huffing out a breath.

I secure the boat to the dock with my free hand and extend my other one to pull Ginger up with us, bringing her to my chest as I hear a silent sob choke in her throat. Always testing her limits, she definitely went way farther out than she said she was going to and, judging by the horror in her eyes, it scared the living shit out of her.

I'm angry, I'm relieved, I'm ready to both yell at her and kiss her everywhere I can. There's time later to talk. Right now, I just need to feel both my girls in my arms, right where they belong.

CHAPTER TWENTY-SEVEN
Ginger

Cole doesn't give me that stern dad voice, or yell at me, like I thought he would. In fact, he doesn't really say anything, which could be worse. The two of us move like wooden people into the cabin, and we all go to change and pack our wet clothes into plastic bags to transport home.

It's just before dinner when Cole finishes packing up the truck. I hand Mabel a sandwich for the road and, as I head back inside for the final bits, Cole's eyes meet mine. This is the first moment we've had alone since he met us on the dock.

"Cole. I—" I try very hard to choke back the tears I can feel coming. He doesn't hesitate for one second.

"Fuck, baby, you're shaking." He pulls me right to his chest, kissing my shoulder through my hair.

"Listen, there is lots to talk about," he whispers, looking toward the porch to make sure Mabel doesn't hear him. He uses his finger to lift my gaze. "You did such a good job of keeping Mabel calm, and from what I can tell, not even fazed, throughout that whole experience. And she should've been scared, Ginger, because that was so fucking dangerous—" He sets his jaw and looks down to try to keep his composure.

He releases me from his grip.

"Let's just get home, and Mabel into bed," he says, sliding his hands down the tops of my arms.

I swallow and nod, and for once, I don't argue. Instead I try so hard not to let the way he says "home" like it belongs to both of us become something I crave, something I need.

Cole turns to get Mabel in her seat and, after giving the cabin one last look, I follow them to the truck and open the passenger door. I slide in and gulp down my remaining tears, talking to Mabel like nothing is wrong the whole way home when in truth I think *I* might be a little traumatized.

By the time we reach Cole's, and unpack the truck, I've stopped shaking and am feeling calmer. Safer. Now that we're in Laurel Creek, the atmosphere is more relaxed. Cole takes Mabel in and gets her ready for bed while I start putting things away. It's not even nine o'clock, but she's exhausted. I promise her we'll watch *Annie* tomorrow, and she seems satisfied with that as she says good night.

After I start a load of laundry, I head to my part of the house and settle in to take the longest, hottest shower I can. It's here that I finally let go, allowing the tears to consume me as the water runs over my skin.

We're safe. She's safe. We're safe, I repeat to myself until the water starts to turn cold.

I step into my matching tank and pajama shorts and blow-dry my hair, taking my time to compose myself.

I pull my robe on, tying it tight. I'm determined to spend the rest of the night apologizing to Cole, but when I open the door to my bedroom, I jump and suck in a breath because sitting on the edge of my bed in the almost dark room is Cole, shirtless in his gray sweatpants.

He stands as soon as he sees me before making his way over. The light glints against the wall as the sun sinks down behind the horizon, and I'm not prepared for the feelings I'm experiencing right now. Fear mostly, guilt, shame, but, as Cole pulls me into his arms, the most prevalent thing I feel is relief.

I mold into him the way I have so many times before, but this time, it feels different.

"Cole, I am so sorry. What I did, choosing to stay out longer, not paying attention to the clouds, was so stupid."

"Yes, it was," Cole confirms, and I know he must be angry, but his next words surprise me. "But it wasn't your fault. I didn't tell you what the weather can be like out there, and I should have. Because I know you, Ginger. I know you're impulsive and so . . ." He flexes his jaw as he searches for the words. "So goddamn giving, and I know you just want to make her happy. If you were having fun with Mabel, of course you'd opt to stay out longer."

He pulls back and places both his hands on either side of my face. My heart feels like it may cease to beat as he stares into my eyes.

"I can't even imagine how afraid you must have been out there."

Tears fill my eyes once more.

"I was so scared," I admit in the tiniest whisper. "Her safety was in my hands, and I wasn't experienced enough to take her out that far. All I could think about was how worried and helpless you would feel."

A lone tear spills onto my cheek, and I look down to avoid his intense whiskey irises. Cole tips his forehead to mine and closes his eyes, swiping the tear away with his thumb. He breathes out a sigh, and the scent of him overwhelms me.

"But you did keep her safe," he says softly.

My breath stills, and I keep my forehead pressed to his. I feel his hands slide down to my waist. His large fingers hesitate for a moment on the knot at my hips, and I stand frozen, as though we're on the edge of a tipping point. The moment he starts gently untying my robe and pushing it open, the decision is made. My pulse thunders in my ears with the loosening of the fabric, so loud I'm sure he must hear it.

He slides his hands in, slowly, as if asking for permission to continue. They feel cool and calloused against my freshly showered skin as he circles under my tank with his thumbs. I open my eyes and look into his. Cole's hands move upward to graze my rib cage and he lets out a groan, tugging me closer, flush against him, before bringing both of his hands up to the sides of my face, tracing my cheekbones lazily.

"In case you are completely oblivious to what is going on here, it wasn't just her I was worried about out there," he says, his voice low and deep.

The heat emanating from his body is all I can feel. His hands move further into the back of my hair, and he pulls me flush to him. His lips hover over mine, forcing me to stop breathing. For a moment, it feels as though we both do. The struggle in his eyes echoes mine, and every cell in my body tingles at his closeness.

Cole tips my head back before bringing his lips down to my neck, kissing me there once, then twice. He moves his mouth to my cheek and dots light kisses along the way to my mouth. His soft lips ignite my entire body, and I clench my thighs together as his lips brush against the corner of mine.

"Every single night is a fight . . ." he says breathlessly, "every goddamn night since you came here, Ginger."

I have no strength to speak as he continues. "It's a constant fight for me because all I want to do is leave my room and come to yours."

I shudder as he pulls me even closer.

"I stop myself because I know if I start kissing you, we'll see daylight before I'm done."

"Cole . . ." I whisper, trying to remember how to breathe.

"Today just showed me it is time to *stop* fucking fighting."

His arms wrap around me, and his lips drop to fully capture mine in a kiss I'm not prepared for. Fire spreads through me as Cole's mouth forces mine open, and I swear the feeling of his mouth on mine causes the earth to shift on its axis.

I'm willing and boneless against him, matching his urgency, kissing him back with everything I have. It feels like coming home.

His lips, his tongue, even his teeth taking in my bottom lip, overwhelm me as his hands move through my hair, tilting my head slightly for better access. He groans into my mouth like I'm his lifeline as much as he is mine. His tongue searches every corner of my mouth as his hands continue to roam. The taste of us together washes through me, and I instantly want more.

I want it *all.*

I shudder, which coaxes a groan from him. And, before I even know what's happening, I'm pressed against the bedroom wall, our bodies flush, fitting together like two pieces of a puzzle.

"So fucking sexy . . ." Cole growls as he pulls my bottom lip between his teeth. "I can't stop this anymore, Vixen."

So don't.

His hands move up my sides and under my tank to my breasts, lightly pinching my pebbled nipples as he presses his lips to my neck and bites me there. The slight pain mixed with pleasure causes me to jolt in his arms. Just as quickly as he nips, he kisses over the sting.

"I don't want to try anymore. All I want to do is fucking bury myself so deeply inside you that you remember me there every single second. I want you to feel *empty* without me."

Oh, fuck.

"So do it," I dare him. *Please, please do it.*

A low sound rumbles through Cole's chest as his mouth finds mine again. He lifts me up against the wall, and I wrap my legs around him. I can feel him hard and pressing between my thighs. I'm past the point of caring, so I push back, searching for the friction I so desperately need. I want him. *God, do I want him.*

Who am I kidding? I've always wanted him.

The air around us peaks with electricity as I melt into Cole, the ache growing more with every swipe of his tongue. My reaction is frenzied, out of control. I can't catch my breath, but I don't even care to if it means missing one second of his mouth on mine. One of his hands holds me up at my hip as the other slides to the base of my neck. Cole massages my throat, gently igniting a trail across my skin. His lips leave mine and move to my neck, and I whimper as they lick over the sensitive spot behind my ear.

"Fuck," he groans, closing the gap between us even further. Never in my life have I felt like this, totally lost in desire. I grip Cole's shoulder with one hand and slide my other to his waist, exploring the abs and the hard muscles of his back I've only just recently feasted my eyes on. Everything is clouded as we move together, his cock pressed against my clit, giving me just what I need. It hits me that he's going to make me come, and he hasn't even removed a single piece of my clothing. Shivers of pleasure race through my blood.

"That's it, so fucking eager . . . take what you need from me," he coaxes, his voice gruff.

"Yes . . ." I whimper, pressing my aching core against his hardened cock. My mind floods with nothing but him and unfiltered lust.

I move against him as his tongue fucks into my mouth. Everything Cole does sends tiny zaps of pleasure everywhere, all at once. His hand at my hips moving me against him, my breasts pressing into his hard chest, my nipples graze him as I ride him, both of us still clothed, but I've never experienced anything so erotic as I move against him in a driving rhythm.

My core spasms, and waves of pleasure pulse through me as the orgasm takes hold. My eyes close as I tighten my ankles around his waist, they shake as I unabashedly grind against him.

"That's it, greedy girl," Cole murmurs as static lines my vision.

"Fuck, *Cole* . . . I'm coming . . ." I moan into his shoulder. He holds me up as I pant uncontrollably, coming down from my high. It's the only sound that cuts through the dark room.

"Coming all over me and I haven't even taken your clothes off yet? Attagirl, Vixen," he purrs into my ear with a chuckle.

Before I have a chance to tell him he's a cocky motherfucker, we hear a sharp thump from the other side of the house. A door? We both suck in a breath.

"Fuck." Cole tips his forehead against mine for a beat, composing himself. He pulls back and lowers me to the floor, squeezing my waist before letting go and adjusting himself. I close my robe, tying it tight. One last desperate look from him in the dark before he swings my door open and goes down the short hallway to the living room. I slump down on my bed and take a breath, asking myself how I'm ever going to live without whatever just happened as I hear Mabel speak.

"I woke up. I had another bad dream."

Cole's voice cuts through the silence. Shaky still, but low and reassuring. "Okay, buddy, I'll be right there."

I'm still shaking, trying not to pass out after coming against Cole fully clothed like a desperate teenager.

"I want Ginger. Can she lie with me?" I hear Mabel squeak out.

"Um . . . well," Cole starts.

I stand and am in the living room in three seconds flat.

"Of course I can, I was just . . . getting ready for bed," I say, moving past Cole and taking her hand.

Cole's eyes follow me as I wander down the hall with Mabel's hand in mine, letting her lead the way. I look back over my shoulder. The same longing and confusion swirling around my head are reflected back at me through his expression.

I snuggle beside Mabel in her bed. She looks up at me in the dark and twists her little fingers into the curls of my hair like she needs something to fidget with.

"I was scared today. I didn't want to tell you," she whispers.

I swallow down the lump in my throat. Her eight-year-old honesty makes my chest tighten.

"You can always tell me anything, sweet girl. And I was scared too," I reply. "But we were brave together, weren't we?"

"We're a team," she says, placing her tiny hand on my cheek.

I giggle. "Yes, we are. A great one."

"We're all a team." She hums sleepily.

I kiss her forehead and pull the blankets up, tucking her tight.

"Me, you, and Daddy," she continues with a yawn, twisting her fingers back into my hair.

I gulp, trying to swallow all the emotion coursing through me. My feelings for her, my feelings for Cole. They threaten to suffocate me as I lie here and try to hold it together.

Whatever is happening between Cole and me, Mabel is the priority, but I can no longer deny these feelings I've always had for him. They are on a freight train heading warp speed down a track. The only thing that will tell whether we land safely or crash and burn is time.

Tonight, I need to let go. So I simply kiss Mabel's forehead and breathe in her sweetness. I need her as much as she needs me.

"Good night, sweet girl," I tell her.

"Good night, Ginger."

TWENTY-EIGHT
Cole

SIXTY-ONE DAYS TO GO

Three things wake me simultaneously:

The sun coming up, which tells me it's way too early, my still painfully hard cock after last night, and the smell of pancakes mixed with the sounds of laughter from the kitchen. I roll over and stretch, forcing my tired eyes open. It's a big fucking day today, and I barely slept. After Mabel asked for Ginger, I went promptly to the kitchen, poured myself two stiff bourbons, and knocked them back. Then, I made a beeline for a cool shower that didn't help at all after feeling Ginger's body pressed against mine when she came, needy and desperate. Even after I fisted my cock for some relief, the dull ache of want was still there.

I have no idea how long I stood in the doorway of Mabel's room after I was dressed, watching the two of them sleep. I'll never get that picture out of my mind; both of their dark hair splayed out around them, as they faced each other, their hands folded together in the center between them. Mabel's free hand was twisted into Ginger's hair, the way she normally does with her Cowey's fur. If one thing had gone wrong yesterday I could've been having a totally different night. But instead, they were safe, tucked up peacefully in Mabel's bed. The way I felt at the sight of them asleep together still has me in knots this morning.

I sit up on the edge of the bed and rub my eyes with my palms. The girls' laughter echoes down the hall, and I know there's no better way to start my day than with that sound. It's only been a few weeks, but Ginger's presence is slowly creeping into this space, and the thing is, I don't even want to try to control it anymore. I *want* to lose control with her.

I pull some clothes on and pad into the kitchen. I'm not prepared for the scene that greets me on the early side of six A.M.

The blinds are open, letting the sun in along with the fresh morning air. The local country station croons Lee Brice, and in the center of the room are Ginger and Mabes, both in their pajamas with big buns on top of their heads. It's as though Ginger did their hair the same on purpose.

Just behind them, a fat stack of pancakes and fruit, syrup, and coffee await. A tight feeling takes over my lungs. I'm not used to help in this house or the idea of someone taking care of us.

"Happy special day, Daddy!" Mabel jumps up with the biggest smile on her face, throwing both hands in the air. It's her Christmas morning smile on a simple Tuesday in the middle of June. Fuck, the sight of them together gives me a small glimpse of what heaven might be like.

"Well, good morning, girls," I say back, making my way over to the cupboard for a mug.

"I have her dress all laid out for tonight. You're going to look so pretty, aren't you, Mabes?" Ginger says to Mabel.

Mabes nods.

"What color is your dress?" she asks Ginger.

"I—I don't think, this is a family thing tonight, honey—"

"You're not coming?" Mabel asks, looking down, disappointment lining her sweet face.

I pull the cream from the fridge.

"Of course Ginger will come with us tonight," I say matter-of-factly.

She looks up at me questioningly.

"I'd have to . . . I'll have to run home for a dress. How formal is it?" she asks.

"Very formal," I say with a smug grin, popping a strawberry into my mouth. I love catching her off guard, making her a little flustered.

She nods, and I can't help but think about those perfect curves poured into an evening dress. Mabel loads her plate with pancakes, then disappears into the living room to watch her favorite show.

When she's gone, I move to stand behind Ginger, running a finger down her neck. Her soft skin instantly breaks out in goose bumps in my wake. I swipe the wispy hairs from the back of her neck, the ones that have escaped her bun, and bring my lips down to the sweet-smelling spot under her earlobe. I let my hands slide farther still, down her shoulders, over her forearms. I lace my fingers through hers and lift them up. The inside of her wrist begs for my lips, so I kiss her there once. If yesterday taught me one thing, it's that life is too short not to take what I want. Maybe this idea is crazy, but I'm hoping, no matter how crazy it may be, she's willing to jump headfirst into it with me.

"You look fucking beautiful in my kitchen, Mrs. Ashby," I whisper, offering another kiss to her palm.

Ginger tenses under my touch, and I feel a shiver run through her. She lets out a contented sigh with my words, and I revel in the electricity between us after last night's unfinished business.

Ten goddamn years of unfinished business. When she turns

to face me, and her light chocolate eyes focus on mine, still sort of sleepy but now lust-filled, I instantly know this spark between us could blow every fucking breaker in this house. Just the way she looks at me makes me hard. Goddamn, I may need five cold showers today.

"This is your special day, Cole, and what happened last night . . . when we . . . you know, kissed and other things . . ." Her words are flustered.

"Other things being you coming right through your panties and shorts?" I ask with a smirk.

She doesn't laugh. "Yes, well . . . maybe living through trauma made us hypersensitive or something?"

I scoff. *This woman.*

"Also, I want to tell you again how sorry I—"

"Ginger." I put a finger to her plush lips, which, in turn, makes my cock instantly wake right up.

"What happened at the cabin yesterday was a freak accident. You need to stop apologizing for something you handled as well as I could've."

I grip both her shoulders and look into her eyes. "You're both okay, and that's all that matters."

I trace her soft shoulder with my thumb, wishing I could slide my hands right under her shirt and rip it from her body, ravaging her until I've had my fill.

Need takes over, need for her to understand. I grip her hips and tug her close, sliding a hand up to her face and losing my fingers to her hair. I lean into her and breathe in her coconut scent.

"I didn't kiss you because I was traumatized. I kissed you because I have thought of nothing else since Vegas. I *wanted* to kiss you. In fact, even with Mabes in the next room, it's fucking taking everything in me not to kiss you right now. Understand?"

She nods once, then turns her face toward my palm, letting

me know she approves of my touch. She looks up at me with the tiniest smirk on her face.

"Well, who am I to stop you from doing what you want? It's your special day. Which means your rules, sheriff." She shrugs, her voice like smoke, and it's a tempting challenge. Fuck, everything this woman does is sexy as hell.

I hear Mabel shuffle in the next room, so I let my hands slip from Ginger's shoulders and put some space between us. It's the very last thing I want to do right now, but I have to control myself.

"That's a dangerous sentiment to challenge me with," I say nonchalantly as I move to the other side of the peninsula and start placing pancakes and fruit onto my plate. When it's clear Mabel isn't coming in here, Ginger leans over the other side, facing me, her cleavage an invitation.

"Never took you for the kind of man to back down from a challenge, Cole," she says.

She pops a piece of pineapple between her luscious pink lips way slower than warranted, and she smiles hazily at me. My cock twitches in response.

Fucking little tease.

I chuckle, then scoop another heap of fruit onto my plate. I can bide my time until I get her alone.

"You don't even like pineapple," she says, reaching to snatch it away from me playfully. I pull my plate back and set it out of her reach, then pick up the piece of fruit. I look right at her, leaning over the island so our faces are only a few inches apart.

"It's yours," I say, popping it into my mouth and leaving it there for the taking. The look she gives in return tells me I'm about to suffer.

I've never wanted to suffer more. Right now, I'd beg for it.

Ginger inches forward, pushing her soft tits purposely against my forearms and resting her elbows on the counter. She tilts her head slightly and looks me dead in the eyes before hers flutter closed. She leans in and brushes her lips against me as light as a feather, encompassing the fruit as she makes a sucking motion to steal it from me. She trails her tongue slowly over my bottom lip to steal any hint of juice, moaning into me softly. Just like she did last night. That sound alone almost destroys me.

Fucking hell. She wins.

"So delicious," she groans in a whisper as she sucks the piece of fruit into her mouth before opening her eyes, flashing me a grin, and chewing the pineapple right up. She backs up like nothing happened, and I'm left standing here, dumbfounded. I give my head a shake. Turned on by pineapple. Another first.

I make my way to the other side of the counter, and she shrinks a little when she realizes I'm coming straight for her. I pull her to me with enough force to make her breath hitch, but she doesn't hesitate. My hard cock presses into her abdomen.

"You like to tempt me, Vixen? Just remember what you said," I whisper, drawing on every shred of willpower I have not to devour her.

She whimpers.

"My day. *My rules.*"

I let Ginger go and move back to the other side of the counter, looking right at her as I call out to Mabel.

"Hey, Mabes, don't forget to pack Cowey tonight when you get your things ready to sleep at Nana's," I tell her, knowing Ginger had no clue we'd be alone tonight for the first time since Vegas.

"I won't, Daddy," she calls back.

I grin all the way through breakfast, and all the way to the shower, because I know no one takes Ginger Danforth by surprise, and I'm quickly realizing I love to be the man who does.

CHAPTER TWENTY-NINE
Cole

"This isn't a good look for any of you boys," I say as I open the cell door and let out the three very hungover kids one of my deputies arrested last night for being drunk and disorderly. They're all underage and were caught drunk and trying to piss into the sewer on Main Street.

"Will this go on my permanent record?" the youngest one asks, pushing his glasses up his nose. I can tell he's never been in trouble a day in his life, which is a good thing. He won't make the same mistake twice.

"No, the town isn't pressing charges. You boys are lucky to be getting away with a warning," I tell them.

His father, the principal of Laurel Creek High School, stands across from us, arms folded against his chest. You just know he's going to give them an earful as soon as they leave.

I process them and send them on their way, but not before I clap the nervous principal's son on his shoulder. I almost feel sorry for him.

"Just agree with everything he says." I motion to his dad on the other side of the glass. I turn to all three of them. "And next time, for Christ's sake, find a bathroom."

"Sorry, Sheriff Ashby," the oldest one says, muttering to his buddy as he passes me, "My dad's gonna kick my ass."

A smile plays on my lips as I turn my back to them. "Be good, fellas."

They aren't even through the lobby before I can hear their parents giving them shit. I chuckle. Been there. Done that.

"What else do I have today?" I ask Bev when I'm back by her desk. All I want is to get home early before my swearing-in tonight.

"Well, you can either attend the two o'clock city council meeting, or take the transport to the county jail with the guy that tried to rob Menders Convenience last night." Bev leans forward and looks at me over the rim of her purple glasses. "I'd do the council meeting. Buddy in the cell relieved himself when he was coming off his high."

I nod. "Council meeting it is. Send Brent to transport. He'll love that."

Bev grins without looking up.

"It would be good to show up and let the town know you're there for them anyway," she says.

"Sounds great."

She glances back up at me again. "You have coffee on your shirt. Might want a fresh one before your first official appearance with council."

I look down. And, sure as hell, I see a coffee stain.

"Shit," I mutter under my breath.

"Fresh ones are in the closet to the left of your desk. Just got your size delivered yesterday," she says, her eyes back on the documents in front of her.

I tap the frame of the door as I leave her office.

"Thanks, Bev," I say, grateful for her motherly care. One

more meeting and I get to go home and see what Ginger has come up with to wear to the banquet tonight. I can hardly fucking wait.

By four o'clock, I've managed to make it home early. I play a quick game of Uno with Mabel before heading to my room to lay out my fancier all-black uniform I wear for formal events. As I get out of the shower, wrap a towel around my waist, and wipe down the mirror to shave, I hear Ginger and Mabel in the living room, chattering away about when to get Mabel into her dress and what hairstyle she wants Ginger to give her. I've thought about nothing but Ginger all day. No matter what I do, I can't get her out of my head.

It's the line I always struggle with, but having her here makes it so much more difficult. This home is where I'm Dad, not Cole. Creating space to be a man in a dad's home might be the hardest thing I've tried to balance. But after last night, I don't have a choice.

A light knock on the door pulls me from my thoughts.

"I think Mabel's hairpins are in there. Can you pass them out?" Ginger asks through the door.

I open it wide, letting her in.

She stands in the doorway for a beat as I pump shaving cream into my palm. I feel her eyes roam over my body, and I relish her stare. I turn to face her.

"Come in. Stay awhile," I say with a grin.

She blinks, and I love that she looks at me the same way I look at her, as though she can't look away.

"So this is you *not* trying to entice me," she says sarcastically, waving a hand over my towel-clad body.

"Working for ya?" I ask, raising an eyebrow.

"Pffft. Not in the slightest," she answers too quickly, but the creep of pink slinking up her cheeks tells me she's lying. After a few seconds of silence, she blurts out awkwardly, "Mabes is watching *Annie*."

"Of course she is," I say calmly, letting her off the hook as I rub the foam along my jaw in small circles.

I pull my razor out from the bathroom drawer and give it a rinse in the sink, tapping it against the marble. I hear her huff out a breath and prepare myself for an earful.

"You know . . . last night was a moment of weakness for me, and just because you know you're hot doesn't mean you can parade it around everywhere you go. I'm aware this is your house, but still . . ." Ginger says in a sort of angry whisper, her hand on her hip. "It's . . . distracting and you not being the least bit upset with me about what happened on the boat, kissing me like that . . . Why weren't you more upset?"

I continue my shave as she rambles on. I know her well enough to let her finish before I try to get a word in edgewise.

"You trusted me with Mabel, and I should've been more cautious"—she taps her nails on my bathroom counter—"and you still trust *me* with her after that? And another thing. You . . . you getting to me like that . . ."

"Making you come," I say, cutting her off.

She narrows her eyes at me. It's fucking adorable.

"Well, it's like you're messing with my head, Cole."

I've had enough.

"Sit." I nod toward the counter, taking a guess that she's finally finished rambling.

"Look, let's get some things clear," I say, keeping my eyes on the mirror as I start to shave. She miraculously doesn't argue for once and pops her perfect ass up onto the counter beside me. She wears cutoffs and a tank, but her hair and makeup are styled for a formal night out. The contrast is perfect.

She looks up at me like she doesn't know what to expect, and I wonder if anyone has ever let her shine on her own. I can tell it makes her nervous when I don't doubt her, but she better get used to being treated right if she's going to hang around here all summer.

I finish up the steady line I'm shaving, feeling the weight of her gaze on me, and breathe out a sigh. I give my razor a rinse before starting again.

"I don't know what the fuck is going on in that pretty head of yours, Ginger," I say as I lean in to the mirror beside her. Her freshly showered coconut scent overwhelms me as I tilt closer.

"And you can keep hiding behind that sassy, standoffish little attitude all you want, but you need to understand two things." I turn my head, rinse, and work away at the other side of my face as I talk. Just having her in here makes the bathroom that much more humid.

"One. No one is perfect, and whoever made you feel like you had to be all the time was wrong for putting that kind of pressure on you. People make mistakes, but that doesn't mean they aren't worthy of your trust."

I know for a fact it is her father who constantly makes her feel this way, but I don't point that out. I finish shaving and turn to look at her.

She looks up at me, breaking free from her trance and giving me the universal motion with her first finger for "come here" and a little grin. That tiny motion instantly turns me on.

"You missed a spot," she says softly. I immediately shift my body toward her, getting close enough to make her breathing increase.

I look down at her and use my free hand to tap her knees. Like the good girl she is, she instantly opens her legs wide enough to accommodate me.

I sink between them, never taking my eyes off hers as I flip the razor over and hand it to her. Her eyes widen.

"Fix me up then," I tell her.

She doesn't say a word, but takes the razor from me, a look of concentration on her face.

"Two," I continue, "I'm not messing with your head. I don't fucking understand this any more than you do, but I do know that, even if you're unsure about me, you wanted me to kiss you last night."

Ginger makes a nervous sound that I know most people don't hear from her. She's always the picture of "nothing fazes me."

"Just stop talking or I'll cut you and I *won't* be to blame." She smirks, intent in her eyes.

Ginger does a little dance of trying to figure out where to anchor her free hand to stabilize herself before she begins.

I don't give her more than ten seconds before I roll my eyes and take her hand into my own, placing it firmly around my waist. We look at each other, and the room around us fades away when we lock eyes this close.

I see her lips part and her thrumming pulse in her throat.

"Shouldn't be afraid to touch your husband, Vixen." I grin.

Her eyes narrow, and she uses her knuckles to raise my chin, rather roughly, which makes me laugh even more. Then, she places the razor at my throat and carefully drags it up, swiping the foam as she goes. She lets out a breath I know she was holding in when she finishes, and I eye up her handiwork in the mirror.

"I'm still alive, so that's a plus," I mutter.

"For now," she retorts.

In truth it's a perfect shave. One that leaves me rock hard beneath my towel.

Turned on by shaving. Another first.

I look down at her at the precise moment she flips the razor and hands it back to me.

She hops down from the counter, inadvertently grazing my hardened cock. Her eyes move down when she feels it, then back up to mine.

"So happy to be of service." She grins. "Better take some downtime before you get ready. But not too much. You can't be late for your own party, Law Daddy."

I look down at my hard-on ready to bust through my towel. The fuck am I supposed to do with that now?

Not twenty minutes later, I stare at myself in my uniform. It's a suit of sorts with a matching officer hat. The gold stars line my collar, and the sheriff badges sit flush on my upper arms. They feel heavy. I'm holding on to all of this by a thread, and now tonight not only will my whole family be there, but Ginger will be too.

I check my watch and straighten my hat. It's go time. I've already been the sheriff for weeks but, for some reason, today it feels real.

"Let's go, ladies, time's a-wastin' . . . " I say as I enter the living room.

Every thought in my head dies as I take in the sight of Ginger standing in the window, fixing Mabel's hair.

My eyes trace her silhouette; from her pretty heel-clad feet to the mass of waves that dance atop her head and fall perfectly out of her carefully placed pins. The black, silky dress she said Liv delivered today fits her like a satin glove, gliding over the hips that beg for my hands. The waist is cinched tight, and the top gives the illusion that one clandestine movement would have her full breasts freed, and hopefully, in my mouth.

The expanse of skin visible from the strapless bodice is dewy and smooth, and looks so fucking soft, just like it felt last night.

"How does this look?" she asks for both of them. I snap out of my trance as she turns her eyes to me for the first time since I entered the room. When she does, her eyes roam over me the same way mine roamed over her. Only she seems to get it together a lot faster than I did. A million thoughts run through my mind as to how to answer her.

Stunning, tempting, exquisite, sinful . . . mine.

I remind myself Mabel is in the room, looking up at me expectantly.

"You both look very beautiful," I say coolly. They look at each other and then back to me.

"We match!" Mabel says. Her little black dress has puffed sleeves and is structured to her knees with white flowers all over. She is adorable, and I couldn't love her more if I tried.

"Of course you do," I say with a smile.

They begin their departure through the front door and, as I place my hand on Ginger's back to guide her, the heat of her skin races up my forearm. I will myself to get through this night without making my first order of business as the sworn-in sheriff pulling her into the bathroom and hiking that dress up over her hips.

The ballroom at the Grand Oaks Country Club is filled with a few hundred people from town. This is always a formal event and one that is taken seriously. I'm not even in the door before people are shaking my hand and congratulating me, telling me how good a job they think I'll do for the county.

Mabel finds my family, and I get through the hordes of

people, thinking about Ginger behind me, keeping her comfortable and making sure she isn't alone.

I turn to guide her to our seats, but she isn't even behind me when I turn around. I scan the crowd but don't spot her as the mayor posts up beside me for a photo opportunity with his media team. He congratulates me on my new position, and we talk for a few moments about my upcoming plans. My eyes are anywhere but on him as I search for Ginger. His publicist pulls him aside and it's then that I see her, standing in a circle with four of my deputies and an officer I don't know, maybe from out of county. She's chatting away, smiling and laughing, while each one of them takes in her body in that dress like they've never seen anyone like her. She either doesn't notice, or does but doesn't mind. Both of which piss me off equally. I set my jaw and get sucked into yet another conversation while Ginger talks with the cop I don't know. He's leaning back against a table, like he's about to pull her toward him.

"Do you think that will work with your schedule?" Daryl Buckner, who runs the community outreach program for the local Salvation Army, asks, bringing my attention back to the conversation at hand. I have no fucking clue what he's talking about. What I do know is that Ginger just laughed and rested her arm on that cop's chest like they're BFFs.

"Uh . . . sure, call my office," I say, patting him on the shoulder as the MC asks everyone to take their seats. The crowd thickens between us, and I make my way to my family's table as someone starts playing a set of bagpipes to open the ceremony.

Everyone is here. My mama and pop are on one side of the table. There are a few empty chairs between them and Nash and CeCe, who sits next to Mabel, playing tic-tac-toe with her on the back of a napkin. I'm perched beside Wade and Ivy, because it's the only spot where there are two spare seats side by side.

Ginger finally makes her way over and sits across from me, at the coaxing of Mabel beside her, leaving the space beside me that I was saving for her empty. Her eyes meet mine across the table.

"Since when do you save Ginger a seat?" CeCe asks in front of everyone, assessing the look I'm giving Ginger that probably says, *Why aren't you sitting here?*

"He's being weird today, maybe something to do with all that sheriff pressure." Ginger smirks. "Anyway, Mabel and I already planned out our seats. Can't play hangman with her across the table."

"True story," CeCe adds. "I could use a break anyway; she's killing me at tic-tac-toe."

Mabel smiles up at CeCe and I grimace, not liking this seating situation one bit.

"You alright? You look like you could use a cuddle, Cole. Is Brent here yet?" Ginger giggles as she normally would when she's ribbing me, but her eyes tell me she isn't having as much fun tormenting me tonight. After our conversation earlier, she seems almost nervous. Which she should be, because I'm ready to snap. I'm about thirty seconds away from pulling her into the nearest hallway and wiping that bratty little smirk right off her face with my cock down her throat.

"You can always cuddle Wade and your badge," CeCe snickers to me.

"Not a chance, I'm not the good sheriff's emotional support puppy," Wade chides.

"And I won't call you sheriff at the dinner table, boy," Pop says with a wink, taking a sip of his drink. "Just because you're the boss at work, don't expect us to treat you any different."

He's as spiffy as Pop gets in a suit I think he's had since the eighties. The whole "if it's not broke don't fix it" sentiment goes hard with him.

"Careful, old man. If you start backtalking me, I'll have to bring you in on account of burning all the brush in the back forty when it's off season." I nod and raise my drink.

"Seriously, though, I'm proud of you, son," Pop says, taking his tone from playful to mushy real quick.

"Thanks, Pop. Still might bring you in, though." I grin.

"My baby," Mama says from across the table, "the youngest sheriff in the county's history."

Fucking hell.

"Aww, listen to all this sweetness." Ginger grins, knowing it makes me uncomfortable when people center me like this.

The cop guy she was talking to sits down at the table behind her and taps her on the shoulder, interrupting my witty retort. She looks back as he speaks to her.

Wade leans over and whispers in an exaggerated manly voice, "Fancy meeting you here, Ginger, I really like the way your black dress looks. You're single and I'm single, let's mingle."

Ginger and the cop both laugh like it's exactly what he just said to her.

I nudge my brother with my elbow. "Fuck off," I say, straightening out my silverware, which is already perfectly straight.

Wade tips his head back and lets out a low chuckle. "You're looking mighty jealous of that cop talking to your summer nanny."

I huff like a child and look away just as I'm called on stage by Bev.

"It's time," she mouths. I nod as Ginger continues her conversation.

I'm sure I look like a grumpy motherfucker, but I don't care. All I can think about is how I had Ginger pinned up against a wall last night, and if she thinks she's going to flirt with some other asshole . . .

She's just talking. Calm the fuck down, I tell myself over and over, wondering if all my sanity has gone out the window.

Ginger turns to look at me when I hit the stage and line up beside my new deputies and Brent, who's here tonight without Gemma. He stands beside me now.

"Looks like the whole family came out to support you, and huh . . . even CeCe's friend too? Wow, so supportive."

He sneers like a cocky son of a bitch. He knows Ginger's name; he's just being a dick. I'm about ready to put someone through a wall with the mix of sexual tension between Ginger and me coupled with what I can only understand is jealousy, something I don't think I've ever truly felt before. The intensity of this emotional cocktail runs through my veins.

It may as well be Brent who takes the brunt of my frustration.

"Mabel asked for her to come. You know, since her mother is constantly fucking absent," I bite out, turning to him and smiling like we're having a friendly chat. "I have to wonder what would make Gemma *not* want to come and see her daughter when she had the chance to tonight. She hasn't visited Mabel since the end of school by my calculations, which is over three weeks ago."

"She's not feeling well." In other words, she was out a little too late last night. *Sounds about right.*

"So who I bring to an event with Mabel and me would stand to be none of your goddamn business, then?" I ask, clapping him on the shoulder. I nod toward center stage. "Looks like you're up."

The mayor announces Brent as the new deputy sheriff, and I grit my molars. He makes his way to the spotlight as I join in the crowd's applause. I can't fucking stand this chump, but I'll clap for him nonetheless. The new deputies are called up one by one until it's my turn. When the mayor calls my name, he talks about my time as an officer, how I've served with honor for this county, and that my plans for the future will take us through the next four years before adding, "Please give a warm welcome to your new county sheriff, Cole Ashby." The room explodes, and the loudest table of all is my family, standing and yelling words of enthusiasm as I meet the mayor and raise my right hand to be officially sworn in. As he does so, it strikes me that the only eyes I want on me are Ginger's. When I find them, she's wearing the world's biggest, most genuine smile as she cheers and just like that, everything around me settles.

CHAPTER THIRTY
Ginger

"Are you ready to leave now?" Cole asks rather gruffly, cutting in while I'm mid-conversation with Ethan an hour after dinner. I've known his wife for years, and it's nice to see a friendly face besides Cole's family. Talking to him is also a welcome distraction from practically drooling all over Cole as he works the room, shaking people's hands, engaging in deep conversation about the county he cares so much for. There's seriously nothing this man does that isn't attractive. I'm having a hard time thinking straight around him more and more every day.

"I'm wrecked, and Mama is leaving with Mabel now," he continues, his jaw set. If I didn't know any better, I'd say he looks a little pissed off. But despite that, he's never looked more incredible than he does tonight. His black uniform suit is molded to the hard lines of his body, and brings everything that happened between us last night to the forefront of my mind for the thousandth time today. I've never wanted him more but, as much as I want to throw myself into this fire, some small part of me is still so afraid to lose the connection we have—the connection we've had for years.

"Sure," I say to Cole. "I'm ready to go when you are."

"Nice to see you, Ginger." Ethan leans in to say goodbye to me.

"I don't think we've met," Cole cuts in from beside me. "Cole Ashby."

He sticks his hand out.

"Hey, yeah, congrats, sheriff. I came out tonight to witness my old co-worker be sworn in as one of your new deputies. Shawn Muller."

Cole nods. "Well, that's mighty nice of you to come all the way from . . ?"

I don't miss the cool edge to his tone.

"I work in Greenview County," Ethan answers, mentioning a correction center in the next county, "but we live in Lakeview Heights."

"And how do you two know each other?" Cole asks not so casually, pointing back and forth between me and Ethan.

Is he *jealous*?

I look him in the eye. "Ethan's son Jesse is in my class. He's one of my favorite students, and his wife is my EA this year."

Looking pointedly at Cole, I raise an eyebrow. He instantly seems to relax. "Their daughter volunteers in the summer for Nash at Olympia for his day camps."

"Oh, I see, very cool. Nice of you to come out," he says to Ethan, a little more genuine this time. I secretly grin as they continue a few minutes of small talk. *Too late; you are totally busted, buddy.*

"Drive safe, deputy," Cole adds before shuffling us over to say goodbye to his family. I smirk the whole way, internally dying a slow death at the idea of Cole being jealous of another man talking to me. Pretty rich considering I spent most of my teen years being secretly envious of every single girl he brought to the ranch. My, how the tables have turned.

I watch the lights of the town twinkle out the window of Cole's truck on our drive back to his place. Laurel Creek is quiet at night during the week, and the silence has been almost deafening since we left the banquet hall a few minutes ago.

"Look, I know you didn't expect Mabel to spring it on you that I come tonight, and it's probably not easy to act like we aren't harboring this whole marriage secret, hiding it from your family," I say as we turn into Cole's neighborhood. He hasn't said a word during the ride home and, instead, has spent the journey tapping his fingers against the wheel to "House Fire" by Tyler Childers. His jaw practically looks like it's going to pop a tendon.

"And I don't know why you're so cranky, but if you want some space I can go to my own apartment tonight," I offer. "I don't want to hang out with Sheriff McGrumperson all night."

I stifle a laugh and, when he doesn't answer, continue to ramble. After all, it's what I do best.

"And I know it's been a weird few weeks. First a wedding, a new housemate, then the scary boat experience; add in a pretty intense, although rather short, make-out session—"

"Ginger, fuck. Just. *Stop*," Cole grunts, keeping his gaze on the quiet streets.

Something about his tone rubs me up the wrong way.

"Stop *what*? Look, I know this isn't easy, Cole. I know we're asking a lot of each other, but all you did tonight was look at me like I've pissed you off. Doesn't make a fake wife feel very fake wanted."

I force a laugh, struggling to lighten the mood as I stare out of the window. The words aren't even out of my mouth before a low, threatening growl rumbles from Cole's chest.

"*Fuck—*" he snarls, swerving into his driveway. The truck comes to an abrupt stop, and before I even register what is happening my seatbelt is unbuckled and I'm hoisted into his lap. The action tears my dress where the slit sits on my thigh, which makes Cole's breath hitch as he looks down to see the damage.

Our eyes meet for one split second before his lips are on mine. Consuming me, leaving me breathless and panting for air. His sunroof is open slightly, but his street is dark and quiet around us. The only sound is our hurried breathing.

His hands cover every part of me, sliding up under my dress and squeezing my ass as he kisses me. I moan into his lips. His fingers move under the lace of my thong, which makes me lose all cognitive function. I moan again and give in completely, rocking against him, pulling him closer, finding he's already hard in his dress pants.

Cole groans into my mouth before speaking. "I'm not pissed off that I had to bring you, or that I'm keeping anything from my family. I'm pissed off that I can't fucking control *anything* when I'm with you. I'm pissed off that I've spent years forcing myself not to give in to the way you drive me crazy."

"Cole . . ." I breathe out.

"What, Ginger?" he asks, a dark undertone to his words. "Go ahead. Do it. Make some more jokes. Avoid the truth and tell me to stop."

His hands creep up my rib cage just under my breasts as he kisses and nibbles my bottom lip. I mewl into him with every little tug.

"Tell me again that this is all *fake.*" He says the last word like it's poison on his tongue as he grabs my palm and slides it over his hardened cock. My memory is hazy of our night in

Vegas, but this time my mind is clear, and I know exactly what line we're crossing.

I whimper involuntarily at the sheer size of him. So big, so solid.

"Come on, Ginger . . . Show me that bratty side you like to push me with," he snarls as his thumbs slide even higher, ghosting my hardened nipples through the satin of my dress.

"I want you, but I . . ." I trail off as he loses patience and pulls the top of my dress down, freeing my aching breasts. He wraps his hot lips around a nipple and finds the other between his finger and thumb. A groan leaves him and vibrates through me. His eyes meet mine, looking up at me as his wavy hair dusts his forehead. My insides churn with desire for him as his teeth graze my nipple as he releases it.

"Tell me you don't want me the way I want you and I'll stop," he challenges.

"Of course I want you, but we're . . . we've always been—"

Cole pulls my bottom lip between his teeth, biting just enough to make me gasp in pleasure. "If you even think about saying this can't happen because we've always been friends, I might fucking blow a gasket here, Ginger." He slides his hand down my center and swiftly pushes my already wet thong aside. His fingers are instantly soaked.

"Do you drip down your thighs like this for all your friends?" He pinches my clit, causing my eyes to roll back. "I don't think you do, because this mess, baby?"

He smirks as he slides a finger up and down through my dripping slit. *Fuck, that feels good.*

"Is *all* for me," he says deeply.

"I've been telling myself . . . it's just the uniform," I say in a whisper.

Cole chuckles into my lips.

"You can lie to yourself all you want, but the only way I'm letting you come tonight is if you admit the truth and tell me this soaking cunt is all mine," he commands, his dark tone a shot directly to my core as he pushes one finger into me, then two.

I cave. "Yes, Cole. It's all for you."

"It's about time you admitted it." His mouth trails my jaw in ragged kisses up to my lips. Any shred of inhibition I have flies right out the window as he whispers into them.

"Ready to find out just how *real* this is?"

CHAPTER THIRTY-ONE
Cole

I'm done fucking trying.

Ginger might be the only woman on earth who gets under my skin, and the way I want her might be the death of me, but, fuck, I'd face the fiery pits of hell just to hear one more of those little noises she's making now. I don't even give a fuck that we're in my driveway. Nothing matters but her right now.

"Cole . . ." she whimpers as I fuck my first two fingers in and out of her tight pussy.

"Say my name like that again," I command. I lift her for better access, and her head falls back, pushing her perfect tits into my face. I've never been so hungry for a woman in my life. Of all people who would drive me to the brink of fucking insanity like this, it's her. Of course it's her.

"Cole . . ." she says in another moan as she shudders, and I feel her sweet, tight pussy clamping down on my fingers already.

"Atta girl." I grip her hair and bring her face down to mine, smiling into her lips as I push back into her, and my thumb makes slow, tight sweeps against her swollen clit. She's about to lose it already, and I fucking love every second of it.

"Yes . . . oh, God, keep doing that . . ." she gasps in that sexy, throaty little voice I'm starting to understand. It only happens when she's full of lust, when she's beyond caring how desperate she is.

"Telling me how to do my job?" I ask her as I bite her bottom lip, then release it.

"No . . . You do it . . . so perfectly," she mutters. She's all mine right now, lost in the way I fuck into her. I pull my fingers from her dripping pussy and suck them clean. My cock pulses as I do, begging to take their place.

"So fucking sweet," I chant, sweeping my tongue against her lips to force her arousal into her mouth. She takes it eagerly, licking it off my tongue as I shove both fingers back into her and let my thumb find that sweet little berry between her thighs once again. Her back arches, and I let her have what she needs. Her nails slide under my uniform jacket and claw at my skin through my shirt. My balls draw tighter with her sounds. Ginger begins to spiral as I move her hips for her against my fingers, pressing the heel of my palm against her clit. She takes me as deep as she can, and the sounds of her wet pussy taking my fingers fills the cabin of my truck as the windows fog.

"So fucking tight," I mutter against her lips. She pushes against my cock every time I thrust into her, making the perfect kind of mess of my hand and almost of my pants since I'm ready to blow in them just from touching her. "If my fingers fill you like this, you don't stand a fucking chance when my cock takes their place."

Her chest heaves as she gasps for air, and her pussy clenches me tight. I feel the orgasm flow through her as she screws her eyes shut and calls my name. Her legs shake as I slide my thumb back and forth over her sensitive clit while she comes down.

"Such a fucking stunning sight, watching you come for me," I say as I grip the sides of her face with both my hands and kiss her deeply.

I can't wait another second. I crack my truck door open, pulling her out and tossing her over my shoulder. She yelps, but it doesn't slow me down. I make my way inside the house as if the fire I feel for her bites at my heels. "Now let's get you inside, Mrs. Ashby, and you can pick which room you'd like the next one in."

CHAPTER THIRTY-TWO
Ginger

The door to the house slams shut behind us, and Cole doesn't even bother to lock it as he sets me down, slides his jacket off, and tosses it on the bench.

We say nothing as I stand before him in my ripped dress that I'm holding up, panting like I just did a grueling workout. My hair is askew, half hanging down my back, and I'm sure my makeup is a mess. But Cole looks at me like he's never wanted anything more. He starts a slow tug on his tie as he stalks toward me. I automatically back up as a dark expression, absorbing every part of me, clouds his features. He towers over me and uses his free hand to pull the clip from my hair.

It tumbles down around my shoulders as his tie comes loose. His hand winds into my waves, and he pulls me close, using it as leverage. I whimper as my body is pulled flush against his.

"So fucking beautiful," he says, the tone of his voice sending little ripples of desire down my spine. His words, and the idea of him naked before me, are too much to bear. I lose all patience and reach up, pressing my lips to his, not wanting to wait one more second, and yanking at his shirt as I kiss his neck. Buttons go flying as it comes open, and we make quick work of pulling it off him. I slide my hands in over his smooth, hard chest as his mouth comes back down to mine.

But I'm desperate for more. I feel like my skin is on fire, and we haven't even made it past the living room.

My hands find his shoulders, his strong arms, the nape of his neck as he kisses me and slides his hands down my back, gripping me tight as he hoists me up and carries me into his room, never once pulling his lips from mine.

He deposits me on the massive bed, my back to his soft duvet as my breasts bounce against what's left of the silk of my dress. He hovers over me, biting the skin he exposes as he begins sliding the dress from my body, kissing back over the sting he leaves in his wake, taking his sweet time.

"The struggle to both kiss you and mark you the fuck up . . . it's damn near impossible to decide which one I want more," he mutters into my neck. "I've never needed someone like I need you. I'm trusting you to tell me if anything I do is too much."

"Fuck," I moan as he continues to trade between both. All the while his hands never stop moving, feverishly roaming over every part of me. "Don't hold back, Cole, you won't break me. I want it *all*."

"Ginger . . ." Cole trails off, a warning.

"I'll tell you, I promise," I say, and then his lips are on mine again.

How many nights have I dreamed about this? How many times have I pictured him as he is now, hovering over me? My dress is pulled off completely before it hits the floor, and suddenly I'm under him in just my thong. His whiskey eyes stare down at me in the lamplit room.

"Jesus Christ," he breathes out as his gaze swallows me whole. He trails one finger slowly between the valley of my breasts as my chest heaves in a shallow pant. I'm normally fairly confident, but being splayed out like this under Cole, the godlike specimen of a man who's had so many women, most of whom are spectacular, feels a little intimidating.

As if he senses my momentary self-doubt, he bends down and kisses me.

"Hey." His brows furrow like he's in pain as he brushes a piece of hair off my forehead. "Don't you dare. You have no idea what you do to me . . . You're fucking mouthwatering, Ginger."

Cole licks his lips, and I let his words wash over me, allowing me to bloom under his worshipping gaze. I reach up and run my fingers through his hair, then slide them down over his muscled shoulders.

Our feverish movements from earlier slow as Cole trails kisses down my neck, cresting one pearled nipple with his thumb while he pulls the other into his mouth. I let my eyes flutter shut and give in to his touch, bucking my hips up to meet his body. I writhe against him as he toys with me for so long it's almost excruciating; licking, sucking, nipping my breasts as his eyes keep a close watch on my face and body, taking in how I respond to his touch. One large hand moves down my center over the lace of my thong.

"Fuck yes," Cole breathes when he feels how wet I am for him. His lips start at my stomach, kissing his way down. "Look at this tight little cunt weeping for me, begging to be used and properly fucked."

I swallow and try to keep my breathing at bay as his middle finger presses firmly against my clit through the lace of my panties.

"These are just in the way," he says as he pulls them from my body in one fluid movement and tosses them to the floor over his shoulder.

"You don't have to rip every single thing I wear," I tell him breathlessly.

"Being gentle just takes too goddamn long," he says, looking over my naked form. "Now, I want to taste my wife." He groans as he moves between my legs.

I feel like I might hyperventilate as he settles there, taking in every stretch of skin and focusing on my dripping pussy. He looks up at me from between my legs. His piercing eyes meet mine, full of hunger. The sight is so organic, so fucking stunning, and right now it's all *mine*.

"Spread these thighs wide, be a good girl and feed me your pussy, Ginger."

Oh my God.

I'm having an out-of-body experience as the flat of his tongue slides through my slit, then flicks tortuous strokes against it. *"Cole,"* I whisper as he repeats the process again before suctioning his lips against my clit.

I can't keep track of his movements as he buries himself against me, then in me, his mouth working with expert precision. I also can't control the sounds that leave me as he makes a meal of me because never, never have I felt a man do *this*.

What even *is* this? Who fucking cares just—

"Please don't stop. You're so . . ." I say as he continues his sweet exploration, thrusting two fingers into me, then pulling my clit back into his mouth.

"So. . . . fucking good," I manage to whine as I feel the tension building. My chest heaves as I gasp for air and I feel the orgasm slowly roll through my center. My back arches off the bed and, just as I think I can't take any more, Cole curves his fingers and hits a spot inside me that makes stars explode behind my eyelids. I cry out as I ascend to wherever Cole's tongue is sending me.

"Fuck," he whispers as he laps both me and the mess I'm making up. "Good girl, fuck my face . . . come all over my tongue."

A low rumble leaves his chest as he rises over me, simultaneously gripping my thighs and yanking me down the bed under him. The raw masculinity and control that Cole exudes as his hands knead into my skin have me desperate for him again already. I want Cole to touch me everywhere and never stop, completely in his element, not a hint of hesitation.

He kisses me slowly, as if he has all the time in the world. The taste of me lingers on his lips, on his tongue, and I start to lose myself again. Craving him already, finding it hard to breathe, finding him intoxicating.

How the hell is it even possible to want him this much?

He stands, and I whimper with the loss of contact.

"Patience, greedy girl," he says as he frees himself from his pants and boxers simultaneously.

"Oh *my God*," I say, my mouth falling open as I take in his size. Cole's eyes follow mine as I blaze a trail over his body. He's not self-conscious as he stands before me, his cock hard and pointing straight at me. A small smile plays on his lips as he wraps his hand around himself, stroking instinctively. Tiny beads of pre-cum leak from his tip, and the overwhelming urge to take him into my mouth consumes me.

"Something wrong?" he asks rhetorically with the smug look I know so well on his face.

Of course this man has a huge dick. Why am I even surprised?

"No. Although now I know why I was so sore the next morning in Vegas," I say, my eyes feasting on the way Cole's flawless abs blend into the deep V that is lined with veins, rigid now and probably pushing all the blood in his body to that perfect cock.

The man is a goddamn phenomenon.

"Ginger," Cole says, tracking my gaze.

Look alive, Danforth. I snap my eyes back up to his.

Cole crawls on top of me with fire in his eyes. It's the type of look that says he knows how hot he is, a look every one-night stand he's ever had has seen. I tense at the thought. I *won't* be the same woman he sleeps with every weekend. One that he takes and has his way with however he wants, only to pat them on the ass and send them packing. I *refuse*.

I prop myself up on my elbows to meet him as he bends down to meet my lips. I slide my hand down and bravely press my palm to his cock. Taking control.

"We'll take it nice and slow. It will feel good, I promise," he murmurs against my skin.

I narrow my eyes at him. I'm two orgasms deep, and he's still sitting in the queue.

"That's right, baby," I purr into his ear as I stroke him. "*I* will make it feel good."

Cole presses me down into the bed, muttering something about me being a "fucking sassy little brat," but I'm quicker than he is and slide out from under him, throwing him off-kilter. I climb on top of him as he flips over, smirking as I slide my soaking pussy against him, taking control as best I can. He looks up at me in shock, as though he's about to try to fight me, but his eyes close with the feeling of me moving over him. I breathe out a moan as the warmth of him presses against me.

"Christ, Ginger, I'm going to come before I even get my dick inside you if you keep that up," he says as I continue my slow, intentional slide. He looks down and watches as my lips hug his cock. The sound that leaves his chest tells me he's had enough. He sits up, wrapping his arms around my waist and winding his hands in my hair.

"You want it? You want to be in control? Then you better be ready to own it and take exactly what you need," Cole says as he lifts me up enough for just the tip of his cock to notch its way into me. We both suck in a breath as the challenge leaves his lips.

"Do it, Vixen . . . I dare you."

"You can't dare me when it comes to sex," I mutter, sinking down onto him that first inch.

"I can and I will. My day, my rules. Now show me just what I've been missing all these years," he half grunts.

I tip my head back and let myself slide onto him a little more. Cole inside me with nothing between us is . . . *shit.* I force myself to gain a little clarity.

"I'm on the pill . . ." I manage to whisper, "and I'm clean."

There's no way I want him to stop now and go searching for a condom, and there's not a chance he isn't safe. It might as well be his middle name.

"I know," Cole says back, his eyes meeting mine. "We had this conversation the first time. So am I. I never go bare. *Ever.*"

He flexes his hips and gives me another inch. *Holy hell.*

"Oh, yeah . . . I-I didn't know if you remembered," I lie as I feel my pussy clench around him.

Cole unwinds a hand from my hair and uses his thumb and forefinger to pull my chin down so our eyes lock as he continues to push into me. I whimper as it all comes rushing back like it never left; the warmth, our slick bodies pressed together, moving effortlessly in sync with each other.

"Ginger. When it comes to you, I don't forget."

He eases into me further, stretching me, filling me, pulling the last loose stitch I have holding back my control.

I completely unravel as he groans and whispers, "I remember every fucking thing."

CHAPTER THIRTY-THREE
Cole

I'm lost with the feel of Ginger's tight, wet pussy begging for me to make her mine. We're both slick with sweat already, and, as I ease myself into her almost all the way, I instantly realize all that control I thought I had was never really mine to begin with. I am the weakest and strongest form of myself in this one moment, inside her.

"Holy fucking *Christ*, Ginger," I grunt as her pussy clenches around me. I give her a second to acclimate as she eagerly meets my depth, her body adjusting to my size like it was made to take me. I lift her slightly and look to where her drenched pussy welcomes me.

"Feels good, like I promised?" she asks, as I do everything in my power to hold it together.

"Fucking Christ, Ginger," I repeat as she rises up and slides back down, her legs shaking.

"You said that already." She smirks as I look into her eyes. Even quivering around my cock she's full of sass. But I don't have the strength to fight it right now. Instead, I let her own the moment, own me.

"Mmmhmm," I agree as my hands squeeze her hips so tight, I'm sure my knuckles are white. "That's it, open up for me. You're doing so fucking well, Ginger," I whisper as she rolls her hips, and it's a fucking sight to behold. She moans as she holds her hair off her back, and I grasp her plump ass, wanting to leave my mark on every part of her, inside and out.

"So fucking pretty struggling to take all of me," I mutter. Watching her work to take every inch of me like this is a high I've never felt before.

"Too big . . ." she croaks out.

I shake my head. "Not a chance. This pussy was made to swallow my cock . . . just breathe," I tell her.

She listens and takes a deep breath, before shuddering as I push the last inch of myself into her. My cock pulses inside her as she starts to rock against me, her hips moving but never rising up. It's almost enough to make me come on the spot.

She continues as I watch her, eyeing where we connect while I graze my thumb over her clit, sliding her arousal up over it. Her head lolls back, and her eyes flutter closed.

That just won't do. "Eyes here, baby. I've waited years to give in to this. I want *all* your attention now."

She cries out when I start to move with her, setting my pace. I lift her hips slightly, then bring them back down again and again as she does what I command and opens those beautiful eyes, focusing them on mine. They're hooded and glassy and *fuck*—

I pinch her clit, and her walls pulse around me. *Fucking hell.* I can't take this little game of hers one more second. Flipping her onto her back, a whole new realm of sensation takes over as I thrust into her from this angle, dragging myself almost all the way out. The sight of me forcing my way into her makes my eyes want to roll back in my head. I'm so ready to fucking unload in her.

I push into her slowly, and the feeling sends a ripple effect through my body, a type of carnal need to claim her. My eyes move between the beautiful, lust-filled expression on her face and the space where her cunt swallows every inch of me as I lose myself deep inside her.

"Look at you"—I push her hair from her sweaty forehead—"stuffed full of my cock. So ready for me to fill you up."

She lets out a throaty moan with my words before her nails reach my skin and slide down my back. It's consuming pain and pleasure. It's euphoria.

I push back into her, bottoming out, not allowing any space between us.

"Yesss." She draws the word out and the sound causes my cock to grow inside her even more as I wrap my hand around her throat gently. She hisses in response, gives me a sassy look, and says, *"Harder."* I'm instantly lost in her. Lost in this moment. Savoring every single second like it's my last. We swallow each other's groans as I kiss her. My mouth finds her neck, her shoulders, her arms, biting her silky skin, devouring her like she's my last meal. Our bodies slap together, and I make a guttural sound against her skin in the silence of my bedroom.

"Cole, I can't take this. You feel . . ."

"The best," I answer for her.

I circle my hips to taunt her, willing myself to last one second longer. I grip her thigh so tight I know she'll be bruised, but Ginger doesn't seem to mind as she looks right into my eyes and cries out, "Come, Cole . . . come inside me."

That's it. I'm fucking done for. My name on her lips as her orgasm rips through her is too much.

"Again," I grunt as fire dances up my spine. I slam back in once, twice, then spill into her, coming so hard I almost pass out.

She knows what I want. "Cole," she chants, "Cole . . ." I keep coming. Fuck, this woman is going to ruin me for all other women.

I pull her bottom lip into my mouth, turning my bite into a deep kiss as I begin to slow my pace, allowing myself to breathe.

"The sound of my name on your lips as you come," I whisper, "is like a drug."

We still as our hurried breathing slows, the room around us quiets like both of us are afraid to move, afraid to let go. I continue to pepper her mouth with kisses and linger inside her, not wanting to leave her. Maybe never wanting to leave her.

"Cole?" she asks, pulling me out of my haze.

"Hmmm?" I tip my sweaty forehead to hers.

"Did we just officially become best friends close?" she jokes breathlessly.

I bend down to kiss her sweet lips. They're so soft my cock jerks, ready to go again.

"I'd say we just became closer than best friends close."

"And that is what exactly?" she asks with the cutest little smile.

"*You and me* close, Vixen, you and me close."

CHAPTER THIRTY-FOUR
Cole

SIXTY DAYS TO GO

I don't know how long I've been sitting here in just my boxers. Since sometime around four A.M. maybe? I woke up in a cold sweat thinking that Ginger and Mabes were on that boat and never came back. That's when I felt her warm foot against my calf, and I settled back down to earth.

But I haven't been able to get back to sleep. I can't stop thinking that all those years of denying myself, growing closer to Ginger as a friend, were worth the wait. Sex with a connection is totally foreign to me, but now that I've had it, nothing will ever compare. Ginger may be my friend, but I'm pretty sure she is quickly becoming my obsession too. I couldn't even make it through a shower that was meant to clean her up without taking her again last night.

I can't stop whatever this is between us. I don't have the strength anymore. But, at the same time, I can't expect more from *her*. Even when the primaries are over and my probation passes, my life comes as a package deal, and I have no idea if Ginger is ready for that.

As the sun comes up and peeks through the blinds, settling

against the naked expanse of Ginger's back, I'm aware that nothing will ever be the same between us again. I take in the tiny little sun and moon tattoo under her left shoulder blade and listen to the little hums she makes in her sleep. I wonder if it's me she's dreaming of. I know I *want* to be the man she dreams about.

Her phone buzzes for the tenth time on my nightstand. I ignore it and make my way over to her as she stirs. I stare down at her from my full height, taking in every part of her; the perfect shape of her eyebrows, her long lashes, the singular freckle under her right eye. Her perfectly straight, slightly up-turned nose, and the exaggerated groove between her nose and her mouth.

My gaze settles on those juicy fucking lips, and I reach down to my cock and adjust. It's been all of five hours since I've been inside her, and I am fucking desperate for her already. Her eyes flutter open, and I smile. She has both hands stretched out as she watches me lazily for a beat before a small smirk plays on her lips as she fully wakes. She says nothing but pulls the blanket down further to entice me, noticing my hand still covering my cock. Always a vixen. I take in the way her waist leads to those full hips, the ones I am going to spend hours gripping while I take her every goddamn way I can. The space alongside her hip bone is like a beacon for my grasp as I slide the back of my knuckle over her shoulder, and all the way down to just under her rib cage, her skin so soft it electrifies me.

She shudders and moans softly, her gaze drinking me in. I ghost her nipple with my knuckle. Her pretty mouth is so close and, as luck would have it, my bed is the perfect height. All she'd have to do is open up, and I could slide right in.

The idea has me reaching into my boxers and pulling my hard cock out, spitting into my palm and swiping the pre-cum that leaks there off the tip with my thumb. I groan as I stroke my cock over her face, not understanding why or how she has this control over me, and not giving a fuck either.

The need to touch her as I touch myself takes over, so I roll her hardened nipple between my thumb and finger.

In true Ginger fashion, she props herself right up on her elbow, her mouth inches from my dick, settling in like she's watching a fucking Broadway show, licking her lips.

"Well, good morning to you too," she says with that fucking smile, the one I want to fuck right off her face.

"It's about to be," I say with a grin of my own.

"Oh, yeah?" she asks, one eyebrow raised. "How so?"

"You can slide those pretty lips over here," I say, pointing to the edge of the bed with my free hand.

"Oh, no, not yet, Law Daddy, I think I'd like to watch this show for a little longer," she retorts with a hazy glimmer in her eyes, licking her lips as she watches me run my hand over my cock slowly.

"You're a bossy little brat in the morning," I tell her. The way her eyes feast on the sight of me tells me I'm right and only makes me harder.

"You have no idea," she says, inching closer toward me, taking her bottom lip between her teeth as she slides her own hand down her center. "Spit on your cock and fuck your hand for me, Cole."

Jesus fucking—

"*Christ*, woman," I say but can't help but follow her orders. I tip my chin down and do what she says. Spit lands on the head of my cock, and I use my palm to glide it over my shaft as Ginger moans, watching every movement.

"I fucking love it," she pants.

"So you like to watch, do you?" I query. Her naked body before me in the morning sun is almost too much.

"Uh-huh . . ." she manages as her chest rises and falls with desire. She takes her plush bottom lip between her teeth, as though it pains her not to claim that inch between her face and my cock.

"Well, the way I see it, if you get to watch, then so do I," I say as I drag my thumb across the corner of her mouth, desperate for my cock to meet it. But I can wait. I'm a very patient man.

"Where do you want me?" she asks in a way that drives me crazy.

"Closer," I order, patting the edge of the bed.

Ginger doesn't waste one second. It's something I love about her; once she commits to something, she gives it her all.

"That's my good fucking girl," I tell her, brushing the hair off her shoulder as she moves into position.

She's laid out along the edge of the bed, so close, her pussy within reach and mine to play with.

Tipping her chin up toward me, I slide my first two fingers into her mouth. She takes them deep and whimpers, not taking her eyes off me. When I feel her spit coat them well enough, I pull them out and slide them just below the tiniest triangle of perfectly trimmed hair, the rest of her smooth and bare. It's like she's looking to win a goddamn award for the world's prettiest pussy.

She shivers when she feels my fingers against her. I grin; she's already wet as fuck. I give her needy clit some attention, and she instinctively reaches down to take over. Her movements are hurried, as though she's as desperate as I am.

I bend down and kiss her sweet lips, never stopping the tug on my cock.

"Slowly," I order. "I want to take my time watching you fuck that pussy."

She does what I say and slows her movements just enough, sliding her middle finger over her clit, then through her already dripping slit to find a rhythm that pleases her.

But it's me that can't help myself. I reach down and add pressure to her fingers with my own, forcing both of us into her tight heat.

"Control freak." She moans as she slides another finger in with mine. Her taunting tone is too much, and I growl as I speed my pace up on both her soaking cunt and my cock.

"It's okay . . . I know, baby," she purrs, "sooner or later, watching just isn't enough."

"Fuck," I bite out as her tongue skims the entire underside of my shaft. My eyes roll back, and I suck in a breath with the contact.

Ginger slides herself even closer, leaving no space between us, before opening her mouth and sticking her tongue out. She looks right at me, waiting expectantly.

"Ready to help when you need it," she says, her voice a husky whisper.

"*Fuck,*" I breathe out, holding her bottom lip open. I drop my aching cock on her tongue. "Then be a good wife and suck."

She moans like those words do the same thing to her they do to me. Her lips close around me and take in my length. My head falls back for a second while I get used to her hot mouth.

She hums in pleasure, and it almost takes me out at the knees.

I reach down and take over for her at her pussy, swiping her hand out of the way so she can focus on her own task. She rises to the challenge eagerly, wrapping her fingers around me and running her tongue down the length of my shaft. Her tongue swipes against the head of my cock before she takes me deep in her mouth, hollowing her cheeks out around me until I hit the back of her throat. She gags as drool escapes her lips but doesn't stop.

I stuff two fingers into her tight soaking pussy as a reward, and she clenches her thighs around them. I push them back open.

"I want to see this pretty pussy clenching my fingers when you fall apart, Ginger. Legs open," I order as I curve my fingers against the place she loves. She's going to make a mess like this, and I'm so fucking ready for it. I think of all the times I wished I was here. I think of every single time I watched her ass walk away as she gave me that sexy smirk over her shoulder. She whimpers around my cock, coming undone as my balls tighten and my release licks up my spine like wildfire.

"Good wives swallow every last drop. Understand?" I say, my voice like gravel.

She looks up at me through her lashes, nodding in submission. Her legs shake, and I push into her one last time, dragging my thumb over her swollen, needy clit. She lets out a muffled cry as she comes everywhere.

I let myself go at the same time and spill down her throat.

"*Fuck, Ginger,*" I growl, holding her head in place by her hair as I unleash, my cock pulsing in her throat as she gags. Her legs shake and her thighs are covered in her own arousal. She practically drips down my forearm. I fucking love it.

When I'm sure she has in fact taken every drop from me, I slide my cock from her mouth and bring my soaked fingers to her lips. Swiping them over her soft mouth, I bend down to capture her lips in mine, tasting us both. She's a mess as she rolls back to the center of the bed to let me in; her hair tousled, her cheeks flushed. What a fucking way to start the day.

"You're going to be late for work," she says, nuzzling into the crook of my arm.

I lie still and look up to the ceiling for a beat, catching my breath because it's been a long goddamn time since I've had that kind of activity first thing in the morning.

"Actually, I took today off."

She leans up on her side so that all her chocolate masses of hair fall over one eye. "Since when?"

"Since this morning when I emailed Bev and told her I'm

taking a personal day. We're going on a date, a real one, before I have to pick Mabes up from my mom's." I stroke her arm. "Oh, and we're having dinner at the big house. Now, go make us some coffee in your crazy-ass coffeemaker while I shower. It's the last finger you'll lift today."

I plant a peck on her forehead and get up, but I can't stay away for long and instantly pounce back onto the bed as she yelps, hovering over her. I bend down to kiss her, and the overwhelming urge I feel for her surges back as my tongue moves with hers, as though I've been kissing her my whole life.

Our mouths connect once more before I stand, satisfied for at least the next twenty minutes.

"Are you trying really hard to make me fall for you or something, Mr. Ashby?" she asks as I pull a fresh pair of boxers from my drawer. I move in the direction of my bathroom, still naked.

"Nah, I would never do something like that, Vixen," I call as I head down the hall, grinning the whole way. Because, right now, I'm just riding this high. And fuck, maybe getting her to fall for me is exactly what I'm trying to do.

CHAPTER THIRTY-FIVE
Ginger

Well, in the spirit of keeping things platonic so we don't ruin our friendship, on a scale of one to ten, with one being a responsible adult and ten being a total fucking slut for Cole Ashby, I'm sitting at about a one hundred and one.

On the other hand, I've had four (or maybe five?) of the best orgasms I've ever had in my life in the last twelve hours. Which means I'm giving myself a little leeway as I head down to make some coffee in one of Cole's black T-shirts and my bare feet.

"Alexa, play I-got-railed-into-next-week-by-a-hot-sheriff-last-night," I call out, happier than I've been in a long time. Of course, Alexa doesn't know that playlist, so I settle for the local country station.

Ten minutes later, the coffee is brewing, and I'm singing along to the radio while slicing fruit. I look up when I hear Cole pad down the hall, still wet from the shower. He has a towel wrapped around his waist, and it hangs low on his narrow hips. His wide shoulders flex as he moves, and those arms . . . those arms are enough to make me wet all on their own. He's freshly shaven, and there are still tiny droplets of water clinging to his smooth chest. He's easily the most attractive man I'll ever sleep with.

"You're staring," Cole says, his biceps flexing as he runs a hand through his thick hair. He moves past me, smelling like the very things sin and dreams are made of, and grabs a mug from the cupboard. "What are you thinking about?"

He pours himself a steaming mug of coffee.

I smile up at him. "I'm wishing this was our date. You, me, and a towel. Or no towel would be even better."

He takes a sip, then sets the mug down, moving toward me. When he reaches me, he wraps his big hands around my waist and hikes me up onto the counter. I yelp when my panty-clad bottom hits the marble.

"You're all clean and I'm not," I say in a mock whine as he tips my head back, licking a train up the side of my neck.

"Best friends don't care about that shit, Ginger," he murmurs into the space below my ear.

I laugh as he continues, "And now I can't stop thinking about just how dirty you are and I'm trying to figure out why the fuck that makes me want you more." He pulls my earlobe into his mouth and bites down. "Just thinking about filling you up with my cum again and again . . ."

I suck in a breath and grind against his body. A loud knock at the front door makes us both jump. My heart drops. On the other side of the glass staring right at us, arms folded over her chest and a smile that says I'm totally busted, is none other than my mother.

"Fuck fuck fuck," I say, sliding off the counter and holding a finger up, hoping by some miracle she didn't actually see what we were doing just now.

"The sun reflects off the glass. That's a thing, right?" I ask Cole as I make a beeline across the living room.

"Uh . . . yeah," Cole says, a smile playing on his lips.

My mother doesn't wait for me to open the door, and instead just makes her way in like she owns the place.

"Hello, bella," she singsongs. "At least I know now why you don't answer your phone. Pffft, working, my *ass.*"

She moves across the kitchen to pour herself a coffee.

"Goddammit, Mother. Can you give us one second?" I huff, heading to my room to find some pants.

"Help yourself," I hear Cole say in an easy tone.

Once I reach my room, I yank my pants on and smooth my hair before running breathlessly back to the kitchen. Cole stands in the middle of the room, still in his towel, and sips his coffee as my mother sips hers.

"So your father was going to come with me, but at the last minute he got called into a phone meeting. Luckily for you . . ." she says, "because this is not what I expected to see when I came to visit you and that little petunia this morning."

"Shit. I forgot you were coming to do the flowers with us." I turn to Cole. "We talked last week, I didn't know Mabel was sleeping at Jo's then, I didn't know . . . anything."

"Apparently not," my mother says, looking at Cole a little too appreciatively. Although I can't say I blame her.

He holds a plate out to her with a smirk. "Fruit, Camilla? We were just about to eat."

She takes it from him, popping a strawberry into her mouth smugly. "I bet you were."

"Mother," I say, tucking my face in my hands in horror.

Cole laughs before turning to go. "You two catch up, I'm clearly not dressed for company."

When he's safely out of earshot, my mother looks at me, folds her arms into her chest, and raises her eyebrows. "So, what is this I'm walking into?"

"Nothing. We're just . . . friends," I stammer out.

"Oh no you don't. This is Cole. Who, unless you've forgotten, you've been talking about since you were sixteen, and, baby, there is nothing friendly here. My eyes don't deceive me. You were practically, as you kids say, dry-humping when I knocked on the door."

She grins as I recoil in embarrassment. "Mother!" I whisper-shriek.

"One more second and you would've needed his towel, no?"

"Oh my God," I mutter.

"I'm just playing with you, darling. I'm thrilled. Cole is a lovely man. So. It's settled."

"What's settled?" Cole asks, coming down the hall looking like a *GQ* model in perfectly fitted black shorts and a gray T-shirt that hugs him everywhere I want to.

"You will come for dinner this week. Bring little Mabel too. The more the merrier!" My mom grins before continuing, "And since we clearly have to reschedule our gardening for a day when the proposed student is actually here, and there's no teacher-parent interview happening."

I look at Cole pleadingly, desperate for him to make up an excuse as to why we can't attend dinner, but he doesn't. Instead, he gives my mother an award-winning smile and says, "We'd love to."

I give him a haughty look behind my mother's back.

Traitor. Best friends my ass.

CHAPTER THIRTY-SIX
Cole

I stare at the still-annoyed little vixen beside me. It's only a matter of time before she breaks; this is going to be the best date she's ever had. Starting with my face between her legs and her coming on my tongue, propped up on my bathroom counter when she stepped out of the shower this morning.

Now, we're in the tack room of our small barn at Silver Pines.

"I haven't ridden in years," Ginger says as I pop a cowboy hat onto her head, swiping some curls off her cheek as I do. It's quiet at the ranch today; my mama took Mabel to the party store in Lexington to shop for CeCe's wedding centerpieces, so the big house was empty when we arrived. The universe is doing me a solid because the weather is perfect for a ride, warm but not insanely humid.

"Then I'm doing you a service," I tell her as I tighten the stampede strings under her chin. I glance down at her. She's wearing cutoff shorts, a loose, flowy tank, and her trademark ivory cowboy boots. She looks delicious.

I'm just about to push her up against the wall when Wade's

right-hand man, Haden Westbrook, comes into the barn. He's a good guy, a lot like me when I was younger, and definitely takes advantage of the whole cowboy thing with the women. He came from the proverbial wrong side of the tracks when he was just eighteen, but he's been loyal to Wade and our ranch for the last several years.

"Shit. Sorry, y'all. I didn't know anyone was here. You just missed Ivy and Wade. They were heading into town for a doctor's appointment." He hangs a picking shovel up on its hook then looks back at us. "I'll be going for a beer later with Dusty if you want to join?"

I shake his hand. "Not this time. Got plans tonight here for dinner, and we're just about to take a ride. Rain check?"

He looks at Ginger than back at me with a sort of all-knowing grin. "Sure, man. It's a nice day for a ride. A little wet near the east side of the river, so watch their footing, but enjoy."

"Thanks, bud," I tell him.

"Have fun, kids," he says with a laugh, like he isn't four years my junior, before disappearing into one of the equipment closets.

"I'm gonna go ass over tea kettle, aren't I?" Ginger says, a little worried.

I lean down to kiss her cheek. "Nah, I've got you, baby, let's go."

I bring her out into the open field at the end of the barn loop where I have two of our tamest horses ready.

"This is Sunflower," I tell her, gesturing to the chestnut-brown horse she'll be riding. "Do you remember how to get up?"

"As much as you do," she replies coyly.

She looks at me defiantly and pulls the little step stool I have leaning against the post over to her horse. I watch as she uses her pointer finger to hold up the rein, loop it down, and press against Sunflower's mane before she pops her foot in the stirrup and swings her leg over, saddling her horse like she does it every day. I'm starting to wonder if there's anything this woman can't do.

"Well, alright, clearly you don't need my help then," I tell her as I mount Smoke, my favorite horse to ride, just as effortlessly. If there's one thing I can do, it's ride a horse. Might as well have been born on one.

"Alright, ma'am," I say with an exaggerated drawl, as though I'm from a fifties Western. "Welcome to Silver Pines. We hope you enjoy your tour. Save all your questions until the end, please, and watch for bandits on your trail. I reckon it's a hot one today."

She laughs as I tip my hat and trot by her to lead. "See if you can keep up. There'll be lunch and refreshments at the end of the tour."

She laughs. "And what tour is that?"

I glance back at her over my shoulder.

"All my favorite places, Vixen. Thought it might be nice to share them with someone," I say, feeling freer than I've ever felt with this adorable cowgirl behind me in the greatest place on earth.

CHAPTER THIRTY-SEVEN
Ginger

The mulch riding trail through the Ashbys' woods is one I haven't ridden since the summer CeCe left for college and she, Liv, and I camped out here in a tent with a few bottles of wine. We hid it in thermoses so her parents wouldn't know. Seeing it through Cole's eyes now shines a whole new light on the area. As we ride through the path of silver pine trees his family's ranch is named after, he takes his time showing me everything that matters to him: the place where he fell off his bike and broke his arm during a race with Wade, the remnants of a teepee fort he made with his dad that still stands at least partially today, the wild raspberry and blueberry bushes CeCe and I used to help Jo pick from every July to make her famous jam.

The thick columns of pines stretch for a good hundred feet to my right and, through them, I can see the spring river that runs along the entire back of the Ashby property. It's buggy and warm, but the canopy protects us, and the sun only filters through. The path stretches on ahead and, at the end of it, we'll reach a clearing and the river where we all used to swim when we were kids. A fishing cabin sits on the bank, where Cole's dad, Wyatt, used to bring the boys, and a little waterfall cascades over a set of boulders just behind it.

As we ride, we pass a smattering of maple and oak trees, the ground below sprinkled with wildflowers and honeysuckle. I should be taking in the beautiful nature around us; the bees fluttering, the birds singing, and the tree frogs croaking. But instead, all I can watch is Cole ahead of me. I know he's ridden his whole life; until he became sheriff, he still helped out on the ranch once a week. But seeing him on Smoke is something else altogether. His body moves with ease on his chocolate-brown quarter horse. His white T-shirt and worn-in blue jeans mold to his body perfectly as his strong arms work the reins. His brown leather cowboy boots and tattered hat, which I know both used to be Wyatt's, complete the look.

I watch from under the brim of my hat as he pats Smoke and bends down to mutter something into his mane like they're the best of friends. I feel myself wishing we could pull off into a bush somewhere just to tide me over until we can make it to a bed. There is nothing Cole does that isn't attractive, but, damn, cowboy Cole might sit at the top of my list.

"This is the tree my friends and I used to sneak beer to when my parents had friends over." Cole laughs as he points to a weathered old birch with a large, low, extending branch that could easily double as a seat. "We'd sit and talk about life, the girls we both wanted, how annoying you and CeCe were."

The closer we get to the clearing, the closer the water gets to the left of us. By the end of the path, the river will only be ten feet from the trail.

"You and your friends were always up to no good," I say with a grin. "I remember one night I slept over, and Wade had to bring you out a change of clothes and new shoes so your mama wouldn't know you had been drinking and trying to swing into the river from that tree right over there."

I point to a big crimson king maple that still has part of an old rope hanging from it.

Cole chuckles ahead of me. "You and CeCe came out to take photos of us. We were drenched. You were gonna use them to bribe us. 'Incriminating evidence for future use,' you called it."

"Hey, I knew your dad would kick your ass if he found out. You were only eighteen, and he wouldn't have taken kindly to you stealing his bourbon. CeCe and I didn't have to ask twice for a ride that whole summer," I say, laughing at the memories.

"You were a little shit disturber even then," Cole comments as he reaches the end of the clearing.

"Had to shoot my shot, you can't blame me for that."

He slows as we enter the clearing, and I ride up beside him. The beauty of the Ashbys' land still takes me by surprise. The space is vast and flat, the grass is long, not really maintained here, and littered with wildflowers.

"Maybe you had to shoot your shot, but I have a secret."

He leans in slightly. When his amber eyes find mine and he smiles big enough for his dimples to appear, my breath hitches. "I would've done it anyway, Vixen. Never could say no to you, even then."

I smile back before he takes off and shouts, "Come on, cowgirl, see if you can keep up!"

I watch him go, moving at increased speed through the flowers.

"Alright, girl, I know we just met and all, but don't fail me now," I say to Sunflower as I tighten my legs against her gently, and she starts to move. Cole isn't going too fast, so I catch up to him in no time, and we reach the grass near the maintenance tree. The waterfall comes into view, and so does a Silver Pines truck.

"Is there someone here?" I ask as I meet him.

"Yeah, us," he says, moving into the shorter grass with Smoke.

The maples are plentiful here along the water's edge. This is the place that the river ends, and where the waterfall rushes into it is almost like a circular pool. It's my favorite spot on the property. When we reach the fishing cabin in front of the waterfall, Cole dismounts and ties his horse to the post, before making his way over to me to help me down. He kisses me when I land on my feet, pulling my hat back for access.

"Fuck, been waiting to do that the whole ride," he says.

"Why the truck, Cole?" I ask with my eyes narrowed. "What are you up to? Trying to butter me up after you sold me out with my mama?"

"Yep. Is it working?" he asks, tying Sunflower up beside Smoke.

"Depends on what's in the truck," I tell him, folding my arms under my breasts. He grins and pulls me by the hand behind the truck. It's there that the edge of the water comes into view, and I see it: a big blanket stretched out under a large round maple, a Yeti cooler holding it down in the breeze. "It's not what's in the truck, it's what I used the truck to bring."

"Oh, yeah?" I ask, intrigued.

"Yeah," he says, wrapping his strong arms around me, "your favorite little sandwiches from the Sage N Salt, and some of their cookies and fruit. The San Pellegrino you like . . ."

I can't help it. That warm, tightening feeling takes over my chest, and I reach up on my tiptoes to kiss him. I kiss him like it may be the last chance I ever get, because the amount of effort this man has put into today might be the nicest thing *any* man has ever done for me. He kisses me back with matched passion, his tongue searching my mouth as heat coils between my thighs. We move so effortlessly together, there's no trying with Cole, we just *are*.

"Easy, Vixen," he says gruffly, pulling his lips from mine, "don't get too eager now, it's the lunch portion of the tour."

He plants a kiss onto my forehead and heads off toward the blanket, leaving me dumbfounded.

"I'm starting to forgive you for agreeing to dinner!" I call out as I start to follow him.

"Yeah, you are, especially when you realize I brought a batch of Spicer's world-famous fudge too." I smile behind him. Cowboy Cole and chocolate? I don't say it, but I sure think it: If I had to have a first date with anyone, I wouldn't want it to be with anyone other than Cole Ashby.

CHAPTER THIRTY-EIGHT
Cole

"You think of all this on the fly?" she asks with genuine curiosity as we reach the blanket at the edge of the water.

"Nah, I can't take that much credit. Been planning it since the day you told me you've never been on a date," I tell her as I take off my hat and toe off my boots. She does the same, her curly hair sticking slightly to her sweat-slicked back.

Her mouth pops open in surprise, and I internally high five myself. Mission "give Ginger the best date of her life" is going exactly according to plan.

The canopy of trees shades us, and the air buzzes with the water and insects, as we eat our lunch. There's not a soul in sight as the maintenance crew isn't here today, and I know my mother and Mabel will be out for hours. I look over at Ginger's beautiful face, free of makeup and slightly flushed from the sun. The waterfall behind her frames her curls, and I'm not sure I've ever seen her look so pretty.

"I'll give you this. Your family's land sure is something,"

she says as she looks out to the rushing water, and then back to me with a light in her eyes. It turns to mischief in one second flat when she meets my gaze. "If you're into that sort of thing, I guess."

She shrugs as she pops her last strawberry into her mouth. She sets her empty food box down, whipped cream glistening on her upper lip, and I launch myself at her to pin her to the blanket below. There's no stopping me from licking it right off.

"Listen here, you sassy little fucking vixen," I growl into her ear. "I know you love this waterfall, and I know you aren't really mad at me."

I lick her upper lip. Fucking delicious. She giggles and mock tries to push me away.

"Stop torturing me and enjoy it. It's one dinner. And you can trust me to be on my best behavior for your father."

I pinch her pert ass as she sighs.

"It's not you I'm worried about, Cole." She looks up into my eyes and, from this angle, at my mercy below me, I feel desire stir within me. *Again.*

"I'm worried about *me.* You've met my father, what? Ten times over the years? In short little bursts? He's a human lie detector"—she sighs—"and after what my mother walked in on this morning, with you looking all hot and gorgeous in your towel, she thinks we're a bona fide couple. You'll charm them at dinner, and she'll tell everyone I'm the sheriff's girlfriend. But she won't stop there. She'll be planning for our babies sooner rather than later."

"Wife," I correct her. She rolls her eyes at me, but I see it, everything I need to know in her gaze.

"My father will be so happy with you as another political ally in his pocket," she rambles on, but I doubt that since I'm pretty sure he didn't vote for me.

"Cole, having a sheriff in his corner is, for lack of a better saying, my father's fucking dream come true. If this all blows up in our face and he somehow finds out the truth, I'll never hear the end of—"

I dip my head down to steal her lips within mine. I've heard enough. She's worrying for nothing. And if she isn't careful about mentioning babies again, *our* babies, I might just try to put one in her.

"You think I look hot in a towel?" I ask as I release her lips. She laughs finally.

"There's my girl," I praise.

"You would hear *that* out of everything I just said," she says.

"Because you're worried for nothing. We've got this," I say. Hovering over her is starting to get the better of me. I slide my hand down over her flimsy linen shorts.

"Reality check? We've always been good at being friends, and we both know whatever is going on with us, this marriage isn't serious or . . . real," she says.

A week ago, maybe two, I would've been able to withstand those words, but today they hit me right in the gut, because the way I'm looking at Ginger right now makes everything between us feel *very* real and not the least bit platonic or friend-like. I swallow down the sucker punch she just delivered me in typical Ginger fashion and keep my thoughts to myself. Instead, I dip my head down and line her soft shoulders with kisses while taking her hand and placing it on my chest. My heart beats faster just having her beneath me.

"Feel this?" I ask her. She nods so I kiss her again. "It's all for you, Vixen."

I slide my hand down over the flat of her stomach, circling the rim of her shorts when I reach them, and dipping my hand below the band. The lace of her panties is the only barrier between me and what I want, but I take my time, just to torment her. I purposely skim over the heat I feel already waiting for me, trailing my thumb down her inner thigh to position myself above her. My cock is already hard and pressing into her leg through my jeans. When she feels it, her eyes meet mine.

"Yeah, that's all for you too," I mutter.

She moans, and her eyes flutter closed. I trace her inner thigh, and when I get to the apex, start over on the other leg. She whines in frustration, and I chuckle against her skin.

"I definitely like you a little frustrated," I whisper as she tries to angle her hips up to force my fingers against her needy clit. She lets out a long breath as I search for the evidence of her need. I skim my finger over the lace of her thong and find her soaked and desperate, just how I like her.

"Please, Cole," she begs, "touch me."

I lick her bottom lip and suck it into my mouth, pressing the pad of my middle finger into her clit through the lace of her panties, and she cries softly into my mouth, "Please . . ."

"Fuck, I love watching this pretty mouth beg," I tell her.

"Why is . . ." she starts as I skim her clit again. "Why is it such a turn-on when you talk to me like that?"

"Like what?" I ask as I pinch her swollen bundle of nerves. The lace is so thin I can almost feel her skin through them. My mouth waters at the thought of her against my lips.

"The swearing. The dirty words. I . . . *fuck*, I don't understand why I like it so much." She groans as I pull her earlobe into my mouth.

"Hmmm . . . seems we all want answers to questions, Ginger." I lick the expanse of her sweet skin at her collarbone. "Like, for instance, why you keep insisting that we're *just* friends . . ."

"We are friends, Cole."

I chuckle at her attempt to convince herself.

"Right . . . we are . . . so that must be why I catch you looking at me when you think I don't notice?" I'll play her game. She doesn't miss a beat.

"Must be . . ."

"Mmmhmm . . ." I mutter into her neck. "Except, you know what you're doing almost every time I catch you?" I add some pressure to where she meets my hand, and she squeezes her thighs.

"What?" she whimpers.

"Licking your lips, Vixen."

Ginger's eyes flutter open. "Cocky . . ." is all she mutters, but she doesn't deny the truth.

"Must also be why this soaking pussy is aching for my fingers right now?"

I continue teasing her, and she writhes under my touch, the sound of her desire echoing against the rushing water beside us. I finally tug her panties aside and push into her; sweet and wet. I bite back a groan as I stroke her G-spot.

"Must be . . ." is all she whispers as I smile into her lips. I pull away to look down at her; sweat glistens on her chest in the Kentucky heat, and the sun beats down in dappled shadows through the trees. I pull her tank top off over her head, and she lies under me, her eyes hooded, hair splayed around her. I watch the little pulse hammering in her throat and the flush of her cheeks increases. As my fingers continue to work in and out of her, I know that, no matter what happens, I will remember her just like this for the rest of my life.

I continue to tease her, never giving her what she fully needs. Toying with her is quickly becoming my new favorite hobby.

"Please, Cole . . ." Her begging words are a shot straight to my hard and aching cock.

"Mmmhmm . . ." I say as my tongue lazily flicks her hardened nipple. "I don't know. The way you're breathing right now . . . doesn't seem on the fake side of things to me."

I pinch her clit, and her back arches.

"It's just because it's . . . so hot out here," she retorts.

I grin into her neck and take a bite. She moans even louder, and I take that as an invitation to lose my jeans with a couple of swift movements. I pull my shirt over the back of my head before tugging her shorts and panties from her body, tossing them aside. She doesn't even flinch at where we are. The sense that she trusts me implicitly to keep her safe isn't lost on me. In fact, it fuels me.

Our hot, naked bodies press together, and I still to revel in the feeling for a few moments while I kiss her. This ache, this need to be inside her confirms she's the drug I'm quickly becoming addicted to. I never want to stop kissing her as sweat covers us both from the midday heat. I slide my cock through her slit and coat myself in her.

"Fuck, the feeling of being covered in you is so goddamn good. You're drenched, Ginger."

"I-it's the heat . . . it turns me on." She moans.

I smirk. It takes everything in me, everything I have, to back away and stand up.

"Got it. It's just the weather you're worked up about? Seems to me like maybe you just need to cool down then," I say as I leave her on the blanket.

She's a literal hot mess right now, and I fucking love it. I saunter without a care in the world naked to the water's edge and make my way in; it's warm after the heat wave of the last two weeks, and I can see all the way to the bottom of the crystal-clear spring. I push off toward the waterfall until I'm waist deep and close enough to feel the spray, before turning and calling back to her.

"Coming in? It will help you to cool down!" I grin, dunking my head under and pushing the water off my face. A look of sheer Ginger determination takes over her expression as she narrows her eyes at me, flicking her hair off her shoulders and stalking toward the spring.

"You're right, Cole, that's just what I need. A nice swim," she calls out.

I take in the show before me as Ginger, in all her incredible naked glory, moves toward the water, a vision of complete confidence and pure sex.

Her nipples are hard, and ready to be pulled into my mouth, and her dark curls bounce off of her back as she walks. That small waist, those full hips, that golden skin. Her perfect tits that bounce as she heads toward me. She's a modern-day Aphrodite. Ginger disappears into the water in a perfectly executed little dive before popping up right in front of me seconds later. The moment her goose-pebbled skin touches mine, it's game over.

She wraps her legs around me, weightless. The heat of her pussy is still apparent against my cock, and I can feel her hot arousal even under the water. Her arms rest around my shoulders, relaxed, and she angles her face with mine.

"So much better," she says, smiling sweetly. "I'm not hot at all anymore." Her pussy hugs my cock, sliding up and down just to torture me. "Perfectly cool now, actually. How are you?"

She licks my bottom lip, and all my thoughts leave my head.

"*Fuck*," I growl as my mouth crashes down to meet hers, and my hands find every possible stretch of her wet, silky skin. Her fingers lace through my hair, and she pulls tight in invitation. I don't waste a second. Her hot pussy is right there and mine for the taking as I drive into her under the water without hesitation. We moan in unison as she clamps down around me.

There's no friction, she's way too wet for that, but somehow the cool water makes her even tighter, and her throaty sounds echo off the falls as I fill her. I take her hard and fast.

"You want to know why I can't keep control around you, Ginger?" I say as we move together.

Her forehead tips to my chin as she slips into the abyss with me. I'm right there with her because there's no explaining this. This feeling of us *together*.

"It's not because we're *just* friends. It's because you were made for me. You know every single button to press. Every single thing you do drives me fucking crazy." I change my tone to a warning. "I could do this all fucking day." I smirk, slowing my pace, filling her to the hilt and holding myself deep inside her.

"Cole . . ." She moans, wanting me to move.

"You can come when you admit it, baby. Admit we're not just friends. Admit this is something so much more."

Her mouth opens, forming a perfect O, but no sound leaves her lips as her eyes close, lost with me as I pull out and then fuck back into her. Deep and fast, like it's possible to make her completely and only mine this way. I let my lips, fingers, and tongue tease her nipples as her perfect tits trade moving between my face and the swell of the water around us.

"Cole . . . I need to," she whimpers almost incoherently as her walls tighten. She tugs my hair just tight enough to make my cock pulse inside her. I slow and still myself. She sure as fuck isn't getting what she wants until I do. Until she admits it.

"What do you need, Vixen? You need me to be a good *friend* and let you come?" I ask.

"Yes," she cries. "Please . . ."

"Tell me you're lying to yourself, tell me how badly you want me." I push on.

"I do . . . I do . . . so badly. All the fucking time, it's so frustrating. *Please*, Cole," she chants.

"Such a good girl." I kiss her and move back to the pace that has her coming apart. She's ready within seconds.

"Honesty feels good doesn't it?" I ask, losing my breath as her legs tighten their hold.

"Yes."

"Look at this tight little cunt milking my cock. Take every fucking drop from me, fucking strangle me," I command.

"Don't stop, Cole . . . please." She pants as her head tips forward and her eyes flutter closed. She's so close.

I grip the side of her face as I fuck her; she opens her eyes, bringing her gaze back to me.

"Eyes on me. I want to be the only thing you see while you fall apart."

Her normally dark eyes are so light, full of lust and fire. Water hovers on her long lashes, and, for a split second, it's like the world stops spinning and there's nothing but us and our unspoken connection. My chest cracks wide open and heats as I slow my pace. Every nerve ending in me is buzzing as our movements turn languid. Ethereal.

"You're *always* the only thing I see, Cole," she moans before her lips are on mine and, motherfucker, I'm coming. Coming harder than I've ever come before. I let go and spill into her as her sweet pussy does just what I ordered, pulling every drop from me as she cries my name.

I give it all to her willingly, kissing her as I do.

The moment washes over me and cleanses me of anyone else I've ever thought about or touched. I know I'll never be the same. From this second forward, there's no one but her. I'll never forget the first time in my entire life that I *made love* to Ginger Danforth Ashby under a waterfall.

CHAPTER THIRTY-NINE
Ginger

"You're getting slow in your old age, are you?" Papa Dean says to me as I try to keep up with the seventy-nine-year-old man kicking my ass in a game of video tennis.

Jo grins over at us as she and Mabel mix salads, chatting away in the kitchen, and Wade prepares the meat ready to grill. Cole and I came to pick up Mabel after our date, but you can't enter this house without Jo stuffing a meal into you. It just so happened that Nash and CeCe were here to talk about this year's festival to help raise money for the underprivileged hockey teams in the surrounding area. Last year, they hosted a very successful Sunset Festival, which raised thousands of dollars and secured the Laurel Creek Lightning's season for another two years. This year they want to go bigger and better, and plans are well under way to do so. This year it will be called Harvest Fest.

"She didn't pop a Viagra and a Red Bull before dinner." Nash snorts from behind us on the couch as "*You beat the high score*" sounds from the TV, and Dean pumps his weathered fist.

"Still got it." He winks at me before tossing Cole the controller. He points around the room. "And hey. You don't need Viagra if you do it right, fellas. Let that be a lesson to you all."

All three men start guffawing at him but, judging by the way he just rolled over me in this game, I wouldn't doubt the old fella for a second.

"If I'm still single when I'm forty, Papa Dean, we're getting married," I say to him.

"Nah, honey, you're too good for me," he calls as he heads into the kitchen to pour himself a bourbon. Nash follows.

"He's kicking!" Ivy says animatedly from her seat, motioning at Wade to come and feel her bump. I turn and take a seat on the couch beside CeCe and watch them. It's truly amazing to see Wade smile so much.

"*She* is kicking," Wade corrects as he crouches beside her to rest a hand on her stomach.

"We'll see." Ivy winks at him.

They chatter for a few minutes about the baby before Wade heads out to start the grill.

"You're very tanned," CeCe says from beside me.

"I've been out in the garden with Mabel a lot," I remind her. "My skin is always sort of a little golden even in the dead of winter."

"Ugh. I've always been jealous of that. Seriously, though, you look relaxed and happy," CeCe says, gripping her chin as though she's a detective and looking to the sky. "I wonder if that has anything to do with my brother. You know, the one you've always had a crush on and are now *living* with."

I nudge her shoulder with mine.

"This meat's ready for Sarge," Nash tells us as he picks up the platter of steaks he was just seasoning.

We all stand. It's an unwritten Ashby rule. The griller never grills alone.

Nash's declaration couldn't have come at a better time, saving me from discussing my and Cole's situation with CeCe. Good thing too, because, at this point, I have no idea what to tell her. That I'm having incredible sex with the man that I've secretly been friends with for years, the only man on earth who truly has my back, and I'm terrified that what we're doing will change everything? But that I'm in too deep to stop? And, oh yeah, that we're married? *Thank the universe for meat needing a grill.*

We make our way into the yard. The Ashbys' patio is wide and seats at least twenty. It's always been a hive of activity, and Wyatt and Jo used to regularly host dinners here when we were younger.

It still somehow doesn't feel complete without Wyatt nattering at Jo, or going back and forth with the boys. Even his Waylon Jennings or Willie Nelson not playing on a night like this serves as a giant reminder that he's gone. When I look over at Cole, I see him glancing around the yard and sense that he feels the loss of his dad in this moment too. I make my way over to sit down beside him and squeeze his knee under the table. He looks at me, and the connection of his eyes with mine drowns out the chatter around us.

"So y'all are going to help with the festival this year," CeCe tells us, pulling me from my thoughts.

"I just assumed we don't get a choice?" Cole replies with a grin.

"Where I come from, that was always called being *voluntold*," Dean says as he sips his drink in the evening sun. I grin at him. He's such a cool old man in his golf shirt, sunglasses, and a fedora-style hat. I wish my own dad was as laid-back as he is.

Nash chuckles. "Welcome to my life, old fella."

CeCe backhands him.

"Ow . . . You didn't wait for me to add how much I love it," Nash backpedals, kissing CeCe down her bare arm.

"You're planning a festival *and* a wedding at the same time?" Ivy asks. "I don't know how you do it."

Nash reaches behind his back to go into his bag and drops a binder onto the table. It's thick and chock-full of all sorts of papers.

"This is for the festival," he deadpans. "The wedding version is more than double this size."

"Jesus, CeCe Rae," Cole scoffs.

CeCe shrugs. "I'm nothing if not organized. The wedding will be here and gone soon enough. And then I'll have lots of time to focus on the festival."

"Well, I'll be either very pregnant or a new mom, so you'll need to have some grace with me," Ivy says. "If it's option A, I'm open to help any way that keeps me off my swollen feet."

CeCe nods. "You can work the ticket counter if you're still pregnant." She flashes Ivy a grin. "And if you're a new mama by then and feel up to it, you can just show up and parade my new niece or nephew around."

CeCe cups her chin in her hands before turning to me. "We've got a few big events lined up already, but we want to book one more thing that will bring a draw in. Whatever it ends up being, I'll have you and Liv help with it, and you can both make sure the hockey players know where their dressing rooms are this year again when they play the townies. We have some new faces this time around. Chris got permission to play."

She talks at a hundred miles per hour as she takes notes for her binder. This woman is a machine.

Nash lets out a laugh. "Last year, Ginger just used that to pick her next victim. Pretty sure I heard you went out afterward with Rod Bordeaux."

Rod did, in fact, take me out. He also took me home and asked me to call him "The Moose" during sex because that was his hockey nickname. It was weird. I did not get off that night.

"Yep . . . you don't need to remind me," I say, feeling Cole's eyes burn into me. I lean back in my chair and sneak a glance at him. He's doing that thing he does when he's jealous; jaw set and flexing like he's trying real hard not to say something he might regret.

"Back in my day, if we wanted to make money, we hosted a car wash or a wet T-shirt contest." Jo winks at me and CeCe from across the table. "But I guess that's not allowed in this day and age."

I smile at her.

"Sex sells," I say, sipping my bourbon. I look beyond Jo to check Mabel is still out in the yard playing with Harley. After spending every day with her for the last few weeks, it almost feels like second nature to check on her now.

"This isn't the eighties anymore. But you have a good idea there, Mama . . ." CeCe says, tapping her pen in front of her. Cole grunts as he stands and makes his way to the outdoor counter for more bourbon. My eyes flit over to him. So do everyone else's.

"It's a family event," he barks defensively as he pops the plug out of the glass canteen.

CeCe looks at him as if to say, *Are you fucking kidding me?* He pours himself a hefty shot and makes his way back to his seat as CeCe chews her bottom lip.

It's her thinking face. I grin.

"Obviously . . . We *could* do something fun, though. What about a kissing booth?" She turns to me, her eyes wide. "You and Liv would bring in a fortune!"

I laugh and shake my head, about to protest. But before I have the chance to say anything, Cole's chair scrapes against the concrete as he slides closer to the table. I flinch.

"Absolutely fucking not," he says.

"Fucking Appollo Creed over there. Settle down, sheriff," Nash says with a chuckle.

"Well . . ." Cole scrambles, "it's not appropriate. It's a family event and . . . germs and shit."

He swallows a sip of his drink. I swallow down a smile.

Nash's laughter grows louder at Cole's outburst. "Germs? Really? That's what you're bringing to the table?"

CeCe swats at him and turns to Cole. "It *will* be a family event. I was thinking a kiss on the cheek, you perv."

Cole shakes his head. "I just don't think it's right. I'm trying to save the girls from kissing a bunch of horny old men."

He wipes the condensation off the side of his near-empty glass as he sets it on the table.

"Kissing booth . . . Christ," he mumbles, scrubbing his jaw as Mabel comes bounding up behind him.

"Dollar, Daddy." She pats him on the arm.

I grin at her. Then at Cole. She really is the best.

"Okay, Captain Valiant. I'll take that into consideration." CeCe looks between me and Cole, and I don't miss the pointedness of it; the way her mouth falls open as if, somewhere in that pretty head of hers, a lightbulb just went on.

Forty-five minutes later. "So, things are going well over there at the Ashby-Danforth house then?" CeCe asks sure as shit after dinner as the boys play ladder golf with Mabel. Jo has headed to her unfinished projects club with Glenda, and Papa Dean is snoozing in the den.

I look into CeCe's questioning eyes. I know this woman sometimes like I know myself. She nods her head toward Cole and waits patiently as though it's been killing her to hold this question in all through dinner. I turn and note how close the boys are to us, eyeing up Cole as he takes his shot. I don't know how it's possible, but he's even more gorgeous now than ever: casual and in full dad mode. He's wearing sage-colored shorts, a white T-shirt that clings to his strong torso, and his damned backward hat that does me in every single time. He's tanned after our day in the sun, and right now he's got his game face on. He takes his bottom lip between his straight white teeth and tosses the two golf balls attached with a piece of rope to the ladder. It lands on the 5 wrung, the highest point he can score. He high-fives Mabes, who jumps up and down, elated at the fact they're taking the lead against Wade and Nash. Cole grins down at her; he looks relaxed, and his jaw is scruffy after not shaving for a few days. He's fucking perfect, really, not too—

"Um . . . Hello!" CeCe says, waving her hand in front of my face. "You're completely zoned out staring at my brother. Stop making sexy eyes at him."

She crumples her pretty face in disgust. I look from her to Ivy.

"You totally are." Ivy backs her up.

I put my head in my hands. "I just . . ."

"Oh my God," CeCe says, gasping so no one will hear. "Something is *actually* going on between you two!"

I pull my head out of my grasp and eye her over my fingers. I can't lie to her anymore. She's my best friend. I'm sure Liv already knows, although she's been MIA lately with inventory and staff shortages at her boutique.

"Wow, Ginger Danforth takes her own advice," Ivy quips, already an integral part of our friend group after less than a year. I look over at her.

"What?" I ask.

"You know," she giggles. "Save a horse, ride a—"

"Cole is *not* a cowboy," I say to them both, remembering how he looked this afternoon riding through the woods.

"Save a horse, ride the sheriff?" Ivy grins.

"It's not like that. This isn't just a hookup . . ." I start.

"Wait, is this *serious*?" CeCe asks, her voice hitting a higher octave. I shrug and look at Cole with his full megawatt smile as he jokes with Nash about something. My core aches at the sight of those dimples every damn—

"You're doing it again." Ivy snickers.

"I have so many questions. I'm half so happy, half *so* grossed out." CeCe wrinkles her nose but immediately reaches over to squeeze my hand, and I breathe out a sigh of relief. "I love you both, and God, there's always been something strong between you."

CeCe looks out at Cole and watches him for a second.

"Be careful, though, Ginger." She continues in a warning tone, "I don't want to know the gritty details, and I have no idea how serious this is or what you're expecting out of it, but I don't want anything to hurt the close-knit friendship we all have if this goes south at the end of summer."

"Neither do I," I say honestly, "and we are being careful, too careful. We haven't even talked about how we feel."

She nods, and I hope that, if she finds out the whole truth someday, she'll be just as understanding as she is now.

"CeCe might not be able to handle the gossip about you and Cole, but I want it all; you better call me." Ivy smirks.

"Deal," I tell her.

CeCe lets out a laugh.

"I'm happy to talk, but details? Not a chance." She turns back to me. "Just take my advice, babe. Cole isn't the serious type. We all know that."

I know she means well, but the sentiment irks me. So I don't answer and turn my attention to Cole instead. I know him probably better than anyone, and I sure as hell know he's capable of a lot more than they think he is.

CHAPTER FORTY
Cole

FIFTY-EIGHT DAYS TO GO

NASH

You bringing a plus one to the wedding? We're finalizing the seating plan today and CeCe and I wondered if we should save a spot for your guest.

ME

Have you ever known me to bring a plus one to anything? and I'm coming with Ginger and Mabel. Obviously.

NASH

Right ok. Forgot how friendly you two are these days.

ME

No you didn't. Nosy prick.

SARGE

Why am I in this conversation?

NASH

Just want to make sure we're all on the same page.

ME

I'm in the wedding party. Which means I sit at your table, right?

NASH

No, you have your own table.

NASH

You and your friend. 👈

ME

You must have something better to do? Dress shoes to polish? Brides to calm down?

SARGE

I'm trying to remember the last time he went to Lexington since his "friend" moved in. 🤭

ME

@Sarge I expected better of you.

SARGE

Just stating the facts, no need to get hostile.

NASH

Seemed mighty hostile when we mentioned his friend in the festival's kissing booth too.

ME

I have a job to do.

ME

Fuck you both very much.

NASH

> I think Cole might need a hug. Do friends hug?

I put my phone down next to me and listen to Brent drone on, just as I have for the last thirty minutes, to every member of the town council about our new budget and how it's going to "get this office on track after Sims was let go" and how "everyone should be accountable and do things by the book." Fucking guy is one of those who loves to hear himself talk.

He eventually stops talking to field questions from our oldest council member, Arnold Dillard. At eighty-two, this man *needs* to retire. Brent kisses his ass every chance he gets. Come to think of it, Brent does a lot of ass-kissing but not a whole lot of actual work.

My phone buzzes again but this time, when I flip it over, it's a photo, mostly of Ginger's backside in a silky lilac dress. She captions the message: *Panties or no panties?*

I zoom in as I shift in my seat and try to appear professional. I could be looking at a spreadsheet, right?

My cock starts to swell at the image; the way her hand rests just above her full hip and the surprised expression she wears on her face. There she goes, looking like a modern-day pinup again.

ME

> Depends. What kind of panties are we talking?

Another photo comes in. This one is of her in the mirror. It's fucking indecent and decent all at the same time. I can see everything from the top of her upper thigh to her naked breasts, which she covers with her arms. Her white lace panties are on full display.

Fuck me.

ME

I'm trying to work.

VIXEN

And I'm trying to make you look forward to coming home.

ME

Mission fucking accomplished.

Home. The way she implies that home is a place we share hits me square in the chest.

"Do you agree, Sheriff Ashby?" Dillard asks.

I'm completely blindsided but attempt to hold it together. I lean back in my chair and say, "Depends on how you look at it."

"True," Dillard replies. "From the town's standpoint, a meeting to go over the new budget, and upping the council's involvement with even the smallest expenses, is helpful and suggests openness. It signals a new era and shows we have nothing to hide. From your office's standpoint, opening the expenses up to every last dollar is a lot of work and waiting for approval on your part."

I jump right in because absolutely fucking not. This was Brent's idea. He's trying to overexpose the department and the things we need to pay for that people will no doubt bitch about. It's one of his attempts to get the town to question me. Normally anything under a thousand dollars doesn't need approval, that way we aren't waiting on the council's okay for a new envelope or coffee creamer.

"From the office side, it's a logistical nightmare," I say. "Where do we draw the line if we're debating every last bill? Things like our electricity bill and toner for the photocopier? There are costs that can't be helped, but people don't always understand that. Everyone always thinks they can do a better job than the person in charge, but very few are actually up to the task."

I eye Brent as I say it. *Yep, I'm fucking talking to you, dipshit.*

I press on. "I say we leave the budget online for now. We can open up statements of our accounts for public viewing, but block all the pertinent account information. That means people can email in concerns, comments, and suggestions, and we are able to weed out who is serious versus those who are just talking to talk."

Brent looks away. *Yep. Still mean you, bud.*

My phone is face up on the table when it buzzes again. Dillard and another associate start talking about the increased electricity bills this year as I read the message on the screen.

CECE

> So listen. You know I love you but I kind of dragged everything out of Ginger when we had dinner at the big house. Cole, she is my best friend, and you better not hurt her. She puts on a strong defense but she's sensitive underneath it all.

My brows knot as I reread the message before responding. I'm not going to argue with my sister, but I think I know Ginger better than she does. *I* was the one there for her when CeCe left for seven years. *I* was there after her first day of teaching, and it was me who sat at the Horse and Barrel with her as she questioned whether or not she'd made the right career choice. Not CeCe.

CeCe's comment, mixed with the fact that these fuckers are still droning on about the electricity bill like there's anything we can do to change it, just serves to irritate me. You know it's going to be a long day when you're already pissed off at ten A.M.

ME

She's my friend too, and she's a lot stronger
than you think.

With that, I mute everyone's messages except any from my little vixen. She can send those panty shots all day long. I take another look at the one she sent earlier to get me through this meeting. It does a good job of lightening my mood. Well, that and the idea of pulling them off with my teeth later. But first I have to get through dinner at Congressman Danforth's house. My less-than-friendly father-in-law . . .

When we round onto Royal Oak Drive at six o'clock that evening, I can feel Ginger's nerves rolling off her in waves.

I look in my rearview mirror at Mabel happily coloring in her princess book and reach over to the console to wrap my pinky finger around Ginger's. She instantly seems to relax and takes a deep breath.

I think back to how I found her and Mabel in the garden earlier. They'd lost track of time so, when I got home, they were still outside, talking about why impatiens like the shade and petunias like the sun. I just stood at the door, watching them work together in perfect harmony, before either of them noticed me. Both of them had spun around when they realized I was there; they were up to their elbows in dirt weeding and pruning flowers in the late-day sun. The golden light had shone on Ginger's face, and her thick hair was pushed back off her sweaty forehead with a bandana. She'd smiled at me then, and the need to burn that image of her into my brain had overtaken me.

The moment didn't last long when she realized she only

had an hour to get showered and ready for dinner. But she's stunning now, dressed in a deep blue sundress that shows off her killer shoulders and upper back. Her hair is piled up on her head and looks as though one slip of a pin could cause it all to tumble down around her in waves. I squeeze her hand in mine as she looks up at the house where she always felt she had to be someone she wasn't while I pull into the massive driveway. Tonight is all about being orderly, prim, and proper. Everyone on their best behavior. It's no wonder Ginger moved out when she went to college, even though she could've easily lived at home. I make a silent promise to myself to always let Mabel be who she wants to be, and to be fiercely fucking proud of her whatever path she chooses. I would never want her to dread coming home the way Ginger does now.

"Are your mom and dad rich?" Mabel asks from the back, staring up at the house in awe.

Ginger laughs. "I suppose so, sweet girl."

I try to give Mabel some social cues fit for an eight-year-old.

"Mabes . . . we can say that in this car between the three of us, okay? But only here. When we get inside, it wouldn't be polite to ask that. Do you understand?"

Mabel nods. "So only if you're on the team you can talk about it?"

I look at Ginger, then back to Mabel curiously. "The team?"

Mabel smiles, the picture of innocence. "Our team. Me, you, and Ginger."

I turn to Ginger, who shrugs. "*The* team. Didn't you know?"

"Daddy and the girls!" Mabel puts both her hands up. I laugh and scrub my face with my hand. Ginger smiles up at me.

"Well, alright then, team. Let's do this," I say with a grin that doesn't leave my face the whole way up the driveway.

When we get to the porch, Ginger knocks on the front door, which baffles me. This is her parents' home. My mother would probably smack me if I felt the need to knock instead of just walking inside. I'm realizing for the first time how different our family dynamics really are.

The door swings open, and Camilla stands before us wearing the world's biggest smile and looking like she's ready for a state dinner. She's wearing an expensive-looking black-and-white designer suit, matching diamond earrings and necklace, and shiny red heels.

She hugs Ginger as she ushers us into their large foyer. "Come in, come in," she says enthusiastically.

Once we're all inside, Camilla crouches down to Mabel's level. "Hello, Mabel, I'm so happy you could come for dinner."

"I had to come." Mabel smiles shyly. "I have to go everywhere my dad goes."

"Of course you do. Why don't you follow me. We have some things for you to play with." Camilla gives Mabel a wide grin before turning to say hello to me, wrapping her arms around me like we're old friends.

"You both look so nice." She pats me on both my shoulders and nods in approval toward Ginger. "Your father will be so pleased."

I nod, not quite sure what to say, when out of nowhere Edward Danforth moves in beside her, pulling Ginger into a sort of awkward side hug and kissing the top of her head. Where Camilla is relaxed, he is stiff; he has a cold air and looks as though he's about to attend a business meeting.

"Darling," he says before extending his hand to me. "Sheriff Ashby. Nice to see you again."

"Cole, please," I say.

He nods. "Well, I should tell you, Cole, I didn't vote for you."

"Wouldn't expect you to, sir, seeing as I ran against your legislative director's husband." I return his firm handshake with one of my own as Ginger looks like she might die.

"You've done your homework," he says, sizing me up, "which shows the markings of a good officer of the law. The public seem to like you."

"Let's hope they got it right," I say humbly.

He looks me up and down like I'm the neighborhood villain instead of the county sheriff.

"Time will tell," he says curtly before he turns and heads down the hall.

Well, this should be fun.

CHAPTER FORTY-ONE
Ginger

I should've known Mabel and my nonna would become instant friends. My father has invited his mother, my always cheeky granny Dan, this evening too. She and my nonna are the best of frenemies; they're always competing for the best grandma award when I love them both equally and for totally different reasons. I stand behind the kitchen island and watch Granny Dan, my nonna, and Mabel play Uno in the next room. My father sits at the dining room table with Cole, talking about his policies to crack down on the vandalism of public buildings in the downtown core. I internally laugh at the fact that there are a total of two buildings that have graffiti on them, and the designs are actually quite beautiful.

"Do you think she likes the game?" my mother asks as we roll out fresh ravioli sheets.

"Yes, I do." I smile, before continuing, "You've really pulled out all of the stops tonight. Even though I told you ten times over not to make a big deal. This is just dinner."

She waves her perfectly manicured hand at me.

"It's not very often my daughter brings . . ." She looks out to the other room to make sure no one is listening, then whispers, "A boyfriend and his beautiful daughter home."

I instantly feel the pressure of what she is insinuating weigh down on me. The expectation to give my parents a perfectly orchestrated future family always creates an overwhelming sense of anxiety. Not because I don't want a family, but because the pressure is to give my parents, mostly my father, the kind of family he can brag about to voters. But, tonight, with Mabel and Cole here, it feels like I have a teammate in my corner, and that makes everything just a little less crushing.

Both my grandmothers return to the kitchen when their game of Uno is finished, and Mabel runs over to Cole with her coloring book. He helps get her situated at the dinner table while he continues to talk with my father. My granny Dan, always looking for trouble to stir, wanders by me and pats me on the shoulder.

"Quite the looker, CeCe's brother." She nods to Cole and winks as she grabs a cloth and begins to swipe leftover flour off the counter and into her hand. "I remember when your granddad was young like that. He was so handsome. I couldn't keep my hands to myself half of the time."

"Granny . . ." I start with a giggle.

"What does CeCe think about all of this?" she asks.

I shrug.

"This is a summer arrangement," I say loud enough for all the nosy women in my life to hear, but not loud enough to reach the next room. "You all act as though we're . . . we're . . ."

"Getting married?" My nonna finishes my sentence and laughs before taking to the stove to stir the beef mixture simmering there. She fishes a spoon out of the drawer and tastes it.

"More garlic, *mia cara*," she tells my mother.

"You're crazy," my mother quips over her shoulder. "It's perfect."

My nonna ignores her and Granny Dan passes her the garlic to add to the pot. Grannies unite.

Mabel walks into the kitchen and sniffs the air.

"It smells yummy in here," she says. "Can I help?"

"Sure. But wash your hands first," I tell her. "I'm done making the pasta, but we have to stuff it now with the filling. You can help me do the hard work."

"That's the good stuff," my granny Dan says as she tastes the ravioli filling.

I smile at her. How she is so sweet and open, yet shaped my father into the man he is today, I'll never quite understand. Though everyone says my dad is just like my grandfather. I don't remember him all that well; I was young when he died. But, if it's true what they say, it seems that the Danforth men have a habit of marrying free-spirited women who soften their otherwise desolate personalities.

I watch my mother and granny giggle over something Mabel says while she washes her hands.

"On Disney channel, the rich people have a cook," Mabel says nonchalantly as my nonna hands her a rolling pin.

Everyone in the kitchen laughs at her honesty.

"Mabes," Cole says sheepishly, overhearing her comment from the table.

I wave it off.

"My family would cook even if they were the richest family in the world," I say as my granny heads out to the dining area to sit with Cole and ask him if he's excited for CeCe's fast-approaching wedding.

"Why?" Mabel asks inquisitively.

"Well, food is part of our roots. We put all our love into it." I lean down to her. "That's why it smells so good."

"Roots like our garden?" Mabel asks as I pull the warm beef mixture off the stove and put it in a cool bowl to scoop into the little pasta parcels.

"Yes, just like our garden," I say.

"How?" she questions as I place a sheet of pasta in front of her.

"Well. My nonna taught my mother how to make this recipe. In fact, she taught her all her special and secret recipes," I tell her. "Then my mother taught me, and now I'm teaching you. So my nonna's roots are now your roots. Do you understand?"

She nods. "So even though I'm not in your family, I can still have your roots?" she asks.

"Yes, babe. That's exactly right," I say with a smile.

She grins up at me, and my heart feels like it might burst. I've never given much thought to having kids of my own, but, man, if they're anything like Mabes, I think it could be pretty damn amazing.

"So, what's next?" she says, clapping her tiny hands together.

Nonna joins in now, showing Mabel how to carefully fill and fold the raviolis before securing the ends.

"Fold and press, fold and press," she chants in the same way she did when I was young.

I take a moment while they work to steal a glance at Cole. He's sitting at the table, listening intently while my father says something to my granny. When our eyes connect across the room, his molten gaze settles somewhere deep within me. It's more than knowing I'm starting to care for him, a lot. It's more than I can explain. It's almost like I can breathe deeper and feel calmer the moment his eyes find mine. He leans back in his chair and sips his drink before flashing me a smirk. It's a smirk that tells me what I already know. When this ends, and I move back into my own house, leaving Cole Ashby is going to fucking destroy me.

CHAPTER FORTY-TWO
Cole

TWO WEEKS LATER—THIRTY-SIX DAYS TO GO

I hear the faint buzz of Ginger's alarm, which tells me it's quarter to five in the morning. Mabel will be up in an hour, and Nash has already texted me twice. I roll over and wrap my arms around her. The sweet scent of her hair hits me, and I breathe it in. Everything about her smells like home, and I feel the overwhelming urge, as I do almost every second of every day, to bury my cock inside her so deep it erases the thought of any other man who found their way there before me. I kiss her shoulder, and she stirs with the tiniest sigh. I groan as her alarm buzzes again, and I know it's time for me to go. We've done this dance almost every morning for the last few weeks: I get up before the sun comes up in case Mabel ever wakes early. Thankfully, she's the kind of kid who sleeps like the dead, so I don't usually have to worry, but I would never want her to find me here without a way to explain it. Which would be impossible because I can't even explain it to myself.

Things are too good right now. And, in my life, when things are going good, bad things tend to happen and ruin everything. Like the time I had just gotten used to being a father when my then-wife decided she didn't have it in her to be the right kind of mother to Mabel. And when I took on the role of deputy sheriff, and started laying down some roots for Mabel, right before my dad got sick.

I'm always waiting for the other shoe to drop when things are going well. And, right now, I'm the happiest I've ever been in my life. So much so, I'm starting to wonder how I ever lived without this soft, sweet, sarcastic firecracker of a woman before.

I'm thinking of all the things I shouldn't be; like putting a baby of our own in her, and how happy it would make me to watch her beautiful body change as she grows our child. I'm thinking about giving her and Mabel a second garden to grow their plants in when they run out of space in their current one. I'm thinking about Christmas mornings, and camping out in the backyard, hosting cookouts, and watching our kids swim in the pool.

But the blaring fact that I am a package deal remains. And asking Ginger to take on the role of being a stepmom to Mabel, and accepting all of Gemma's bullshit on top of that, is a lot. Besides, who actually marries their friend, drunk in Vegas, and then turns around a few months later to say, *Hey, I actually really like you, wanna stick around?* And even if she does stick around, how can I be sure she will stay for good? I can't bear to have Mabel's heart be broken by another woman she loves.

I kiss Ginger's shoulder one last time, reminding myself that she is nothing like Gemma. She would never hurt Mabel. She groans in disapproval as I make my way out of bed, taking all this fucking emotion with me.

"Coffee," she mumbles sleepily.

I chuckle as I pull on my sweats, willing my hard-on to disappear so I can start my day. I'll save my fucked-up feelings for another time. Today, I have to focus.

I look down at my phone as it lights up.

NASH

Were you nervous before your wedding
because I'm not nervous.

NASH

Should I be nervous? This is a good thing,
right? Fuck I hope you were nervous.

I toss my phone on the table.

Today Nash and CeCe are getting married, and on Sunday
Mabel goes to Ernie and Trudy's, Gemma's parents, cottage
up north for almost a week. There is a lot to do to get ready,
but first, I must make my secret wife some coffee. *Husband,
brother, and dad mode, activate.*

CHAPTER FORTY-THREE
Ginger

It feels as though it's just my luck that the universe would send me the man of my dreams when I was a teenager, only for me to marry him as an adult by accident and then start to fall in love with him.

Would it also be my luck that both of us are so stubborn that we haven't properly talked about any of this, and what it will all mean by the end of the summer? *Yes.*

And would that same universe also plant his ex-wife in the very salon I'm getting my hair done in for my best friend's wedding? Of *course.*

"I didn't even know she worked here until two days ago," CeCe hisses to me. "Apparently, she just started in June. She was supposed to be off today, but they had two people call in sick. She isn't working on any of us. Don't worry."

All of us girls are sitting in a row at the upscale Elegance Salon in Laurel Creek's bustling July downtown. I watch Gemma over my shoulder as my hair gets tamed into manageable curls so it can be upswept in the style CeCe wants.

Gemma is pretty, I suppose. Her blond hair is cut shorter

than the last time I saw her. It's now styled into a smooth bob with bangs, and she has wide, almond-shaped blue eyes, high cheekbones, and a pretty smile, when she isn't scowling, that is. I can see how Cole could be attracted to her once upon a time. I chew my lower lip as my hair is tugged in every direction by my own stylist. CeCe sucks back a half glass of champagne beside me just as the door to the salon opens and Ivy comes forward with yet another card, passing it to CeCe as Wade follows behind with a massive basket of white roses.

This isn't the first time the bride-to-be has received a card and gift during our salon trip. Earlier, a giant vase of Hershey's kisses was delivered to her. The card read:

"A wise man once told me to always kiss the woman you love. In this vase is a kiss for every day since you came home. Since the day you walked back into my life and stole my heart."

Wade told us there were 381 of them in that damn vase, and I think I've eaten at least ten since Gemma walked in the door.

CeCe starts to tear up before she even reads the latest note.

"Who knew Nashby had all this romance buried under that bruised heart?" Liv says from my left side as her red hair is pulled into a half-up do by her stylist.

I squint at the side of her neck, which is left exposed with the movement. Are those . . . teeth marks? I make a mental note to ask her who the hell has been biting her.

"A wise man once told me to never go a week without bringing the woman you love flowers. Here is a rose for every week since you've been back with me. For every week you've shone a bright light on the darkest parts of my soul."

Mama Jo, who is sitting beside CeCe, swipes tears away from her eyes and gets up to hug her daughter.

"That wise man was your daddy," she says as CeCe starts to cry again. "He never missed a week. In fact, when he knew he was in his final days, he had Smith Landscaping come in and plant a row of bushes along the fence at the big house so that every week, and all season long, I'd have fresh roses."

She kisses CeCe on the head, and turns to Liv and me before saying, "Nash learned from the best."

Liv flashes Jo a teary smile and squeezes CeCe's hand. Goddammit, even I feel the tears creeping in. We all look at each other, and I shake my head. If CeCe can find her soulmate in her brother's best friend, can I be lucky enough to find happiness in my best friend's brother? I'm just about to tell CeCe how much I love her when the devil herself chooses this second to come in and ruin the moment. My stylist heads over to a cart for some supplies, and Gemma sneaks right in between CeCe and me.

"Congrats, CeCe Rae," she says in a sugary voice that sounds like nails on a chalkboard. Her crooked smile is almost a sneer. "And, Ginger, fancy seeing you here. I heard through the grapevine that you're my daughter's nanny this summer. That's *so* sweet of you to do that for Cole. Don't suppose you two are a little more than friends, huh?"

I shrug and try to keep my voice steady.

"I'm helping my *friend* out, yes," I say calmly, "and I'm happy to spend time with Mabel. She's an incredible girl, and Cole is just the best daddy."

"Don't you have foils to cut or hair to sweep up, Gemma?" CeCe asks with a smile. "I don't see you acting too interested in what Cole and Mabel are doing any other time. What makes today different?"

I want to high-five her for her sass.

"There's no need to get your panties in a twist," Gemma says to CeCe, while pulling a lipstick out of her pocket and turning to me. "I'm just saying, Cole gets friendly with a lot of women. Of course he'd get friendly with you too, Ginger. *Finally.*"

Gemma angles her face to me over her shoulder as she moves to the mirror in front of me.

"You've been waiting on that for a long time, haven't you?" she says before putting on her cherry-red gloss, rubbing her lips together, and fluffing her hair. "I suppose it makes sense now. Especially since you're doing *exactly* what he needs you to do for him. He can be very accommodating when it works to his advantage. Ask the editor at the *Laurel Creek Gazette* that posted all those favorable online articles about him right before the election for sheriff."

I grit my molars and will myself not to get sucked in by this woman. Cole is not just sleeping in my bed, eating almost every meal with me, snuggling up with me on the couch every night, and giving me more orgasms than I know what to do with because I'm helping him with Mabel and his probation.

Is he?

I smile at Gemma in the mirror, but my eyes shoot daggers into her soul. I clench my fist and feel my nails biting into my palm. *Be an example for Mabel,* I tell myself. *Do not do anything stupid.*

"I don't know how you'd have any idea about what Cole is really like. From what I understand, he never let you know the real him. Which is too bad, because he's great." I smirk at her. "Guess it all worked out, though. You've got Brent now. He's *perfect* for you."

She leans down toward me with a smile, but my work is done. She's definitely pissed I hit a little too close to home.

"You think you're so smart, Ginger, but a word of advice, darlin'," she hisses at me. "Cole goes where life suits him. And, right now, you suit him. You know I'm right. Stop lying to yourself."

One of the other hairdressers calls over to us before I can bite back. "Gemma, your three o'clock is here."

"Coming!" she says, but her eyes stay on mine as she walks away.

"Bitch," CeCe mutters under her breath once she's out of earshot. "Don't let her get to you."

I scoff as my hair stylist returns and starts tugging again.

"As if," I say, pouring myself some more champagne, sounding way more confident than she just made me feel.

Of course, CeCe and Nash's wedding is the most beautiful event I've ever been to. The décor is stunning, and the atmosphere is magical. The front of Nash's property is usually vast and green, but tonight it is full of people. The creek behind his house sparkles as the sun begins to sink, and the massive tent where we will eat is glowing with lights, foliage, and flameless candles. To the right there is a perfectly placed aisle complete with a white runway and scattered teal rose petals. Sixty chairs face the imported archway, which is covered in Kentucky honeysuckle and more fairy lights twinkling in mason jars.

My breath is shallow as I move toward Cole at the end of the aisle. I breeze past Chris Bell, who is also a part of the wedding party. I haven't seen him since Vegas, but he doesn't fail to look me over appreciatively. I walk past, and he brushes my arm to get my attention.

"You look beautiful, Ginger. Dance with me later?" he asks.

"We'll see," I say with a shrug, attempting not to be rude but also not wanting to commit.

Cole and I have been placed behind a very pregnant Ivy and a beaming Wade. I haven't seen Cole since eight o'clock this morning when I left to meet CeCe. His satin lilac tie matches my dress, a strapless number that is structured at the waist before flowing downward and resting, loose and billowy, on my knees. It screams simple elegance. Which is exactly what CeCe wanted. Any hope in hell I ever had of not admitting I'm crazy for this man dies as I drink him in; he's wearing a perfectly fitted three-piece suit, his hair is styled back and, as he stands behind his daughter, his brow is furrowed in concentration. My ovaries go firmly into overdrive as he tightens her bun, making sure all her hairpins are in place, while telling her not to be nervous about walking down the aisle. The warmth that spreads through me tells me that I'm definitely falling in love with my husband, and I have no fucking idea what to do about it.

Cole sends Mabel to the front of the line with a kiss to her forehead, and his eyes flit to mine as we come together. They rake over every single stretch of me before coming up to meet my gaze again. My cheeks heat, and I feel the flush under my skin as his stare burns into me.

"What did our friend Chris want?" he whispers, attempting to sound casual.

I keep my eyes forward as I quietly answer. "He wanted to tell me I looked nice and asked me for a dance later."

"Mmmhmm," he says, angling his head closer to mine. "He won't have the chance. We'll be leaving as soon as we can, because the fucking things I want to do to you right now . . ."

His words are a whisper in my ear and instantly turn my skin to gooseflesh.

"Uh huh," I whisper through my smile as I wave at a teacher from school in the crowd. I lock arms with Cole, and we begin our journey. A fleeting moment of regret passes through me with the knowledge that I already got married and that I can't undo the fact that the first time I said wedding vows to someone, it wasn't real. I promise myself in this moment, arm in arm with Cole, that the next time I walk down an aisle like this with my husband, it will be the real thing.

Three hours later, and Nash and CeCe are officially married; dinner is done, dessert has come and gone, and speeches are almost over. I'm pretty sure there isn't a dry eye in the place. There's a short break in the chatter as Chris Bell does his best to chat me up from the other side of our table. He sits directly across from Cole while I'm next to Cory and Anna Kane on one side, and Avery Pope and her boyfriend, Jacob Riley, Olympic bronze medalist for snowboarding, on the other.

Avery is only here for the weekend, but it's so good to see her. She became a central addition to our girl crew last summer when she worked for Nash as his head figure skating instructor until she was called away midway through August to work with the US Olympic Team. She's been in Louisville on and off ever since, which is where she met Jacob.

Chris isn't shy about the way he tries to flirt with me, and every time he does, Avery's eyes catch mine in question. Cole is obviously less than happy about the situation, and makes this clear through his jaw-flexing jealous tell.

I answer Chris's question about how my summer is going, telling him about working with Mabel and everything we've achieved in the garden. Then I turn to Avery, and we talk about everything she's been up to during the last year.

We're only interrupted when CeCe's "aunt," Jo's friend from school, decides that, after three glasses of wine, she wants to say a word to the bride. Cole leans back in his chair beside me in our dark little corner of the wedding party table and we listen to Aunt Daisy drunkenly ramble on as CeCe flashes her best fake smile at her. Jo sits with Wyatt's sister on the other side of the tent, and I can see the grimace she's giving her longtime friend from here. Mabel is sleeping inside the house while Nash's extended family's kids play video games and eat snacks in the next room. Everyone in the tent is clearly itching for this woman to stop talking so we can get to drinking and dancing.

"Who is this woman?" I ask Cole in a whisper. "I've never met her before."

"I don't even think *I've* met her before," Cole jokes quietly as he sips his whiskey.

He places his hand on my thigh as he speaks, and just this simple touch ignites me. And, even though they're blowing air-conditioning into this tent, I'm suddenly very warm as he slides his hand up under my dress and rests it between my thighs.

"At least she's stopped Chris from doing his best to get you to sleep with him for the time being," Cole says under his breath.

I nudge him with my elbow. Aunt Daisy finally stops talking, and everyone claps. Cole removes his hand from my thigh to join in.

"So, Ginger, did I tell you what I'm doing for the Harvest Festival? Will I see you there? I was so glad when Nash and CeCe asked me to help out . . ." Chris starts talking to me again, but I can't focus on his words as Cole's hand lands back on my thigh.

My heart pounds in my ears as Cole's grip creeps slowly higher. I should want to shoo him away, but I don't. He's doing this on purpose, and I'm sure he's getting off on the fact that Chris is trying to keep my attention, even though he's the one commanding it. As if there were ever any competition.

My mind wanders back to the first night Cole and I spent together as his fingers trace the sensitive spot just under my hip bone. The memory resurfaces in flashes; how we barely made it into the hotel room before he was pressing me up against the wall, how the texture of the wallpaper felt against my skin . . .

"And in New York we helped out with the Fourth of July celebrations at St. Jude's. That was my favorite. The kids were adorable, and the way their faces lit up when . . ." Chris rambles on while I nod politely.

Cole's hand meets the apex of my thighs. The tablecloth reaches right down to the floor, and the flickering candle is our only light. My back is to the tent wall, which means Cole can touch me without anyone seeing a thing.

Jacob grabs Chris's attention momentarily, and Cole uses the moment to lean down and whisper in my ear.

"Should I make my wife come while she plays nice with the guests?" His hand slides higher. I start to shake my head, but my body has other ideas, because I open my legs further. Cole's lips turn up in a smirk and practically graze my ear as he pushes my thong aside. It's loud in here, but his voice is level and clear.

"Don't fight it. Open right up for me," he groans as his fingers skim over me. "You're fucking soaked, Vixen."

I stifle a moan but do what he says.

His middle finger finds my clit, and he starts to strum in tight circles using the perfect amount of pressure. Just the thought of us doing this here adds a certain buzz to the already charged atmosphere. I drown Chris's voice out as he turns to tell me about a teenager he helped mentor. His words and face fade away, replaced instead by the image of Cole driving into me the night we got married, both my hands tucked behind his head in his hair, his eyes holding mine.

I fist the tablecloth as Cole continues his rhythm, fucking into me with two fingers in a slow, steady roll, his broad palm adding delicious pressure to my clit. It takes everything in my power not to cry out when that tight coil of heat begins to build within me.

"Nash and CeCe say you offer free tutoring throughout the year for any kids that are behind. That's so sweet of you," Chris says, bringing my attention back to the here and now, right at the same time my body ignites. Cole pinches my clit and I clench my thighs together as I come all over Cole's fingers, fast and furious.

"Yes!" I cry out. "Yes, I love it."

Chris laughs at my outburst, shaking his head at me.

"Helping others really excites her," Cole says as he pulls his hand away and squeezes my thigh one last time. I offer Chris a sweet, breathless smile as I tug my dress down under the table. I see my phone light up as I start to regain my composure.

AVERY

You have a lot of explaining to do at girls' night tomorrow.

I look up at her; her arms are folded across her chest, and she wears a smug look on her face. I shrug before I look back up at Cole, ready to shoot daggers into his soul for making me come apart like that in the middle of Nash and CeCe's wedding reception. He knows I'm about to read him the riot act.

He bends down to whisper in my ear. "Don't look at me like that. You wanted it. This pussy is *mine*."

A chill runs through my spine, and I can't decipher if it's a wish or a memory that suddenly comes crashing down around me. A hazy vision of Cole on the night we got married, long before we crossed any lines sober, fills my mind. His molten eyes bore into mine, and I swear I hear him whisper.

"You're mine, Ginger. You've always been mine."

CHAPTER FORTY-FOUR
Ginger

THIRTY-FIVE DAYS TO GO

"But you will still be here when I come home?" Mabel asks as I secure her first braid and start on her second. She's all packed and ready to go to Ernie and Trudy's cottage for the week.

"Yes. I will be here," I say.

I can't tell her that I'm also worrying about the impending "end of contract" that is approaching faster than I want it to. When Mabel gets back from the cottage, I'll have just under a month before I'm due to leave.

"I will be here until after we pick all the peppers and the tomatoes, remember?" I remind her, figuring the easiest way to give her a timestamp is with our garden.

"Can we check them before I leave?" she asks, and I can sense her nervousness. Over the last few weeks, I've learned that, as tough as Mabel is, she seems to carry a lot of anxiety around leaving Cole for any length of time.

I squeeze her hand.

"Of course we can," I say. "Would it make you feel better if

I sent your grammy Trudy a picture of the garden every day while you're gone? Or I could even video call you?"

"At the same time every day?" she asks, looking for that stability she craves.

"Yes, definitely," I say. "How about every day after dinner?"

Her response is a hug, and one I'm not totally prepared for as her little arms curl around my neck. I wrap her up and squeeze her tight.

"I will miss you," she says, and warmth floods my chest.

She pulls back and grabs her Cowey, gripping him tightly to her. Something about this brave little girl makes me want to pick her up and put her in my pocket for safekeeping.

"I'm going to miss you too," I tell her. "But when you come home, we're going to do all sorts of fun things."

"Can we swim?" she asks

"Of course."

"Can we eat ice cream and have extra chocolate sauce?"

I laugh. "Yes, baby. Now, let's check on those peppers," I say as I pick up Mabel's bag and lead her out of her little en suite bathroom.

As we walk toward the garden, we're met by Cole leaning against the doorway of her bedroom. The sight of him sucks all the air from my lungs. He's dressed in his sheriff's uniform, ready for his once-a-month Sunday shift. It just so happens to coincide with our traditional Sangria Sunday and, even though it's been a busy summer and we haven't gotten together for it lately, tonight all of us girls are going. CeCe and Nash are leaving for their honeymoon in Alaska tomorrow, and we're celebrating Not Angels style, which means we'll be dancing and drinking sangria all night while trying our best to stay out of trouble.

"I didn't even hear you come in," I tell him. His eyes say something I can't place as he clears his throat.

"You ready, half pint?" he asks, scrubbing his freshly shaven jaw with his hand.

Mabel nods in response.

"You're going to have so much fun with Lolli and Pops this week. They're taking you to Waterworld and you can play with Sara Ann. She's there for the whole week too," Cole tells her.

"She is?" Her face lights up before turning to me. "Sara Ann is my friend who lives next door when her mommy comes. Come on, Ginger, we need to check on the garden."

Mabel skips out of her room, leaving me to stand here awkwardly while Cole drinks me in. I look away because there are times when his gaze still makes me nervous, like he's trying to figure out what to do about our little domestic situation just as much as I am. I'm not sure I'm quite ready to have him remind me my days are numbered with this little game of house we're playing.

I move past the bed and grab Mabel's bag, then make my way to the door. Cole is leaning against the doorframe and grabs my arm as I pass, pulling me in close and kissing me. Cole and I kiss, a lot, but this feels different . . . deeper and urgent somehow.

"Thank you," he says when we break apart. He kisses me again, more gently this time, before saying, "For being so incredible with her. She really loves having you here."

I look out to the living room where Mabel skipped off to only moments before.

Cole bends down to whisper in my ear. "She's not the only one who loves having you here."

A shiver runs down my spine, and I push further into him. "You planning on showing me how much *you* love having me here when you get home, sheriff?" I ask, before planting my lips on the base of his neck in a kiss. He smells so damn good I can't help myself, flicking my tongue upward against his skin just once like he's my favorite flavor of ice cream.

He growls in response. "Fuck." He squeezes my jean-clad ass with his big hands as he says it, lifting me off the floor slightly before releasing me. "I can't get hard before I go to work, Ginger."

I smirk, pressing my palm to his chest and looking him straight in the eye.

"For the record, being with Mabel is easy and . . ." I stand up on my tiptoes to kiss his lips softly. "I like you too, Cole."

I slip from his grasp, throwing one last glance his way, before I head out to join Mabel in the yard.

We spend the next ten minutes checking all our plants in the garden.

"Should we tie these ones up?" Mabel asks as she spies two stalks of tomatoes that are leaning hard to the left.

"Yes, good idea," I tell her, looking around me for our supplies. "Shoot. I forgot the twine."

I turn to Cole, who's still in the doorway, his muscular arms crossed over his chest.

"Be a good teammate and get us the twine from my purse? It's on the kitchen table," I say with a wink.

"You almost ready to go, Mabes?" he calls a few minutes later when he comes back outside. "I have to go to work soon, buddy."

"We just need to tie these, and then she's ready," I answer for her, meeting him in the middle of the yard. "You're the one that took so long."

"There's lots in that purse, Ginger. I had to dig around through lip balms, hand creams, bar menus . . ." Cole whispers with a grin.

I look up at him, and the smug facial expression he's wearing tells me he saw the letter I wrote to myself on the bar menu in Vegas. The one where I declared I would quit Cole cold turkey. I mentally berate myself for never cleaning out my purse.

Shit.

Cole doesn't say anything; he flips the menu over and notes where it's from, all the dots connecting in his head as he stares deep into my eyes. I narrow mine at him in response.

"What?" I ask. "Why are you looking at me like that?"

A flush of embarrassment creeps up my neck.

"Just doing my best to turn you into a puddle of scientific matter," he says with a grin, using my own words from the pact against me. I make a scoffing noise as I turn away from him.

"I wrote that as a joke," I say, walking back to Mabel.

"No, you didn't, Vixen," he notes confidently. "And we're going to talk about that."

"No, we aren't," I retort.

Mabel and I finish what we're doing in the garden and, when I turn around to guide her to the door, Cole looks like a rooster puffing his chest. Though the look he's wearing isn't cockiness as I move toward him. It's . . . pride?

He knows I'm crazy about him, and he seems to *like* it. I saw this look yesterday too; every time he glanced at me during Nash and CeCe's wedding, as we danced through the night together, and especially when we got home and he took me twice before he got up and made us our coffee at five. There's no denying these deep feelings between us. I give in and smile at him, shrugging as I walk by. "Guess you know my secret," I tell him, not even ashamed to admit it anymore.

We started this summer as friends with a clear plan to rectify a drunken mistake. But now? Now Cole Ashby is looking at me the same way I've been looking at him for years.

Fucking hell.

That sangria and my girls can't come soon enough.

CHAPTER FORTY-FIVE
Ginger

The Horse and Barrel is packed with the usual crowd that frequents ladies' night. There are also quite a few men here who I can only assume are on the prowl, a bunch of Silver Pines cowboys included.

Haden Westbrook, Wade's right-hand man, and three others take up a booth in the far-right corner.

"He gets better looking by the year, doesn't he?" Avery says to us. "I mean Haden's no Jacob, but he's sure got that whole rugged cowboy thing going on."

I look over at their table to eye Haden up. He's worked on the ranch for a few years now and has grown close with all the guys during that time. He's definitely good-looking: dark blond hair, scruff along his wide jaw, that enticing kind of cowboy mustache, and a tattered old cowboy hat perched atop his head. He's got the whole if-Charlie-Hunnam-was-a-cowboy thing going on.

He's certainly using that cowboy draw to his advantage tonight as some buckle bunny sits on his lap and whispers into his ear. It's clearly working for her.

"Looks like ladies' night brings out all kinds." Liv grins, nodding to Brent Wilson in the other corner of the room as he drinks in the women on the dance floor.

"I trust that man as much as I trust a dog with my plate of steak," I say and CeCe, Liv, and Avery laugh as I gulp down my sangria.

"Of all the people for Cole to get stuck working with," Liv says, tapping her nails on the table. "Hopefully he can make it through his term without pummeling him."

"Cole will keep him in line," I say confidently.

"Okay, so I'm going to just bring up the giant elephant in the room here," CeCe starts. "Now that I'm a happily married woman, I have a little more time on my hands. Which means I can help with what we've all been ignoring all summer."

She flashes her massive diamond ring and matching band at us.

"That thing is blinding," Liv says with a laugh.

"The elephant being the fact that something is clearly going on with Cole and Ginger?" Avery says with a grin. Her long, chocolate-brown hair shines in the bar lights.

"The very one," CeCe agrees. "You two were stuck together like glue all night at the wedding."

I tuck a rogue hair behind my ear and shrug, not knowing how to explain what Cole and I are and feeling protective over what is going on between us.

"It's something that appears to be serious if Ginger Danforth is speechless . . ." Liv comments.

"You guys want what I can't give you right now. I have no explanation for y'all other than the fact that things are oddly easy between us, and I'm . . . happy," I say.

CeCe smiles at me across the table. "Some part of me knew this was going to happen with you two living in the same house," she says. "Though I can't say I'm not worried."

"I get it, but I've got this," I say, hoping I'm right but also feeling a little defensive.

Thankfully, one of our favorite Shania Twain songs, "I'm Gonna Getcha Good," comes over the sound system, giving me a much-needed break from their scrutiny.

CeCe jumps up and looks at us all expectantly. Of course, we all gulp down the rest of our drinks and follow her out onto the dance floor. One is simply not allowed to turn down dancing to Shania.

We get through the song, and another good one starts. Typical Sunday night. The Horse and Barrel DJ knows how to keep us and every other woman in this place dancing.

We spend the next hour on and off the dance floor until I'm sweaty and a little tipsy but having the best time with my girls. I needed a night to not think about Cole, my father, or the fact that I'm going back to work soon. A little girl time to gain some perspective.

CeCe, Avery, and Liv move off the dance floor to the washroom, so I take a moment to head back to our table and chug some water before I start on another sangria. When I get there, I see my phone light up. It's my dad. So much for a night off.

WARDEN

> I need help going door-to-door on Tuesday.

ME

> I can come.

WARDEN

> Good. There is a team of us to canvass. I'll have Kate contact you.

Kate's his administrator.

ME

Can't wait.

WARDEN

Sarcasm isn't becoming, Ginger, and it would
be nice if you were on stage with your mother
and me for my speech next week.

So cocky and sure of winning his primary. I sigh. I know if
I don't go, I'll never hear the end of it. A pang of dread sits in
my stomach like a rock.

ME

I'll be there.

WARDEN

Good. I'll be in touch.

Just as I roll my eyes at his response, a new text comes in.

HUSBAND

I think pineapple is growing on me.

I smile at his newly appointed name in my phone. Even if
it's short-lived, it makes me happy to see it.

ME

That so? Why?

HUSBAND

Read an article.

ME

On pineapple?

I start laughing. What the hell is this man talking about?

> **HUSBAND**
>
> Apparently if you eat a lot of pineapple, it makes your cum taste really fucking good. I'm testing the theory, but I'm gonna have to rely on you for the study and conclusion.

I take another sip of water as I read his text and suck it straight down my windpipe. I don't respond as I attempt to calm my coughing fit. Another text comes through.

> **HUSBAND**
>
> Looking it up, aren't you? 👀

> **ME**
>
> No, you made me choke.

> **HUSBAND**
>
> Title of your sex tape. 😉 And I love making you choke, Vixen.

I play along.

> **ME**
>
> What do you expect? It's huge. 🍆

> **HUSBAND**
>
> It is a good size, isn't it?

I can practically see him patting himself on the back from here. Cole would have the world's most perfect dick.

> **ME**
>
> Stop making me think about such things when I'm out with your sister and the girls.

HUSBAND

Such things = my cock.

HUSBAND

Stop kidding yourself, Vixen. You'd be thinking about it anyway. You're always thinking about it.

ME

That so?

HUSBAND

Yes.

ME

You been reading my diary, Cole?

HUSBAND

No need, purse letters say it all.

Fucker.

ME

Pretty confident to assume you know what I'm thinking.

HUSBAND

Don't need confidence, baby. I know for a fact that just talking about this is making that tight little pussy wet for me.

A rush of heat filters through my core at his words. *Dammit.* I have no idea how this man makes me feel this way. Oh, wait, yes I do. It's because he's fucking incredible, and the literal definition of hot-sheriff-daddy-big-dick-energy.

HUSBAND

Tell me I'm wrong.

I bite my lip and start to type, honesty and my second sangria driving me on.

ME

I can't. You're right. I'm always thinking about it.

HUSBAND

Want to know what I can't stop thinking about?

I take the bait.

ME

What?

HUSBAND

Only three more hours until I get to kiss those beautiful lips, prop them open, and stuff my cock down my dirty little wife's throat.

I shift in my seat. Any more of this and I'm going to have to take care of myself somewhere in the bar. It's at this moment that I realize Liv, Avery, and CeCe are back from the bathroom and in front of our table, watching me sit here and grin at my phone like an absolute idiot. I have no idea how long they've been there.

"At the risk of me making myself feel grossed out at the thought, that's my brother, isn't it?" CeCe asks.

"I . . ." I sip my sangria.

"You're practically making love to your phone." Liv giggles, before turning to CeCe. "Cover your ears!"

"Why do I feel like I'm always covering my ears?" She gets up. "I'm going to kiss my husband. Talk about the gross stuff while I'm gone. You have two minutes."

She saunters over to the bar, seating herself on a stool in front of Nash. So maybe I have three minutes.

"Well?" Liv asks.

I glance over at CeCe and decide to give Liv and Avery the one-minute CliffsNotes version of what has happened between me and Cole this summer, leaving out the fact that we got married because Cole's becoming my ride-or-die and we promised to keep that part between us.

"But now it feels more serious and . . ." I put my head in my hands. "I don't know. Ugh, I think I might . . . Things are just more complicated now."

I trail off as I catch a glimpse of Brent standing at a table one over, wrapping up his conversation. He looks at me with a grin, which instantly unsettles me.

Liv's eyes grow wide as saucers.

"Wait . . . No you didn't. Ginger Lily Danforth, did you let yourself fall in love with our best friend's brother?!" she asks, her voice hitting a higher octave.

"Shhh," I hush her. "I . . ."

I drop my head into my flattened palms and muffle into them. "I think I did."

"But it's *Cole*," she says.

"Sometimes these things just happen, and no amount of trying to prevent it would've helped if it was meant to be," Avery offers. "It's how you handle it now that counts. You need to make sure he's on the same page. From what I remember, Cole isn't the serious relationship type."

"I know," I deadpan, looking up at them both.

"Wow. That is a lot of information to take in. I thought you two were just having a fling. Getting it out of your system." Liv looks back at me, and a serious expression crosses her face. "Avery is right. Do you think he feels serious about you?"

"I don't know . . . maybe? Sometimes he looks at me like he does," I answer honestly, draining my glass.

Liv snorts.

"He's been looking at you like that for years," she says. "I've been telling you that this whole time, but you never listen."

"Even I noticed it last year," Avery adds.

I nod, starting to think that they might be right, but that still doesn't tell me how serious he is about me. It just tells me he's desired me physically.

"I don't need to tell you, but, Ginger, you *have* to have that talk with him," Liv says. "You have a best friend who just happens to be his sister, and he has a *daughter*. One it seems as though you're getting very attached to and vice versa."

I catch eyes with Asher Reed, Nash's always a little intimidating bartender, and hold my empty glass up. He knows the drill. I should have a new pitcher here in less than five.

"Oh, I'll go get us more," Liv offers. I watch her stand up and smooth her hair. "Be right back."

"Okay . . ." I say. She's being so weird lately, but right now I have my own problems. I can't deal with hers too.

"Take my advice now that they're both gone," Avery says, leaning forward. "If you have a shot at being happy, Ginger, don't pass that up to please anyone else."

I smile at her nonjudgment.

"Thanks," I say as her phone rings. She pulls it out and smiles.

"It's Jake," she explains, before standing up to answer it and moving outside.

I blow out a breath and sit at the table, now alone. I pull my phone out and type a message to Cole.

ME

Only two hours and fifty minutes now.

And Cole? I've eaten a ton of pineapple today. If
I test your theory, you're testing mine.

ME

And you're right. I am already wet.

I smirk down at my phone as I watch the three dots appear then disappear. I picture the look on his face right now, the way he'll be shifting in his seat at work.

Liv is right. I need to have that talk with Cole. And this week, with Mabel away, is the perfect time. I start planning how I'll bring it up. Maybe I'll make a nice dinner. I could cook us something special, and we could hash everything out. I will myself to believe I can put my fears aside and have an honest conversation with him. As bold as I try to be on the outside, I've never been the best at putting myself out there.

I take a deep breath as I watch Liv make her way back from the bar, fresh pitcher in her hand. My phone lights up just before she reaches me.

HUSBAND

Be naked when I get home.

I'm definitely going to have to start that conversation with Cole this week. But first, because I'm way too turned on to do anything else, I'm going to let him have his way with me tonight. I mean, what kind of dirty little wife would I be if I didn't?

CHAPTER FORTY-SIX
Ginger

"*S hit*," I mutter, smacking my shin as I drop my purse on Cole's front bench just after midnight.

I straighten up and listen for him. The house is dark, but I hear the telltale sign he's home before me: water running. I make my way through the house and set my phone down on the counter, his last message still glaring up at me.

HUSBAND

> I'm home and you're neither here nor naked.

In my defense I had to wait for Nash and CeCe to come back from whatever it was that they were doing. Okay, I know what they were doing, but, still, I had no choice. Nash was my ride home after one too many sangrias. So I quickly run to my room, determined to make it up to Cole for being late.

I pull out a flimsy black lace lingerie set that would make even the most seasoned porn star blush and throw it on while simultaneously freshening up in the bathroom at record speed. By the time the water stops running in Cole's bathroom, I'm in the middle of my bed, lamp on so he'll see the light under my door. The two sets of handcuffs I stored away when I moved in are hanging off my first finger, and my legs are slightly tipped open to reveal just enough of the set's almost crotchless core.

My heart rate accelerates when Cole comes in through my door, a towel wrapped around his narrow hips, little droplets of water still clinging to his muscled chest and shoulders. I practically come at the sight.

It takes him all of three seconds to register me lying here and what I'm holding. He doesn't even flinch at the scene before him. The fucker just casually raises an eyebrow, looks to the cuffs in my hand, then back to my body. His eyes set me aflame as he takes in the expanse of my skin, adorned in lace and straps, not to mention all the pushing up that's going on.

"You're late," he comments, his voice doing that lower octave thing it does that brings my core to life.

"You want to arrest me, officer?" I ask as a smile plays on my lips. How many sangrias I've had tonight must be evident in my voice, because Cole smiles coyly back.

"I think so," he says, pulling the towel from his body and letting it fall to my wooden floor.

My mouth waters at the sight of him in all his hard, inked, naked glory before me. God, he's perfect. His cock bobs, already pointing straight at me.

"Public drunkenness . . ." He stalks toward me, using his hand to stroke himself.

"Three sangrias . . . not intoxicated," I say in a sassy tone, just tipsy enough to make me want him tenfold.

"Theft of an officer's handcuffs . . ." he says, crawling onto the bed and pulling me down roughly under him. I yelp as he forces my legs wide and sinks between them; hovering over the top of me, he groans.

"And this . . ." His eyes rake over me one more time as a finger slides under a strap in the dim light of my room. He lets it go with a snap as it falls back into place. "Goddamn, woman, this should be fucking illegal."

His mouth is on mine before I can think, rendering me dizzy as his tongue plunders my mouth in sweet desperation before he pulls away.

"Fuck . . ." I mutter, unable to withstand this kind of torture.

"I'm about to destroy this pretty little number you're wearing, and then I'm going to fucking devour you, Ginger." Cole pulls my almost crotchless thong from my body and tosses it over his shoulder.

His large middle finger skims my already soaking slit, spreading my arousal over my sensitive clit.

"I can't get enough of you. I've been dreaming of how you taste all fucking day," he says. "So fucking wet, so fucking ready for me."

The urge to take control washes over me with his words. I place my hands inside his shoulders and curl my calf around his. I flip him over onto his back. "All the years of self-defense my father made me take just served their purpose."

He laughs out loud in shock when I land between his legs on top of him, the sound cutting as I kiss him deeply. A smirk plays on his lips as I slide my hand up and secure one end of the cuffs to each of my bedposts.

I sit up as he rips the back of my lace bralette open. The sound of the fabric tearing fills the air as he pulls it off and tosses it to the floor. His hands palm my breasts, and I almost lose my train of thought.

"What do you think you're doing with those cuffs, Vixen?" He looks at me through narrowed eyes.

I grin back, pressing my pussy against him. His eyes flutter closed as a deep groan escapes him.

"Do you trust me? Or is *authority* on the tip of your tongue, sheriff?" I ask him, grinding against his rock-hard cock.

"In this situation? Not a fucking chance, but I don't use safe words when it comes to sex, Vixen. Do your best," he answers as I grin. He asked for it. I take both his hands and pin them, outstretched, to his sides. I wrap one cuff around his wrist and lock it in place, tight. The sound is a warning in the quiet room. I slide a finger down his arm.

He lets out a low rumble but doesn't protest as I lock the other cuff securely. I kiss him lightly on his lips. The idea of him below me at my mercy courses through my veins, and my pussy throbs.

"Good boy . . . I wouldn't trust me either," I whisper as I sit up and grin at him.

"Ginger . . ." he warns, not looking as sure as he was a minute ago, but it holds no merit. I'm the one in control here.

"Yes, baby?" I ask.

"Where are the keys?" he says, realizing the power he's just turned over to me.

"Right there on your bedside table, safe and sound," I tell him. "See, Cole, I'm the one in charge . . ."

I slide down him as he lets out a tortured groan. I run my tongue over every crevice of his freshly washed skin, his cock hard and inescapable against me.

"Fuck," he growls as I kneel between his thighs and my hot mouth finds him. I lick a slow trail up his shaft just to torture him. When I let him finally sink into me, he raises his hips to force himself in deeper, hitting the back of my throat. I hollow out my cheeks and open up my mouth wider to take all of him.

"Patience, baby," I purr.

"This was a bad idea," Cole says, pulling at his wrists as if he can free himself.

"You have no idea . . ." I reply as I lean over to my bedside table, pulling out the cuff keys and Mr. Always Ready. I run my thumb down the thick wand and turn it on. The low hum fills the air.

"*Fuck*, Ginger," Cole says, looking both a little afraid and really fucking turned on as I slide the toy down his neck. His skin breaks out in gooseflesh as I straddle him naked. He lets out a breath of air as he feels the pool between my legs press up against his cock.

"So *hard*, so fucking ready for *me*," I whisper, using his words against him.

It's clearly working as his eyes screw shut and a sound rumbles from his chest that borders on animalistic. I use my own arousal to coat him, and then I scoot back a little to stroke him against my pussy with my free hand. Cole mutters something I can't understand as I ghost the end of the wand over my nipple and shudder, before trailing it down my waist and toward my core. I rest it against my clit and whimper. It hums against us both, and I let my head drop back as I speed up the pace.

"That's it, baby. Make yourself feel good," Cole says as I circle the wand against my swollen center.

"Fucking Christ," he murmurs as the vibrator touches him every time I move it, every time I slide it down to graze him too.

"Look at me, Ginger," he commands. I almost lose it when I do. He's like my own personal Roman god lying beneath me, helpless and vulnerable to my actions.

"You can use that silicone against you all you want, but it will never take my place. It will never fill you like I do," he says.

Cole's eyes are dark and stormy as he thrusts his hips up. The feeling of his cock against me and the vibration at my clit is too much. I give in and lift my hips, slinking down onto him. We both breathe out in a huff as I let him fill me, inch by perfect inch. He's so big from this angle that it takes a moment for me to stretch around him.

"Cole . . ." I shudder, almost ready to unlock him and let him have his way with me.

"Oh no you don't," he says fiercely, thrusting his hips up to fill me to the hilt. I cry out, and my arms slink to my sides.

"You're not going to give up now. You want to cuff me?" *Thrust.*

"Then fucking own it, Ginger." *Thrust.*

"I'm going to stuff you full, and you're going to ride me until you drip down the sides of my cock." *Thrust.*

"And don't you dare forget that needy little clit while you do." *Thrust.*

I cry out as he hits the spot inside me that threatens to ruin me. He continues to chant to me.

"Use your toy. Use your fingers. Use whatever you need." *Thrust.*

"It's my name on your lips every time you come. It's *me* that makes you come."

I move my wand against my clit, and we both groan with the vibration. I set my pace, and he meets me with his hips every time I sink down.

"Such a good girl, Ginger . . ." He praises me as my speed increases with the wand. I can't take all of this; his words claiming me, his cock filling me, and the wand stimulating me. A tight coil of heat and pressure builds in my lower belly. It feels uncontrollable.

"This fucking pussy." He grunts as he works his hips up again to somehow take back control even though he's the one cuffed to the bed. "That's it, take all of my cock like a good little slut. You might be in control, but remember this pussy is *mine.*"

Goddamn, those words.

I clench around him and work my clit with the humming wand. He thrusts one more time and I lose it. I lift up off him as my body shatters from the inside out. I never stop the wand, and I soak them both in the process as I cry out his name.

"Fuck . . . Ginger . . . *Fuck.*" His voice cuts through my whimpers.

But Cole gives me no reprieve, and I practically strangle his cock as he thrusts back into me, all cares lost and the bed soaked. I'm like a boneless heap above him as he fucks into me.

"Unlock me, Ginger. *Now*," he orders.

I don't argue, I can't. My body is his as I reach for the keys in the center of the bed and unlock one arm, which instantly flies to my throat as he grips me tight.

Cole sits up as best he can with one arm and hovering his lips over mine.

"Faster," he commands darkly as I fumble with the key for his other hand.

I manage to set him free, and nothing could prepare me for the vengeance Cole unleashes upon me. First his mouth claims me as his arms encircle my body, kneading every part of me in a bruising grip. Like he can't touch me fast enough.

"That was a dirty little trick, Vixen," he rasps into my ear. "I'm going to *fucking* ruin you."

He tosses me off of him and flips me over so I'm on all fours, before hiking my ass up and pressing my upper body into the bed. It's wet with the mess I made earlier. Cole grabs the wand, still humming, and skims it up my inner thigh. I moan as my pussy throbs, already wanting more. Already begging for him to fill me.

"Cole . . ." I whimper.

"You want to tease me, hmm?" he asks as the wand finds my clit. "You have no idea how I can tease *you*, Ginger. How many years I've waited to do fucking depraved things to you, to this body. This body I've imagined in my hands, against my lips. Between my teeth."

He wraps his free hand in my hair and pulls my body up to bite my neck in multiple places before he releases me, gripping my hips, hiking me up and notching my knees farther apart. The wand rolls over my ass, then against my back hole, and I mewl into the bed, not used to the foreign sensation.

"So do it," I coax, wanting all the things he offers, desperate for him to own me completely.

Cole growls and sheaths himself in me with one fluid movement that almost causes me to collapse against the sheets. I fist them as he keeps the toy between my cheeks and holds me up with his free hand.

I'm helpless now as he drags himself almost all the way out, then slams back into me, a guttural groan escaping him. The sound ripples through me. I love him out of control like this, I love holding all the power and surrendering it to him all at once. He pushes the wand against me with perfect pressure, stimulating something in me I've never experienced as he fucks me with a kind of brute force he hasn't unleashed on me before.

"My dirty little wife likes to be fucked *and* toyed with?" he asks as he slams into me again.

"Yes . . ." I whimper as he grips my hip tight, thrusting into me over and over.

But it isn't enough. Cole is unhinged now; he lifts my body and moves me up the bed so that he can grab the headboard for leverage. He picks up the wand again and, when I glance at him over my shoulder, he flashes me an all-knowing smile as he glides it over my back hole again. In this moment, it becomes instantly apparent that I've never really known what it means to be taken by a man.

But it's this; Cole driving into my pussy hard and fast, unforgiving and animalistic, as he offers pressure in tight circles against my asshole with my vibrator. He turns it up to max and spits above the cleft to coat the head before slipping it into me just enough to send me reeling. I all but scream into the bed, moaning his name and begging him for everything and nothing all at once.

"*Holy fuck,*" he says, sensing the hum against him from inside me. "That feels . . . *fuck.*"

He starts to move faster, and I grin in a moment of clarity.

"My dirty husband likes to be fucked *and* toyed with?" I ask.

Something about my words sends him over the edge. He pulls the wand from me, and I hiss at its loss. He tosses it onto the bed and grips my hair, sliding his other hand around to pull me up by my throat. My back is flush against his front, and I turn my face to meet his in messy, urgent kisses.

"Call me your husband again," he orders.

"Will my husband make me come, please?" I say, ready to ignite around him. His hand squeezes around my throat, pulling the breath from my lungs just enough to make me lose all control. Dots line my vision as he thrusts into me so deeply I see stars.

"Fucking mine," he growls as he grows inside me. "*My wife.*"

He spills into me just as my vision goes static, and I free-fall with him, calling out his name as he calls mine. I come harder than I ever have in my life. We both moan and pant as we ride out our high, our sweat-slicked skin pressed together.

A few minutes later, as we lie in a tangled mess, he kisses me gently through my hair and onto my shoulder.

"Guess we'll have to test that pineapple theory later . . . ?" I grin.

"You're going to be the death of me, woman," he says, still breathless.

I peck his lips. A warm feeling spreads through my chest as he wraps his arms around me and hugs me close.

He whispers into my ear. "But, Ginger, this? Us? It's fucking *everything.*"

I sigh. Maybe that talk I told the girls I'd have can wait until tomorrow . . . or even the day after that.

CHAPTER FORTY-SEVEN
Cole

TWENTY-EIGHT DAYS TO GO—
PRIMARY VOTE DAY

I wake to the sound of Ginger's phone vibrating on the bedside table. My bets are on it being her father. He's called her three times in the last twenty-four hours to remind her of all the things she needs to do for him, never once asking her if she *wants* to. I've been biting my tongue, but one of these days I'll be reminding him she is his daughter, and that her job isn't to help him win an election.

My brow furrows as I roll over and wrap my arms around her soft, warm body. Not only is it primary day, but today marks the first step in our divorce plan. Mabel is also coming home from the cottage later, and this protectiveness I feel over my and Ginger's situation has only increased tenfold over the last seven days.

For the past week, we've barely worn clothes when we're together. We've talked, we've eaten every meal at home, we've swum, with and without bathing suits. We've watched movies and turned some heads during our grocery shopping in this small, gossipy town. We've managed household chores, and we've fucked, a lot, in every crevice of my house and yard, yet still I never seem to get enough of Ginger. It's given me a glimpse into what life might be like if I can convince her to stay. With Ginger by my side, I feel . . . whole.

I go to work and deal with everything there with an ease I've never experienced before. Even Brent seems less annoying because I know that, at the end of every day, I will drive home and she'll be here, waiting for me, lounging by the pool in one of those skimpy bathing suits that turn me savage, or tending to the garden so as not to miss a beat while Mabel is gone. Hell, I even came home and found her on FaceTime with Mabes the other day, and the feeling I got when I heard them talking almost knocked the wind out of me. I'd watched her from the patio door as she paced around, asking Mabel whether she was remembering her pleases and thank-yous, her sunscreen, telling her that the coloring page she held up was beautiful. I watched as they talked about what they'd do when Mabes got home. It wasn't like how a nanny would talk to a child in her care, but how a mother would address her daughter.

I've witnessed how Mabel blossoms under Ginger's attention this summer. Their relationship fills the void she misses from her own mother, who only went up to the cottage last week for four hours. The whole time Ernie and Trudy have had Mabel, Gemma couldn't even be bothered to spend one night with her.

Now, lying here in the morning sunlight starting to filter through my blinds, I'm a ball of nerves. Because, over the last week, it's fucking hit me. Somewhere along the lines of friends to best friends to fake wife, I've fallen in love with Ginger Danforth. Deep fucking in love with her. And this isn't a fake marriage we're both trying to get through. In many ways this is more real than the marriage I did my best at living in for years.

I make a pact with myself to figure out how to tell this woman how I feel, how to get her to stay longer, to convince her to be a mother to my daughter, to tell her that she's the final piece to our puzzle.

Ginger hums beside me as she stirs, and her phone buzzes again just as I'm about to slip a hand between her silky thighs.

"Fuck," I mutter, "he's called twice already."

Ginger groans. "I have to answer it or he'll just keep calling."

I grunt and move to get out of bed while she picks the phone up to talk to her father.

I slide my sweats on over my hard-on and make my way to the kitchen. Ginger joins me twenty minutes later to work out the timeline for the day. I stare at her as she talks; she looks way too enticing in just my T-shirt and her bed hair falling around her shoulders in waves.

"So Mabel comes home at one P.M.," she says, typing on her phone before looking up at me. "And you'll be home when?"

I hand her a coffee, which she takes eagerly. "I'll be home at four-thirty," I say. "I'll grab a pizza for me and Mabes on the way back."

"Okay. I have to be at the Masonic Temple at five or so, and it'll be a late one, whether he wins or not," she says while chewing her bottom lip. She takes a sip of her coffee as she stares out of the window.

"Do you need Mabes and me there?" I ask. I am fully prepared to be there for Ginger tonight, but I also don't want her to feel overwhelmed with questions from the press and her parents about *why* I'm there.

"Um . . ." she says.

She looks way too stressed, and I'm not having it.

"Come on, let's start the day right," I tell her.

I pull her by one hand to my bathroom, her coffee in the other. She sits up on the counter and takes a sip, a look of curiosity on her face. The tops of her silky thighs flatten against my counter and, naturally, I want to push them apart. I do my best to control my urges for five goddamn minutes to make this moment about her. It is not without effort.

The large ivory claw-foot bathtub in the middle of the room looks out over the backyard through a frosted glass picture window. The morning sun streams in while I start running a bath.

"Why am I in your bathroom, Cole?" Ginger asks.

"Just sip your coffee and stop asking questions," I tell her, adding some Epsom salts and bubbles to the water, letting the tub fill while I head back to the kitchen to bring my own coffee mug and the pot back in.

I bend down to kiss her lips, taking her cup and setting it down beside her. I peck her once more before pulling her shirt off over her head, lifting her off the counter, and turning her to face the mirror. I stand behind her and, using both of my hands, sweep her thick tresses into a high bun, all the while trailing my lips down her neck and shoulders just enough to relax her. She lets out a sigh.

"Tonight is going to go well," I tell her as I reach into my bathroom drawer and pull out a black hair tie, securing the bun and using my hands to smooth her hair. "You don't have to be his entire support system."

"Not bad, Law Daddy." Ginger smirks at me in the mirror, most of her now on display, her pink nipples pearled and ready for my fingers . . . my mouth.

"If the sheriff thing doesn't work out, you could always go into hairstyling," she says.

I smack her panty-clad ass and turn away from her. If I look at her in the mirror for too much longer, it will be game over. I slide the teak bath table over to sit beside the tub, setting both our mugs on it before losing all my clothes and sinking into the hot bath and shutting off the faucet.

"Truth or dare?" I ask as she pulls her panties off and climbs in to sit in front of me, her back to my chest.

"Always a dare, Cole," Ginger says as I begin to move the bubbles up over her shoulders. She sighs, and I reach over to hand her her mug of coffee. She takes a sip as I trace lines over her shoulders, her neck. She instantly relaxes into me, and the feeling pushes all the blood in my body straight to my cock.

Fuck, focus, Cole.

"I dare you to tell me what's going on in that pretty head of yours. What are you afraid of?" I ask.

"That's cheating, sheriff. I didn't say truth." She laughs.

I kiss her neck, once, fuck it, twice. She smells like coconut and the sun, and *me*. I can't tell which note I like best.

"That's the nice thing about being sheriff. You get to make the rules," I tell her as I slide my fingers over her arms, penciling circles in the bubbles against her skin.

"You're being very convincing," she muses.

"Then start talking, Mrs. Ashby," I tell her in my best cop voice.

"I'm . . . nervous," she says, draining her mug and setting it back down on the table.

"About what?" I ask as I start to draw words into the bubbles on her back: *wild, light, loving.* Anything that comes to mind about her.

I kiss a line down her warm neck as she tips back farther, exposing the smooth column of her throat to me. When she doesn't answer, I lean forward and take a nibble out of her shoulder. She flinches and swats at me as I kiss her in the same spot.

"About what?" I repeat.

"This. You . . . Us . . . Why the hell I seem to care about you so much. It's annoying and hard to understand . . . and . . ." She trails off as my tracing continues.

Sweet, proud, grace.

"And what?" I press her for her honesty. I don't have to look at her to know she's biting into her plump bottom lip in thought.

"How I'm going to adjust . . . when I leave," she says, "and go back to work. How I'll cope when I'm away from Mabel."

Goddamn, I did not expect that much honesty, and Ginger's rawness causes a tight feeling to take over my chest. I say nothing as I trace another word: *beautiful.*

"You owe me one," she says, angling back into me but still giving me enough space to trace her upper back and shoulders. *She likes it.*

"Truth or dare?" she continues, tilting her head to look up at me. Her fiery eyes meet mine, and I'm a goner. I kiss her once because she's too perfect to resist.

"Truth," I say.

"Tell me something *real*," she says, skimming her fingers over my thigh.

I take a deep breath.

"You asked me why this G is branded into my skin?" I start.

Her body instantly stiffens.

"Each moment . . ." she says, trailing off when she can't finish the rest of the saying inked in Italian under the G.

"Each moment only once," I tell her, still tracing what comes to mind: *friend.*

I push the bubbles away and lean down to her ear with a kiss as I trace the last words. *Soul, love.*

"It's *you*," I whisper.

CHAPTER FORTY-EIGHT
Ginger

My mouth falls open as I blink and try very hard to string a sentence together that makes sense, which is near impossible because not only are my emotions out of control, but I struggle to think when Cole's lips are pressed against my skin.

"C-come again?" is all I come up with, as the pads of his fingers continue to draw little designs on my back.

"I said, Ginger Lily Ashby. This letter, it's *you*," Cole says. "You turned my world upside down when you kissed me that summer. I spent the whole time at Grosvenor thinking about you, telling myself why it could never be."

He nips his lips along my shoulder; and I whimper at the contact.

"*Ogni momento solo una volta*. Each moment only once," he purrs.

Cole's hands slide up my arms to grip my face and turn my lips up to meet his. Italian rolling off of Cole's tongue while we're naked in the bath together might be the sexiest experience of my life. He licks a slow trail over my bottom lip, and I squeeze my thighs together under the water as he kisses me.

"I didn't kiss you back that night in my truck *because* of the way it felt," he says, laying everything out on the table now. "I always knew I cared about you, but I didn't know what to make of how it made me *feel*. How *you* made me feel. You were my little sister's best friend."

"Cole," I manage to choke out as he strokes my face.

"And then, I went to work at Grosvenor and had to look at that fucking G everywhere. All I could think about was how it felt to kiss you . . . to hold you," he says, kissing me now and looking into my eyes.

Mine flutter closed as he steals all rational thought from me. He continues on, obliterating the imaginary line in the sand between us with his words.

"Midway through the summer, with you consuming my mind . . . my every thought, I had Carson McKinney pull out the fucking iron after a couple of beers, heat it up, and sear that G into my ribs." He takes a breath before adding, "Right where I felt your hands for days after you slid across my truck seat. I searched for that feeling for a long time, but I never ever found it with anyone else," he whispers. "It's been you for so fucking long, Ginger . . . you're the baseline I compared every woman to. You're the one I sought. I sought your attention, your sass, your fucking beautiful smile. Always."

"Oh . . ." I manage, as soft kisses dot my shoulders, my hair, everywhere he can plant them.

"Even when life handed me a twist in fate, the greatest gift of my life, I still couldn't let you go," Cole says. "I couldn't let you go, Ginger. And for some fucked-up reason, you never let go either," he rasps as his lips move down my neck. I hang in this suspended moment of bliss.

He maneuvers his body a little so he can pull my hand over and place it on top of the G at his side, *my G*.

He looks into my eyes as he says, "I wanted you. I never admitted it, not even to myself, but I knew if I kept spending time with you, if I could just keep you in my grasp, one day you'd be mine."

He lets out a growl, and then his lips are on mine: tasting, searching, claiming.

"That day is now," he tells me. "You are *mine*, Vixen." His kiss sears his words like the brand at his side. "That real enough for you?"

"Yes," I whisper.

"It's always been you, Ginger," he mutters into my lips. "And I have no fucking clue what to do about that. Besides maybe keep you."

I take a moment to let everything he's just admitted sink in before kissing him back and snuggling against him as he wraps his arms around me.

"I don't know what to do either," I say. "Besides maybe let you."

I sit here, with him, in the knowledge that I wouldn't think twice about moving into Cole's house the way he and Mabel have moved right into my heart. Wholly and without any hesitation.

CHAPTER FORTY-NINE
Ginger

I pace around the house at five minutes to one, making sure everything is ready. I've baked her favorite cookies, straightened up her room, and bought her a new stuffed toy to be Cowey's friend. The little golden retriever sits patiently in the center of her bed.

I'm doing anything to keep moving. Anything to shut my mind off.

Cole branded *my* initial into his skin. I think back to the end of that summer. CeCe left for Seattle the day after Cole came home from Grosvenor. I brought Brock to the ranch for her going-away party. I think back to the way he was with me then, curt and fleeting. I thought it was because he was upset with me for kissing him. I was so mortified after that night. We had no contact. Then he went back to school and, by Christmas, Gemma was pregnant with Mabel. I think about how long he's held all of this in as I straighten up Mabel's bed for the third time.

I hear the car door shut, and I'm in the foyer before the front door is even open, holding the stuffed dog. The moment the door opens, Mabel is in my arms, and a sense of peace washes over me. I squeeze her tight, her new toy wedged between us. I'm so excited to see her I don't even realize it's Gemma delivering her back until I hear her clear her throat.

I stand up.

"Mommy came to have lunch at the cottage and ride back with us," Mabel tells me.

Convenient. Doesn't visit her for more than a few hours all through the week but comes to bring her home. If I had to guess why, I'd say it's so that Gemma can see what's going on here.

My suspicions are confirmed when Mabel finishes chatting animatedly about the week, Sara Ann, and how much she loves her new dog.

"It's until Daddy breaks down and gets you a real one," I tell her as I rustle her hair.

She grins up at me, and my heart swells. It's amazing how much I missed this child over the last eight days. A pang of fear hits my heart when I remind myself I have no idea what the future holds. Cole's words this morning were strong, but once I don't *have* to be here, will everything change between us?

"Making yourself right at home, Ginger?" Gemma asks as Mabel heads to her room to start putting away her things.

I turn to face her, holding in everything I have to not verbally pummel her because Mabel is in the next room, and I won't do this with her here.

"For the summer, yes," I say.

Gemma nods. "That's good. Don't get too attached now. You'll be back to your own side of the tracks soon enough, and Cole will do what Cole seems to do best lately."

I narrow my eyes. I may not be ready to get into it with her, but I certainly won't tolerate her insulting Mabel's father while she's in the house. I move closer, close enough to smell her flowery perfume and the faint hint of weed.

"And that would be?" I ask, low enough that there's no way Mabel could hear from the next room.

She smirks at me.

"You know," she says. "I heard he hasn't made any trips to Lexington in a while. I wonder why?"

She winks and I flex my palms, digging my nails into them to control my anger. I shrug.

"If you knew him, you might know why. But you don't." I lean in a little closer and whisper, "Lucky for him."

"Oh, sweet naïve Ginger," she says with a laugh, tightening her half-up bob in its hair clip.

"This one's gonna sting, babe," she continues before calling, "bye, Mabey-babey! See you one night next week."

"Bye, Mommy," Mabel singsongs from her room.

It says everything to me, but nothing to Gemma, that Mabel doesn't even bother to come out and give her mother a hug goodbye. She's become indifferent to not seeing her.

Gemma turns and heads for the door.

"Oh, and, Gingey, I'll see you tonight. Brent is such a strong supporter of your dad," she says and then she's gone, leaving me stunned. I push her from my mind and focus on Mabel.

I will not let Gemma get to me.

"Mabel!" I call.

Mabel tiptoes out to the living room.

"Is she gone?" she asks.

"Yep," I say back, trying to figure out how she's feeling from the look in her eyes.

"Can we go see Daddy?" she asks. "I really missed him."

I smile. Cole was supposed to sneak out of work to be here when Mabel got home, but there was a massive accident on Highway 6, and he had to go to the scene an hour ago to help out. I assume he'll be back at the office by now. I smile down at her.

"Sure," I say. "That's a great idea. Let's bring him some lunch, and then we'll come back for some swimming."

I reach for her hand, trying to forget the fact that Cole's ex-wife is a heinous bitch, and I'm going to have to spend the evening with her. Right now, Mabes is my priority.

The sheriff's office is bustling when we arrive ten minutes later. I warned Cole we were coming before we left the house. He said he was run off his feet, but wanted us to come anyway.

Cole's office administrator, Bev, is running multiple phone lines, so Mabel and I sit and wait in the reception area of the station. She gives us a friendly smile and waves through the glass wall. I teach her niece tenth-grade English.

ME

We're here.

HUSBAND

Just on the phone, be right out.

I look down at Mabel with a grin. "He's coming."

I tap my fingers on my thigh with one hand while we wait and hold Mabel's hand with the other. The street outside is full of tourists shopping in Laurel Creek's quaint stores, and I watch as a little girl skips down the street carrying a stuffed toy version of the town's mascot, Archibald the Tiger, while holding her dad's hand. I smile at the scene; it reminds me of Cole and Mabel.

I turn my attention back to watch for Cole when something catches my eye on the other side of the glass behind Bev. I realize that what's grabbed my attention is Brent, who seems to be milling about the mail area. Maybe it's just my mistrust of him, but he always seems suspicious to me. He looks around and down the hall toward Cole's office before he starts rifling through the open mail slots that hang on the wall. He pulls a pile out of one slot and brings them down, out of sight, below the half wall. Only, just a moment later, he places the same mail he was holding back where they came from. He looks around again and my spidey senses tingle as I count the mail slots. Two over from the left. Top row.

"Girls!" I hear Cole's voice call out as he comes from the door that leads to the offices.

"Daddy!" Mabel springs up and runs to him, launching herself into his arms and squeezing tight. He showers her with kisses as she giggles, and it gives me the tiniest glimpse into a future where there are children of our own running around. You know, the ones we aren't planning but that I can't stop thinking about. This fatherly side to him, totally separate from who he is as a man, is intoxicating.

Cole asks Mabel all about her week, and I struggle to tear my eyes away from his strong arms, their shape emphasized by his short-sleeved uniform that clings to him in literally all the right places.

"Come with me," he says as I approach. "Let's have some lunch."

He rests his hand on the small of my back as he looks down at Mabes.

"Lunch with my favorite girls. There can't be anything better than that."

Mabel smiles.

"The whole team!" she says happily.

As she snuggles into his neck, Cole's eyes meet mine.

"Damn good team," he says as he squeezes my hand.

"My first dollar." Mabel grins.

"Right. Guess now's a good time to tell you Ginger's been cussing the whole time you've been gone," Cole says.

"I'm going to be rich!" Mabel giggles.

I laugh with her. And, as I follow the two of them down the hall to Cole's office, I'm definitely feeling as rich as can be, almost like everything is perfect.

CHAPTER FIFTY
Cole

I button up my suit jacket and look in the mirror.

"You look like Mr. Stacks," Mabel says to me, mentioning Jamie Foxx's character in *Annie*.

"Why, thank you," I reply, raising an eyebrow. "Ready to get your hair done then, Annie?"

She giggles as she hands me her hair tie. I carefully braid her hair and ask myself if I'm doing the right thing, showing up unannounced at Edward's election results party. Ginger never really answered me this morning when I asked if she wanted us there. But when she got to the Masonic Temple at five-thirty P.M., she had messaged to say she might need to pocket text me all night just to make it through. She'd told me how her mother had started frantically smoothing out her blouse as soon as she'd arrived, and that her father was having her parade around to every person in the press to tell them about how wonderful he was. I knew in that instant that Mabel and I had to make an appearance. Mabes is excited because she gets to stay out past her bedtime. Plus she gets to wear a fancy dress. My mom has promised me she'll pick her up when she gets tired so I can stay until the end of the night.

The Masonic Temple is teeming with people when we arrive. There is security out front, and local media trucks line the street leading up to the ornate building.

Luckily for me, being the county sheriff means you're automatically on most guest lists, which means Mabel and I breeze through the door with ease. I'm stopped by multiple people almost the moment we step through, and Mabel instantly makes a little friend she skips off to play with.

I've been here for more than ten minutes when I finally see Ginger through the crowd. Her hair is in a knot at the nape of her neck, and she's wearing a white blouse tucked into a fucking mouthwatering pencil skirt. Her outfit is finished off with a prim little black cardigan sweater and a string of pearls. This is the neatest I've ever seen her. Usually, she's dressed in all things billowy and wavy but, tonight, she sort of looks like a hot buttoned-up librarian, and everything about that makes me want to mess her right the fuck up.

I watch her. I have no idea for how long because I'm mesmerized by her grace, her beauty, and her ability to always put everyone else first, even her self-centered father. She is smiling and talking to the local news anchor when Mabel spots her and runs over. Ginger looks so surprised to see her but doesn't hesitate to pull her in close and snuggle her tight while she continues her conversation while looking around. I wonder if it's me she's looking for. I can't hear what they're saying, but I hear her laugh at something Mabel says to the reporter. Just the sound of it makes me smile. It might be the thing I love the most about Ginger. Her ability to *always* make me smile no matter the circumstance, no matter where we are, no matter what shit I'm going through.

It's in this second that I swear to Christ the sky opens up and what feels like lightning rains down on me. I'm so fucking in love with this woman. In fact, the word *love* doesn't even cover it. How can you be only in love with someone who feels like they've been a part of you forever? Like you need them to breathe? Ginger has always been in my heart, but it's taken less than two months for her to sink into my bones and every goddamn nook and cranny of my soul.

Just like the sunflowers she's growing along my back fence with Mabel, you can't miss her. Her personality is larger than life and she commands the attention of everyone around her, but hell, she's so beautiful you can't help but want to breathe her in.

Her eyes finally meet mine from across the room and, when they do, she sighs, tips her head to the side, then smiles at me. It's like maybe, just maybe, she feels the same way when she looks at me as I do her.

She holds up a finger to me to signal she'll be over in just a moment as she and Mabel start talking to an older couple. The room that's filling up by the minute explodes with cheer. It's eight P.M. and the polls have just closed.

I'm so transfixed by her that I don't hear Brent Wilson post up beside me. I turn to face him and wonder why he's wearing such a stupid grin on his face. He folds his arms across his chest, waiting for me to speak.

"How's your night, Brent?" I grit out through my teeth. The last thing I want to do is make small talk with this fucker.

"It's going pretty good, Cole. And that *wife* of yours sure looks beautiful, doesn't she?" he asks with the world's slyest smile.

I've gotten so used to thinking of Ginger as my wife that it takes me a moment to realize that he shouldn't know this information. When it registers, I feel all the color drain from my face.

"What the fuck did you just say?"

"I think we both know what I said, sheriff. You know, I could've broken this news earlier while the polls were all still open and given good old Edward Danforth a nice little scandal on election day." He takes a moment before pushing on. "But I figured if I showed up, played the doting supporter, he might back me for sheriff when you get the boot."

I turn to him as rage seeps into my muscles. I flex my fists at my side to keep from hitting him.

I keep my voice low and say, "The fuck are you threatening to ruin my job? You fucking—"

"Don't need to *threaten* to do anything." He waves me off, all cock and no balls. There are so many people and so much chatter around us, I wonder if anyone would notice if I gave him a knock right in the middle of the crowd.

"You ruined *yourself* when you got married drunk at two in the morning in Vegas. And I mean *very* drunk as that beautiful bride of yours hoisted a close-to-empty bottle of champagne over her head like it was the Stanley Cup."

"Did you have me followed?" I ask, not understanding how he knows any of this. Out of the corner of my eye, I spot Gemma all dressed up and talking to the mayor's receptionist like she wasn't out sucking lined-up tequila shots off the Horse and Barrel bar last weekend. I instantly get the feeling she's in on Brent's little scheme.

"Mr. and Mrs. Ashby, a true love story for the ages," he says, framing the words like they're up in lights.

I grind my molars and will myself to remain calm.

"It's not unheard of to get married," I snarl, ready to attack.

"Maybe not. But the way I see it, you have two options here, because, shoot, at first I just thought this was a drunken mistake, but I have a feeling by the way you were just looking at her that you may in fact love that woman—" he says, chuckling, and I've never wanted to pummel someone more.

"Option one," he continues. "Step down as sheriff and offer your strong backing for me to take over. Save her the shame her father will lay on her and her reputation."

"Fuck you. I'll do no such thing," I say to him, my jaw so tense I could pop a tendon.

He ignores me as he opens his mouth to speak again. "Or, come clean with the public and hope for the best," he says. "You know I talk to the public every day to ask the residents of this fine town, the ones who are trying their darnedest to have confidence in you, what it is they hope doesn't happen. Do you know what their answer is nine times out of ten?"

I say nothing, so he presses on.

"Another scandal. Even if it's just the gossipy kind that paints our sheriff as the least bit flighty or irresponsible. Normally this might not be enough to make them lose faith in you. But considering what happened with our predecessor . . ."

Brent grins at me.

"Fuck you," I say. "I won't be blackmailed into anything, you sleazy little—"

He cuts me off before saying, "Oh, you will, or *I'll* be leaking this info to the public, and trust me, I have my proof." He blows out a whistle. "And that proof paints your bride in an unbecoming light. I'm not afraid to drag her and her father's name through the mud, just for the clout."

The fucker shrugs and makes a tsking sound.

"Laurel Creek's sheriff, already the most notorious—how should we put it?—bachelor in town," he says, "goes to Vegas, gets drunk on a whim, and marries the congressman's daughter? Then there's me, the stand-up guy who swooped in and took your ex when you left her to whore around with half of Kentucky. Who *will* they choose?"

He has it all ass-backward, and we both know it. Gemma is the one who slept with every available guy in town after we split up, including this fucker. My mind reels as he continues his folklore.

"Might not be enough to lose the confidence of the fussy townsfolk," he purrs in a low voice, "but it sure wouldn't look good for our stand-up congressman or his daughter. Not to mention I doubt Mabel would want to hear her dad got married to her *nanny*."

That fucking does it. I push Brent in one movement into the corner of the room against the paneling, away from the crowd. His soft body flops backward, and I fist his shirt, ruining his tie in the process.

"If you threaten to hurt my wife or my daughter ever again, I'll fucking gut you like a fish," I seethe.

Brent shifts underneath me, trying desperately to escape my hold, but he's no match for the fury coursing through me. His confidence wanes under my chokehold, but he does his best to appear strong. He holds his chin up, and I smell the whiskey on his breath.

"I *will* send it to the press. Anonymously. I should've won anyway." He spits the words out the way a ten-year-old would. Like a sore loser. Actually, fuck that. A ten-year-old would have more class than this guy.

I chuckle. "Oh, yeah, and why is that, you piece of shit?"

"I've been a cop longer than you, and the only reason you won is because you're an Ashby," he says. "Everyone in this town loved your pa, and now you've got a hockey hero in your family. Not to mention you walk around flashing that shit-eating grin everywhere you go."

"You're wrong, Brent," I retort. "You didn't win because you're fake, impulsive, you drink too much, and the town knows I'm the better man for the job."

I push him back into the wall and let him go as a few bystanders notice us struggling. I turn, refusing to let him think he has any kind of effect on me.

"You have until tomorrow night," he calls out after me. "If you haven't stepped down by then, this will be in the next day's paper along with my proof. Photographic proof."

I flinch. *Fuck.*

I disappear into the crowd, no direction in mind, just knowing I need to get away from Brent before I do something really newsworthy, like pummel him. He's right in some way; it wouldn't bode well for Ginger or her father if the town found out about our drunken mistake. And I would never want Mabel or my family to discover our secret from anyone but me either.

I realize that I'm searching for Ginger as I make my way through the crowd. I head down a hall where I assume she'll be waiting with her father beyond the stage.

I stop before I round the corner, hearing their voices, and freeze, not wanting to eavesdrop, but wanting to make sure she's okay.

"It would have been nice if you had let me get ahead of it, Ginger," I hear Edward say. "I could have prepared something in my speech to welcome the sheriff and his daughter. You know I don't like surprises."

I grit my molars and flex my fists to stop myself from moving. *Let her handle it. She's got this.*

"I didn't know they were coming," Ginger says quietly, and I ask myself why this strong woman who doesn't take shit from anyone takes this crap from her father.

"Well, that is just unacceptable," Edward presses on. "I didn't back him for sheriff, so how do you think it looks—"

"You know what, Dad, for once, I don't *care* how it looks," I hear Ginger say a little louder this time with a laugh. It's enough to stop Edward from speaking. "This is my *life*! Until five minutes ago I was happy, surprised that Cole cared enough to come and support you, support me. It's a pretty romantic gesture, if you ask me. But all *you* can think about is how you can spin it to make yourself look good."

"In my line of work there can be no surprises," Edward offers.

"And heavens, Ginger, don't be so dramatic," he says. "It's not about romance. This is about optics. His past is less than favorable where women are—"

"That's just it, Dad." I hear her voice shaking, and it takes everything in me not to go to her. I have to let her hold her own. She needs this, but more than that, she's got this. She doesn't need me to fight her battles.

"For once, just once, I wish you thought of how I feel, my happiness, what I want instead of how it makes you look. I don't *work* for you, I'm your daughter," she says defiantly.

"What does that mean? Being a part of this family carries a responsibility, Ginger—" Edward tries to reason, but she stops him in his tracks.

"There's no need to rewrite your speech. You'd be best to leave Cole and Mabel out of it. They are here for *me*." She sounds as though she is about to cry. I can hear it in her voice, but I'm so fucking proud of her right now, so I stay where I am.

She starts talking again. "Oh, and by the way, I've been really fucking happy these last couple of months. Cole is incredible, and he's finally made me feel *seen*. In case you're interested, which clearly you aren't. Maybe you shouldn't call me until you are, Dad," she says.

With that, I hear her heels click down the hallway and my chest fills with pride.

That's my girl.

CHAPTER FIFTY-ONE
Ginger

My father has just won the congressional primary.

I stand backstage with both of my parents, waiting for it to be announced. Cole has just returned from walking Mabel out to meet Jo for pickup. I see him before his eyes find mine. He's tense, and I can't understand why. He looked so relaxed earlier. The crowd falls to a hush as my father is announced and takes to the stage, motioning for my mother and me to follow behind him. My mother turns and fluffs my cardigan, then reaches up to smooth my hair before we head out.

"Mama," I hiss, pushing her hand down. "They don't care about how I look. I'm twenty-six years old, not ten."

"Everyone cares how *we* look, bella. We must be at our best. Come now, straighten up," she tells me as I feel Cole's eyes on me from twenty feet away. I turn and look at him; he gives me a nod and mouths, "You've got this."

He gives me a small smile, but I can tell something is off. I want to go to him, to ask him what's wrong, but there's no time because the room explodes in celebration, and we're already moving onto the stage.

My father stands in front of the crowd and turns on the Edward Danforth charm.

He addresses the hall.

"Thank you all so much. We're very humbled and overjoyed by this support and by the trust you put in us. I love representing your voice and hope to continue this path in November. This job isn't easy. My wife goes through a lot: late nights, early mornings, a lot of pacing and problem-solving. To say you can be a congressman and not bring your work home would be a lie. I care so much about this district and the great state of Kentucky. I live and breathe it for all of you. My wife"—he pauses and then turns to me—"and my beautiful daughter put up with more from me than they should most days, but I hope they know how much I appreciate them." He grins at the crowd. "I must remind myself that the special things in life are worth savoring, so I'm going to go off script a little here."

He takes a beat before flashing me a smile then angling his head to look at Cole beyond the curtain at the side of the stage.

"My daughter brought her new boyfriend to us a few weeks ago, and he is here tonight."

Oh, God, he didn't just call Cole my boyfriend on local television.

"The good sheriff Cole Ashby has come out to support us, and we are all so grateful to have him in our corner," he says, looking straight at Cole. "Even his lovely daughter Mabel joined us for a little while. We're all so happy to have you here, sheriff."

The crowd goes crazy with applause.

I look at Cole, and the expression he's wearing isn't one I can place. I glance back at my father, who is clearly oblivious to what he's just done. Using Cole and Mabel to gain votes is the lowest he could go, and I'm seething. So I do what I've never done before when it comes to Edward Danforth; I put myself first and turn and walk right off the stage.

My father's speech continues while I stare at myself in the mirror of the ladies' room. I swipe the tears away from my cheeks. The pressure he has just put on Cole is causing him to shrink backward. I can feel it. I hear the roar of the crowd as the address comes to a close, and I put my best foot forward. I will deal with my father later. But first, I need to find Cole.

It doesn't take long to find him sitting at the bar. I move through the crowd to meet him.

"I'm so sorry," I say when I reach him. "He can't help himself. He has to go for the crowd's love no matter who's in his path. He shouldn't have put us on the spot like that."

I prop myself up on the seat beside Cole, leaning my elbows on the bar. Cole looks over at me, his eyes dark, his jaw tense. I can see how much my father's speech bothered him.

"I talked to him, Cole," I say, "and I plan to again. Using you and your position in this town is off-limits."

The bartender comes over to us, and I order a cocktail.

"And bourbon neat here, please," Cole says as he holds up a finger. She nods at him and gives him the look of appreciation most women do. He doesn't seem to notice.

"I will make him understand—" I start.

"I know you will. I know you talked to him, I heard you and I'm so fucking proud of you, Ginger," he says as he angles his body to me and grabs my knees, pulling me and my stool to him.

He leans in, his hands on my thighs.

"Your father can say anything he wants about me. But if he treats you for one more minute like you need to be managed, I'm going to have a real hard time keeping my mouth shut." His voice is almost a growl as he speaks. He gestures toward the stage. "And yeah, he owes me an apology for that, but I have other things to worry about tonight."

The bartender puts my drink down in front of me and hands Cole his shot. He knocks his back before I can even pick up my glass.

"Nobody should ever make you feel like less than what you are." His eyes bore into mine as he talks. "Which is fucking perfect. Promise me that, no matter what happens with me, with us, you'll always remember that."

He stands up and throws a fifty on the bar. My mouth falls open.

"Cole . . ." I say, "what the hell happened between the time you got here and now; what other things are you worrying about?"

"I have a lot to figure out—" he replies.

I know what he's doing. This is Cole's language for *I'm pushing you away.*

"What happened?" I repeat. This time, my tone is a little firmer.

"Nothing I can't take care of," he says, loosening his tie and running a hand through his thick hair.

I step forward into him and place my hand on his forearm. His whiskey eyes look up to meet mine, and he starts to flex his jaw. His eyes are dark.

"My head's just—fuck, it's a mess right now. I need some time to think," he says to me, pecking me on the cheek. "I'll see you at home when you're all done here."

Then he turns and walks right through the hall and out the front door, making a beeline for where his truck is parked.

Even though I have no clue what just caused this knee-jerk reaction from Cole, I don't wonder *why* it happened. I'm pretty sure I *know.* My father talking about us made everything real to him, and now Cole's doing what Cole does best: searching for an out.

Part of me, the part that realizes I love him with my entire being, begs me to chase him out the door, grab him by the shoulders, and shake him, to tell him I'm not letting him run away, not this time, to remind him that this is *us*.

But the other part? The part that wondered for years why he didn't kiss me back when I could feel that he wanted to? That part tells me to sit my ass down and drink my cocktail. So I do just that; I drop to the stool and pick up my glass.

Cole wants me to stand up for myself, so I will. Ginger Danforth doesn't chase any man, not even Cole Ashby.

CHAPTER FIFTY-TWO
Ginger

TWENTY-SEVEN DAYS TO GO

CECE

Goes on honeymoon, comes home to find out
my brother and my best friend are boyfriend
and girlfriend. 😒

ME

Ugh. I will set my father straight. Cole and
Mabel came to support me, and of course he
turns it into something about him.

CECE

Typical. We all know Edward; any political
association in his back pocket is a good one.
I'm sorry he put you on the spot like that, babe.

ME

I'm used to it at this point. I just never thought
he'd put Cole or Mabel in the middle of it.

CECE

I have to ask . . . Is this thing with Cole serious?

ME

That is exactly what I plan on finding out
tonight. Mabel is going to your mama's, and
Cole and I will be having a long-overdue talk.

CECE

I know, I'm heading there after work. I'm having
dinner there and watching movies with them.
It's a girls' night.

CECE

Side note, I'm sure my mama knows about you
two. She called me last night during your
father's speech on the local news. Her words,
and I quote, were: "I always knew those two
would end up together."

I breathe out a sigh and roll onto my back, the early morning
light seeping through my blinds.

ME

I'm scared, and the truth is, we kind of stayed
closer than we let on after you went to Seattle.
There's a lot of history between us and I don't
want to ruin that.

I have no idea why I'm telling CeCe this other than the fact
I'm tired of not being honest with everyone, myself and Cole
included.

CECE

I know.

ME

How? Why didn't you say anything?

CECE

> Cole got a little drunk two Christmases ago. It was when my dad was at his worst and he told me you two were friends, and that you helped him through everything with Gemma. I never said anything because I knew you'd tell me when you were ready. No pressure, but whenever that is, I'm always here. Just leave out the mushy details.

I grin.

ME

> Thank you.

CECE

> For what?

ME

> For constantly being there but never judging.

CECE

> Always, babe. Men come and go but you're my kindred spirit. Not Angels for life. And if you need to talk later, I'll be at the big house.

I take a deep breath and set my phone on my bedside table. I'm desperately trying not to read too much into Cole's cryptic attitude last night and the fact that, for the first night in almost two months, he never came to my bed. When I got home, which was not long after him, he was either in with Mabel or in his own room. I couldn't tell because both doors were shut.

As I get up, the face he made when my father spoke his name in his speech keeps playing in my mind. I know, no matter what Cole's going to do, I have to do what he said: get out in front of it and not let anyone fuck with me, even him. Enough is enough.

I put on my robe and make my way to the kitchen. When I get there, Cole is already at the table. Mabel is in the living room eating a muffin and watching TV.

"Morning," I say, as if him not coming to my bed last night doesn't bother me.

He looks up at me. That same pained expression from last night lines his face.

Mabel calls out to me that it's pruning day and time to pull the last of our raspberries. We were planning to make jam with our little harvest. I grab a mug down so I can pour myself a coffee and mentally tell myself to put on my big-girl pants. I'm just about to lay down the law and tell Cole we need to talk tonight, but when I go to turn around, he's already there.

His arms encircle me as he grips the counter at my sides. I look up at him, caged in, breathing in his delicious scent. He takes my mug, sets it down, and looks into my eyes like he has so much to say but can't bring himself to do it with Mabel in the house. His knuckles graze my cheek before he slides the pads of his warm fingers into my hair and his thumb traces the line of my cheekbone lazily, before he tips his forehead down to meet mine.

"Favor," he says.

"You want to tell me what's going on, Cole?" I say as I look up at him, a million questions in my eyes.

He must sense my unease, because he slides his hands down my arms and holds my hands, tight. He speaks in a hurried whisper, so Mabel doesn't hear.

"I made a mistake with you, with us, with all of this," he says. "I fucked up. This is all my fault."

He waves toward Mabel in the living room, and I recoil at his words. A *mistake*?

"And last night it . . . came to a head. I need you to let me sort this out. I need some time. That's my favor."

The words tumble out of him, and I gulp. Panic rises up my throat. I knew this would happen. I knew things would get real, and he would run—

"Daddy, I need more juice, please!" Mabel calls.

"Coming, buddy," he says, his eyes still on mine. Cole drops his lips to my cheek, kissing me like he would a friend.

"Look, I'm on no sleep and I have a lot of shit to sort out today." He's talking to me but glancing at the clock on the wall. There is hesitation in his every action this morning, just as there was last night, even in the way he moves to brush the hair off my forehead and kiss me there.

"I've got to go," he says, squeezing my hand, and I feel his angst in his touch.

I nod, not knowing what to say, and discovering that all my nerve to make him tell me exactly what's going on has somehow gone out the window. He gives me one last look before grabbing Mabel's juice and taking it to her. And then he's gone.

I hear the door close behind him and I lean on the counter, placing my head in my hands. Gemma's words play through my mind. But it's not just Gemma's words that I remember, it's CeCe's and Liv's too.

Could I have been completely, and utterly, wrong about him? Panic rises in my gut. I should've thought this through more. But the way I felt, the way we felt together. It was perfect.

I spin around and look out the back window to the pool beyond, contemplating how I let this happen. How I let myself fall madly, crazy, insanely in love with Cole Ashby. All I can do is hope I'm wrong about what's going on in his head, because if I'm not, I have no idea how I'm getting out of this with my heart intact.

"I'm still hungry, can I have another muffin?" Mabel says, startling me as she stands in the doorway.

I turn to her and smile. "You're hungry this morning."

"I had a tummy ache last night. Daddy stayed with me," she explains.

Oh.

"Is your tummy all better now?" I ask.

"Yes. Sometimes it hurts when I'm nervous," she says, looking down, twiddling her fingers.

"Do you want to talk about why you're nervous?" I ask, pulling another blueberry muffin from the package from Spicer's Sweets. She looks up at me, her amber eyes full of honesty, and way too much maturity.

"I like when you're here and . . ." she starts and then looks at the backyard. "Our tomatoes are so big . . ."

Her bottom lip starts to quiver. *My heart.*

I immediately set down the muffin in my hand and go to her, putting my arms around her. My heart shatters into a million pieces, and I squeeze her tight.

"Listen, sweet girl, me and you?" I say, pushing the hair off her forehead to look at her properly. "We've become good friends, haven't we?"

She nods and winds her little fingers in my hair like she did the night we came back from the cottage. It's a comfort thing, I'm sure.

"You're my best girl, and no matter what happens when those tomatoes are ready to be picked, you're still going to see me all the time, okay?" I tell her with a sense of certainty I'm not sure I feel. "Because if I didn't see you, I'd miss you way too much."

I tweak her chin, and she nods and smiles up at me.

"Okay. Will you still see Daddy?" she asks. "Will you miss him too?"

"Of course I will," I tell her, squeezing her again. "Now let's eat, we've gotta fight those thorny bushes and make some jam."

I tickle her and she giggles, knowing how hard it is to pick all those berries without getting pricked by the thorns.

We get ourselves dressed, and I remind Mabel to put on pants to avoid getting poked. I grab our clippers, tossing them with gloves for both of us into picking baskets, and we head out into the yard.

The sun is already warm, and there is a light August breeze as we move through Cole's yard. Mabel skips ahead of me and picks a few wildflowers that have seeded from our garden into the grass and pops them into her basket for pressing. Two bunnies munch on clover in the corner of the yard and don't move when we pass them, even though Mabel does her best tiptoeing so as not to scare them. I smile at her; she's so carefree, so happy. I hope this is the way she'll always be. Worry knots in my stomach about leaving her and heading back to my own place at the end of the month. How am I supposed to pretend I haven't fallen in love with her too?

Mabel is animated with chatter as we drive to the ranch, her morning nerves long forgotten and, when we pull down the driveway to Silver Pines, I breathe out a sigh of relief the way I do every time I come here. In a lot of ways, this ranch was like my home when I was younger. Unlike my own house, it was a place of no judgment. A place where parents just loved their kids. A lot of the time it was like the entire place ran on laughter and inappropriate humor.

I look at Mabel in the rearview mirror. She's watching the horses out of her window, and I smile at the beautiful scene that surrounds us. Ivy and Wade are sitting at a picnic table near Silver Pines' largest breaking pen, eating their lunch. The thick brush of trees sway in the distance, and just beyond them, I see Rowan McCoy working with Wade's derby horse, Angel's Wings. Ivy is so pregnant she looks like she might burst any moment as she kicks her sandals off and runs her feet through the cool grass. I'm guessing she's uncomfortable in the late summer heat, but even so, she's beautiful and manages a little smile and wave to us as we drive by them the extra few hundred feet to the big house.

"There's my girl," Jo calls, coming into the foyer in shorts and an old Shania T-shirt of CeCe's. Her long blondish-gray hair is in a big bun tied up with a scarf. Mabel hands her a jar of our jam and Jo takes it like it's the most precious gift she's ever received. She looks down at the label stuck on the top: Daddy's Girls Jam and the year. Mabel wrote everything herself.

Jo's eyes meet mine questioningly, but she says nothing.

"I can't wait to eat it, daddy's girls! Let's pop it open and put it on some biscuits," she exclaims, her eyes moving back to Mabel.

What am I doing?

My phone vibrates in my pocket, and I pull it out.

IVY

Saw the news. Just letting you know my house is a safe space as a nonrelated member of the Ashby clan, and I've always got chocolate.

I laugh before replying.

ME

I just might take you up on that soon.

IVY

> Anytime, girl. I'll be here folding little clothes and waiting for this baby to stop kicking me in the ribs.

I smile and put my phone in my pocket, hating how much I wished that it was Cole texting me, cracking some joke or sending a dirty message. Anything that will tell me everything is fine between us.

"Let's put these snacks together, and I've got all your bracelet-making stuff out back, darlin'," Jo says to Mabel.

"Will you make a bracelet with me?" Mabel asks, looking up at me hopefully. I tuck a rogue strand of hair behind her ear, feeling the need to be close to her too right now, the same way she seems to feel about me.

"I don't know how."

"I'll show you." She smiles and takes my hand, leading me into the yard.

"Constantly looking at your phone isn't going to make that call come any faster," Jo says, nodding toward me a little while later as I make my way through my bracelet, trying my best to copy Mabel while simultaneously looking to see if Cole has messaged me. I glance down to read my screen.

WARDEN

> Hearing how upset you were last night showed me what I've been doing wrong, Ginger. I let my work consume me and put it before you and your mother. I have no excuse other than the

pressure of this job is unfathomable to anyone on the outside.

WARDEN

Why have you never told me how you feel?

WARDEN

We need to talk, when you have time. Please call me.

WARDEN

And I was wrong to judge your sheriff. I can see he really cares about you.

That gets my attention.

WARDEN

I only want what's best for you. I am a proud man, but I can admit when I'm wrong.

ME

Who is this really?

I smile and experience a flicker of hope that he might have actually listened to me last night. Finally.

WARDEN

Just a dad who isn't perfect.

WARDEN

Can we have lunch next week? Just the two of us?

ME

Of course.

I breathe out a sigh as I turn my focus back to my bracelet. My dad's apology doesn't change everything between us, but it's a start.

I reflect on the way my father has tried to control every choice I've ever made, every friend I've ever had; the way he talks to everyone around him, his staff, even my mother sometimes, as if they're almost beneath him. It's how he treats me too, the only difference being that he calls me "darling" or "bella" when he pushes me toward all the places and people in my world that are right for him but not for me.

Cole encouraging me to say how I feel has made me grow more powerful. He's pushed me to take my place, wherever that is, and however it may be received by those around me, including Edward Danforth.

With Cole and Mabel in the most unlikely situation this summer, I've felt needed, trusted, wanted for exactly who I am, and honestly? It's the closest thing to true love I've ever felt.

Our arrangement is up in a few weeks, but I don't want to leave. Like anything else I've ever wanted, I know I have to take the bull by the horns and tell him how I feel. If we're going to crash and burn, at least I'll know I did my best to give us a real shot.

"See, you wrap this piece over the top of these other two strands," Mabel says beside me, pulling me from my thoughts and directing me how to make the simplest bracelet in her kit.

"I only have one other strand," I say, holding my wonky bracelet up in defeat. Jo and Mabel laugh.

"No, darlin'," Jo says, eyeing what I'm doing. She scoots over beside me, reaching down to my bracelet and comparing it to hers.

"Here's your problem," she says, her eyes meeting mine before she takes my bracelet into her own hands. "See, you've got this one little strand here and two here, you need to weave them through the loom and into each other."

She crosses the one through the other two, repeating the action a few times before I get the hang of it. Mabel munches happily on our delicious, still slightly warm jam on toasted homestyle biscuits.

"You were missing a step. Leaving your one lonely little strand out there on its own," Jo says, taking a bite of her own biscuit. "You can't make anything strong like that, honey. Three strands together make an unbreakable cord, much better than one can make on its own."

She winks and smiles at me. Suddenly, I feel like I'm no longer taking bracelet advice. Maybe CeCe is right; maybe this woman really does know everything.

"Makes perfect sense," I say.

"What do we have here?" Wade calls as he makes his way out the patio door.

"Uncle Wade! Try my jam!" Mabel squeals, picking up a jam-covered biscuit and handing it to him. He eyes up the label before taking a bite.

"Who is the Daddy's Girls Jam company?" he asks as he chews. "I'd like to invest."

Mabel giggles.

"Me and Ginger and Daddy. That's our team."

"Sounds like a pretty solid team," Wade says with a small smile.

Jo pats my shoulder then scoots back to the other side of the picnic table.

"I thought so too. And you know, sometimes all a team needs to be the very best at something is a leader to steer them in the right direction," Jo says, though she doesn't look at me this time. She doesn't need to. I understand every word. I smile and weave myself a perfect bracelet as Mabel shows Wade how to make one for himself.

"I'll be the leader," Mabel says as she concentrates on her bracelet.

"Then you'll be the best team there is," Wade says, his eyes on me. I flash a grin at him from across the table.

Suddenly, just a little sun, some homemade jam, and a bracelet-making session affirms everything I already knew.

I am not a teenager anymore, and I want this life with Cole and Mabel. As scary as having this conversation with Cole and risking changing *us* forever is, I'm going to do it, whether Cole's ready or not. Because I'll be ready enough for both of us.

CHAPTER FIFTY-THREE
Cole

"Why is your tummy sore, baby? What's bothering you?" I ask as I lie down beside Mabes and tuck her in, Cowey and her newest stuffed dog from Ginger, Goldie, between us.

I'd only been home long enough to have a quick shower and see my mom off before Mabel woke up and said she had a stomachache, which usually means something is bothering her.

Tired as I was, and desperate for a few hours to think over everything that happened tonight, she always comes first.

"I think Ginger will be lonely if she has to go to her old home," she says, twisting her fingers in Cowey's fur.

"Well, that's not for a little while," I say, trying to make it sound like it's in the way far-off future even though it's mere days, or even less, away now. I don't want her to leave, but the last thing I want to do is give her an ultimatum. I'd be asking her to commit to a life with Mabes and me, which is huge for someone who has their whole future, and possible future family, before them.

"She lived by herself before she came here for the summer," I say to Mabel. "And I'm sure she'll come visit."

"But that was before she was used to us," Mabel croaks out. "Can she stay while I go to school?"

I sigh and brush her bangs back.

"You like Ginger, don't you? It's nice to have her around, especially when you miss Mommy?" I say.

Mabel shrugs and looks down at her fingers.

"Sometimes I miss Mommy," she answers honestly. "But I will miss Ginger all the time. She always plays with me, and she smells nice."

I grin. "She does smell nice, doesn't she?"

"And she gives me hugs like you do. Plus she cooks yummy food," Mabel continues sleepily.

"She does do all those things," I reply.

"Rachel's daddy got married, and now she has a new mommy." She mentions her little friend from school. "You could get married to Ginger, and then she'd be my new mommy."

She trails off then, before turning her eyes up to mine in the dark.

"I like Ginger on our team all the time," she whispers, and my heart sinks. "But you're the best daddy." She says this with a yawn. She's already an incredible caregiver and would never want to hurt my feelings.

"You're the best daughter; and you want to know a secret, little one? I like Ginger on our team too," I tell her, taking her hand as she closes her eyes.

I snap out of my daydream of last night's chat with Mabel when my in-office phone buzzes. I pick it up.

"You got some news for me, Bev?" I say into it.

"You have space at town hall for seven. You want to tell me what's going on, boss?" she asks. I tap the pads of my fingers on my desk.

"Not just yet, Bev, soon. And thanks," I reply.

"'Course," she says before hanging up.

I stand and start to pace again. I've been doing this for most of the day. Like the true pussy he is, Brent called in sick this morning, clearly not wanting to face me.

I have spent hours setting everything in motion for later. I have the use of town hall now if I need it, and the local news is on standby for a seven o'clock press conference. I've racked my brain, I've retraced my steps, trying to remember every place Ginger and I were that night in Vegas, but I still can't figure out how Brent discovered our marriage, unless he did in fact have me followed. He says he has proof. I'd like to believe he's full of shit but, in my profession, I can tell when someone is lying, and I know he's not.

If it was only about me, I'd tell Brent to go fuck himself. But it's not. I have Mabes and Ginger to think about, as well as Ginger's family. Plus my own. If I step down, Ginger and her father won't be talked about or dragged through the local news. It'll be gossip at best. But I feel so protective of her, I would never want anyone saying anything less than noble about her. And as for Mabel, chances are she's too young and wouldn't hear about this, but it's possible. Parents gossip in front of their kids sometimes. I would never want her to think her father is just as unreliable as her mother, and maybe, if I step down and give Brent what he wants, I can keep my little family just as it is, give Mabes everything she deserves, and keep the scandal for Ginger at bay.

Just when I think I have my mind made up, my phone buzzes again.

"Ginger is here," Bev says through the speaker. Of course she is. She knows something is going on, and if I know Ginger, she's about to come in here and read me the riot act about keeping anything from her.

Thirty seconds later, my door swings open, and Ginger is standing there, a hand on her hip, the sass and determination I love with everything in my fucking soul pulsing through her.

"Cole Weston Ashby. I am not leaving this office until you

tell me what the hell is going on," she announces before slamming the door behind her and stalking over to the other side of my desk. She's wearing a little pair of flimsy linen shorts and an off-the-shoulder shirt. Her hair flows in loose waves down her back. She's the complete opposite of how she looked last night and exactly how I love her: wild, fresh-faced, and free.

"Now, you once told me that we're closer than best friends close." She makes her way over to my side of the desk, leans back, and presses her palms against the surface. The tiniest sliver of skin peeks out from under her cropped tee, just in line with my face. My cock twitches at the sight.

"We're you and me close. Remember?" she says, raising an eyebrow and gesturing between us. "And as Mabel reminded me this morning, we're a team, whether you want to admit it or not."

I lean back in my chair and take her in. She's fucking sensational when she goes after something she wants.

She's in full flow now as she continues her speech.

"I'd say two people that close wouldn't have secrets, so it's about time you cut the shit and tell me what's going on, don't you think?"

Ginger's breath is heavy, and her eyes are full of fire, but under all of that is the tiniest flicker of uncertainty, and I'm not having it. I stand to wrap my arms around her, crushing my lips to hers, leaving her breathless when I drop to my knees in front of her. I yank her loose shorts aside and pull one leg up to rest on my shoulder. I push one finger in, and her tight pussy clenches around me.

"You won't shut me out, Cole," Ginger says as her head tips back.

She didn't expect me, so she isn't ready yet, but it won't take long to get her there. I watch her spread her legs wider without questioning my actions. That trust is like a spear to my heart. Her eyes flutter closed when my tongue finds her with one slow, languid lick. She squirms, and her fingers find my hair. She pulls my face back.

"You *won't* shut me out, Cole," she repeats. "Everything or nothing."

I smirk. I like bossy Ginger.

"I will tell you anything you want to know but, first, I'm going to bury my face between these thighs, Vixen, because I missed you last night and I'm hungry as fuck," I tell her as I suck her clit into my mouth, and she gives in, either satisfied with my answer or wanting my tongue too much to argue.

Whichever one gets her pussy in my mouth faster will do.

"Can't have you hungry, I guess . . ." She trails off in a moan.

I glance up from between her thighs and see her eyes have fallen closed again. She's a goner. Instantly for me. *Me.*

I lift her other leg and plant it firmly on my shoulder so she is straddling my face. My fingers dig into her flesh, hard, holding her in place while I make a fucking meal of the sweetest pussy I've ever tasted. I start slowly, lightly tracing over each side of her before finally reaching her center. By the time I'm there, she's panting and writhing against my lips. She moves shamelessly against me, fisting my uniform shirt, searching for her undoing.

I don't give it to her. I take my time, tasting her arousal, sensing the tension that builds within her. I slide a hand down and crook one finger inside her, then two. She's soaked, no friction now.

She grips my hair tighter and moans softly; her body quivers and begs me for more.

"Cole . . . please," she chants. "Please let me come."

"My polite little vixen," I murmur, looking up to see her watching me, her eyes glassy and hooded. I smirk against her pussy and offer her some pressure against her clit with my teeth. She jolts around me.

"You come in here so bossy and controlling. Filled with fire. Do you know how incredible you are?" I ask her.

"Yes," she agrees, and I smile into her.

"Good girl," I whisper, flicking my tongue against her clit to reward her honesty.

"Fuck," she whimpers.

I'm pretty sure she'd agree with anything I say right now if I let her come, but at least she acknowledged that she is incredible. I'll take it as a win.

I push my fingers into her expertly and give her my tongue, taking her all in, giving her what she needs. She cries out, clamping her own hand over her mouth so no deputies hear her as they pass down the hall.

Her hands twist in my hair as she gives in and pants my name, probably louder than she should as she quickly comes apart, but I don't give a fuck. My door is self-locking, and something about anyone knowing she's mine gets me off. After years of pretending I didn't want her with every fiber of my being, the idea of not giving a fuck is *very* enticing.

"Not fair," she whimpers as her legs shake. "How am I supposed to be quiet through that?"

When she turns boneless, I stand, hiking her even closer with one arm and unbuckling my pants just enough to free my rock-solid cock with the other.

I sheath myself in the only pussy I'll ever want as her legs wrap around me.

"Fuck, Ginger . . . you're a fucking dream on my office desk with my cock buried in your tight little cunt." I groan. My core tightens as I buck my hips, driving into her again.

It's so effortless. She's so wet, so fucking *tight*.

"Fuck, Cole," she whines. Her eyes open; her pupils are dilated and they shine at me as she takes her bottom lip between her teeth. She readies to come again, and her eyes start to roll back.

"Uh-uh, I want those pretty eyes," I tell her. My hand palms her throat and gives it a squeeze, pulling her back to me.

Ginger's eyes meet mine. There's fire in them.

"Harder, Cole. More," she whimpers.

Her gaze burns into my soul, and I lose it. I'm uncontrollable.

The deep and unrelenting sound of our skin slapping together fills the room. There's nothing soft or sweet about this, but it's what we both need. Those loving, soft moments come when her eyes meet mine across a full room. It's the feel of her skin in the night when I turn over to touch her, the brush of her feet against mine as we lounge on the couch. It's the years of just being there for each other.

But this? This is cathartic and raw. It's perfectly us.

"Fuck, I love you. I have loved you for so goddamn long," I tell her without thought as I fuck into her perfect pussy on my desk. *My* perfect pussy. Her nails digging into my skin and her silent cries of pleasure tell me that the tight wrap of my hand around the slender column of her throat is what she craves. Just as it is for me, this moment is exactly what she needs.

My lips come down on hers, and everything turns hazy around us as I fuck her.

"I love you, Cole. You're the only man I've ever loved," she says between kisses, and I'm free-falling, spilling into her hard and fast. I growl her name into her lips as my cock empties, fighting to stay in the moment as I come, because we're so in sync, so perfect, and, right now, I know there isn't a hurdle I can't overcome with her by my side. My movements become sloppy and unorchestrated as my cock jerks inside her. Her breathing slows as she pulls my face down to kiss me once more.

When we're spent, I lean back, collapsing in my chair. She falls with me, right into my lap.

"Everything or nothing equals you taking me like a cave-man on your desk?" she asks with a giggle.

"Yes, because I fucking can't resist you," I say as I stroke her hair. She nuzzles her head in the space between my collar-bone and my jaw.

"You *love* me," she says, and I feel her smug smirk against my bare skin.

"I do." Goddamn, it feels good to say it out loud. Did I picture myself balls deep inside of her when I thought about the moment I'd tell her I loved her? Definitely not.

But I'll give her as many soft, romantic moments as she needs. I'll spend the rest of my life giving her those, but *that* was something more. Something animalistic I had no hope of controlling.

I kiss her head.

"I've wanted to tell you this for weeks," I say. "I don't want you to leave at the end of the summer, Ginger, I want you to stay, but I can't *ask* you to stay. Us together . . . with Mabes. This is a lot for you . . ."

She tilts her head up to me, her eyes questioning.

So I continue. "Taking on the role of being a wife and a partner is one thing, but a stepmother? A role model for a child who isn't yours? That's a totally different—"

She silences me with a kiss.

"Stop right there, Mr. Ashby," she says. "We can talk about the semantics later. But if you think for one second I went into this lightly, not realizing that you and Mabel were a package deal? You're dead wrong. I love everything about that little girl. And besides, we're a team. Remember?" She grins. "You don't *have* to ask me. I volunteer. I know exactly what it means to love you, Cole. I think on some level I've always loved you. And I want it *all*. Every last piece. Especially Mabel."

I kiss her lips, not wanting to come up for air, because I've never felt happiness like this before. I never thought it was possible. It's overwhelming. This isn't just my happiness, it's Mabel's too. Because she deserves someone like Ginger in her life. I let my mouth stake its claim on my wife, reveling in my newfound wholeness, until a cold shiver runs the length of my spine as I remember why she's here today.

I sigh as I plant a peck on her forehead.

"You were right to come here today. We do need to talk about something," I say to her.

"I gathered," she replies, rising, seemingly unconcerned as she pulls her shirt back over her head while I disappear into my private bathroom for a cloth to clean her up.

"Brent Wilson found me last night at your father's reception," I tell her as I wipe her down. Her eyes meet mine as if to ask me why that matters.

"He knows about us. He called you my wife," I say.

Just that word has more meaning now that I've told her how I really feel about her. Our marriage no longer feels temporary. She's my wife and, as crazy as it seems after only a couple of months, that's how it's going to stay. Even if she doesn't know it yet.

Her mouth falls slack for all of ten seconds, and then her mind is working.

"How?" she asks.

"I don't know, but he's demanding I step down as sheriff or tell the public. I'm wracking my brain trying to come up with an option three where I don't have to do either," I admit.

I tell her all the details I can and, by the time she's dressed and we're sitting across from each other at the desk, my beautiful spitfire of a wife is wearing an emotion I rarely see: anger.

"I think he had me followed," I tell her. "There's no other way. There's no documentation of this marriage."

A thought occurs to me as I talk. "Other than the certificate, which should be here anytime. I remember they said it would take eight to ten weeks, but I haven't seen it yet—"

Ginger's eyes move to mine, and she holds her first finger up to stop me from speaking.

"This marriage certificate, Cole. Did you have it sent here, to your office?" she asks.

I think for a moment. A memory flashes through my mind of doing just that the moment she asks the question. Because in my half-drunken stupor I remember thinking it would be better to have it come to the office instead of home.

"Yes, I didn't want to risk Mabes seeing it," I tell her. She looks thoughtful. "What is it, Ginger?" I ask.

"It may be nothing," she says, chewing her bottom lip. "But what mailbox is yours?"

"Second one in. Abbott's is before mine," I answer her, mentioning a deputy.

"Goddammit," Ginger mutters under her breath. "He took it."

"What?" I ask.

Her eyes flit to mine. "I saw him the other day, when I brought Mabes down for lunch. I don't know why, but I remember thinking he looked . . . suspicious." She keeps talking as she stands and starts to pace. "He pulled mail out of that slot, and I couldn't see if he took anything. But it was odd because, after just a few moments, he put the stack of envelopes back and left."

"Motherfucker," I breathe out.

Ginger stops pacing and looks at me to say, "He's been stealing your mail, Cole. He has our marriage certificate."

I scrub my jaw and lean back in my chair. She puts her hands on her hips.

"Teamwork, baby." She smirks. "If you can prove it, there's your option three."

I stand and look out the window, gathering my thoughts.

"You're a genius, by the way," I tell her. "And, in case I haven't made it clear to you, you're *my* genius."

She giggles as I grab my ID badge off my desk.

"Where are you going?" she asks.

"To get my proof," I say.

I go to call over my shoulder as I turn to leave but, instead, I stop and walk back to kiss her again.

"I love you. Thank you for being in my corner," I say.

"I love you too, Cole, and I'll always be in your corner," she whispers back, filling me with every bit of encouragement I need to nail this fucker to the wall.

As I blast through my office door and down the hall, I make sure to tell Bev to put a hold on that press conference.

CHAPTER FIFTY-FOUR
Cole

"What are you doing here, Cole?" Gemma asks, arms folded across her chest. The front door sits partially open. "I'm in the middle of making dinner."

She flips her hair over her shoulder. She's nervous, but I don't want her. I want her slimy boyfriend.

"Where's Brent?" I say, my jaw set, my tone easy. I'm nothing but calm, and she can sense it. It's making her uneasy. *Good.*

"He's . . . sick," she says, her voice faltering.

"Uh huh," I say as I push the door open and breeze through it. "This will only take a second," I assure her.

I stalk through the house I know well, the house I lived in miserably for four years. When I hear the sound of eighties rock coming from the backyard, I follow it.

Sure as shit, not looking the least bit sick, there is Brent drinking a beer and working on a dilapidated dirt bike in the backyard.

"Feeling better?" I ask.

He smirks, snide motherfucker.

"Hey, sheriff. Or should I say soon-to-be deputy?" he asks. "I will be feeling much better after your resignation letter is handed in. I'm guessing that'll be by the end of the day?"

He points toward a cooler.

"Beer?" he asks, sipping his.

"Nah." I grin and take a seat on one of the chairs in the dusty patio set. The table is littered with flyers and a few beer caps.

"Don't care much for cheap beer in the middle of the afternoon," I tell him, extending my arms behind my head. I'm too relaxed, and he's hating it, but he does his best to fake his confidence.

"Why are you here?" he says slowly.

"Thought you'd never ask," I reply with a wide smile. "You really had me over a barrel all night and all day today. That is until my *wife* told me that, the other day, while she was waiting to bring me lunch, she noticed you rifling through the mailboxes."

"So?" he says, folding his arms over his chest. "I'm allowed to get my mail. That's not a crime."

I look down. "That's true but the funny thing is that she said you were picking up mail from box two, which is my box." I pause for a beat but don't wait long enough for Brent to chime in. "And stealing my mail. Now that is a crime."

He gulps down a good portion of his beer. His plan is foiled, and he knows it. But he hasn't even heard the best part yet.

I stand and start to wander their overgrown yard.

"So then I got to thinking. What if those cameras I installed last month to catch the kids that keep spray-painting the side of the building could *also* record someone rifling through my mail through the side window?" I'm in full flow now, and Brent is silent. "And the fucking craziest thing is, it can. Technology is so good these days, it even picked up my name on the envelope."

I toss a thumb drive onto the table and stalk toward him, gripping him by the collar.

I keep my voice low as I look straight into his eyes. "Every day, right around the same time, there you are, rummaging through my mail when you think no one is looking, stuffing anything you think might be interesting into your pockets just so you can try to push me out of the job I earned, the job *I'm* good at."

I let him go, giving him a little shove, and he slumps down into the chair below him. I reach into my pocket and toss another thumb drive on the table. I should've known this fucking guy was into nothing good when he was so adamant about monitoring me.

"Funny thing about cameras is they not only catch when you steal mail, they catch everything," I say, nodding toward the last drive. "You remember Holly Shaw, the nineteen-year-old we've brought in more than once for possession? Meth, I believe?"

All the color drains from Brent's already pale face as I continue.

"She was brought in last week, after being picked up by Deputy Davis for soliciting at the Husk." I mention the local truck stop off the highway notorious for drug activity.

Brent is a statue as I plow on. "You can have a look if you want to confirm, but I'm pretty sure this is her with you, early the next morning, right before you released her, no charges filed. Doesn't show you doing anything corrupt per se, but it does show her getting up off her knees and leaving you to do your fucking pants up in the corner of the hallway."

I shake my head. "Guess you gotta know your camera angles, you sick fuck."

It's a video I can't unsee. I stumbled across it while looking for proof that Brent was stealing my mail. It shows Brent's back and bare ass at four A.M., him moving out of the way to make way for Holly to stand and straighten herself out.

"Sexual favors for no charges laid? Seems like something the town might care about a lot more than my marriage," I say. "And now it makes a lot of sense why you're so hell-bent on proving I'm doing something wrong. To cover up your own wrongdoings."

Brent chucks his beer bottle across the patio. It shatters everywhere, and Gemma comes to the door.

"S-so what are you gonna do about it?" His voice booms, waiting for his fate. He's all bark and no bite. What's meant to intimidate me, I just find funny. I rub my jaw as I think.

"*You* are going to resign and get the fuck out of here. I can't stand dirty cops like you. You give us all a bad fucking name. You will never work in law again, and if I find you anywhere near the office, Ginger, or Mabel, so help me God."

He snatches up the thumb drives and puts them in his pocket. I have two other copies if he tries to pull anything. Bev made sure of that.

"You . . . you're gonna tell them anyway. You can't make me leave town," he barks.

I move closer to him and flex my fists to keep calm.

"Brent, you have no idea what I'm capable of when it comes to the well-being of my wife or my daughter," I say.

He shrinks with my words a little more, knowing I mean them. He storms past me into the house, and I follow behind.

"I'll be making the announcement that you've left our district first thing in the morning. Feel free to go somewhere else. If another county is stupid enough to hire you, you're their problem," I lie. There's not a shot he's working as a cop anywhere again. I'll see to that. But I need something from him first.

"I'll expect all copies of my property back before you go. You can set up a time to clear out your office, supervised. Aside from that, I don't want to see you again," I say from behind him.

It's then that Gemma comes storming out of the kitchen, cutting Brent off from leaving.

"You son of a bitch," she shrieks at him. "You weren't supposed to do anything that would hurt Mabel. You said you would get him out *fairly*. This isn't fair."

She pushes at his chest, and he swats at her hands to move past her.

"She never would've known. And you're the one that told me I'd make a good sheriff," he says, before blasting through the front door, leaving us with "Fucking shithole town."

I breathe a slight sigh of relief when I hear his Bronco start up. I look down at Gemma, who is crying, or doing a good job of pretending to. At least she doesn't appear to have been in on the blackmail plan, although I'm pretty sure she was involved in the rest of it. It's not about her fear of being a shitty mother. She just hates that the town knows she's one. When it comes to Gemma, it's always about winning. Nothing more. Nothing less.

"I didn't know, Cole, I swear. I had no idea that he would try to blackmail you or involve Mabel finding out—" she says through her tears.

I turn to her.

"I don't give a shit about your domestic issues, Gemma, or what you did or didn't know," I say, my voiced raised but steady. "But Mabel is going to have some new structure in her life now, and that fucking guy, or any guy like him, better *not* come anywhere near my daughter." I point at the space Brent just left moments before.

"I'm done babysitting you where Mabel is concerned," I say, more calmly now. "I won't keep you from seeing her, but I'm giving you one last chance. If you don't start showing up to your afternoon visits every week, consistently, and really put some effort in, or if I find out you say one negative thing about Ginger to her, I'll be filing to restructure," I tell her.

"I'm just . . . not . . . I've never been good at being a mama, Cole," she says, fiddling with a string on her shirt.

I realize it's probably the most honest thing she's ever said to me. But it's not enough and she's not my problem.

"You *choose* not to be a good mama, Gemma. There's a difference between can't and won't." I pat her shoulder as I say, "It's up to you how you move forward now. Mabel is the priorty or you're done."

I push her screen door open and breeze through it, feeling more free than I have in, well, maybe ever.

ME

You can cancel that press conference.

BEV

On it, boss. You better find a way to thank that lovely wife of yours.

Oh, I'm going to. Every day. For the rest of my life.

CHAPTER FIFTY-FIVE
Ginger

FOURTEEN DAYS TO GO

"I think we can dunk Daddy if we try," I say to Mabel quietly, two weeks after my father's election. We're deep in a game of Marco Polo. It's Saturday, Cole has taken the day off, and Mabel is going to Ernie and Trudy's tonight for her last sleepover before school starts with the promise from Gemma that she will be coming to dinner there.

Cole and I are heading to the big house after Mabel leaves to let Cole's whole family in on our little secret. After two idyllic weeks of just existing together, we've really found our rhythm, and I think Mabel suspects we might be more than friends.

Brent came into the office with his tail between his legs the day after Cole found his proof. Cole heard he's on a bender, apparently unable to secure any kind of transfer. Probably because Sheriff Ashby has talked with every local county head and is working to have Brent stripped of his badge.

The bulbous, almost red tomatoes in the garden remind me every day that we need to have a talk with Mabel soon. But I'm following Cole's lead on this. All that matters, in this moment, is the three of us, swimming lazily in the hot August afternoon. It's as easy as it always is. It's a little piece of heaven.

"Okay." She giggles, not so inconspicuously, as we start to swim toward him.

"Marco," Cole calls, his eyes closed in the center of the pool.

"Polo," I call back, trying to make my voice sound like it's coming from much farther away. This stunning man grins with his eyes closed, his dimples appear, and I die a slow death at how incredible-looking he is.

But even his gorgeousness won't prevent his demise as Mabel and I stalk toward him, look at each other, and each take a shoulder, shoving Cole under the water, then doing our best to swim away from him. He chases after us, catching Mabel in one hand and me in the other. He kisses Mabel's chubby cheeks into fits of giggles.

"It was Ginger's idea!" She laughs as he turns to playfully kiss my cheeks while I yelp. This makes Mabel laugh even harder before he sets us both free.

"What happened to Daddy's Girls? The team? The team doesn't work against each other!" He grins as Mabel and I swim to the side. Mabel covers her mouth in an attempt to stop her laughter from spilling out.

"Me and Ginger have our own team!" she says as Cole feigns shock.

"Traitors," he gasps, pushing his hair off his forehead before climbing out of the water. "And what is this team called?" he asks.

Mabel and I look at each other.

"The Garden-istas," I say as Mabes and I side five, without even looking at each other. It took us three days to be able to do that.

Cole chuckles and opens his little outdoor fridge near the barbecue on the patio, pulling out the sandwiches Mabel and I made earlier.

"Okay, Garden-istas. Come and have some food," he says, drying himself off.

Ten minutes later, we're seated and eating our lunch. Cole polishes off his sandwich first.

"So, Mabes, can we have a talk?" he asks, his eyes on mine, telepathically telling me that the time is now.

Mabel dips a berry into whipped cream and shoves it into her mouth.

"Yep," she says.

Cole fidgets in his seat.

"Do you like having Ginger here with us?" he asks.

I smile into my lap as I pop a berry into my mouth, loving Cole so much in this moment for caring so intensely about what his daughter thinks of him. Of us.

"Yes," she says as she continues to eat.

"How would you feel if Ginger were to stay for longer?" he asks.

"Happy," she says without hesitation. I smile at her.

"I'd be happy too," I tell her.

"Why?" Mabel asks. "And what will happen to your house?"

"Well." I take a breath before answering her. "Someone else would live there, and I would live here."

"You'd help my dad take me to school?" she asks.

"Ginger will help me look after you, I'm sure. But there's something else too, Mabes," Cole tells her.

Mabel looks at both of us and tries, in her little eight-year-old mind, to understand Cole's beating around the bush.

"Sometimes when grown-ups spend a lot of time together," I say, "they find they get along very well."

Mabel nods and looks up at me. "Like me and you?" she asks.

"Yes, sort of, but also in a different way," I tell her.

She picks up another berry and thinks for a second.

"Like how Grace is always around when Annie comes to Mr. Stacks's, and they fall in love?" Mabel asks, referencing *Annie* and sounding way too grown up.

"Exactly," I tell her. *Smart girl.*

"Do you love my dad?" she says bluntly.

Cole almost chokes on his iced tea from the other side of the table. I look at Cole.

"Yes, I do, very much."

Mabel smiles, looking genuinely thrilled.

"My dad loves you too," she says, matter-of-factly.

Cole shakes his head and smiles before popping a grape into his mouth.

"How did you know that, half pint?" he asks.

Mabel shrugs. "Because you look at her like Mr. Stacks looks at Grace."

Cole's eyes meet mine over Mabel's head.

"You totally do," I tell him as I steal a grape of my own. He doesn't even deny it, he just shrugs with a grin.

We all clean up and then spend the obligatory fifteen minutes after lunch listening to Mabel tell us all about decorating the house for fall, and what teacher she hopes she has, and all about her friend Alex's new cat.

Midway through the conversation, her eyes light up like Christmas morning.

"Now that Ginger is going to live here, can we get a dog?" Mabel asks as I help her put her water wings back on.

"Every team needs a mascot," I say to Cole with a grin.

"So, is this how it's gonna be? You two ganging up on me?" he asks, pointing between us. Mabel and I look at each other. We both nod and shrug.

"Better get used to it, Daddy," Mabel tells him, turning to cannonball back into the pool.

I nuzzle into Cole's neck as she jumps.

"Yeah, Daddy. Better get used to it," I murmur.

A low growl rumbles in his chest, before his arms are around my waist and he's launching us both into the pool. Mabel is hysterically laughing as we pop up to the surface and our blissful afternoon continues, the conversation we just had making us no more a family than we already are. We may not have done things the conventional way, but we did them our way, and I wouldn't change a thing.

CHAPTER FIFTY-SIX
Cole

"Married?" CeCe's jaw falls open across from me at the dining room table. Everyone is staring at us, speechless. Even Nash has nothing to say. Mama smiles and leans back in her chair, sipping at her glass of spiked lemonade.

Ginger gives her a small smile back. I place my hand on Ginger's thigh under the table, and no one speaks for at least a minute. We let them absorb the news.

"You guys have been married for longer than I have?" CeCe, the only one who apparently knows how to talk, asks. "You're my *sister*?"

The table erupts with laughter as Wade pats me on the back.

"Most people date first." He chuckles.

"Of course, if anyone would do things the totally ass-backward way, it would be them," Liv says, smiling at us, then at the rest of the table.

"We weren't planning on staying married," Ginger says softly. "We didn't want to take anything away from your big day, CeCe. But then, something just happened . . ."

She delves into the entire story from start to finish. I speak when appropriate, adding in my take here and there, plus the wedding Polaroids to prove it, which make everyone howl with laughter. Pop says things like "This one's a framer for sure" as he holds up one of me kissing Ginger on the cheek while she flashes the camera her champagne and a peace sign with her tongue out.

Finally, we finish the tale with how I ended up confronting Brent.

"So, if Brent is gone and you don't have to worry about him, what's the next step?" Mama asks.

"I fucking knew that guy was a piece of trash," Nash mutters, gritting his molars.

"He isn't gone yet," I tell them, "but last I heard he was staying at the Motor Court Hotel after Gemma kicked him out."

"Gemma kicking him out makes sense. She can't get anything from him anymore," CeCe scoffs.

"Enough about Brent and Gemma. I want to bring up the question no one has asked yet. Are you two just going to stay married?" Liv says abruptly, directing her gaze toward me and Ginger.

"Oh, we haven't really worked that out yet." Ginger trails off, the faint blush of her cheeks making my cock twitch. "We've known each other for so long, and it's always been . . ."

"You against the world?" Ivy finishes, a soft smile on her face.

"Yeah . . . sorta," Ginger answers with a sigh.

"Watching Ginger with Mabel has been amazing," I chime in, looking at Ginger while I say it. "And the three of us together, it feels . . . like we're already a family. There are times when I think I can breathe easier when Ginger is with me. I love her with everything I have."

"Holy fuck, break out the violins." Nash chuckles.

"This from the guy who handpicked almost four hundred silver Hershey's kisses out of the damn bin at the Candy Shack so they would match the wedding colors at his wedding reception," I reply.

Nash mutters something about being a good husband as Mama reaches across the table to put her hand on mine.

"You two have always been like family to each other"—she wags a finger between us—"and if you all think I didn't know about this secret friendship you've had going all these years, you're wrong," she says, polishing off the rest of her lemonade.

"Same," Wade says, raising his hand. "Knew it when I drove by one night after Gemma left and saw you two sitting on the porch eating takeout. Drove by a week later and you were there again."

"I had my assumptions too," Ivy adds with a giggle, "and I've only known you a year."

"I knew something was up when Cole's face went from zero to a hundred in one second flat when Chris asked you to dance in Vegas," CeCe says, raising her glass toward Ginger and letting out a laugh.

"I knew it when you said *fate* while you were talking about him at the Horse and Barrel," Liv pipes up.

I smile. "Well, aren't y'all so fucking smart then," I say, squeezing Ginger's thigh.

"Ah well. Eloping, weddings on a whim, happens to the best of us," Pop says nonchalantly as he sits forward.

Every eye in the room turns to him in question.

"What? We all have our secrets." He grins as he turns to Mama. "I was nineteen when I married your mother. Who has money for a wedding? So we eloped. Pissed your granddad right off. Even though everything turned out just fine. We were married for over fifty years when she passed."

He slaps both his thighs like he didn't just drop a bomb on us. "So, who wants a drink?"

"Jesus, Pop," I say, scrubbing my face with my hand.

"What? Back in those days you waited until your wedding night to, you know . . ." he says as he stands. "And your grandmother was a little devil."

Ginger leans over to me. "I can't unhear this."

I shudder.

"I'll take a drink," Ivy says as she gets up to make her way to the bar.

As she does so, a gush of water hits the floor. We all look down, and it takes us a second to realize what just happened.

Ivy turns to Wade, a horrified expression on her face.

"I think my water just broke," she says, clutching her massive bump.

It's at this declaration that several things happen at once. Mama and Ginger sprint for the linen closet in search of towels to clean up the mess on the wooden floor. CeCe rushes to Ivy to offer reassurance. And Wade—Wade goes into dad mode instantly.

"What do you need, bro?" I ask him, clapping him on the shoulder.

"I'm not leaving her for a second," he says, turning to Nash. "Go to my house. When you get there, open the front closet and grab the blue bags. They have everything we need. Get two waters from the fridge and bring my truck up here."

"On it," Nash calls out, already making his way toward the door. Ginger and Jo move about the kitchen while Wade and I help Ivy to the comfortable chair in the den.

"And get my mama!" Ivy adds. "She should be almost home now. She was at the local market with her blankets this afternoon."

Nash nods and heads out.

Her face winces in pain. The expression tells me she might not be in the early stages of labor. I was trained for deliveries when I became a cop, and I've witnessed a handful during my time. Including Mabel's.

"Ivy, have you been experiencing discomfort today?" I ask, offering her a cup of ice Ginger has just handed to me.

"You said your back was sore," Wade cuts in, looking down at her. "I thought that might have been the start of it."

"Well, that's a good thing. You could have been in labor all day," I tell them. "Which means this should be faster than expected."

"Doc told us that, since it's her first labor, it might be on the long side," Wade says.

I nod. Gemma was in labor with Mabes for twenty-six hours. But Ivy's face is contorted in that strange way again, and it's only been five minutes. I pull Wade aside after another ten minutes go by.

"As soon as Nash gets back, you should take her to the hospital," I say. "She's had three contractions in a row five minutes apart. Has her back been bothering her all day?"

"Since this morning," he says.

"She could have been in labor the whole day then," I tell him. "Gemma had back labor with Mabel." Wade's face is half panic, half determination.

"You're gonna be a father today, man," I say, smiling wide.

"Yeah," he says. "You're all coming, right?" he calls to the room, then looks back at me.

"Wouldn't miss it," I say.

Forty minutes later and we're all pulling into Pendalton Community Hospital in our respective vehicles.

"Never a dull moment," Ginger says, looking so beautiful I can barely stand it. Who wears a pink sundress that fucking torturous to a family dinner? I take a moment when we pull in to kiss her.

"I've been waiting to do that for hours," I tell her, sliding my hand up her thigh. "We did good tonight, telling them everything."

"They all seem happy about it," Ginger says as I trail my lips down her delicious neck.

"Yep," I say, not fully listening to what she's saying because, fuck, she smells like goddamn dessert, and the thought that we have the whole night alone makes my cock throb in my shorts.

"You better cut that short, sheriff, or we'll be in the back seat before we can go inside," she scolds.

"Shouldn't have worn this dress then."

She laughs and turns her caramel eyes on mine with a look of warning before opening her door.

"Fuck . . ." I say, selfishly hoping this baby comes quickly so I can have my wife all to myself.

CHAPTER FIFTY-SEVEN
Ginger

"How is she?" CeCe asks Ivy's mom, Glenda, as she exits the delivery room. We're all piled into the small waiting room just outside, and Jo gets up immediately to get her a coffee. Glenda hasn't wavered; she's been at her daughter's side for hours.

"She's eight centimeters dilated," she tells us. "The doctor said she was six when we got here. Probably been in labor all day."

Just as Cole thought.

"She wanted to have a completely natural birth, but she's regretting that choice right now." Glenda grins. "Keeps asking every intern that comes in for drugs. Though she'll be glad she did it this way when it's over."

Ivy's mama sips her coffee. "I can't believe I'm going to be a grammie," she says with a sweet smile on her face. Jo pats her hand, and we all sit in a sort of happy bliss.

The clock ticks on, and a marathon of *Property Brothers* plays on the waiting room TV. We've watched a few episodes when Glenda comes out to give us the update that Ivy is about to start pushing. We sit for another thirty minutes as we watch the end of another episode before Wade comes out of the delivery room, leans his hand on the wall, and takes a deep breath.

"She's almost there," he says, looking as white as a ghost. He takes a sip of water, and Cole gets up to talk to him. I watch as he claps him on the shoulder.

"Just needed a second. They're checking her as we speak. It's so fucking hard to see her in this much pain. All I want to do is fix it for her," Wade says to Cole.

"You got this, man," Cole reassures him. "She's so fucking strong. Trust me, the moment your baby is born she won't remember the pain. She'll be so in love and so will you."

Wade nods and pats his brother's back before heading back into the delivery room.

"Next time we see you, you'll be a dad," Cole calls after him. Wade flashes him a wide grin, a truly rare occurrence until Ivy came along. He has the same dimples as Cole. I smile as I watch them, imagining the two of them when they were younger.

Then my thoughts turn to what it would be like to give Mabel a sibling one day. Someone who can be her best friend. Half Cole, half me. The thought electrifies me.

It isn't fifteen minutes later when a breathless and teary-eyed Glenda rounds the corner wearing the biggest smile on her face.

"It's a girl!" she cries. Jo is instantly out of her seat and hugging her. They both cry into each other's embrace.

"She's perfect," she continues. "They're just getting everyone cleaned up, and then you can all come and meet her. Give us fifteen minutes." The whole waiting room erupts in cheers.

The wait feels a lot longer than fifteen minutes, but I'm not prepared for the scene that awaits when we enter Ivy's room. Nor am I prepared for the emotion that overtakes me when I see her. She's beautiful, with tearstains and flushed cheeks, her hair pulled back in a big messy bun. The look she's wearing is one of pure, unfiltered joy. It's the look of true love.

"Congrats, Daddy," I say to Wade, who is a puddle when Ivy hands him his daughter.

"Thank you," he says, staring down into his daughter's eyes. She stares intently back at him, and it feels as though they recognize each other from another life.

"How is it that Ivy gives birth and still looks better than you?" Cole says, patting his brother on the shoulder. "Welcome to the dad club. She's beautiful."

The look the two of them share in this moment makes me wish I had a sibling of my own.

Mama Jo hugs Glenda, then Ivy, before the three of them start discussing the details of the birth. Nash wraps his arms around CeCe and whispers something inaudible in her ear.

"Do you want to hold her?" Wade asks Cole after a few minutes.

"Of course," Cole replies, arms outstretched.

Wade places the tiny pink bundle into my husband's arms and makes his way back to Ivy, determined to kiss her everywhere he can. I just stand dumbfounded, unable to take my eyes off Cole. What a fucking sight he is: a little scruff, backward Yankees hat on his head, and a black T-shirt, rocking this newborn babe.

He grins down at his new niece and runs a big finger over her cheek.

"Her name's Billi Grace," Wade announces proudly.

"After my daddy," Ivy says, giving her mom a knowing look.

"Well, hi, Billi," Cole croons, cradling her in his strong

arms. "Welcome to the family, beautiful girl. We're gonna have all kinds of fun, you and me, just to piss your daddy off. And you wait until your cousin meets you."

Cole's dimples are at full wattage as he converses with Billi like she can fully understand him. They're in their own little world. And me? I'm ready to become a full-on baby-making machine for this man if it means I get to see him like this with our children.

Cole glances up at me before slowly making his way over with Billi in his arms.

"You're next, auntie." He smirks.

He places her in the crook of my elbow, and I'm instantly in love. She's all wrinkled pink, heaven-scented goodness. Her bottom lip moves like she is suckling away as her eyes flutter closed in sleep.

"You've had a busy night, haven't you, little peanut?" I say to her. "That's a lot of hard work coming into this world."

I can't understand why, maybe it's the creation of life in my arms or the way Wade and Ivy look right now, but I feel the tears start to well. Everything around me right now is so beautiful. So intimate. An overwhelming sense of gratitude washes over me.

"The fortress of strength and sass cries?" Wade jokes as a tear slides down my cheek. Cole is next to me instantly, swiping it off.

"Shut up, Daddy Wade," I say. "I'm just so grateful to be here with you all."

Cole's arm goes around my shoulder, and his lips hit my temple.

"You're so fucking next," he whispers. His hand grazes the small of my back, and I look up at him.

"Can't wait," I say softly. His eyes darken, and I know he means every word he says. With him, I want it all.

Cole kisses my cheek.

"Still not used to *that*. Who's with me?" Papa Dean asks, coming in the door, his hand raised. The room gives a collective laugh.

"I think it's beautiful," Jo says, winking at me. "Always knew you two were destined to be together."

"Of course you did, Mama." Wade side hugs her and kisses the top of her head. "You know everything."

"Sure do," she says with a grin as she tightens her ponytail. "I'm seeing a lot more grandchildren in my future." Jo winks. "And I love seeing you all happy."

"Who'd have fuckin' thought?" Wade chimes in as the room laughs.

I make my way to Ivy with a sleeping Billi and place her in her mama's arms.

"You did so good," I tell her.

"Thank you," Ivy says, still emotional. "It's like taking a piece of your heart out and praying for it to always be safe and happy. It's the best and the scariest feeling in the world."

"I bet," I say, feeling the tears start to build again.

"I was so nervous," she says quietly while the room chatters around us. "I didn't know what it would be like. I kept wondering if I would feel a connection with her instantly. Whether she'd know me. But now that she's here . . . it's like she knows I'm her home and she's mine."

She smiles down at her daughter and kisses her forehead. I look back at Cole, ready to go home with him after this emotional night.

His eyes meet mine across the room, and it's as though he can read my mind. He pats Wade on the shoulder and makes his way over to me, stopping to speak to Ivy as he does, telling her what a great job she did.

"Love you both," he says to Ivy and Billi as he kisses Ivy on the top of the head. "Let us know when you get home tomorrow. Mabes will be dying to come by when she gets home from Ernie and Trudy's."

Ivy nods. "Of course."

Cole closes the space between us.

"Ready to go home?" I ask quietly when he reaches me.

"Nah. Not waiting that long. There's a utility closet down the hall. We're going there first," he replies, dropping a kiss to my cheek. "I'm gonna practice filling my wife right the fuck up, and then I'm going to take you home so you can properly scream my name."

He says this in the lowest whisper so no one can hear, his breath hot on my neck.

Yep, that does me in.

I say congratulations to everyone one more time, then, like the dutiful wife I am, I follow my husband out the door.

CHAPTER FIFTY-EIGHT
Cole

ONE DAY TO GO

SARGE

Did you just pay over $800 to have rush hockey jerseys with your name and number made for Ginger and Mabes?

ME

Maybe. Gotta have them wearing my number when we obliterate the Rocket.

NASH

This guy's a total goner.

ME

I learn from the best.

NASH

I am the best, aren't I?

I don't deny Nash's accusations. I am a goner. And tonight, everyone in this town will know it. Including my beautiful wife.

NASH

> FYI, she could wear a jersey lined with gold and you fuckers still wouldn't beat me.

SARGE

> I taught you everything you know.

ME

> @Nash you got everything set for me?

NASH

> Yes, bro, I told you. It's all taken care of. Just show up and do your part.

NASH

> Also you fuckers will never beat me. See you at noon.

I breathe out a sigh and mentally make sure I have everything I need for tonight. I grin when I see Wade's message come through in our private chat.

SARGE

> He has no idea we have half his old teammates playing with us?

ME

> Not a clue.

SARGE

> It's going to be so fun to beat his ass. Thank God we have the help. Fuck, babies are tiring.

ME

> You got this, old fella.

SARGE
You're next.

ME
Hope so.

I turn and pull two jerseys out of their bags, laying them over the back of the couch ready to be packed and taken to the girls. They're helping out at the Harvest Fest until three, working at Glenda's booth. She's become quite the sought-after artisan for all things crocheted or knitted.

When they're finished, we're all heading to Nash's Olympia Sports Center for the game: Pros vs. Townies: The Rematch. Only the Townies have some surprises up their sleeves. We recruited six of Nash's former NHL and Dallas farm team players, which gives us a fair and fighting shot at kicking their asses this year. I run my hand over one of the crisp white jerseys. Ashby 18. The number I wore through my years of hockey and football in high school. Looking at it now unlocks memories of Ginger with CeCe in the stands when I played, reminding me of the way she was always there, cheering me on, always in my corner like I've always been in hers.

On the back of both shirts, under the number, is the small banner patch that says "Daddy's Girls." They're going to fucking love them.

I shake my head in disbelief. Three months ago, I never would've guessed I'd visit Vegas for the weekend and find the love of my life in Ginger Danforth. Everything has changed since that trip. Now, instead of thinking about how I'm going to make it through the day, I fucking look forward to it. It's a thrill never knowing what the day will bring, but always knowing it will be an adventure with her around. The babies I'm ready to start putting into her . . . Fuck, I want that too. The idea of watching her grow with my child does something to me I can't explain. I've told her I'd love to have at least three and that I want everything that comes with a big family. It's not something I'd ever thought about much. But, with her, it seems like my own personal kind of heaven. Mabes is the happiest she's ever been and grins whenever she sees me kiss Ginger on the forehead or hug her, and I'm so fucking happy I can give her this life. Like the life my parents gave me. One where all our roots just grow together as a family, each at our own pace but always counting on one another to be the best version of ourselves. Those roots are ours, mine and Ginger's together, and I'm realizing that the life I wasn't even looking for is the best damn one I could ever ask for.

CHAPTER FIFTY-NINE
Ginger

The carnival atmosphere of Nash and CeCe's Harvest Fest is everything I love about living in Laurel Creek. There are people everywhere; all you can hear is the sound of kids' laughter, and all you can smell are food trucks, funnel cakes, and popcorn.

It's still technically summer, but you can tell fall is imminent, and I'm beyond excited to start my school year soon. This summer has been life-changing, yet I've never felt so refreshed and ready to shape young minds. Being with Mabel has brought back my love of teaching just to teach. So much so, I've already been in to start setting up my classroom. Everything else has started falling into place too; I was able to sublet my apartment in less than a week, and tomorrow Cole and I are heading there to pick up the rest of my belongings. But, today, we're all just ready for some small-town fun.

"I love them," I tell Cole as Mabel squeals beside me when he holds up two matching jerseys for today's game.

"Gotta have my name on your back while you watch me play. There's no other way." He grins at me.

Mabel and I hug Glenda and thank her for letting us help out at her stall. She cleaned up today, sold a dozen blankets and a bunch of fall hats. Her story is one I hope ends happily; she's doing so well and is just in love with Billi Grace.

Ivy approaches us to visit her mama, and Mabel and I start packing up our things so we can wander the booths before they close. CeCe has been in and out of the festival all day, checking on vendors, making sure they all have water and good shade in the late summer heat. She was born for this, and everyone is saying this festival has been an even bigger hit than last year's. Even my parents and grandmas have ventured out for the festivities.

When my dad and I had our lunch two weeks ago, he apologized for his behavior again, promising to remember I'm his daughter first and foremost from now on. It was the first step to mending everything between us. He also told me that, after this term, he is officially retiring, and when Cole and I went for dinner last week on our own, leaving Mabel with Jo for the evening, it was a pleasant experience. I've almost worked up enough courage to tell my mother about my and Cole's accidental marriage. Nah, maybe I'll tell my grandmothers first.

My father had apologized to Cole that night too about using him and Mabel in his primary speech *and* told him how he thought Cole was a stand-up man, and that he could tell how much he cared about me.

Two-week-old Billi makes the cutest little grunts from her stroller, snapping me from my thoughts. Mabel is right there to tend to her, and Ivy watches them with the sweetest, most relaxed smile on her face.

"How are you feeling, Mama?" I ask, bringing her close for a little side hug.

"Tired but . . . complete," she replies, smiling. Her long black hair is pulled back in a ponytail, and her pretty face is free of any makeup. "And trying to rest up as best I can."

"We all gotta rest up." Glenda smiles from behind her craft table as she packs up. "The whirlwind is coming for a visit next week."

I look back at Ivy.

"My sister, Cassie," she explains. "She's finishing up the tour with Red Dirt Roots. It's been a busy summer for her. Success kind of came out of nowhere, and she's about to head into the studio to record her next album."

"I bet it's been a bit of an adventure," I say. "She's skyrocketing right now."

Cassie's single, "Friday Night Lights," has been climbing the charts all summer. Since its release, it became the sort of slow creeper hit played in every bar at a slow dance time, and now she's finishing up a tour with one of country's hottest bands. It doesn't hurt that she's drop-dead gorgeous, and even through a screen you can tell she's just full of charisma. She's been playing the outdoor festival circuit since April. Ivy and Glenda are intensely proud of her.

"She's a bit of a tornado," Ivy warns with a smile. "But she loves so hard. I can't wait to see her. Can't wait for her to meet Billi and all of you."

I smile back at her before turning my gaze to Mabel, who is gently pushing Billi's stroller back and forth, soothing her to sleep.

"Well, just remember, those Sangria Sundays make house calls if you want a girls' night," I say.

"Sure, as long as my sangria can be virgin, since I'm a food source right now." She laughs.

"You got it," I say. "While Cassie's here, we'll find some ways to keep her entertained. How long is she staying?"

"I'm not sure, a few days maybe," Ivy replies.

"It's good to have family around," I tell her with a squeeze of the hand. I'm so grateful for this crew. "You need anything, you just ask," I continue, tilting my head toward Mabes. "Looks like you'll have a built-in babysitter right here for the next few years anyway."

Ivy nods as we watch Mabel, utterly enamored of Billi. She's so attentive and helpful, a natural-born little mother hen, and I can't wait to give her a little brother or sister to love in the same way. But that will be down the road; Mabel needs time to adjust to me as a more permanent fixture in her life, and we all need time to grow as a family before we add to it. As much as it pains Cole to admit it, he knows I'm right.

We all pile into the arena, and it seems as though the entire town has come out to watch the boys play.

I'm not prepared for how my body reacts to seeing Cole in his hockey gear. He looked good playing when we were young. But now? He's like a walking wet dream. So big and ominous when he approaches me. I stand on my tiptoes to greet him. I'm not a short woman at 5'7", but he's got at least ten or eleven inches on me right now in skates.

The look on Nash's face as he greets the players who make their way out of the dressing room is priceless. "You mother-fuckers," I hear him whisper to Cole and Wade as he realizes they've stacked their town team with former NHL players.

"Gotta get a win in for my daughter's first game," Wade replies.

"I think I might need to have you keep that jersey on later," Cole mutters in my ear as he reaches me. "Goddamn, that does something to me."

Mabel skips over to us, and Cole ruffles her hair.

"Ready for the show, half pint?" he asks with a wink. She nods excitedly.

"Good luck, Sir Peanut Butter Cups." She winks back. He

winks again, and then they high-five, signaling that they share a secret. I look between them.

"What am I missing?" I ask them both, folding my arms over my chest. Mabel looks at Cole and giggles. I turn back to Cole and see his finger against his lips, before he swiftly pulls it down.

I narrow my eyes at him, and he shrugs sheepishly. Something is definitely up, but I have no time to figure out what because suddenly my shoulder is being tapped, followed by a chorus of "Miss Danforth?" I turn to find three of my students from last year's homeroom class standing beside me. We chat for a few minutes about our summers, and what we've all been up to.

"Would you help us for the school socials?" Josie Grass, one of my favorite students, asks me. "We're going to sing the national anthem and wondered if you would record it for us at ice level? My mom was supposed to do it, but she's running late."

CeCe arrives next to us at exactly the right time.

"Go for it, Ginger. Mabes can come with me. Right, Mabes?" She smiles at me. "You can find us after the game starts. We'll be on the right side, ice level."

I thank CeCe and turn back to my students.

"Sure," I tell them. "Whose phone am I using?"

We head over to the rink so they can get set up. The game is due to start in ten minutes, and the whole arena is packed. The second-period music class from last year are on the ice, and I'm surprised when I realize that I've taught almost every one of them at one time or another. I had no idea they were doing this.

The crowd falls into a hush as the students begin their version of "The Star-Spangled Banner." I record dutifully on the ice in my cowboy boots and watch with pride as the crowd sings along. When they're done, the lights suddenly cut out, and the entire arena turns black. I look around as my eyes adjust to the lack of light and wonder if there's been a technical difficulty when the opening strings of "H.O.L.Y." by Florida Georgia Line begin to play through the sound system. The jumbotron in the middle of the ice lights up with a *giant* photo of me at fifteen, sporting braces and looking slightly awkward sitting on the Ashbys' patio with CeCe. Cole is standing behind me, holding up bunny ears and making the goofiest face. Then another image appears onscreen. This time it's of the three of us eating cotton candy at the town fair, followed by another of us at my and CeCe's prom. It's a candid shot of us girls waiting for our dates. Cole stands behind us, wearing casual clothes and holding my clutch purse while CeCe fluffs my dress. The photos continue to roll: Ashby Christmas movie nights when we were young, backyard fires, always Cole and me near each other, as natural as can be. There's one where I'm in my first year of college, his arm around me, and another of him, CeCe, Jo, and me at one of Nash's games in Nashville. Each memory flashes onscreen in time to the song, and the crowd is silent.

The photos showing now are of just Cole and me, a little older than before, and mostly selfies from the beginning of our friendship after CeCe left. I'm looking at one where he holds a baby Mabel at the Ashbys' and I'm leaning in with a big smile on my face. Then I'm watching us on his couch on any random night, before a picture I sent to Cole pops up; I'm pouting as I order his pizza during the Reds–Yankees weekend in 2021. Soon, we're on the dance floor at Nash and CeCe's engagement party, and back in Vegas, beaming and slightly tipsy.

After the evidence from the weekend we got married fades away, photos from the last three months start, photos I never even knew were taken. There are so many of Mabel and me: in the pool, in the garden, at the cottage. There are snaps of Cole and me in the backyard too, me taking a big bite out of a burger he'd made. They're never-ending, and they're totally and completely us.

At some point, the song ends, and a spotlight drops to the center of the ice. Tears are streaming down my cheeks when I see Cole standing under the light in the center of the rink. He skates over, stopping just before me. When he kisses me, a dizzy sort of haze takes over.

"How did you? What is . . ." I whisper.

He grins.

"Ginger. You're the love of my life. And this"—he points to the screen—"is only the beginning of our story. You're the face I want to see every single morning, the one I want to share my thoughts with, my needs with. You're the one I'm always talking to even when I'm not with you, the one I dream about. And if you let me . . ." He drops to his knees before me, and I gasp. Cole holds up the most beautiful ring I've ever seen, a perfectly cut round diamond encased in a double band. I instantly recognize my Vegas band incorporated into the new design.

He covers his mic.

"Buried in your wallet, right?" He grins, uncovering his mic.

A tear slides down my cheek. I swipe it away.

"I never thought I'd be lucky enough to end up here on my knees before you, Ginger, but I know without a doubt that when my lungs pull in their last breath, my final thoughts will be of you and our family. Thing is, it's always been you, and it always will be. So what do you say, baby? Will you do me the incredible honor of being my PIC forever?" he says. "Will you marry me?"

"Yes!" I cry as he stands and lifts me up, crushing his lips to mine.

"It's always been you too, Cole," I whisper. He covers the mic and leans in.

"Let's make this marriage official," he says softly into my ear, sending goose bumps down my spine. The crowd explodes around us, and I'm momentarily stunned by the flash of cameras. Once my eyes have adjusted, I see my family in the stands clapping and cheering. Then I see Cole's family doing the same, laughing and smiling. But mostly I see him. Those amber eyes I've loved for so long. And when Mabel comes from the sidelines, I hug her too.

"You knew about this, didn't you, sweet girl?" I ask.

She nods and wraps her little arms around me.

"Will you be my mommy in my heart?" she says, and I pull her closer.

"Of course I will. Daddy's girls?" I ask, tears streaming down my cheeks.

She nods, beaming, and when Cole picks her up and kisses me, I feel it. The peace I've been searching for. The place I'm meant to be, with my very best friend.

All the years of twisted and broken paths that unconventionally led us to each other now behind us.

Only one day left in our contract, but forever to go.

EPILOGUE

SEVEN YEARS LATER

"I don't like it. I don't like one thing about it."

I stare at my husband as he comes in the door, knowing the exact words that are going to come out of his mouth next.

"She's too young."

And there we have it, folks.

"She's fourteen, Cole, and they're just friends. Unless you have something against her being friends with a nice young man?" I say, raising my eyebrow. "A boy she's known since she was nine? A boy who is your deputy's son?"

I know he can't argue with me. Cole's deputy sheriff, Wayne, who took over when Brent left, and was elected again with Cole two years ago to his second term, is a great man. He and his wife, Lisa, have become two of our best friends, and Mabel and their son Max have been close since the day we all met. Might they have a little crush on each other now that she's fourteen and he's fifteen? Probably. But they're both great kids, and I, for one, am not against them spending time together.

I smile at Cole and watch the tic in his jaw as he mentally gives in. Dads of daughters will be dads of daughters, and my husband has three of them to worry about. Thank God he finally got his beloved boy when our son Luca was born.

"Friends isn't what I'm worried about, Ginger. Max is almost sixteen, and I remember being sixteen," Cole says, running a hand through his hair. I notice the way his arm flexes as he does so. His left one matches his right now with a full sleeve, inked over the years to incorporate all our children's names. At thirty-five, Cole has never looked better, and I still often catch myself staring at him.

I laugh off his worry and pin up another balloon, a red one because today is Luca's second birthday, and it just so happens to fall on a Reds–Yankees weekend. Which means, of course, that the entire house is decked out in Reds décor. Advantages of being home during the summer and having free rein to decorate the house with Mabel's help. She had warned me Cole wouldn't like it if she went swimming at Max's and came back to the party with him and his parents. I assured her that her dad is just overprotective sometimes. As much as I worry about Mabel too, I know she's a trustworthy, sweet girl.

"This is blasphemy by the way," Cole says, taking off his badge and pulling out his keys and wallet, setting them down in the basket in our entryway. I watch him as he takes in all the Reds balloons, streamers, the custom "Happy 2nd Birthday, Luca" banner.

"Hard to believe he's two already," he continues. "Hard to believe how old Isla and Sofia are too. Soon they'll be fourteen and bringing home strange men."

He grimaces.

"They're five and three," I say with a laugh before walking over to him.

"Sofia is almost four," Cole corrects me. I have no idea how, but I still get little butterflies in my stomach when he wraps his arms around me like this and drops his lips to mine. It's probably why we have so many kids.

There hasn't been one day over the last seven years where I've woken up and not felt grateful for my decision to play a drunken game of truth or dare with Cole.

We got married for the second time in front of all our family and friends a year after he proposed. I was pregnant with Isla at the time and our two golden retrievers, Mabel's babies, Jake and Amy, had walked down the aisle with the rings tied around their necks. The wedding itself was simple and Vegas-themed old school to remind us of where we started. We hosted it at Silver Pines. It was the first wedding to take place in Wade's pet project, the newly built rustic wedding barn. We had a makeshift casino in the back quarters of the hall, complete with carnival games for the kids, but left the front candlelit, rustic, and beautiful. It was the perfect way to celebrate with everyone we love. Not long after, we announced we were having our first baby. And the rest, as they say, is history.

"Cake cake cake!" Isla squeals, burning through the living room. She runs right between us at warp speed as Jo comes through the door with Luca's cake.

"Your turn," I tell Cole.

It's well known that there's no stopping Isla. Someone has to wrangle her at all times. And, right now, that's Cole's job. He makes his way over to her and scoops her right up, her long, dark hair tumbling around him as he tickles her into oblivion. If I thought I loved Cole before we grew our family, I had no idea what was in store for me when he became a dad again. He thrives as a father, and together we make the best team. Our life is hectic, messy, and chaotic, and about to get even more so. But we can handle it.

"Oh, this man must love you," Nash says as he comes through the door eyeing up all the Reds décor. He's carrying my almost six-year-old niece Ruby, and CeCe follows with my brand-new nephew Rex.

"Please. He couldn't live without me." I smirk.

"I'm thinking about making her sleep in the garage," Cole cuts in with a laugh before setting Isla down. She and Ruby scamper off to find Billi in the backyard.

All the girls are so close in age, they're almost always getting up to mischief. Their main pastime is tormenting Wade and Ivy's one-year-old, Wyatt, and our younger kids.

There's a large, loud group outside, and Cole greets everyone after changing into his civilian clothes. He carries out the meat ready to be grilled, and it's in this moment that he realizes not only did I decorate the whole house in Reds paraphernalia, *and* dress our three kids in Reds jerseys, but that I decorated the entire backyard too, and made the whole family wear their Reds gear.

"*Motherfucker*," he mutters under his breath

"I got you, Dad," Mabel says, coming in behind him with Wayne, Lisa, and Max.

All four of them are wearing Yankees jerseys or T-shirts, and they stick out like sore thumbs in the crowd of red. Cole's grin spreads across his face as he shakes Wayne's hand.

"You're the only ones I trust," he says. "The rest of these assholes are traitors."

"Hey, I've always been a Reds fan," Nash calls out. "It's the one thing in sports that your dad and I ever agreed on."

"I was forced into this," Wade adds with a shrug as Ivy nods, bouncing little Wyatt on her knee.

Cole and I make our way to the grill.

"I'm liking Max a little more now," he says.

Cole starts cooking up a storm, and the smell of food fills the yard. The chatter is loud around us, accompanied by the sound of laughter and water splashing as the kids jump in and out of the pool.

Papa Dean prepares buns for Cole to toast as I talk with Glenda while rocking baby Rex in my arms to give CeCe a break.

"Does he have any idea?" CeCe asks me in a whisper as Glenda heads off to talk to Olivia and her man.

I grin. "I don't think so."

"This is going to be fun." She giggles.

Cole calls everyone to eat with a whistle, and we all seat ourselves around the giant outdoor harvest tables he built three summers ago. They each host sixteen people, and Ivy says that, at the rate we're all producing offspring, he'll need to add to it within a year. She may not be wrong.

"Who wants presents?" my mother calls from the patio door. I turn to see her holding a giant stack of gifts, way more than are warranted for Luca, which tells me she's done it again.

"You don't need to bring presents for all of the children every time someone has a birthday!" I say as I get up to give her a squeeze.

"I keep telling her we're on a budget now that I'm retired," my father jokes, carrying his own stack of gifts. He kisses the top of my head. Things have been so much better between us during the last few years. He has been enjoying tinkering on a project car and spending every winter in Florida with my mother. I finally feel that, after years of not really knowing my father, I understand him as a person. I'm grateful every day for the relationship we've developed.

"And he still supports me," my still-vibrant nonna says with a giggle, turning to give Papa Dean a squeeze.

"They forget we supported them their whole lives. It's about time they gave something back," he jokes.

"We really are just a trio of freeloaders, aren't we?" she says to him and my granny with a wink.

I hug my nonna before turning to pull my granny Dan close.

"Don't think you're going to keep the only eligible man in this place to yourself," Granny says to my nonna, wagging a finger with a grin as she gives Dean a hug after me. We're all used to the friendly flirting between them.

"Alright, ladies, no need to fight over me. I've got a chair on either side of mine. Let's get a drink and give these grandkids presents and way too much candy," Papa Dean says with a mischievous grin.

"Pop . . ." Cole warns. "They'll be up all night."

"Payback, son." Pop winks, and Cole rolls his eyes.

"Let's eat, before the kids have no appetite left . . ." Cole says to me, loud enough for the grandparents to hear, before turning to shake my dad's hand and help my mom with all the gifts.

"We've got bookings every weekend for the entire summer," Wade tells us as we eat.

"He's going to have to hire someone to either run the ranch while he handles the hospitality side or vice versa. It's getting too much," Ivy adds.

"I've offered multiple times!" Liv pipes up. "The moment I can find a buyer for my shop, I'm all yours."

"Why do you think I haven't hired anyone yet? Will you get on that?" Wade says with a grin before his attention is diverted to Billi beside him making a mess with Ruby and Isla.

"I've offered my services too, but for some reason he doesn't take me up on it." Papa Dean sighs.

"Yeah, 'cause you'll be making inappropriate cracks at all the brides and their friends." Cole chuckles as he sips his drink.

"Besides, you're too young and carefree to settle down to one career." CeCe smirks.

"That is the truth." Dean grins. "Gotta decide what I want to do when I grow up first."

"Alright, let's get this cake show on the road," Mama Jo says, coming out from the kitchen with the slab cake in a box. Behind her trails my second-best PIC, Mabel, with a little surprise cake of my own. She winks at me and I at her. After seven years together, our mother-daughter relationship has blossomed into something so special. Her own mother still comes around, I will say a little more now than before, but I sometimes feel like I know Mabel better than even Cole. Our late-night chats about boys and school, talks about her future and what she wants to do, it all just flows so easily between us, and I wouldn't trade it for the world.

The whole crew sings "Happy Birthday" to my dark-haired, amber-eyed little man, who claps his hands and shows off his adorable dimples as we all cheer. Ivy takes photos of all of us together, and Cole, Sofia, Isla, and I help Luca blow out his candles. The girls must, at all times, be involved in everything we do.

"This cake has your name on the box, Dad," Mabel says with a grin.

Cole looks around the table, and then at me.

"What is this?" he asks. "Should I be opening this?"

I shrug. "Yes. In fact, I dare you to, baby," I tell him with a grin.

Cole's eyes narrow, and he makes his way to the end of the table to pop open the box lid. I move to stand beside him.

There, written in pink and blue icing are the words:

"Boy, Girl? Maybe both?"

Cole looks down at the cake, then back at me, as our family clamors to see what we're looking at.

"Both?" Cole asks with a gulp.

I nod.

"Twins?" he croaks out as the tables erupt in a chorus of

cheers. I look at my husband and smile. I didn't even know they ran in our family until my nonna told me her mother was a twin.

"Might be time to add on to this house." I giggle

"Would you take it easy on the woman? Jesus, Cole," Papa Dean calls from his seat.

"Six kids?" Cole asks.

"You wanted a big family." I shrug and kiss him.

"Well, we're on our way to that now, aren't we?" Cole laughs.

The moment his initial shock has worn off, he's scooping me up in his arms and spinning me around as Mabel laughs.

"You knew about this, didn't you?" he says as he turns to face her.

She nods, and he kisses the side of her head.

"Just don't expect me to babysit them all at the same time!" she replies with a wide smile.

The sound of our family and friends laughing and talking fades into the background as that hazy kind of bliss I only get when Cole dips his lips to mine takes over.

"So that add-on to the house . . . can we consider that a favor? Add it to my tab?" I whisper into him.

He kisses me lightly on the lips.

"A whole house addition?" he responds, moving his lips to the spot on my neck he loves.

"You're gonna owe me big-time for that, Mrs. Ashby," he says. "Get ready to take it all."

"Title of your sex tape," I reply with a soft laugh as he kisses my lips, my shoulders, anywhere he can. I hug him tighter.

Is having five kids under six scary? Hell, yes, but attempting anything in this life with Cole Ashby by my side is okay by me. Nothing can really be considered a risk when everything we do together makes me the happiest I've ever been.

And every bit of my history with Cole from the kiss in his truck to that chance game of truth or dare in Vegas that led us here? It all just reminds me why I *always* take the dare. Because you can't always wait for the perfect time to risk it all. Sometimes you have to just close your eyes, slide over to the boy in the front seat, and kiss him like your future depends on it, because maybe someday it will.

Acknowledgments

What an emotional journey Cole and Ginger took me on! One that had me laughing, crying, and kicking my feet!

To my amazing husband for taking a back seat to Cole Ashby, as he always does with every MMC I write. For always taking care of me as I create endlessly, some days placing food in front of me when I'm in the "zombie zone."

To Tabitha, for the incredible character development that comes so naturally to you. For the deep dives into Cole and Ginger's connection and for being my sounding board always. I could not have made this book (or any books) what they are without you, your mind (which is my mind), and your sparkle.

To Rose, for being my unofficial assistant with all things Paisley.

To Jess, Alicia, Shauna, Deborah, and every single person who has a hand in making the Silver Pines books come to life within the Penguin Random House family: I love you and appreciate each one of you so very much for believing in me and these stories!

To my ARC readers and all readers alike, thank you. I may not do it better than anyone else, but I pour my whole soul into these stories and every comment, like, share, edit, and mention is noticed and loved wholeheartedly.

PLAYLIST

PAISLEY HOPE is an avid lover of romance, a mother, a wife, and a writer. Growing up in Canada, she wrote and dreamed of one day being able to create a place, a world where readers could immerse themselves, a place they wished was real, a place they saw themselves when they envisioned it. She loves her family time, gardening, baking, yoga, and a good cab sav.

Instagram: @authorpaisleyhope